Traitors

Jake Corey

DISCLAIMER

Except for the extract from the book by Dr./Col. Philip ('Tom') Cobley MBE late PARA, **'The British Infantry'**, this is a work of fiction.

Unless otherwise indicated, all the names, characters, businesses, places, events, and incidents in this book are either the product of the author's imagination or used in a fictitious manner. Any resemblance to actual persons, living or dead, or actual events is purely coincidental.

Copyright © 2022 Jake Corey
All rights reserved.
ISBN: 979 8 4163 9009 9 ISBN:

ACKNOWLEDGEMENTS

Thank you!

All my supporters who have encouraged, read, advised, and criticised this work, thank you.

Particularly John, a fellow soldier from our 'Death or Glory' days, who gave me valuable advice on prison life, on military aspects and advised me on the cover, and who described the final version as 'rivetting'.

Tom, with whom I served and who is a brother in arms. We have almost 90 years military experience between us. We discussed the many military aspects for hours. He is always supportive and forgiving. Tom kindly and generously allowed me to include an extract from his book 'The British Infantry'.

Sharon, who gave me sage advice on the plot and told me to remove 'procellous'*. Despite my protestations, I removed it.

Doug, who kept me sane and listened to numerous plot options, always with an encouraging word.

Carol, who (thankfully) advised me to get rid of the long words, which I did.

Angie, who gave me useful advice, after which I revised parts of the plot.

Linda, for supported me over the years in the SHAPE Writing Group.

And of course, Else-Marie, who read my manuscript several times, encouraged, advised, and repeated the process until we were both satisfied with it and who is the love of my life.

* **Procellous** - stormy; tempestuous, tumultuous.

Usage – The sea had a procellous air about it; not altogether stormy, for the sky was clear, but tempestuous, and alive with malicious energy. The sea around the Kent coast is often procellous..

ABBREVIATIONS AND ACRONYMS

AN Other
British military term for an unnamed person yet to be revealed, or unknown. (Another)

ANA
Afghan National Army

CASEVAC
Casualty Evacuation

CIA
The USA's Central Intelligence Agency.

Clean Fatigue
Stripped out of personal armour and other clothing (usually down to combat trousers and T-shirt) and anything that might snag during a swift exit. This is sometimes necessary to facilitate a quick escape through a small space.

CO
Commanding Officer

Cpl
Corporal

DMRC
Defence Medical Rehabilitation Centre

Egg Banjo
A fried egg sandwich. A staple for soldiers in the field. When cooked to perfection, egg yolk squirts onto the eater's front. This causes the eater to raise their egg banjo to ear height whilst they 'strum' the egg from their shirt with the free hand.

GPMG also 'Jimpy'
British colloquial term for a General Purpose Machine Gun or GPMG

HQ
Headquarters

IED
Improvised Explosive Device

ILS
Internal Locking System on the Glock 17 handgun.

ISAF
International Security Assistance Force

Izba
A traditional Slavic countryside dwelling. Often a log house, it forms the living quarters of a conventional Russian farmstead.

KGB

The Soviet Union's security agency from 1954 to 1991. (*Komitet Gosudarstvennoy Bezopasnosti*)
LSW
L86 Light Support Weapon used by the British Army. An SA-80 weapon.
M240
A 7.62mm General-purpose machine gun used by US Forces
MI5
The Security Service, known as MI5 (Military Intelligence, Section 5) is the United Kingdom's domestic counter-intelligence and security agency.
MOD
(UK) Ministry of Defence
MP5
Maschinenpistole 5. A Sub Machine Gun (SMG) made by Heckler & Koch GmbH. It fires 9mm Parabellum rounds.
Mufti
Civilian clothes, when worn by one who normally wears, or has long worn, military uniform.
NAMP
Not A Morning Person
NATO
North Atlantic Treaty Organisation
NCA
National Crime Agency
NCO
Non-Commissioned Officer
NKVD
The People's Commissariat for Internal Affairs *(Naródnyy komissariát vnútrennikh del)* 1917 to 1946, when it was renamed the Ministry of State Security (MGB)
OGFOT
Only Good for One Thing
PACE
Police and Criminal Evidence Act 1984 (PACE). It provides a code of practice for the exercise of police powers in England and Wales as well as the rights and freedoms of the public.
PTSD
Post-Traumatic Stress Disorder
RAPTC
Royal Army Physical Training Corps

RPG
Rocket Propelled Grenade. The term 'RPG' is a backronym and derives from the Russian '*Ruchnoy Protivotankovy Granatomyot*', meaning 'handheld anti-tank grenade launcher'.
SA-80
Small Arms for the 1980s. Standard British Army, personal weapon.
SA80 (L85A2)
An A2 upgrade of the SA80. Modified by Heckler and Koch and brought into service in 2001.
SBS
UK Special Boat Service.
Sgt
Sergeant
SITREP
Situation Report
Snatch Land Rover
A protected patrol vehicle based on the Land Rover Defender. Used in Northern Ireland, Afghanistan and elsewhere.
SNCO
Senior Non-Commissioned Officer. Usually, Sergeant to Warrant Officer.
SOP
Standard Operating Procedure
Spetsnaz
Soviet Union and Russian Special Operation Forces. Formed in 1941.
SVR
The Foreign Intelligence Service of the Russian Federation. Operated from late 1991. (*Sluzhba vneshney razvedki*)
Tango Uniform
Broken beyond repair. Dead. From the NATO Phonetic Alphabet 'T' 'U' 'Tits-Up'
TCP
Traffic Control Point
TM-57 and TM-62
Tank Mines
USB
Universal Serial Bus (A computer memory device otherwise known as a 'memory stick')
WIA

Traitors

Wounded-in-Action

Extract from 'The British Infantry'
By
Dr./Col. Philip ('Tom') Cobley MBE late PARA

Chapter Seventeen
War in Afghanistan
Battle of Musa Qala (2007)
Perseverance

Afghanistan is often called the crossroads of Central Asia and early humans were living there at least 50,000 years ago, creating some of the earliest farming communities in the world. In 328 BC Alexander the Great entered present day Afghanistan, then part of the Persian Empire. In subsequent centuries invasions by the Scythians, White Huns, and Turks followed. However, in 642 AD the Arabs invaded the whole region and introduced Islam. This Arab rule was followed by various princes attempting to govern various parts of the country. That is until Genghis Khan led the Mongol horde in their invasion of 1219. In the 14th Century Tamerlane incorporated Afghanistan into a vast Asian Empire, and in the 16 Century Babur, a descendant of Tamerlane and founder of India's Moghul dynasty, made Kabul the capital of his Afghan principality.[1] During the 19th Century the collision between the expanding British Empire, and Czarist Russia influenced Afghanistan in what was termed "The Great Game." This resulted in two Anglo-Afghan wars; the first in 1839-42 saw the destruction of a British Expeditionary Force and is an example of the ferocity of the Afghans to foreign rule. The second Anglo-Afghan war was from 1878 to 1880, after which the British and Russians officially established the boundaries of modern Afghanistan.

The recent history of Afghanistan has been dominated by the Soviet invasion of the country in December 1979, after which a force of up to 120,000 Soviet troops were unable to establish authority outside Kabul, with as much as 80% of the countryside being outside effective government control. An overwhelming majority of the Afghan population opposed the Soviets, and their puppet communist government, either actively or passively. The Afghan freedom fighters called "mujahideen," although being poorly armed initially, were soon being rearmed, trained, and assisted financially by the U.S., Saudi Arabia, Pakistan, and other outside powers. By the mid-1980s the tenacious Afghan resistance movement was exacting a high price from the Soviet military, and as well as this, the war was souring the Soviet relations with the western and Islamic world. It was finally in 1988 that the Geneva Accords were signed between the Governments of Pakistan and Afghanistan, with the U.S. and Soviet Union serving as guarantors, which settled the major differences, and more importantly agreed a timetable that ensured a full Soviet withdrawal from Afghanistan by 15 February 1989.[3] It is estimated that 14,500 Soviet troops, and one million Afghans lost their lives in the war between 1979 and 1989.

However, significantly the "mujahideen" were not party to the peace negotiations or the agreement, so understandably they refused to accept the terms of the accord. Consequently, a new civil war started after the Soviet withdrawal, as with the demise of their common enemy the warlords, ethnic, clan, religious, and personality differences became irreconcilable. In reaction to the anarchy created by the warlords, a breakaway movement of former "mujahideen" arose, which became known as the Taliban. This name arose as most of the Taliban had been educated in madrasas in Pakistan, with the name "Talib" meaning pupil.[4] The Taliban dedicated themselves to removing the warlords, imposing Islam throughout the country, and providing order. In this endeavour it received considerable support from Pakistan. By 1994 it had developed enough military strength to capture the city of Kandahar, from where it expanded its control throughout the country capturing Kabul in September 1996. By the end of 1998, it controlled 90% of the country, with the only remaining opposition being from the Tajiks, who were concentrated in the north east of the country and particularly in the Panjshir Valley.

During the mid-1990s the Taliban provided sanctuary to Osama Bin Laden and allowed him to establish bases for his al-Qaeda terrorist organisation. Accordingly, the Taliban received financial and political support from Bin Laden, whose al-Qaeda terrorist group claimed responsibility for the bombing of the U.S. Embassies in Nairobi and Dar es Salaam in 1998, as well as the 9/11 attacks on the Twin Towers in New York. After the latter attack the U.S. demanded that the Taliban expel Bin Laden and al-Qaeda from the country. At the same time they also demanded that the Taliban end their support for international terrorism. The Taliban refused both these requests. Therefore, on 7 October 2001 the U.S. led anti-terrorist coalition began targeting terrorist facilities and Taliban military and political locations throughout Afghanistan. The combination of U.S. air power and the support of the anti-Taliban Northern Alliance ground forces resulted in the Taliban rapidly disintegrating militarily, with Kabul falling to the Coalition Forces on 13 November 2001.[5] In early December, sponsored by the UN, the anti-Taliban factions met in Bonn, Germany and agreed to restore governance to Afghanistan by creating an interim government. Under this Bonn Agreement an Afghan Interim Authority was formed, which took office in Kabul on 22nd December 2001, with Hamid Karzai as the Chairman. He was officially elected as the President in the general election that followed in 2004.

No sooner had the Taliban, Bin Laden and al-Qaeda been routed than the Coalitions military and financial resources were funnelled toward the forthcoming invasion of Iraq. The troop levels were never high enough to completely dominate the topography, and thereby provide a "safe and secure environment." Instead, the Coalition forces that remained were forced to chase the ever elusive enemy back and forth, as they emerged from their safe havens in the mountain ranges of the Hindu Kush, and increasingly from the tribal lands that form the border with Pakistan. Due to this lack of troops the Coalition could only "seize and clear," but more critically they could not "seize and hold" the ground, as the troops were required to redeploy on another operation, where the enemy had miraculously reappeared.

These of course are the tactics, as described by Mao Tse Tung in his famous book 'On Guerrilla Warfare' written in 1937 where he describes:

> "Guerrilla warfare has qualities and objectives peculiar to itself. It is a weapon that a nation inferior in arms and military equipment may employ against a more powerful aggressor nation. When the invader pierces deep into the heart of the weaker country and occupies her territory in a cruel and oppressive manner, there is no doubt that conditions of terrain, climate, and *society* in general offer obstacles to his progress and may be used to advantage by those who oppose him. In guerrilla warfare we turn these advantages to the purpose of resisting and defeating the enemy."

Mao stated that the fundamental axiom of combat on which all military action is based could be stated as: "Conservation of one's own strength; destruction of enemy strength. In operations the guerrilla fades away when confronted by overwhelming enemy strength, only to re-emerge to attack where the enemy is now at his weakest." Mao further described that if your enemies:

> "...military power is inadequate, much of the territory her armies have overrun is without sufficient garrison troops. Under such circumstances, the primary functions of guerrillas are three: first, to conduct a war on exterior lines, that is, in the rear of the enemy; second, to establish bases, and, last, to extend the war areas. Thus, guerrilla participation in the war is not merely a matter of purely local guerrilla tactics but it involves strategic

considerations."

In January 2006, NATO announced that Britain would lead the International Security Assistance Force (ISAF) in Helmand Province, which is in the south of the country. This was after fresh outbreaks of violence had occurred in the province. The British force was to be 3,300 strong, but this soon rose to 10,000, with Camp Bastion being built near the provincial capital of Lashkar Gah, as the HQ for the ISAF personnel. In April 2006, the then Defence Secretary, John Reid visited Afghanistan and stated: "We would be perfectly happy to leave (Helmand Province) in three years without firing a shot." This statement displayed the total naivety with which Britain decided to volunteer to take on responsibility for the Taliban stronghold of Helmand Province, as it was soon found that Britain had inherited a viper's nest, with this new commitment witnessing the heaviest fighting seen since the Korean War.

The vast majority of British casualties in Afghanistan took place after this redeployment of British forces to Helmand Province, as prior to this time only five British servicemen had died between April 2003, and March 2006. However, this was all to change dramatically as by 24 July 2015 there had been a total of 454 British Armed forces personnel Killed-in-Action (KIA), and 2,116 Wounded-in-Action (WIA). A total of 6,663 British personnel were aero-medically evacuated from Afghanistan, to the UK on medical grounds, these being both battle, and non-battle casualties.

Thanks to Dr./Col. Philip ('Tom') Cobley for permission to reproduce an extract from his Best-Selling work on Military History:
'The British Infantry'

Chapter 1

Sergeant Georgina Stone of the Royal Army Physical Training Corps sat behind the driver in the second of two M1151 High-Mobility Multipurpose Wheeled Vehicles, or 'Hummers', as the troops called them, and watched. Her family and friends called her 'George'.

They were heading across Afghanistan's arid and rubble strewn desert towards Lashkar Gah. She held her SA-80 loose, uncocked but ready, as a Chinook helicopter thundered overhead, preparing to land at the base they'd left one hour ago. Unlike most soldiers, who thought Afghanistan was the arse end of the world, George saw its breath-taking beauty. But this South East corner, with its twenty-metre-high sand hills, was as deadly as it came. A sniper or even an ambush team could lie in wait for hours for an easy target to pass, ready to trigger an Improvised Explosive Device (IED). A soldier's survival then depended on preparation, training, guts, and a little luck. George appreciated the beauty and the danger with equal awe and caution. She was with a team assigned to meet with a group of Afghan locals who might offer Intelligence. The Taliban had been active in the area for months. They'd capture Lashkar Gah, as they did Nawa and Nad Ali Districts on the edge of Lashkar Gah, but she doubted the Afghan National Army (ANA) could hold the area on their own without Coalition support. She was thankful she didn't have to make those decisions.

Twelve years of military experience had taught her that ninety five percent of soldiering was planning, preparing, training, and waiting. And that was how her first tour in Afghanistan had been. She'd arrived in Helmand for her second tour a week ago. If this tour turned out the same as the first, she'd be disappointed. However, her mother, and her twin sister, would be relieved.

In the hour they'd been on the road, they'd passed through three Traffic Control Points (TCPs); the Headquarters Controllers tracking their progress throughout the operation. As the Hummer rounded a corner, George peered through the thick reinforced glass side window of the vehicle. The village for their liaison was in the distance. A sand hill bordered the road, less than fifty metres in front and a hundred metres off to the left. It had become visible as they turned the corner.

George saw something appear from the crest as the Gunner/Commander bellowed, "STOP-STOP-STOP! CREST LEFT!"

She grabbed the radio mic and reported, "Contact, Wait out"

The driver stamped on the brake and the gunner tensed and swung the M240 7.62mm machine gun towards the potential target. Momentum is an unforgiving force and the four-ton vehicle stopped as the front left wheel rolled over the explosive device. A bone crunching explosion hit the underneath and left side of the Hummer and lifted it several feet off the ground. The Hummer shook, rattled and complained like an angry camel with a broken leg. It slammed back onto the hard rubble, landing at an acute angle. She guessed the blast had blown off the left front wheel, and probably also shredded the back left wheel.

George's head connected with the armoured window and for several seconds, she saw black, until her eyes refocussed. The driver slumped over the steering wheel, his arms hanging down, lifeless, blood dripping from his ears. The driver's chest moved, confirming he may be alive, for the moment. The gunner was most likely dead or injured, otherwise he would have opened fire on the hill. She looked across at his feet standing on the gear train running the length of the vehicle down the centre. His knees sagged and George guessed the explosion had neutralised him, which meant she was the only one in her vehicle left in the fight. Burnt explosive invaded her sense of smell and she guessed it was an Improvised Explosive Device or IED, and not an anti-tank mine. The latter would have caused more damage. Anyway, an anti-tank mine would likely have been pressure triggered, and she was sure she'd seen someone watching. This was a simple decoy for a bigger attack. The Taliban may want to take the crew alive. That would happen over her dead body.

She'd last seen the lead Hummer about sixty metres in front. She'd expect the Commander to head back and make a contact report. But 'hope' is fickle in war, and a last resort. The driver and gunner needed Casualty Evacuation. She snatched the radio mic to send a SITREP, no response. That wasn't surprising, the blast may have wrecked the antennae on the outside. The ringing from the explosion lessened, and the silence deafened her. Blood dripped into her eyes from a head wound and she wiped it away with her combat jacket sleeve. A disabled Hummer was a death trap; safe enough if left alone, but a sitting target for the Taliban. A Rocket Propelled Grenade (RPG) at 100 to 150 metres could destroy the vehicle and more than likely kill the crew. That would be the Taliban's normal modus operandi. She needed to get the crew and herself out if she could, and quick, seconds counted.

The enhanced armour of the M1151 Humvee meant the vehicle side doors weighed over a hundred kilograms each. The ground to the left of the Hummer jammed the left door closed, making escape impossible by that side door. The right-hand door sloped towards her, and was far too heavy to open manually with muscle power. It could only be opened if another heavy vehicle hooked to the 'D' ring on the outside of the door and ripped it off. There was one other escape route, which was blocked by the gunner. She scanned the terrain through the front and side windows, no sign of attack or rescue. At this moment, her Hummer and its three occupants were sitting ducks. The usual Taliban Standard Operating Procedure or SOP was to mine the vehicle with a tank mine or improvised explosive device, disable the vehicle, and attack its occupants in force. The enemy knew where the driver sat, and an explosion under the left side would stand the best chance of a kill. They'd also know the gunner had been 'neutralised'. But they didn't know about a third crew member.

George stripped out of her armour and combat jacket, down to 'clean fatigue'; she'd need the extra space to crawl out through the turret. She checked her SA80, cocked the weapon, put it on 'safety' and placed it next to her. George thumped the legs of the gunner, which elicited no response. Struggling to place a hand under the gunner's feet, she heaved and squeezed her body under his booted feet. The difficult part was to heave the eighty plus kilos out of the turret and eject him to allow her to leave by the turret. A couple of minutes later, she was sweating like a weightlifter on a heavy workout, but she'd pushed the gunner out like a sack of potatoes. The gunner was now a dead weight behind the turret. She'd check him later.

George dipped back down and heaved on the driver's webbing, but he was too heavy to manhandle via the turret. The driver's pedals were trapping his feet. He'd have to wait and take his chances for the moment. So long as the Taliban didn't overrun the vehicle, they'd be safe, but she expected the enemy would attack soon. She reached down for her SA80, went up into the turret, dropped the back armour plate and slid along the roof, dragging the gunner as she went. She lowered the gunner to the ground over the side of the Hummer away from the hill. The other Hummer took up a firing position using the protection of the reverse slope of a rise. They'd offer covering fire for her. As one of the crew of the other Hummer raced over to check the gunner, George climbed back onto the turret to dismantle the American made M240 from its mounting bracket. With the vehicle at a crazy angle, she must dismount the weapon from the vehicle by pulling the 'retaining pin' and lifting the gun away, but it was a two man job. The M240 from the second Hummer barked short bursts and its rounds struck the hill where George had seen movement earlier. Empty cartridge cases rattled into the ammunition bin.

"Gimme a hand here," she yelled to the guy from the other Hummer. "I'll take the MG; you pull the pin."

On the ground with the MG, she placed herself in a gully, spread the bipod legs and sighted the weapon. She'd never fired this weapon, but she'd fired the British General Purpose Machine Gun or GPMG and known as a 'jimpy', also the Light Support Weapon, how difficult could it be?

"Get inside and see to the driver, he may be alive but

he needs attention. He's trapped, see if you can free him. I'll cover you with the jimpy."

The other soldier nodded, climbed onto the vehicle, and disappeared inside.

The 'Whup', 'Whup' of a chopper some distance away suggested a rescue. Their mission now was to observe, prepare to hold the enemy off, and provide the CASEVAC helicopter with covering fire. The Taliban usually dissolved into the desert when reinforcements arrived. Unless this was a complex attack, and the attack on the Hummer was a 'come on' to draw in a helicopter and attempt to bring it down. The Taliban were awash with Stinger anti-aircraft missiles, courtesy of the CIA, which had provided them to the Mujahideen to destroy Soviet helicopters and aircraft. A complex attack might also lead to a heavy attack on any surviving troops coming to the rescue. She familiarised herself with the M240, cocked the weapon and sited on the crest of the hill where she'd seen the head bobbing up. George lay behind the M240 as the machine gun on the other Hummer fell silent. She looked across to see the gunner struggling with the weapon, probably a blockage. She let off a short burst to check the fall of shot and, adjusting her aim, then fired a longer burst.

***

Back at base, she had a medical, which gave her the all clear. Then a solo debrief, written and verbal, followed by a debrief with the convoy crews. The initial consensus was that an IED caused the explosion. Had the enemy set an Anti-Tank Mine, such as the TM-57 or TM-62, it would have been endgame for the crew of the Hummer.

Now back in her quarters, George began her evening ritual. Looking up from her book, 'Combat Command' by

Colonel Philip (Tom) Cobley, she checked her watch. George commandeered a laptop available for emails to family. She maintained contact with her mother, Julia Stone and her twin sister, Charlotte, who everyone called Charlie. If she could, she wrote a letter to each once a week, and a daily email together.

Hi Mum and Charlie,

Hope you're both OK and enjoying the rainy summer in the UK. Here it's a modest 32 degrees. Good to know you're together at home and Charlie's working from home for the summer. Mum, I hope she's looking after you! Has she brought a boyfriend with her? If so, I want a full report, I bet he's one of her designer friends, who says things like "Darling, you look scrumptious in chiffon".

Charlie, don't let Mum wait on you. You're an idle sod when you're home. You two should have a girls' party and invite Aunt Sheila. Have a drink on me. And Mum, don't let Charlie get pissed, you know what she's like; she gets carried away and makes a fool of herself, dancing around like she did when she was five.

Mum, say hello to Aunt Sheila when you next speak to her, please give her my love, and ask how Postmistressing is going and when she's going to retire. She's been threatening to retire for years. Tell her I'm OK and I'll write to her soon.

Mum, you asked when I'm coming home; not sure, I've just arrived. Can't say where I am, but maybe home for Christmas, who knows? As soon as I know, I'll tell you. We'll have a party and a few drinks.

Little has happened today. Took a trip in a Hummer, but not much to tell. Bloody hot in those things. Got a ride in a helicopter too. Beat that, Charlie. Don't worry about me, either of you. It's safer here than walking down some streets in the UK.

Tell me all the local gossip, and I'll contact you both again tomorrow.

Love you both, email me soon.

Traitors

George
X

Chapter 2

4 Months later

Three knocks at the door brought Julia out of her daydream, and thoughts of spending Christmas with her daughters, although it was weeks away. She looked around the curtain. The wind was blowing autumn leaves all over the place. She'd have to sweep them later.

A thin, officious looking man, wearing a decades-old suit, stood on her doorstep. Julia Stone looked in the mirror to reassure herself that she looked presentable. Satisfied, she opened the door with a cautious smile.

"Yes, how can I help you?" she said, sounding like someone from an abandoned era. Outdated or not, she'd taught her girls that manners cost nothing.

"Good morning to you, Mrs Stone," said the caller in a nasal tone.

She waited. Her question remained unanswered and her smile remained fixed.

A slight cough from the man. She sensed his discomfort as his hands fidgeted at his jacket collar. An air of a 1960s bank clerk enfolded him.

"My name is Pinchin, Wilson Pinchin. Could you spare me a few minutes? I'm here on a matter of some import, which I must discuss with you."

Pinchin offered Julia his card, which she grasped but didn't look at.

With a name like Wilson Pinchin, he must be a solicitor.

"You'd better come in, Mr Pinchin."

She led the way to the dining room and pointed to a chair at the table. Old barber shops and over-applied rubbing alcohol insulted her nostrils. Pinchin laid his briefcase at his feet, and adjusted it to his satisfaction. Julia tried to disguise her worry. Her only relatives were her precious daughters, and any harm to which they might come would tear her world apart. There was Tony, her ex-husband, but she hadn't heard from him for decades. Perhaps he'd died. Waiting was her forte, and she felt no need to put Pinchin at ease. He was reminiscent of a dark alleyway on a drizzly January night; or a cobweb she'd remove the next time she cleaned. She shivered.

"Mrs Stone, I have a matter of delicacy and urgency to bring to your attention."

Julia sat straight and stared at Pinchin. The threat was subtle, but certain. Pinchin studied the grain on the wooden table.

"What is it? My daughters, are they alright? I spoke to Charlie yesterday and George is abroad." Her voice trembled, giving away her concern.

Pinchin raised his gaze to fix Julia's. The corner of his eyes twitched, giving her a hint. Something had piqued his sensibilities.

"As far as I know they are fine, Mrs Stone. No, this is something my client wishes to request of you; a favour."

Julia sighed and immediately regretted her earlier show of emotion to a stranger, or anyone, except family. It revealed weakness. What did this man want? It filled her with dread. Pinchin stretched it out, a master of timing, a performance perfected over years.

"My client is familiar with your former predilection and vocation, and wants to avail himself of your work and expertise, Mrs Stone, for a generous consideration, of course."

The Soviet Union had fallen decades earlier and Julia Stone had hoped she and her colleagues could quietly 'retire'.

She pressed her hands flat on the table to hold them steady, held Pinchin's gaze and lowered her voice by an octave, "Mr Pinchin, whatever I may have been, whatever I did, whatever my earlier beliefs, I am not that person now. My kind is obsolete, our usefulness has lapsed. My compliments to your client, but the answer is, 'No'."

It was Pinchin's turn to sigh with a perceptible shake of his head. "That is a pity. You have skills for which the person I represent would make a generous remuneration. You can also help retrieve certain… information he would find… useful."

Pinchin sounded tired, boredom etched across his face. He'd lingered on the last word, waited, and held Julia's gaze. There was no reason to repeat herself. Half a minute passed, Pinchin and Julia each waiting for the other to break.

"I'll show you out, Mr Pinchin."

"Thank you. I will convey your answer. My client will be disappointed. He has the means and the inclination to ensure his desired resolution and your acquiescence, but if you change your mind in the next forty-eight hours, please telephone me, otherwise…."

He paused, leaching menace. "Good day, Mrs Stone."

Julia Stone led Pinchin out and closed the door, which shuddered, then leaned against it, wrapping her arms around her body.

As Pinchin sat in his car on the track leading to the road, she watched him take out his mobile phone and speak to someone, and wondered who it was, a shiver revealing her trepidation. The time she'd dreaded had arrived, and 'preparations' had to be completed.

Chapter 3

Sergeant George Stone, stood between the 26 Engineer Regiment being physically fit for the forthcoming battle to establish a new joint forward operating base near the Nahr-e-Seraj canal and a lazy day. Her mission today was to take the troops on a gruelling two-hour beasting, a light lunch then first aid training with the medical NCOs whilst the rest did essential maintenance on their armoured vehicles and their kit.

But at 0630 hours with the sun baking the ground, her immediate mission was to slake her camels arse thirst, complete her ablutions and look as if she meant business, instead of a woman trying her best to unfug her brain, which after a pint of shandy the night before and a laugh with the lads, shouldn't have been difficult. A woman sharing her tent snored in a manner suggesting she'd be out for at least a couple of hours. The other sleeping bag lay empty.

She'd usually be the first to arise in the morning, but Corporal Faiza Mirza, her assistant, had beaten her to it. Cpl Mirza's orders for the day included assisting the close protection team for an incoming Brigadier. Mirza, a newcomer in her first tour, was lazy as hell and a loner, frequently talking to her family back in Leicester in Urdu. Mirza had explained that her mum and dad spoke only Urdu, but her constant gibbering in Urdu annoyed her colleagues and Stone spent time neutralising squabbles.

As she made her way over to the female showers, the Squadron Sergeant Major ran towards her, returning from his morning run and sweating like an Afghan squaddie in a fire fight, his chest heaving.

"Morning, George. Change of plan. Cpl Mirza reported sick last night. Cancel training today. You're going with the away team to support close protection for that one star. Okay?"

"Roger, Sir. Who'll take the training?"

"AN Other. The OC picked you from a cast of one. Get your kit sorted and prepare to move at 0900 hours. Clear?"

"Clear, Sir."

***

The Puma pilot kept the helicopter blades turning as the team deplaned. Sgt Stone followed Brigadier Wyson, the British Army's Director of Support Services, out of the chopper. At that moment, he was one of the most protected people in Afghanistan. The Brigadier stood at five foot six inches, his escort swamped him and, at a little over six feet, Sgt Stone was one of the tallest of the team. She looked down at the back of Wyson, less than a metre in front of her. His head was level with her shoulders. The Puma lifted and created a back draft, disturbing sand and debris and making visibility almost zero. As they marched at a brisk pace, the sand settled and Stone closed in behind Wyson. Seconds later, an impact made her stagger forward, knocking her into Wyson. A scything burn hit her right rear shoulder and Sgt George Stone's body shuddered from the shock wave of a high velocity round.

Silence. Then, a microsecond later, she sensed rather than heard the 'zing' of the high-velocity projectile slicing the air, the round pierced her right shoulder and exited near her collar bone. Stone felt little after the shoulder impact. The round, now slowed by the impact with Stone, carried on its trajectory and clipped the side of Wilson's head. A serious injury but probably not life threatening.

Before Wyson hit the ground, a second round entered the back of the Brigadier's head. The bullet entered, tumbled and span, ripping out spine, throat, and connective tissue and coming to rest in the base of Wyson's skull. A moment later, the supersonic crack of the second high-velocity round resonated. Sgt Stone collapsed onto Brigadier Wyson in a ballet of death and guilt. Her body slumped and straddled Wyson. It wasn't Stone's fault, although she'd trained in Close Protection, she'd come along for the ride. Despite George's shoulder injury, seeing Wyson transition from living to dead in the time to blink, triggered indelible and inexorable trauma and guilt. They lay together in a bundle of pink grey gore with most of the fluid coming from Wyson.

A third round sliced along the back of Stone's thigh. She guessed it was a flesh wound, but it hurt like hell and far more than her shoulder. Stone attempted to return fire, but her body refused to obey and her assault rifle, the SA80 L85A2, lay out of reach, a metre away.

"Contact, wait out," came the shout from Sergeant Stan

Ford, the Platoon Sergeant, over the Personal Role Radio.

Not yet in shock, Georgina's mind cleared. A sniper was likely positioned beyond the crest, a few hundred metres away. She had to order suppressing fire, then the pop, pop came from the 5.56×45 mm rounds from her section's SA80s and sustained automatic fire from the support weapon. Sgt Ford had read her thoughts. The sniper knew he'd made at least one kill. A sniper's standard operating procedure was to withdraw down the reverse slope. However, another sniper may wait. They remained vulnerable.

"Contact, sniper 500 metres north of our drop point. Two casualties, CASEVAC, immediate, am engaging," Ford reported, urgent but calm.

George had started her Afghan tour with Sergeant Ford, and they'd hit it off from the get go. They were as close as Army mates could be. If this had to happen, best to happen on his watch.

Despite George Stone bleeding from the shoulder wound, she still considered Wyson as her charge and her responsibility. But one glance at him told her it would take the combined efforts of the saints to resurrect him. Whoever the sniper was, he was skilled and knew his target. But when he'd hit her shoulder, was it a sudden movement causing him to hit her shoulder instead of Wyson's head, or was he trying to be flash. In her experience, professional and experienced snipers rarely made mistakes and were never 'flash', so it must have been a sudden and unexpected movement. But why the third round into her thigh? A third possibility spinning through her mind like a high velocity round, was she the target? Ridiculous, why would she be a target? If Cpl Mirza had taken this assignment, she'd be lying in the Afghan dust with bullet holes in her, or would she? She dismissed it in an instant.

Someone pressed a field dressing to her shoulder. She lay still and guessed morphine was coursing around her body, deadening the pain but not the mental wound. It felt like mere minutes, but she'd done the calculations, a minute to report the contact, fifteen minutes for the chopper to get to them, seconds to load and fifteen minutes to return to relative safety. If she was lucky, she might not bleed to death.

The 'wup wup wup' of rotor blades and the smell of high-octane aviation fuel revealed the passage of time. Someone heaved her onto a stretcher and into a Lynx helicopter.

"Brigadier Wyson?" George mumbled, trying to turn her head in Wyson's direction.

"Never mind him, George. We'll be at Boost Hospital in a few minutes," responded the medic, slipping an oxygen mask over her face. The answer confirmed what she already knew. She'd failed in the worst way a soldier could fail, he'd died and she might yet live.

"Fuck, we'd better move it, we're losing her. She needs blood," the medic told the pilot.

"Don't swear," George murmured. "No need."

George thought about her Mum and her twin sister. The three were close, especially since her dad had left them years earlier. Mum taught Charlie and George they should fight like lions and act like ladies, including manners, amongst them no swearing, which men tolerated, women ignored, and ladies never uttered. Pain no longer wracked her body, more morphine she guessed, and despite the surrounding noises, she needed her Mum. Someone shouted 'Mum', and it may have been her mind playing tricks. Although weakness dragged at her, she tried to sit up, but a reassuring hand pushed her down. Training didn't cover this part of Army life; only living and fighting, never dying.

The thwack, thwack, thwack of the overworked Lynx rotors beat air, demanding height. It pummelled her head, and the machine banked hard. Her survival was now with the Lynx crew, her Methodist God, and the thought of her Mum and sister.

Chapter 4

Some weeks after suffering from her injuries in Afghanistan and after several operations to restore her right shoulder, Sgt George Stone was moved to Stanford Hall near Nottingham to the 'Defence and National Rehabilitation Centre'. Their aim was to rebuild both George's body and mind to something approaching full fitness. In comparison, mending the body was relatively easy, but the mind is an altogether more difficult and complex organism to mend. George had heard of Post-Traumatic Stress Disorder before her first deployment to Afghanistan. She'd attended lectures and even paid attention to some. But it wasn't something that would affect her, and perhaps all soldiers thought that way. It wasn't something soldiers talked about openly. Few soldiers admitted it, but most thought only the weak succumbed to PTSD.

During her worst moments following her move to Stanford Hall, George raged and cursed, but the Defence Medical Rehabilitation Centre (DMRC) staff talked through the events that led to her state, raising her self-esteem, and taught her how to cope with the negative thoughts and blame. But PTSD is a wily enemy and can strike when it's least expected, especially during the quiet times and at night. A single thought, smell, touch, or word could trigger George into fits of crying, rage, despair, or paralysis. The prescribed meds helped her insomnia, but the regular nightmares persisted.

Jerking to a sitting position in bed, she gasped and listened for the helicopter rotors. It took a minute to quieten her thumping chest and control her breathing. As she filtered out the pounding, it left her with the sound of radiators creaking, heating for the day ahead. Her hand rubbed across her face. Another nightmare.

The nightmares were a constant companion since she'd been shot three months earlier. Even during the surgery to rebuild her shoulder, and the blood transfusions, which seemed to take days, her mind floated between guilt and anguish at Brigadier Wyson's death. The torment of knowing that her Mum, and Charlie, her twin sister, were waiting for news, and the agony it caused them.

Sweat soaked the bed sheets. A bandage covered her left leg and the flesh wound to her thigh. She reached down and massaged it before dressing in a tracksuit. Sometimes her titanium shoulder felt like an alien clawing its way out. No point in complaining, she knew what she'd signed up for.

The darkness and rain greeted her as she limped out and gritted her teeth to start her two-mile run. The staff at Stanford Hall, the Ministry of Defence's Rehabilitation Centre, told her to stick to a slow fifteen minutes, but George needed to push herself, to show her Mum and Charlie she could be 'normal' again; whatever that meant after Afghanistan.

A counsellor told her to concentrate on the positive, to see each step forward as progress. The pain was weakness, trying to escape. She believed some of it. George thanked the Army Medics for saving her life. It was enough for her to live, without complaining. But, no one saw the pain, only the scars and her veterans' tortured gait. Her injuries were no excuse, but a reminder of her strength and determination to succeed. She'd tasted failure when Wyson had died, and facing it was a painful necessity, but it offended her self-respect and probity.

George increased her speed, pulling her right shoulder across her chest for comfort, and tried to limit the pressure on her left leg to prevent it bleeding again. Ordinarily, she would have looked deformed, but at Stanford Hall it was normal. She passed one other person and exchanged a nod. Looks weren't important right now.

She ran through the gates of Stanford Hall, pondering the day ahead. She had a medical and fitness Assessment Board in one month. They'd decide whether she had a future in the Army.

Chapter 5

Templeton Maudlin preferred his women elegant, beautiful, and dead. His contact assured him this coming event would deliver that. The shadows in the alleyway concealed him, but he stepped back, his enthusiasm for his work, his anticipation of the pleasure to come and his eagerness spurred him forward, and he restrained himself. The outskirts of Grain, in Essex at 11 p.m., was almost deserted. Even during the day, it was so quiet, some locals called it 'zombie central'; others called it 'Bliss Bay'.

A physical distance from the 'wet work' was essential, and uppermost in his mind. Even with an overcast night sky, he could see the van parked across the road, twenty metres away. It had neither side nor back windows; but emblazoned on its side was an advertisement for 'Stone Cold Air Conditioning'. Maudlin thought it rather clever. He used a different one each time.

Michael, his idiot but strong and loyal assistant, sat behind the wheel of the van. His head bobbed, and Templeton assumed he was listening to music. He hoped the boy was paying attention. Close to the vehicle, across the road, was the park, its gates open. A lone female dog walker, in her late sixties with a pug type dog, strolled towards the gates to exit the park. Her dog walked off the lead, which hung from her hand. She carried a bag to clean up after the animal. Templeton shuddered. Some people would do anything for their pets. He couldn't understand such devotion, neither to animals nor people.

As she headed for the park gates, she called 'Puggins', and Templeton curled his lip in a sneer. The dog ran after her. She bent to attach the lead and stroked its head. She may have whispered tender words.

A man appeared from Maudlin's left and strode across the pavement towards the van, tall and well-muscled, his movements fluid; a killer by profession. Seeing the killer gave Templeton Maudlin goose bumps. The man looked casual, but not furtive, his hands in his pockets and his jacket collar pulled up. The dank weather and overcast sky complimented the man's mission. Woman and dog exited the park, turned right, oblivious to the man's presence. A few steps out of the park, she walked past the unseen killer, who drew close behind her. If she felt his presence or smelt his cigarette breath, she showed no sign. Maudlin inched back into the alleyway, wishing to have a ringside view of the next minute.

Templeton Maudlin described himself as a voyeur. He thirsted for this moment, but he was no scopophile, but an unfettered artist and metaphysician. Templeton was a self-declared coward who dreaded exposure and incarceration. He was also a respected Funeral Director. He gained great pleasure from his work, a deserved bonus, and a service to society.

A woman's transformation from one state, vibrant and alive, which he loathed, to the obverse; pure and dead, which he cherished and revered, was spiritually and intellectually stimulating. This was no fetish, which implied a sexual motivation. This was far removed from mere concupiscence. Philistines would consider it a 'foible', but the more enlightened, 'high art'. Each time he experienced it, it left him drained but invigorated.

The killer removed his hands from his pockets and withdrew a wire loop, hand grips at the ends. His female victim gasped as the loop of wire dropped over her head and rested along the line of her neck. The unfortunate woman issued the slightest protest, silenced by the loop tightening. Terror replaced her 'normal' life.

The dog, now forgotten; her hand went to her neck. Satisfied he'd set the garrotte correctly, the killer twisted his body 180 degrees, back-to-back with his victim, bent forward, and lifted the woman off her feet by her neck. His hands grasped the hand grips, his arms taut and straight by his sides. The woman's feet kicked, not in panic but in death. The dog ran into the park, disappearing into the night.

The van's side door slid open, and the killer slung the limp woman onto the floor of the van. He removed the scrag from around her neck, pocketed it, and walked down the road. The van door closed with a 'bang', as final as the death of the woman. A couple of minutes elapsed between the woman exiting the park and the killer resuming his walk. As the killer disappeared into the dank darkness, Templeton Maudlin stepped out of the alleyway and walked on unsteady legs across the road towards the van. Attempting to stop his hands shaking, he opened the van's passenger door with difficulty.

Behind the wheel, Michael smiled at him and put the vehicle into gear. Templeton Maudlin glanced in the side mirror as the van pulled out and a woman's shadow exited a shop doorway. For a moment, he felt the woman's stare, but dismissed it as the after effects of his latest experience.

"To the Funerarium, Mr Maudlin?"

Templeton nodded, and breathed deeply to calm his nerves. Michael drove the van as if nothing untoward had happened.

***

Julia Stone had watched it all whilst standing concealed in a shop doorway. She expected the killing. If she wasn't next, she was moving up the queue. She might have helped her long-time 'comrade by circumstance', but it would have achieved nothing, except her own premature demise.

After watching the killer dump the unfortunate woman in the van, Julia watched him slip his weapon into his jacket pocket and continue down the road, looking neither left nor right and passing less than three metres from her. She noted his features, thin but athletic, muscled but not muscular, relaxed but taut, focussed but undisturbed. Not a regular murderer, but a professional assassin.

Julia watched a short, wiry character appear from an alleyway and walk unsteadily towards the van. The man dressed like a throwback to a 1950s black and white film. From his movements, he was drunk, drugged, or mentally deranged, and complicit in the killing, or his timing was impeccable. The little man boarded the van.

Julia Stone remained hidden, certain no one had seen her arrive, and if she kept quiet and hidden, no one would see her leave.

Chapter 6

The killing Julia Stone had witnessed gave her a fretful night, but by morning she'd decided what she must do. She might have days left, not long to prepare. She'd reduce it to essentials. The priority was the 'safeguard', as she called it. Most of the work she'd completed over the years since the 1970s, ever since she realised making copies of detailed, confidential records, might save her own life, and any family she might one day have. Now she considered herself expendable, but others may reason, her death was desirable, even essential. She'd ensure it would come at a price. She worked tirelessly for over twenty-four hours without a break.

Her precious daughters were now her only family, and this final work would ensure they wouldn't suffer the same fate awaiting her. Nothing more to do than copy, collate and format the information. Her final task was to write two letters, one to each of her daughters.

The farm house's East-facing window looked out over the fields, a track, and fences and further on, the sea. She gazed out as she'd done for years. She never tired of seeing the sun rising and feeling the warmth massaging her ageing skin.

As usual, the kettle boiled for tea; the radio tuned to John Humphreys on Radio 4. A couple of slices of bread were in the toaster. She leaned back, exhausted, but satisfied. The clock on the mantelpiece showed 7 a.m., too early to phone Sheila Wallis, her friend at the village Post Office. A bleep from the computer told her its work was complete. Now, only the packaging and letters to write. She enveloped the memory sticks, ready to go with the letters. As an afterthought, she wrote a brief letter to Sheila Wallis, if she didn't see her again. She'd know what to do.

John Humphreys told his audience, Russia had blockaded Sevastopol, killed several Ukrainians, and an EU official. Nothing changed. By 1990 the West thought the Cold War was over, they'd tamed the Russian Bear. Fools, she scoffed to herself. For Putin, the Cold War wasn't even halfway through. Anyone with common sense, and a sense of history, could have predicted this. She prayed for her daughters' safety in a dangerous world.

George could look after herself. From being a little girl, she'd possessed an inner strength and determination. She insisted on attending the Methodist Church, despite other children teasing her at school. After two tours in Afghanistan, she'd proved herself. She stayed positive, even as she recuperated at Stanford Hall after being shot. George was more like her mother, but she worried more about Charlie, the naïve hothead who would argue with herself.

She liked her toast lathered in butter, decadent but delicious, and the smell of melting butter, scrumptious. After one bite, she laid down the toast and wrote the letters to her daughters using her fountain pen. She thought it disrespectful to write a personal letter on a computer. They had their uses, but personal letters weren't one of them, something she'd instilled in her girls. Computers also left traces.

She spent about ninety minutes writing the letters, and placed an old photo of herself and her daughters in each of her daughters' envelopes. She placed the envelopes with her pile of early Christmas cards and sighed. It was so final, inadequate, but the best she could do. How do you tell your twin daughters, who you've raised on your own, that you've been leading a double life, without it appearing that you've deceived them? Which she had? She'd tried to be a decent mother, but had her efforts been good enough?

A shiver down her back told her she'd never again see her children. They were twenty-nine years old, but to her, they were children. Such a shame; so many things she had to explain to them, so much she needed to apologise for. The letters would have to do. Charlie and George were both bright, but different. They'd get together, fill in the pieces and not judge her too harshly.

After breakfast, she glanced at the clock. By the time she reached the Post Office, it would be after 9 a.m. As Julia adjusted the curtain, she looked across at the gate and track. The dark blue Mondeo hadn't moved. The car appeared empty, but she knew better. A simple trick to cover yourself with coats or bags, lie between the front and back seats, and stare at a smartphone connected to a tiny camera on the dashboard. But, even the slightest movement in the car caused its suspension to shift.

She gathered the letters and cards, placed them in her bag and left by the side door, closing it so quietly that she couldn't detect a noise. If someone was waiting in the lane, she'd face them when she came to it. Hopefully, the man in the car would assume she was still in the house.

Julia hurried, controlling her breathing to avoid panic. Even after all she'd done, this was the most important thing she'd ever do. As she turned onto the street, she didn't look back, but heard soft-soled shoes closing with her. Despite her even pace, the person gained on her. She clutched her bag and prepared to run towards the Post Office. Unlikely she'd make it, but she had to try, for her daughters' sake. Slap, slap, slap on the tarmac, a little faster. He'd soon be on her. Her mind revisited the killing she'd seen two nights ago, imagining the garrotte encircling her neck. It would all be over within thirty seconds.

"In a hurry, Julia?"

Her steps faltered, and her body refused to move. She prepared to run, but her mind and body failed her, struck by paralysis and indecision, whether to run or fight.

Clutching her bag to her body, she stuck out her chin and turned to face the man following her. Her best bet was to use her feet if she got a shot between his legs, but his smell made her hesitate, sweat and bad breath. The local Postman faced her. Julia let out a breath she'd been holding.

"You alright Julia, you look like you want to kill me?" asked Alf, the ever-cheerful Postman. Today, he looked concerned.

"Sorry, Alf. I thought you were following me. Are you going to the Post Office?" she said. "Can we walk together? Would you take my arm?" she added.

"You're fair shaking; I'll be pleased to escort you."

The two caught Sheila Wallis opening the Post Office. Sheila stood in the doorway, a motherly woman in her seventies with a gravity defying, mantelpiece bosom. Her apron gave her a WW2 look, but her sunshine smile welcomed Julia Stone. They'd known each other since Julia had first come to the town in the early 70s and remained close friends. Even though Sheila Wallis knew her friend's faults, background, and failings, she didn't judge, but rebuked her with a tender-heartiness some may have taken as motherly, others as a weakness, and some as naïve. Sheila was neither weak nor naïve. As Postmistress, she had more than a passing knowledge of everyone in the village. She'd nursed some, knew most of the villagers' secrets, and kept them to herself. She'd even babysat George and Charlie, who considered her a second mother.

Julia held onto the Postman's arm until they entered the small shop.

"Come into the back, love. I've put the kettle on. Alf, get three mugs out please, and warm the pot. You can hold the fort in the shop for half an hour, can't you?"

Alf took the hint and disappeared to man the counter. Sheila sat facing Julia and took her hands. "Tell me what this is about and how I can help."

"The time has come, Sheila. Can you take care of this lot for me?" said Julia, her voice shaking, handing over the pile of Christmas cards.

"Are you sure? It could be your imagination, love," said Sheila, taking the pile and looking into Julia's eyes.

"No, I'm sure. I saw them kill one of us."

Julia looked at the older woman tearfully, they threatened to stream down her cheeks. It was rare, but not the first time. She swallowed hard, coughed, and attempted to be business-like. The Postman's voice filtered through to the back as he served customers. Over the next half hour, Julia reiterated what they'd previously discussed and agreed over the last twenty-five years. Sheila nodded, resigned to the inevitable departure of her closest friend.

Julia took three envelopes from her bag.

"We discussed this. These are the letters to the girls." She handed over the two letters for her daughters and her own letter to Sheila, who put them in the safety of her apron pocket. "You know what to do with these?"

She didn't need to ask Sheila if she'd do it, or if she minded breaking the law and abusing her position as a Postmistress. "When it happens, please give the girls the letters, when the time is right."

"Right you are, love. I hope you're wrong, but you rarely are."

They hugged, and Sheila pulled Julia into her arms. This wasn't the first time Julia had sought respite by putting her head in the fortress of the shorter woman's bosom. Her body fitted there as if it belonged. Sheila stroked her hair and whispered to her. Although they both knew this day might come, they assumed it would come later rather than sooner.

"Be brave, Julia, and fight to your last breath. Don't let them have you, girl. You're strong."

Julia nodded and pulled away.

"Watch the girls for me, Sheila, and if they have questions, try to explain."

"Yes, of course I will."

"Oh, can you post all those Christmas cards, please, Sheila? I don't have stamps, I'm afraid."

"Don't you worry; I'll take care of them."

"I'd better go,"

"Should I ask Alf to go with you?"

"No, I'm better on my own. There's no point in him getting hurt."

Sheila used the corner of her apron to wipe Julia's face, as a mother would to her beloved child.

After a final hug, Julia left the Post Office and headed towards her house. As she did, her mobile rang.

"Hello?" hesitation exposing her worry.

"Hi, Mum, It's Charlie. Where are you? Great news, I'm home early."

"Where are you, Charlie?"

"At home, lying on my bed. Can't wait to see you. Where are you? Who's the guy sitting in the car outside?"

"Charlie, listen to me. I'm a few minutes away. Leave the house. Now! Do you hear me? Now!"

Panic almost overtook her.

Chapter 7

Bradley Maudlin - Aged 7

Since his childhood, Bradley Maudlin had considered his father, Templeton Maudlin, weird, if not downright monstrous. However, his mother was as saintly as his father was weird. Seven-year-old Bradley Maudlin listened from the balcony, cowering behind the rails, as his father's van pulled into the parking area of the funeral parlour. The house side door slammed shut. His father dropped something, a bag. A war of words ensued between his mother and the monster. By the sounds of it, at least one of his parents would be dead by morning.

"It's past midnight. I don't need to ask what you've been doing, you…," said Bradley Maudlin's mother, searching for a sufficiently vitriolic word, then settled on, "excuse for a man," she sobbed.

"You know, I have no choice," said Templeton Maudlin.

"No choice? Did you enjoy tonight with… with… and

do I need to ask what's in your bag?" said his mother, spitting the words.

"I'll do what I want. Get me a drink and go to bed."

More sobbing and a wailing scream.

"I despise you, Templeton. Once more, I'll call the police. I'm sick of it."

Bradley saw shadows at the bottom of the stairs. Despite his father's short stature, his shadow loomed over the thin, frail shadow of his mother.

"You'll be next before then, and I'll add yours to my collection."

Bradley heard a slap and a cry of pain, which he also felt. Another thud and a slap. It wasn't the first time his father had hit his mother. A slap was usual, but this level of brutality had a malignant energy previously absent. He wanted to run down the stairs and protect her, to whisper to her, "I'll take your beating". But at seven, his father would give him the same treatment. Instead, he crept behind the banister, hid, listened, waited, and cringed.

"Tell the police about this," shouted Templeton Maudlin. More thuds accompanied his father's grunted words. Boot or fist, Bradley couldn't tell. He curled into a ball and shook. He must have made it to his bedroom because he awoke in the morning, his pillow wet with tears and bed sheets wet with urine.

Bradley remembered his father threatening to take one of his mother's fingers for his 'collection'. It didn't take long to work out where his father kept this collection. A few weeks later, his father made the mistake of leaving the door open and Bradley gained access to his father's 'Display Room', as Bradley called it. Despite his tender years, although it disgusted him, it didn't scare him. But the rows of fingers were a testament to his father's depraved derangement.

By the age of ten, Bradley challenged his father regarding his behaviour and his excursions. Templeton Maudlin explained to his son with a calm understanding, that it was none of his concern. Bradley's second, more forceful enquiry eight years later met with a bad-tempered response and a similar concluding message.

"Sometimes I do things you might think are strange. I am a Funeral Director and sometimes things aren't what they seem."

He poked his bony finger at Bradley's chest to punctuate his point. "My business is my business. When I want your concern or your interference, I shall tell you. Clear?"

Bradley nodded, but he hadn't explained why he had to 'stay in his room', or the strange phone calls and fevered activity on these nights, or the morning after, when his father was as carefree, calm, and happy as a hippy on laughing gas. His father had always been his persecutor. Templeton had trampled his son's heart and spirit to stultify him, but Bradley loved his father as a prisoner comes to love his jailer.

He never enquired again, and saw no advantage in pursuing his father's strange aberrations. And so, things remained, until now. Over the years, Bradley's opinion of his father hadn't changed, but it had inured. His father was criminally weird.

On each occasion his father received such a call, he disappeared with Michael, his idiot helper, and returned hours later. On his return, he forbade young Bradley to roam the house at night.

***

Present Day - Bradley Maudlin aged 30

The door between the library and his father's study was open. Bradley Maudlin sat reading, watching his father, whose peculiar traits disgusted him. But Bradley showed no reaction. Frequency made it familiar and eventually desensitised him. His father showed telltale mannerisms, which he seemed unable to control.

Templeton Maudlin pressed the house phone to his ear and adjusted his black horn-rimmed glasses on the bridge of his hawk nose, then gripped the bowl of his pipe and ground the stem between his teeth. One corner of his lip curled and quivered, anticipating a forthcoming pleasure. Templeton Maudlin let go of the pipe bowl, gripped the edge of his desk, then rubbed his thumb and first two fingers of his right hand together, his excitement rising.

Templeton Maudlin placed his unlit pipe into a small box, which he locked in his desk drawer, depositing the key in his waistcoat pocket. As his father left the 'Funerarium', Bradley slipped on his parka and left by a side door. Michael sat at the wheel of the van, his father riding shotgun. Michael's presence and his father's reaction confirmed this would be another one of his father's 'strange events'. Today, Bradley Maudlin might discover what 'strange' meant.

Bradley's nerves jangled as he stepped from his concealment. He followed the van in his own car, his hands shaking. A sheltered upbringing and a university degree in Social Engineering did not qualify him for this. He'd thought about it for years. But 'planned' would be to overstate his preparation. There was nothing wrong with him driving along the same stretch of road as his father. And anyway, it's a free country. He'd take it one step at a time and if threatened, he'd run like hell.

He parked behind his father's van as his father strolled through the five-bar gate, carrying a holdall, and walked down the dirt track towards the back of a farmhouse.

Bradley followed at a safe distance, pulling up his parka hood and hunching his shoulders as he walked past the van. Bradley's height and ungainly manner made him stand out. He was aware he looked like a giraffe on an outing from the zoo. But music leaked from the van, and Michael was intent on making the most of the music, his head bobbing to the beat. Michael was ideal as a helper, short, strong, innocent, and slack minded, leading to insensitivity to the dead and an indifference to his employer's activities.

Following the route taken by his father, he entered a conservatory at the rear of the house. As he slipped inside, a shuffling sound came from the front room. His father was not stupid and might see him, but he gathered his courage and waited, concealed.

A smell of lavender permeated the place, reminding Bradley of obsessive cleaning, an aged and ripened housewife, a home tended for an absent but loved family.

Shadows in the front room showed someone other than his father in the house. Breathing sharply, he held his breath, hands shaking, legs weakening and palms moist. He feared his father may have sensed his presence. He looked around for a weapon, nothing. What was he thinking? Could he beat his father to death? After all, his presence may be innocent and legitimate. His best strategy was to hide and wait. He hadn't taken a breath for a while and gasped.

A woman shouted from the front room and Bradley forgot about his breathing.

"Jesus Christ," shrieked his father.

"What the bloody hell are you doing here? What have you done to my Mum, you bastard?" a girl's voice, half sob, half in anger.

Expecting a reply from his father, a scuffle ensued, then silence. Hands still shaking, Bradley took out his phone. Knowing his father's history of violence towards women, there could be no question; his father had attacked the girl, and maybe killed her. He dialled 999 and whispered, cupping his hand around his mouth and the phone.

"My name's Bradley Maudlin and I'm at...," he hesitated.

"On West Lane, Grain. I don't know the address. An old farmhouse near the firing range on the coast, going out of Grain. I think someone may have died," he guessed, but it would get someone's attention.

"I think police and ambulance. Quick."

The phone clicked off, leaving him alone. His face broke out in a cold sweat. What now? Should he barge in on his father or stay hidden? His father spoke to someone on a mobile phone. Bradley Maudlin's next decision changed his life.

Chapter 8

George took a few seconds' break from physiotherapy as sweat leached down her body and her tracksuit stuck to her. She took out a handkerchief and wiped her cold, damp face. A year ago, she'd have lapped this up and begged for more. Even now, the cardiovascular exercise didn't cause the cold sweat, but the strength training to bring her right shoulder and left thigh closer to her pre-injury level, hurt like hell. A final push, she'd finish her press-ups, medicine ball, parallel bars, and physiotherapy, shower, then lunch. Water therapy after lunch, otherwise known by the staff as 'waterboarding'. They knew how to make her work.

The communal mess was busy, and the smell turned her stomach, but she had to eat. George took a salad from self-service and searched for a seat.

"Hi George, how's the recovery going?" asked Allan, a support staff member, and someone with aspirations of extracurricular activity with George. Although built like a wrestler, he was a head shorter than George and not her type. She liked the opposite sex as much as the next woman. But she had rules; no spitting on her own doorstep, no attached men, and he had to be taller than her. Above all, they had to have 'chemistry'.

Allan was a mate with a girlfriend, so she'd let him down gently. Unless, he insisted, then things may get 'knotty', as Charlie, her sister called it. She had a job, and Stanford Hall was her job. Work and sex don't mix. She enjoyed both, but not together.

"Hey, Allan. Not bad, getting stronger. How's Mandy?" asked George, referring to his girlfriend.

He cast his eyes down, his brow knitted. "She's fine. Do we have to talk about her?"

"She's a nice girl and I like her. You're lucky."

George's mobile rang. She looked at Allan apologetically, then at the caller ID. It was Charlie, her twin.

"Hey Charlie, how is it? Ready for Christmas? Where are you?"

When they were little, they'd compete for the broadest cockney accent. They'd even played rhyming slang. George had lost her accent, until she got excited, which was a rare but unforgettable event, with a voice like Brian Blessed.

"Hi George, I'm at 'Gates'. (Gates of Rome - Home) I took a day off. In my bedroom with the door closed. Got something to tell you," said Charlie.

George's eyes rolled.

"Boyfriend?"

"Yeah, sort of. I'll tell you when you get home. How's it going?"

"Better than a few months back. Another month or two, and I may box again."

"Stop it, George," said Charlie. "You don't need to win the Army title again to prove something," she said, giggling.

"Still give you a good beating," George laughed.

"In your dreams. You here for Christmas, I hope?"

"Christmas? Yes, I'll be there in a few days. How's Mum?" asked George.

"She's downstairs, Mumsying, cooking, etcetera. Someone's at the door, a friend probably. Although I can hear them talking, she's arguing, or something. My money's on Mum."

"Speak up, I can't hear you."

"I can't speak up; I'm trying to listen to why they're arguing. Anyway, you know what Mum's like. Even with the door closed, and talking to someone else, she can hear an ant fart at a thousand paces. If she hears me, she'll interrogate me until I 'fess up."

They both giggled.

"Got to go, there's a commotion downstairs. Sounds like Mum's beating the caller beyond recognition. See you Thursday. Kisses. Bye."

"You too, Charlie. Stay safe, bye."

She disconnected and turned to her lunch.

"Your sister, is she as nice as you?" asked Allan, almost grovelling.

"Like me, but smarter. She runs her own interior design company."

"Wow, she got a boyfriend?" asked Allan, with a cheeky grin.

"Maybe, but she's not your type."

"My type?"

"Yeah, she likes her men to take a good thrashing on the first date. You wouldn't enjoy it," she laughed.

"Got to go, swimming in half an hour."

She felt Alan's eyes on her as she walked out.

Chapter 9

Bradley Maudlin could leave the house the same way he'd entered; no one would be wiser, except the police. He inspected his watch. The police would be here within ten minutes, enough time for his father to kill the girl. Templeton Maudlin had turned Bradley into a self-declared coward. Bradley pocketed the phone and strolled into the front room with more bravado than confidence.

The woman lying on the floor looked like she may be the lavender lady, oldish, with short blue-rinsed hair. A few years ago, she would have been a good-looking woman. The dent in her head, the matted blood, and the gathering pool on the floor suggested she was dead, and the bloodied chair leg on the floor was probably the weapon. Her eyes were open, but Bradley had seen enough dead bodies to know 'dead'. The other female, a girl in her late twenties, lay on her side, her back to him. Bradley watched the movement along her upper back, concluding she was still breathing.

His father lost the power of speech. "Br… Bra…"

"Dad, what are you doing here?"

Under different circumstances, his father would have berated and bullied him, but now Templeton Maudlin shook, and his face was a picture of turmoil. Templeton coughed and found his voice.

"Bradley, get out. Someone's coming to finish the job."

"What job? The police are coming. What have you done?" he said. "Did you do this?" asked Bradley, pointing at the lavender woman.

"No, no, it's not like that. Someone else. I…," he hesitated, drew himself up to his full five foot five inches, and gave Bradley a stare, which caused his Pavlovian reaction. Bradley stiffened and stared at his father.

"It's your fault. I told you not to interfere. I told you. Now see what you've done!"

"I can't help it; I followed you to see… What did you do, dad?" almost in tears.

His father stared at Bradley, lambasting him. "You did it. You will take the blame, not me. If you hadn't interfered, everything would have been fine."

"The girl, what did you do to her?"

Templeton poked his son in the chest with a bony finger. "Not me. You. You slapped her, you hit her. Tell the police you did it," said his father, his voice rising by a few octaves. "I'm going; you're on your own. Tell them you hit her when you were breaking in, you lost your nerve," said Templeton Maudlin.

Bradley looked down at his desperate father. Templeton Maudlin didn't hesitate. Composure restored, he grabbed his holdall and walked past Bradley.

A minute later, a noise behind Bradley caused him to turn to face a man moving with the grace of a dancer but might have been a gymnast. The man was average height, wearing dark overalls and black leather gloves. He scanned the scene.

Bradley cringed; a sparrow tormented by a cat. He assumed the man wasn't police, which left few alternatives.

"I've called the police," Bradley muttered, backing against the sofa.

"I'll make it quick,"

It wasn't in Bradley's nature to start a fight with one outcome.

"What are you…?" Bradley asked, fearing the worst.

'Gymnast' reached for the bloodied weapon, a chair leg. Bradley, thinking he would be next, raised his arm to deflect a blow. Gymnast tossed the piece of wood to Bradley, who caught it with the sticky end. Bits of blood and matted hair stuck to his hand. His fingerprints all over the weapon; his hand shook as he dropped the chair leg.

"Good boy. One minute," said Gymnast, hefting the weapon with his gloved hand and turning to the girl.

Bradley had little doubt that the man had returned to kill the girl. Even the coward in him couldn't accept it. The girl was alive, and he couldn't stand aside and allow this thug to finish her. He stepped between Gymnast and the girl and raised an arm in fright, not bravery.

"If you want it as well, okay," said Gymnast, raising the weapon.

Instead of the thud of the chair leg on his skull, the welcome sound of the police siren rang in his ears, whilst Gymnast cursed in a foreign language. He may have been calculating whether he had time to kill Bradley and the girl then escape. Flashing blue lights from the police vehicles filtered into the room.

"You're lucky," said Gymnast, pointing at Bradley. He tossed the weapon to Bradley, who fumbled and caught it. The killer pushed Bradley away, leaving with the urgency of someone late for an appointment. Bradley sagged on the sofa and dropped the weapon at his feet. He covered his face and waited to face the police.

Chapter 10

As George walked to the accommodation block, the base Sergeant Major called to her, his steps short and rapid. "Sgt Stone, a moment. The CO wants to see you."

It was unusual for the Commanding Officer to see a 'recuperee' without warning. Maybe he wanted to wish her Merry Christmas whilst he had a chance.

"What is it, Sir?" asked George.

"Best get it from him, lass. He's waiting, so get across to his office now."

His tone wasn't unfriendly, but George sensed he knew something, although nothing would drag it out of him. She also knew eventually, she must see the CO for 'a chat', which would either reset her career or spell the end. But they'd agreed on the end of January. She was making excellent progress with more than a month to go.

She tried to avoid limping. The Commanding Officer would watch her. Clenching her teeth, she walked slowly, but purposefully. Each step was a knife slicing along her thigh. It helped if she relaxed but the thought of the imminent meeting with the CO added to her stress. Had the CO called for her directly after physio and swimming to see how she coped? Out of her peripheral vision, she saw movement through his office window, a shadow, or his current appointment.

The CO's Adjutant, Captain Andrew Pritchard, managed the outer office. He sat chatting with the CO's wife, Melanie Syman, who'd probably visited the CO. Pritchard saw George enter and tapped Melanie's hand, and they stopped talking. This could be bad.

"Hello, dear. Here to see Robert?" asked the CO's wife.

Melanie looked at George; the angle of her head, her eyes squeezed together, and a twisted grin. She tried, but most of the base saw through her; even seasoned soldiers could have a fake wife.

The Adjutant opened the door to announce her to the CO, then returning to his desk, brushed his hand along Melanie Syman's back.

Most residents of Stanford Hall avoided Colonel Robert Syman, the Commanding Officer. Some feared him, most respected him, and a few adored him. George was in the latter category. Unlike most of the staff, he was neither Royal Army Medical Corps nor Rehabilitation Support Staff, but Infantry. Colonel Syman had served his time, and rumour had it, this was his last posting before retirement. His gravelly voice led some to think of him as an old warrior looking for a last battle, but George saw him as a friendly old warhorse. He had nothing to prove. He sat behind his desk, and as she entered, he fixed her with a thin smile, revealing crossed teeth. His pock-marked complexion was reminiscent of a bag of crisps, probably from a childhood infection. He didn't stand, but looked George in the eye when he spoke to her. She liked that about him.

Some staff members called him Ugly Syman, but not to his face. His saggy eyes told of too many nights without sleep. Facial disfigurements suggested war wounds, Northern Ireland, The Falklands, or Iraq. He had hair sprouting from his nose and his ears, which looked like shrubbery. Someone else was with him, a woman sitting across from him.

"Sergeant Stone, good to see you, you're looking well. Sit, please, take the weight off your feet. Come from physio, I understand."

It wasn't a question. He knew her programme.

"Right, Sir. A good workout and I'm improving my strength."

She took a seat and focussed on the CO. Charlie and her Mum must be okay, but she sensed bad news. But it couldn't be Charlie; George had spoken to her that lunchtime.

"George," he said. That meant bad news. Rarely did the CO use first names, regardless of how long he'd known them. "This is Constable Shaw, local constabulary, and I'm afraid she has bad news. Someone attacked your mother at her home, probably during a burglary. She died, probably a couple of hours ago. I am so sorry."

George opened her mouth, tried to speak, but failed. She stared at the CO.

Eventually, she spoke. "But Charlie's okay. I spoke to her, she's with Mum. It's not funny, Sir. What's wrong?"

The policewoman looked about George's age. This woman had told the CO, someone had attacked and killed her Mum. That was wrong. Charlie was with her. The woman was mistaken; it happened all the time, it had to be someone else. "Charlie," she said.

"Charlie's your sister?" asked the policewoman.

"Yeah, my twin, her full name's 'Charlotte'. Mum's okay, Charlie's with her."

Each word uttered caused pain to cut through her like a scalpel. She gasped for breath and leaned forward, grasping the CO's desk for support. He'd said there'd been a break in at their home in Grain. Her Mum attacked, dead. What about Charlie?

These words removed all sense and rational thought. The policewoman's voice sounded distant, talking about Charlie being in a coma in hospital.

"It can't be right. You're lying. No. No. NO!"

The woman reached for George, who pushed her away, clamping her hands over her ears, trying to block out the sound to render it untrue. George stood and hugged herself, death in her eyes and desolation in her heart.

"I'm sorry," said the policewoman.

George barely heard those two words, but their quietness made it even more real. They sliced away a part of her and tossed it aside. They had finality to them, leaving no argument, and no reasoning could make them wrong. George couldn't bluster, or bully the policewoman or the CO into saying 'it's a joke'.

The clerk brought a mug of tea, forcing it into George's hands as if he knew what to expect.

"When did you speak to your sister?" asked the policewoman.

George gave her phone to the Officer, who tapped at the screen.

"The call would have been before or during the burglary. We'll keep it for a couple of hours."

"We should go straight to the hospital."

George slurped the tea, then placed it on the CO's desk with numb hands.

"Toilet?" asked George.

As George left the office, Melanie stood in front of Pritchard's desk, ready with fake sympathy. George pushed past her and walked along the corridor to the toilet, and locked the cubicle door. As she slumped on the toilet seat, tears streamed down and through her fingers like rain on a window on a wet afternoon. George had watched Army colleagues die; she'd comforted others with bodies damaged by war. Wyson died in her arms. But it didn't prepare her for this, nothing could, but she clung to what she knew, a soldier first, so she'd tackle each crisis as it arose. A tap on the outer door startled her. No one must see her cry; Mum and Charlie wouldn't want it. She wiped her face, unlocked the cubicle door, and looked in the mirror. She looked like crap and washed her face.

Minutes later, George emerged and stood in front of Melanie with as much bearing as she could muster. The CO's wife went to hug George, but she didn't need a hug, not from the profligate Melanie Syman. She sidestepped Melanie and returned to the CO's office.

Syman said, "George, there's nothing I can do to ease your pain, and God knows you've already been through too much. I'm giving you indefinite compassionate leave, return when you're ready. You're due for reassessment at the end of January. So, come and see me then, but stay in contact and if there's any way I can help, call me. You know my number. Gemma will escort you."

Leaving the CO's office, the Adjutant lingered. George scowled. Promiscuity and the Army didn't mix.

"Tell me if there's anything I can do, dear, you know I'm here for you anytime," Melanie Syman said.

George ignored her to the point of rudeness.

In the car, the policewoman reached for George's hand, which she shrugged off.

"The CO told me you're Royal Army Physical Training Corps. How long have you served?"

"Twelve years."

"I read, you were the Combined Services over 65 kg boxing Champion and almost made the Olympics."

George nodded. Normally, it would start her talking. The CO must have told Shaw; but not now. George turned away from Shaw and stared through the window. In a minute, her world had turned 180, from getting back on track and looking forward to Christmas with Mum and Charlie, to this.

"What's next, hospital?" asked George. It sounded callous, but she wanted to at least appear business-like. "If there's been a mistake, the sooner I find out, the better."

Things happen, so they could also unhappen, and she clung onto that thought like a frightened child clinging to a blanket.

The smell of hospital gave her the heaby jeabys. The claustrophobic sterility of hospitals, the sense of lurking disease and broken bodies gave her the shakes. But George hardly noticed it and allowed the policewoman to lead her along corridors to Charlie's room.

"This is Dr Wheeler, George. He's looking after Charlie."

He smiled, which she resented, but if he'd said, 'Well, Miss Stone, it looks as if your sister is for the Grim Reaper,' she'd have punched him and called him a callous bastard.

Instead, he said, "Charlie is stable but, in a coma, she suffered head wounds. She may have disturbed the burglar and tried to tackle him."

With her Mum dead and Charlie in a coma, ten rounds with Mike Tyson would have been easier.

"Can I stay with Charlie?"

"Yes, as long as you like."

Besides the instruments, giving an occasional bleep, the

catheter in her nose and the bandages around her head, Charlie looked normal, serene. Her sister's dyed, dark hair against the pillow made her look composed and more tranquil than she'd been in real life. She wanted to run to her, take her into her arms, and tell her everything would be okay. But it would be a lie.

"Charlie, who did this to you?" George asked, taking her hands.

The twins were tactile. Compared to her own, Charlie's hands were soft, whilst her own were rough, her nails bitten to the quick. George talked to her, watching her sister's eyes, hoping for movement. Hoping she'd stretch and say, 'Hey George, fantastic sleep.'

Charlie had always affected their moods, and her sense of humour had them in stitches. She was strident, hot-blooded, the dominant one, although she was younger by two minutes, and George a soldier. George convinced herself there couldn't be too much wrong with her; otherwise, she'd look a mess. She sat and talked to her until sleep prevailed.

George woke as a nurse, and another woman entered with tea. She lifted her head from Charlie's bed covers and wiped saliva from her mouth, which tasted like rotten eggs. The light peaked from beneath the curtain. Morning. She rubbed her eyes, smiled at the nurse, then remembered why she was here.

"The doctor has arrived, he'd like to talk to you," said the nurse.

"Is it morning?" asked George, bleary-eyed. She rubbed her aching shoulder. "Where's Constable Shaw, and who are you?" asked George.

The woman's smile didn't falter. "I'm Sarah from the National Crime Agency. I've been assigned to this case. Constable Shaw returned to normal duties."

George took exception to her use of the word 'case'. Her family was not a 'case'. Perhaps the woman wanted to appear professional.

"Sarah who?" asked George, looking down at the National Crime Agency (NCA) woman, who looked fit, but not muscular.

"Detective Sergeant Sarah Frolic."

The woman didn't produce a warrant card, but George accepted her word.

"I'd like to speak to you when you've finished with the doctor, please," said the NCA woman.

George ignored her request and turned to leave. "Thanks for the tea."

The doctor stood as she entered his office, with a 'you can have confidence in me, smile'. He rubbed his bearded chin and beckoned her to a chair. He reminded her of her dad before he walked out. Was he about to deliver a doom-laden prognosis, or was he hopeful? His expression remained unchanged as he leaned towards her. George wanted to shake him and tell him to tell it straight.

"George, I've looked at the scans, and it's not good news, I'm afraid."

It summarised the situation, and she had no response. As the next few minutes, or maybe hours, passed, George understood without really listening. Charlie in a deep coma. Part of her brain damaged by the blow to her head, not helped as she fell against the corner of the stairs. May deteriorate, with a slim chance of recovery, but don't give up hope. Be realistic. Advances in medical science, etc. The doctor was managing her expectations. Comforting words, but George sensed they wanted to get down to business.

She sensed silence and left the doctor's office.

The Sister took George's arm and stood facing her. "George, your sister is in a room with a second bed. If you want to stay with her for a couple of days, it's fine with us. You won't be able to go home right now. It'll be a crime scene. Stay here for a few days. Okay?"

"Thank you. I appreciate that. And thanks for all you're doing."

Another sympathetic smile, this time a genuine caring smile.

Chapter 11

After three days, night and day blurred into each other. George constantly checked Charlie, and the staff brought tea, food, and sympathy. On the fourth day, George awoke to Sarah Frolic standing at the foot of her bed.

"Sorry to wake you, George."

George slid out of bed and dressed at a speed that seemed to shock Sarah, the NCA woman, who stood waiting for George to compose herself.

"Alright, what can I do for you?" asked |George with more than a slight hostility in her voice.

"Look, my choice of words wasn't great. I can be sharp. I'm here to help. Can we start again?" asked Sarah Frolic.

Better, at least she was sensitive enough, and from her eyes, bright. The woman led George into a small office to ask questions. None of which applied to her Mum's death. She told Sarah about the phone call with Charlie and about the noise downstairs, which disturbed her.

"Do you want us to contact your dad and other relatives? If they're alive, we'll find them."

The only family was on her dad's side; an aunt in Scotland, a granny in a nursing home, and a cousin somewhere in the Far East. Mum had no relatives. She had nothing to say to her dad, and now she'd lost her last real relatives. She tried to control her shaking. George shook her head.

"I'm afraid you must identify your mother's body, George," said Sarah. "Are you okay with that?"

"Yeah, I'll be fine," she said, standing and leading with her chin. Although she felt far from 'fine', she'd work on autopilot until she could function again. Her emotions would wait until she was on her own.

Sarah drove George to the police morgue. She glanced sideways at the NCA woman. So why was the NCA involved? They took jurisdiction when the crime had national significance. Was this more than a simple burglary gone wrong, or was it organised crime? Anyway, how come they'd targeted her Mum? They had nothing of value in the house, and Mum didn't believe in collecting valuables. She always said her two daughters were more valuable than any object. Sarah looked like a hard nut, sharp thin lips, hair pulled into a ponytail, uncared for skin, and dark edges under her eyes. Those eyes had cried a great deal. George sensed the women had problems, but nowhere near George's suffering.

The morgue wasn't busy. The only sign it was a morgue was the young couple leaving. A man held the woman, leading her to a car as she wept, dabbing her eyes.

Leading George along the corridor, Sarah stayed close to her, ready to catch her if she collapsed. Their footsteps echoed like she imagined they would on death row. The place smelt of disinfectant and the faded green walls with no corners or edges were grubby, but sterile.

They sat in a waiting room. Sarah touched George's hand, perhaps for comfort, but George pulled away and instantly regretted it. She touched Sarah's sleeve and tried a smile. One human seeking comfort from another.

The morgue attendant entered, giving a practised nod. George took it as her queue to identify her Mum's body, which lay on a hospital trolley. She recognised her Mum's shape under the white sheet. But she inwardly begged for this not to be her Mum, to be someone else's mother, daughter, sister, friend. Let someone else suffer the pain. She clung to the hope of a mistake, although it would mean another woman lying dead.

Sarah took George's arm and drew her to the head of the trolley. At a nod from Sarah, the technician lifted one corner. As the cover lifted, inch by inch, George prayed for it to last for an eternity, simply to delay the inevitable. Uncovered, the lifeless face of her Mum lay there. That face in life had shown joy as they grew up, sadness when Mum broke the news their dad had walked out on them, and mock anger when she fought with her sister. George nodded.

The technician replaced the cover, and George took her Mum's hand and whispered, "Thank you."

This wasn't her Mum; she'd gone. This empty shell contained nothing more than a shadow. Wherever her mother was, she'd left this aseptic room. As they left the room, she didn't look back, her pace slow, deliberate. She shook off the hand offered by Sarah.

They walked down the corridor and into a small canteen.

"You think I'm heartless, don't you?" George asked.

"No, I can see you're not. I know what you're feeling."

No, she didn't. She knew nothing. She couldn't guess what dad leaving had been like, when Mum had hugged George and Charlie together to comfort them. Mum had held the family together. George and Charlie were closer than twins. They finished each other's sentences, giggled, and anticipated something funny. George met Sarah's smile with folded arms and clenched teeth.

"Who did this? If you know, tell me. Now!"

"We're not sure. We arrested a man at the scene, but he's saying nothing."

"The burglary may not be as straightforward as it looks. The bloke who we've arrested called the police. He may have disturbed the burglar and saved your sister's life."

George stared at Sarah, as if she was an alien, her eyebrows squeezing together. Did she not understand? "I'm supposed to be grateful?"

For George, dying wasn't the worst thing. Seeing your mother dead, your sister in a coma and knowing there's nothing you can do; that was worse.

"He was at the scene, so arrest him. Force the truth out of him. He may know who did it."

"We have arrested him, but we stopped beating confessions out of suspects in the 80s."

She guessed that, but she demanded the impossible, hoping for something, anything.

"So, Mum's killer may still be loose?" George said through gritted teeth.

"For the moment, yes."

"If this man who called the police didn't kill Mum and didn't injure my sister, he knows who did, and he let it happen. Either you catch her killer, or I will, and if you can't get at the truth, I will. And when I do, I won't be as merciful as you."

Sarah grimaced, shook her head, and held George's stare. "Not a good idea. Let us do our work. Your house is now clear and no longer a crime scene, so can I drive you to the house? Otherwise, we can arrange a B&B for you."

George had no problem living in the house where she and Charlie had grown up, shared secrets, been chastised, and cherished by their Mum, and she didn't believe in ghosts. Her Mum had never hurt her, and she never could. There was only love in the house.

Leaving the morgue, George tried to think positively, but the image of Charlie pushed out thoughts of 'letting the police do their job'. She had three tasks; look after her sister, discover who killed her Mum, and make them pay. There were questions, such as, who had killed her Mum? The police seemed certain it was a burglary, but why? They weren't rich, the opposite. Since dad left, life had been simple with rare luxuries. Despite her Mum's work for the government, she'd also taken a night job at the supermarket to pay Charlie's university fees.

As Sarah stopped her car outside George's Mum's house, she gave George a card with her contact details.

"Call me if you think of anything, and I'll keep you informed. Would you like me to come in with you?"

"Thanks, but I'm a big girl," said George.

As she walked away from the car toward the house, she realised she was being a bitch and regretted having a poke at Sarah. She had bigger things to think of. Sarah would get over it.

She closed the door behind her, slumped behind it, and wailed.

Chapter 12

For the first time, Bradley Maudlin sat in a police cell and gagged. It stank like a doss house on a Friday night, the stench masked by bleach. After a few hours, it was 'normal', but it gave him a blinding headache as he sat on the thin plastic-covered mattress, head in hands. An abusive drunk threatened him from the cell next door. The hourly grating, metal against metal interrupted his sleep, as the door shutter opened revealing the eyes of the duty policeman checking he was still alive.

But the spasmodic noise disturbed Bradley Maudlin, as did the quiet. Jerking awake, the image of his father standing over the girl with a weapon in his hand assailed his imagination. Whether a dream or a waking figment of his imagination, he wasn't sure. Bradley lay awake thinking, trying to figure out why 'that man' would, or even could, get into this mess, combined with his usual preoccupation, his father's unexplained activities. Retrospect is a potent weapon in the paranoid's arsenal. Despite his attempt to stay focussed on damage limitation, his thoughts returned to past opportunities to rid himself of the man. His mother left his father a note, which told him she'd gone.

He could contact her via a relative, and he might have taken the opportunity, if not for his father being a control freak.

After university, paid by his father, he should have started a new life on his own. But he returned, hoping the man had changed. But he was even worse, obsessive, disliked people, his surreal relationship with the dead, and the times he worked all night, doing whatever he did.

Bradley feared Templeton Maudlin in a way a controlling parent can. Bradley hated his own reaction when his father raised his voice, and his time-tested intimidation techniques. He didn't know why he accepted it. Wiping a hand across his face, feeling stubble, he flopped onto the thin mattress.

Most saw Bradley as having a sign around his neck screaming, 'I'm a coward, please humiliate me'. His hand swept across his forehead to flick his black hair out of his eyes, which suggested an affectation, but it was a nervous habit. He was tall enough to look down on most men, but his thin build and good looks led some to see him as epicene, almost feminine. Or, as a few called him at university, 'a ponce'.

The kindest nickname he'd ever received was from a university friend who called him 'Tony'. Even when he reflected on the positive, a gloom overshadowed it. Stella, a friend from university, was drawn to his serious, almost morose nature, although he was far from humourless. Celluloid memories from his university resurfaced; a late-night study session in Creative Arts, more alcohol than was good for him, Stella and him watching old DVDs of the seventies and eighties comedians. His favourites were Peter Sellers and Norman Wisdom, which endeared him to her, and she appreciated his humour. As they watched the comedians, he chuckled, and she laughed and threw popcorn at him.

"Bloody childish," he'd said, but stroked her hair and squeezed her hand.

"Like that," she'd snorted, imitating Tommy Cooper, and snuggling against him.

Stella wasn't his only romance in his twenty-five years, but she was his first, and she was special. Brushing off 'creepy' comments, he'd once heard her tell an old friend, "I like him. If it's a problem, too bad. Bye."

Their romance developed from attraction to carnal lust to close friendship to inseparable, platonic soul mates. Bradley felt he could use Stella's comfort and support, but she'd moved on. A husband, two kids, and she didn't need Bradley's problems. He'd told his father about Stella. His father had scoffed and made a banal comment.

If he'd left it alone, Templeton Maudlin might have been sitting where he sat now. It should have been easy to predict; his father's anti-social behaviour, temper tantrums, and a controlling streak reminiscent of a dictator, would one day land him in trouble. His father had inherited the funeral business from his father, and he no doubt expected Bradley to take over one day. Templeton Maudlin's occupation matched his character.

In retrospect, following Templeton Maudlin had been stupid? Why hadn't he left when he'd sensed trouble, and why did he risk his neck to stop the killer from finishing his job? It wasn't bravery, and despite his curiosity, he should have left when he could. These and worse thoughts ravaged his mind. It became worse as he thought about them. A crazy reinforcing spiral.

The door hatch opened and someone left breakfast in the hatch tray for Bradley to either eat or not. Bradley left it. Sometime later, he was led down a corridor to an interview room, a double tape deck on the table. He sat on one of four chairs around the metal table and waited.

He clasped his hands together on the table and looked around. Waiting reinforced his nervousness. Did they know he was as skittish as a schoolgirl on a date with Elvis? The artificial lighting hurt his eyes, and he rubbed them, trying to remove the grit. No window, faded magnolia gloss paint, and a torn and faded poster on the wall 'Warning Notice', underneath 'We are watching you,' and a pair of staring eyes.

He might change things. Why should he take the blame for someone else's wrongdoing? Why let Templeton Maudlin drag him into his weird world of necromania? He'd come clean, tell the police everything, including his father's 'peculiarities' and to hell with the consequences. Feeling better, he chanced a weak smile.

The door clanked open. A tall woman entered, who may have been good-looking at one time. She didn't look at Bradley. He used the time to inspect her, trying to read something from her body language, the way she held herself. Her indifferent silence was a ploy to make him think he didn't matter, and beneath her attention.

The woman looked bedraggled and tired, perhaps called from her bed to the police station. No wedding ring, a boyfriend maybe, and he recognised 'downtrodden'. He may have been staring, and forced himself to relax, his mind wandering. When she spoke, it jerked him into the present, and he again stared at her.

"Mr Maudlin, Bradley Maudlin, can you understand me?"

Bradley said. "Err, yes, yes I can."

"I'm Detective Sergeant Sarah Frolic."

Bradley glanced at her with Labrador eyes.

"You do not have to say anything, but it may harm your defence if you do not mention…" No change since his Caution.

"You understand, Bradley Maudlin?"

"Err, yes. Yes, I think so."

"Do you want a solicitor? Or do you have your own?"

His father had his own solicitor, Mr Wyne, a nice enough chap. He needed to call his father, who would be vexed.

"No, I don't need a solicitor," he said, looking up, pleading.

A man, loose tie dangling from his neck, entered and sat next to the woman. He looked like he'd been on desk duties for too long, thick around the waist, a bright red face, and a bulbous red nose, suggesting to Bradley he had either high blood pressure or a weakness for alcohol. At least he was unlikely to get violent. Would the woman play the bad cop?

"Cautioned?" he asked the woman.

"Yeah," she replied.

She pressed a couple of buttons on the tape deck.

"Mr Maudlin, I'm Detective Sergeant Thomas, this," he said in a London accent, pointing a thumb at Sarah, "is Detective Sergeant Frolic from the NCA. Tell us what happened, your own words, please; it wasn't your fault, right? Wrong place, wrong time? Got caught up in something?" He leaned forward. "Or did you slaughter the woman, and then attack the girl? Which was it, Bradley?"

Bradley sat straight. "I want to make a statement. I didn't do it, but I can explain," said Bradley, trying to stay neutral. He pressed his hands palms down on the table.

They both stared at Bradley, as if their worlds depended upon his next words. Under their stare, Bradley sweated, palms wet, panic in his eyes. What if he's found guilty and gets life? Best to come clean and tell the truth. His father couldn't kill, could he? He gulped and settled, calm.

"You know, I made the phone call to the police?" They nodded. "I heard some of what happened, someone attacked the girl, but I didn't see the attacks."

Bradley paused, licking his lips. Sarah Frolic left to get a glass of water. When she returned, a storm of a scowl covered her face. She whispered into Thomas's ear and put the glass in front of Bradley, who gulped the water. A man followed her into the room and sat next to Bradley.

"Mr Maudlin, this is Mr Wilson Pinchin. He's been engaged to represent you, and has requested a few minutes alone with you," said Thomas. Looking at Pinchin, he said, "Two minutes, and you're on the clock."

Bradley hadn't seen this man before. He wasn't his father's usual solicitor. So, if not his father's, whose? His features were reptilian, black eyes plucked from a corpse. Pinchin turned, smiling, and Bradley expected to see a forked tongue. The man inspected his face for a moment before sliding his gaze down the length of Bradley's body. Bradley felt 'weighed up'; with a practised eye. He pulled his chair over towards Bradley, encroaching on his personal space.

"Who sent you?" asked Bradley.

"An anonymous benefactor; someone who has your interests at heart."

The man's smile and his eyes remained fixed. He leaned towards Bradley conspiratorially. Bradley's hands clenched into fists; his throat constricted. He whispered to Bradley, his warm, foetid breath assaulting Bradley's face, causing him to shiver. Bradley imagined the man had a brain as sharp as a soprano's High C.

"Time is of the essence, so I'll make it brief. You have a friend, Stella, with a charming, happy family. If you wish them to remain charming and happy, you will do precisely as I say," Pinchin said, in a matter-of-fact manner.

His explanation was graphic, showing the consequence of defying his advice, but with Bradley's compliance, the alternative would be tolerable and above all, it would meet with Mr Maudlin senior's appreciation.

"Do we understand each other and do I have your agreement Mr Maudlin?"

Bradley nodded; his head bowed.

"This will be your line of narration. You will explain nothing, give no statement, remain silent. Is that clear?"

Bradley nodded again.

A few seconds later, Thomas and Frolic returned, taking their places opposite Bradley and Pinchin.

"Mr Maudlin expressed a wish to make a full statement. Please continue Mr Maudlin," prompted Thomas.

Bradley looked at Thomas, then to Frolic, his mouth frozen open. Finally, he looked at Pinchin, who smiled back; a cat protecting its injured prey. Receiving no respite, Bradley looked down at his hands.

He hissed. "What did you say, Bradley?"

"Mr Maudlin said 'no comment', clear enough," said Pinchin. "Whilst I appreciate this is a serious crime, and you cannot release my client, I would reiterate, Mr Maudlin has nothing to say, and I must be present for all future interviews."

"Bradley," said Frolic, "you can still make a statement, even though Mr Pinchin advises against it?"

"No," said Bradley, still studying his hands on the table.

"Bradley," Thomas spat, as if he'd bitten into a piece of gristle. "You understand? You are in a pile of trouble the size of an elephant's dump."

"No comment."

"Your prints are on the murder weapon. You were present at the scene of the crime, and you sat over the girl with the murder weapon at your feet when the police arrived. How do you account for that?"

Sarah rolled her eyes, and Thomas sat back. Bradley was thankful for the silence. They all stared at him, and he wondered if they were waiting for him to speak first. He waited, not daring to.

Frolic snarled at him. "I hate men who attack women, they make me sick, and I bet they make you sick too, don't they Bradley?"

"I didn't attack the women, I was there… but…."

The comment elicited a cough from Pinchin, and Bradley murmured to a halt.

Sergeant Thomas leaned forward, across the table, and spoke in a secretive tone, as if giving Bradley fatherly advice.

"Look, Bradley," he said, stretching towards him, "Let's talk about how this happened, man to man." He waved a pointed finger at Frolic and Pinchin as if creating a separation.

"I don't think you did it. You don't look like the type of bloke who'd do this. For the life of me, I can't think why you're acting dumb. You know who did it, right? If you tell me now, we can talk about leniency, know what I mean?"

Thomas looked at Bradley, eyes wide, waiting. Bradley's father and Pinchin would be angry if he told the police what happened. And Stella, poor Stella, he couldn't bear it.

"I've said all I'm going to say. Do what you have to

do." His voice didn't match his words.

Silence, the spinning tape deafening; he waited. He'd go to prison if it meant avoiding Pinchin's threat. Despite this, his eyes watered, and he hung his head in shame and self-pity.

What's the worst they could do? He didn't think they could charge him with murder. He'd called the police. They'd take that into account. His father scared him, but Pinchin was in a league of his own. He'd do his jail time, and then make a new start, on his own.

"Mr Maudlin, let me spell it out what's going to happen now, okay? If you don't make a statement on what you saw or heard in the house," he pointed a thick stubby finger at Bradley, "I will charge you with breaking and entering, murder, grievous bodily harm, for starters." he counted them off on his fingers. "You'll be remanded in custody, pending a high court trial, and we'll ensure you don't get bail. Your pre-trial time in nick will be commensurate with the seriousness of the charges, and pre-trial time could be considerable. Are you okay with nick?" his voice gravelly and spit landing on Bradley's face.

"You can't make these outrageous and inaccurate claims, Sergeant, and Mr Maudlin has told you all he intends to tell you," said Pinchin.

Thomas ignored him, pushing his chair back, and leaving the room with Sarah Frolic. Pinchin followed them, leaving Bradley alone. He imagined the conversation between Pinchin and the police officers. He pitied the police officers. Finally, he covered his face with his hands and made a painful mewing sound, thinking about spending time in prison.

Chapter 13

George Stone took a chair at the side of Charlie's bed and ran her hand through her unwashed hair then picked gunk from her eyes. A bad night, and coming straight to the hospital from her bed, bypassing her normal routine of shower, run, and breakfast; she felt like a wet rag. She wiped her sweaty hands down her jeans and took hold of Charlie's hand.

"I'm still having problems believing this, Charlie," George whispered, half to Charlie and half to herself. "I was talking to you a few minutes before it happened, before you went downstairs to see Mum. The police asked me about that, but then they shrugged. I've been listening to your voice messages; yes, I know, weird. I've moved into our house, but it's so big and lonely now. But I can visit you anytime, and when you come out, I'll take care of you. That's the first sensible thing I've said. Don't start disagreeing with me," said George, smiling. "Eventually, I'll start clearing out Mum's things, but right now I can't, and you are my priority."

George sat next to her twin's bed, squeezing her hand.

A nurse hurried in to take Charlie's pulse, change the bags of fluid and medication, and examine Charlie's pupil dilation. After writing a few words on a check sheet, she smiled at George, which she assumed meant 'no change'.

George dreamt of being free. Nothing to tie her down, no commitments. No one to say, 'spend Christmas with us, we have a goose'. Even if her sister recovered, their relationship would change, she must be the dominant one now. She was used to Charlie saying, 'Come on Georgie, let's go to the fair.' or, 'We're going to Paris, us two, a weekend away'.

One of the few decisions she remembered making on her own was to join the Army. Even then, Charlie insisted on her phoning every day to check on her, see if she needed rescuing. Everything changed once she found her own confidence, but Charlie still took over when she came home on leave, and she loved her for it.

She wondered about the dream last night. A condor flying over the Grand Canyon, looking down on those struggling to survive. Was it connected to recent events?

She squeezed her sister's hands but held back tears.

"Charlie, I want to ask you something. Did you rush downstairs, when Mum shouted for help? Who killed Mum, Charlie? One minute she's Mum, our sole relative, the next she's dead, and for what? The police think it was a burglary, but they stole nothing."

What would have happened if, as planned, Charlie had arrived later? She wouldn't now be sitting next to her comatose sister. Did the burglar think their Mum would be alone? Burglars recce these crimes, so maybe they didn't reckon on Charlie.

"How am I going to mend this? I always rely on you because you're smarter than me. You always decide for both of us, but you usually get it right."

Tears tracked down George's cheeks, even through her smile.

"Remember when Auntie Jill and Uncle Tony came to see us? We were four and swapped places and clothes and pretended to be each other. You said, 'My name's not Charlie, it's George. Anyone can see that.' We laughed until Mum sent us to our room and told us to keep quiet. Mostly, only Mum could tell us apart."

The smile left her. "I'm not sure I can do this on my own, Charlie. I'm not smart like you and Mum. You can do anything. All I wanted was to join the Army, travel the world, meet a nice guy, save the world, live on coconut milk, and have loads of brilliant, free-spirited kids. Not much to ask."

George stared at Charlie's face. "I'd do anything to swap places with you now. Not because it's easier, but you'd deal with this better than me."

George lifted Charlie's hand to her face and brushed it against her cheek.

"Is our family cursed, do you think? First Dad walked out, although I can't remember him; now this."

A tear ran onto Charlie's hand, and she brushed the wetness into her skin.

"I doubt Mum's dream retirement included this. You remember teasing Mum when even she couldn't tell us apart, and we convinced her we could communicate without speaking, feeling pain when the other hurt. 'Go on, slap me across my hand. I bet Charlie feels it'. You sat in the other room peeking and yelled when you heard a slap. We laughed like hyenas when Mum realised we were making fun of her; or maybe she knew all along. The three of us rolled on the floor, laughing. Mum made us promise not to do it again, and we loved her."

George held onto Charlie's hand but sat straight, alert as she felt Charlie's fingers flicker. "Charlie, I can feel a movement. Can you hear me?" George said, eyes wide with joy. "I'll get someone. Stay there," she shouted, elated, wiping her eyes dry.

George pressed the alert button and rushed into the corridor to return a minute later with a nurse.

After checking Charlie's eyes and pulse, the nurse said, "Sorry to disappoint you, love, but sometimes it happens, it's simply nerves and muscles, I'm afraid. The doctor was right; it may take a long time."

"I could have sworn…" her voice trailed.

When the nurse left them, George took hold of Charlie's hand again. "False alarm. It's a good job you can't see my face, it's a mess. You'd tell me to get a grip."

For over one hour she held onto her sisters' hand, waiting for a twitch, anything. But nothing.

"I need to pull myself together and get through this. I'll find out who did this, and why. Then I'll make them pay. This guy in the house, either he's responsible or knows who is. Whoever it is, whatever it takes, I'll find him. Then I'll do to him what he did to you and Mum."

A Sister stopped George on her way out. "Can we have a chat, Miss Stone? In my office, please."

The short, stern-looking Sister pointed, and led the way.

George followed without answering. The Sister closed the door and sat behind her desk. She clasped her hands, placing them on the desk as a statement of resolve. Here comes the real prognosis, thought George.

"Look, George," she paused, as if she might have second thoughts. "We don't know what happened to your sister. We worry about our patients receiving the right treatment, and where we can, we get them well again; although I understand the suspicious circumstances."

George focussed on the words 'where we can'. It suggested grim prospects for Charlie. Best let the Sister talk; no doubt she was well-intentioned.

"Your sister is in skilled hands, and we've all taken her to our hearts. She's in a coma, so any change will be gradual. If she wasn't in a coma, we'd put her in a medically induced coma for her own good, to help her heal. We will keep you updated, daily. Give me your mobile number, and we'll call you. There's nothing you can do here. It might be weeks or years before we see signs of improvement. We don't know."

"Could it be days?" asked George, realising she was too abrupt.

"It's unlikely, but the doctor told you the nature of your sister's trauma. It will take weeks to heal physically. But we don't know," she shrugged.

"Don't get your hopes too high. Charlie looks well, but she is not. She may never recover, I'm afraid. Also, you need to take care of yourself. You are no good to your sister if you feel the way you look."

George ignored the last comment, although she was probably right.

"So, you don't know. She may recover sooner?" asked George.

"It's possible, but not likely."

"Sister, here's my phone number. Thanks for your efforts, I appreciate it, but we're a strong-minded bunch, and I won't go quietly, and neither will Charlie. I'll come to visit when I can, but I have a job."

The Sister looked at George, aghast.

"You have a job. I understand…"

"No, you don't understand, Sister. Someone did this to Charlie and killed my mother and I intend to redress that wrong. If there's nothing else, you must be busy."

"George, listen. You must leave this to the police. I know your background but don't get yourself in trouble doing the police's job for them."

She fixed the Sister's stare and left. Walking away from the hospital, she realised she'd been harsh, she'd apologise the following day.

Chapter 14

Periods of skewering pain, which felt as if the metal plate was exiting through her shoulder, punctuated a restless night. But the flesh wound in her thigh fared better. George's interoception forced her into a waking nightmare, so she relived the Afghanistan incident constantly. Her mind reran the episode, trying to find a solution. What went wrong, why did something still plague her? The medication the Stanford Hall quack had prescribed helped but left her dull headed. Regardless of the nightly pain, she resolved to free herself of the medication. She needed to be sharp, focussed, not wandering around in a smiling haze.

She took the Sister's advice and an early morning run along the beach helped to clear her head and the scar tissue on her leg loosened after a mile. She was improving, but not quickly enough to face the challenges ahead. The light rucksack aggravated her shoulder despite the padding. Sweat from exertion mixed with a cold muckment from pain, but she dug in and moved on. The fitness Assessment Board was important. She couldn't miss it, and she couldn't fail. Steep steps marked the path from the beach into the town and George stopped to do sit-ups, press-ups, and bunny hops.

A bowl of porridge later, she was ready to face the world. Colonel Syman would cut her some slack and not demand her presence in Stanford Hall, but there'd be time for crying, regret, and bitterness later. Now she needed to start on her 'to do' list. There were the death certificates, the funeral arrangements, and a visit to the solicitor. But Charlie was her priority. She needed to see Mrs Wallis at the Post Office. Aunt Sheila, as George and Charlie affectionately called her, worked like Google; George could ask her anything. She wasn't a real Aunt and as far as George knew, she had no family. George and Charlie always called her Aunt Sheila, and she was more like a second mother to them. She'd babysat the twins, changed their nappies, and collected them from school. Besides her Mum and Charlie, she was always a lighthouse in a storm. She'd see her before going to see Charlie.

She pulled the net curtain to one side. Her mother liked her privacy, and she'd fitted nets and curtains. A light frost covered the ground like dandruff, but a dark saloon parked a hundred yards along the road and pointing away from her house was frost free. It wasn't there when she'd left for her run, so someone was waiting. This road led directly onto the military firing range, so few people came this way. She made a mental note and left the house for the Post Office.

George hadn't visited Sheila recently, but her house had been a second home to her and Charlie, and she knocked on the back door and entered.

"Hello, Aunt Sheila, it's me," she shouted.

Despite the recent tragedy, Sheila came through from

the Post Office smiling. Her eyes betrayed her pain and although being barely five feet tall, enfolded George in her arms and pulled her head into her neck. Aunt Sheila was friendly with everyone in the village, but her Mum had been her real friend.

George hugged Sheila's old-age spread as Sheila silently, tearlessly, trembled. George waited until Sheila looked ready, placed a hand on her arm, and eased away. She felt she needed to explain her lack of emotion.

"I can't, you know, not yet."

Sheila nodded and smiled.

"Have you had breakfast?"

George nodded but welcomed toast. She sat in an old straight-backed chair. Both she and Charlie had continued their habits from childhood. They even had their own chairs. George looked across at Charlie's empty chair.

Sheila walked through with tea and toast on a tray, placing it on the kitchen table.

"Your Mum came to see me just before she died. She was frightened, which wasn't normal for her. You know it wasn't a burglary, right, George?"

Sheila crunched into a slice of toast, then sipped tea. George thought Sheila had something to say.

"What is it?"

"George, you've got to believe this. Since your dad left, your Mum did everything for you girls. When you hear what I have to say, don't judge her. On the day she died, she told me she loved you both," said Sheila, waiting for her reaction.

George couldn't help thinking for the second time, her world was again tipping upside down.

"You know your Mum, worked for the government?"

"Sure, she worked at the camp as an accountant. We didn't take too much interest."

"She wasn't an accountant, George, she was a Research Technician, recording data on weapons tests. A real boffin was your Mum. She sometimes had to go to London for meetings."

George scrunched her forehead, nodded, and waited, sensing the tempest bringing destruction.

"So what? I suppose she worked on secret stuff and didn't want us to get involved."

Sheila put her hand over George's and fixed her stare.

"It was far more, love. The stuff she worked on was secret; I think she was killed because of it."

"I'm not shocked. Remember, I've done back-to-back tours in Afghanistan. Mum was no Pussy Galore. What do you mean?"

"That's right, love, but it's not the whole story."

Sheila glanced out of the window and drew closer to George, whispering. "Your Mum was a spy, George. Not for us, but for the Soviets. Until the 1990s, she spied for the Soviets and passed information to them. It went quiet after the Berlin Wall fell. We thought the Russians had forgotten her, and the others like her. But your Mum was much brighter and knew better. She told me, 'I'm still on their radar'. A few weeks ago, she received a phone call from a friend warning her, and she had a visit from a lawyer asking her to resume her work, she told me she refused."

It shocked George. She hadn't lived through the Cold War, and the Russians were no big deal, although she knew the history and had read about the period. As a Senior NCO in the British Army, she loved her country and was still prepared to die for it. Now Aunt Sheila, a second mother, accused her Mum of betraying her country. Sheila was mistaken or lying. Why?

"It's not true, Sheila. Mum was as loyal to her country as Charlie and me; she was no spy for the Russians. Who told you this? Why are you saying this?"

George worked into a rage and clenched her fists to stop herself from slapping Sheila for saying such rubbish.

"I have something for you," said Sheila, leaving the room. George sat, her head in turmoil.

George gathered her wits, trying to make sense of this mess. Mum was the greatest Mum any girl could have, and if she had half of her talents, she'd be happy. George struggled to accept what Sheila had told her. She trusted Sheila with her life, but this didn't sit right. She'd vowed not to grieve until after, but this was testing her.

Sheila returned. "I know it's hard for you, but it can't wait. Your Mum saw me the day she died. Someone was following her. I've never seen your Mum scared, but the day she died, she was. Years ago, we discussed what we would do if this happened."

"Were you a spy as well?"

"Me, a spy?" she laughed. "I'm simply a Postmistress, and I was your Mum's closest friend. Your Mum needed someone to confide in, and I was there. She swore me to secrecy until she died, and she asked me to ensure you received this."

Sheila took an envelope out of her apron pocket and placed it on the table between them, but kept her hand on it.

"This is your letter and I have one for Charlie too, which is in a safe place, waiting for her. I'm the Post Mistress, so I know how to keep things safe," Sheila tittered, as if to underline the statement. "Read the letter from your Mum, I've a good idea what's in it and I hope it'll help you make sense of this. Then we can chat."

George opened the sealed envelope with more vigour than she'd intended and removed a folded letter, which enclosed a black and white photo of Charlie, George, and her Mum, and a credit card thickness USB stick. Her Mum's handwritten letter said to look after the photo and mentioned 'a precious family moment'. The twins must have been ten or eleven and George remembered it well. It was a holiday on the south coast, Charlie splashing in the sea, George pointing to something out of view of the camera, and her Mum's arm around their shoulders. Mum is also pointing in the same direction, their fingers almost touching. It was a WW2 Spitfire from RAF Manston, whizzing past to give the holidaymakers a thrill. George's mouth curled at the corner and her eyes softened when she remembered the perfect 'oh' her mouth made when she saw the plane. Her Mum had the same photo on her bedside table at home.

Sheila went into the Post Office to serve customers and poked her head around the door half an hour later. George barely looked up and read the letter again.

It was her Mum's handwriting; she'd recognise it anywhere. Mum had written the letter. The sentiments and sorrow were all Mum, but the detail she didn't recognise. But the letter was genuine. It said someone would give her more information on her career, both legitimate and working for the Soviets. She explained, she worked for the Soviets and that's why she worked for the UK Ministry of Defence. George's mouth and throat turned as dry as the Sahara, her mind whirling. Did their mother love them, or were they a convenience for her 'legend'? Had she betrayed Britain for the money?

Her last words to George were to love her country and stay loyal to it, but above all, to look after her hot-headed sister, and for them to love each other. So which country did her Mum consider as 'her own country'? And which country was George supposed to be loyal to, the Russians? Never.

George folded the letter, returned it to the envelope, and saw Sheila standing over her. Besides Charlie, Aunty Sheila was the closest she had to a friend and family. She bore the same smile she used when George and Charlie were kids, when they were hurting and needed motherly sympathy. Besides Charlie, there were two people her Mum said to trust; Sheila and one other, 'James Chance'. She should contact him if her death looked suspicious. She'd included a London phone number. James Chance would explain more.

"Don't forget, George, I've been here for you as long

as you've lived, and so long as I'm alive, I'll be here for you. I hope the letter answers some of your questions?" Sheila was expressing concern, rather than inquisitiveness.

"Sheila, why didn't Mum tell us this? Why?" George demanded. It answered a few weird things about her family, and perhaps why dad walked out. Did he discover his wife's deception and her activities and couldn't accept it? Also, why had Mum encouraged George to join the Army?

"She knew this could get you killed. You had enough to worry you. Now it's your turn to settle the score. Okay?"

George nodded, not sure what to do. She enveloped the letter and the USB stick and put them in her bag.

"Right. What do I need to know? Mum referred to more information, which would explain her career."

"Okay, you'll have to ask the contact your Mum gave you. Ask him for the file."

Chapter 15

George strode towards home along the road, thinking through the issues and contradictions. She supposed it was hers and Charlie's house now. She had difficulty understanding how her Mum could spy for a Cold War enemy, even though she said in the letter she didn't look upon it as betraying her country. Why had their Mum raised them to behave properly and in George's case to serve her country? Was it protection, part of an act, the 'legend' as spies called it? Why had neither Charlie nor she spotted it? Why hadn't Mum given herself away? No doubt Mum excelled at her job. Above all and despite what she'd just learnt, George resolved to set the score straight and avenge her Mum and Charlie.

What a spewy mess. And now it was all hers to sort out. She clenched her fists, quickened her pace, and felt a slight twinge in her shoulder. A casual onlooker might have thought she was heading for a fight. Bushes bordered the lane leading to her house. Mum had been asking the Council to cut them down for years because it hid her view of the road. They had a fantastic view of the sea. If you walked across the fields, in a few minutes you could be swimming. The gate to her house stood open; even though she was sure she'd locked it.

The car she'd spotted earlier was still there, a hundred metres short of the gate. It was clear of snow, even though there'd been a slight snowfall, which meant someone had sat inside with the engine running to keep warm. But she could see no one in the car now. She'd investigate later.

Mum had been strict with house security, and it all made sense now. She'd planted blackthorn hedges outside the house, told her daughters to stay away in case they became snagged in them. George liked the tart taste of sloe berries, but sometimes became entangled in the spines. Mum didn't like night latches which locked when you slammed the door closed. She said even a twelve-year-old could get past one of those, insisting on a five-lever mortice deadlock with several locking points along the frame. Mum had even researched and explained the different locks to them. Now, George realised she'd probably had professional advice.

George became as preoccupied with security as did her Mum, even more so since she'd joined the Army. Something her mother approved of. She stopped in the doorway, key in hand, looking at the open front door. There was no question of her having left it unlocked, let alone open.

Standing against the wall alongside the door, she listened for a sound inside. Maybe they'd left. This could be the man who'd killed her Mum. Aside from the possibility he may be here to finish George, which was reason enough to introduce herself violently, her recent surprise had inflamed her. Violence is better executed with a cold mind and a warm heart. But right now, she'd settle for a cold heart and a hot head.

The sound of a man humming. Did the door squeak when it opened? She planned to push it open, then slide into the house. A man appeared in the doorway. He pulled the door open and saw George. Taller than him, she looked down at him and scowled. His eyes wide, a deer caught in the headlight. He looked up with surprise and attempted a smile, his mouth open. George wasn't interested in the whys and wherefores. The man's eyes fidgeted. He didn't look like a murderer or a burglar. In the quarter-second before she seized his wrist in her right hand, wrenching it down, and twisting it against the joint, she'd decided she wasn't interested in whether he was legit. Height on her side, and the man out of shape, with a stomach extended from his neck to his groin she applied more pressure. He emitted a gravelly wheeze, and a squeal accompanied by a surprised and pained grunt.

His open jacket flapped as he bent forward to ease the strain on his elbow and shoulder joints. The squeal turned to a gasp as she may have heard the word 'Police'. She twisted his arm, punching the back of his head with her free hand. He grunted, his legs sagged, but the pain in his arm held him up. George yanked his jacket down over his back and part way down his arms, then dumped him in the entrance way.

Her knee pressing gently into the middle of his back as he landed face down. He lay on the ground groaning, which was a plus. For a second, she considered breaking his arm at the elbow, but kept the pressure on instead. She'd be in her right. He may have murdered her Mum. But she wasn't sadistic, and it wasn't right. Murder or no murder.

"Who are you, and what are you doing here?"

Another grunt, presumably as a pretext to answering her questions. With one free hand, she reached inside his jacket pocket, pulled out a leather folder, dropped it on the ground, and flipped it open. It told her he was, 'Detective Constable Douglas Freer, NCA'.

George heard hard-soled shoes on the driveway and saw a pair of legs coming down the path. She'd disable the man on the ground, and then tackle the approaching woman. George glanced towards Sarah Frolic.

"You've met Doug," said Sarah. "He's harmless, you can let him up."

"Not until he tells me his business in my house. You have a search warrant, 'Dougie'?" asked George.

He wheezed through his bruised nose, "It's a crime scene, and you've assaulted a police officer."

"Being a police officer doesn't give you the right to break in and I used minimum force. So, you thought you'd chance your hand?"

"Sorry, can we play nice now?" asked Dougie.

"I am playing nice. Your arm isn't broken, yet. Make a complaint if you're not happy."

She let go of his wrist and stood. 'Dougie' made an undignified scramble to his feet, rubbed his arm, and dabbed at the blood on his face.

"I think you've broken my nose," he said with an exaggerated lisp.

"Stop whining, Doug. It's not even bruised."

Sarah turned to George. "Can we go inside and sort this out? Doug can be an arse."

George frowned, then nodded and let them inside. She pointed to the sofa, but remained standing over them.

"What's this about, you first?" George said, pointing to Doug who had taken out a handkerchief and dabbed at his nose.

"I wanted to look around. The locals may have missed something," said Doug, staring at his shoes.

"I'm supposed to accept stupidity and enthusiasm took over. What were you looking for?"

"Anything unusual, anything to give us a clue?"

George didn't believe him. She slipped a hand into her coat pocket to feel for the letter containing the USB stick. It was still there. She'd look at it as soon as she could. Sarah's eyes went to the hand in George's pocket and George withdrew it.

"Why is the NCA getting involved in a burglary?" she asked, turning to Sarah.

"You know it wasn't simply a burglary. They were after something else. The NCA has been investigating a series of suspicious murders; your mother was the latest. What we don't know is why. We have a link between the murders. All the victims previously worked in sensitive government jobs. But why your mother was murdered is a mystery. We even have an idea who's doing it, but not why. But it's getting way above our pay grade."

"Do you want to share your insights with me, or are we on opposite sides?" asked George.

"It's a police matter. Leave it to us," Sarah said with little conviction.

George looked at Doug and pointed. "With police like him working on the case, you may need my help. This looks more like Laurel and Hardy than 'The Professionals'."

"You," said George, pointing to Doug, "leave and don't come back. You can't help."

Sarah looked down, embarrassed, and Doug shuffled off the sofa and left the house.

"I'm sorry. He's not the brightest star in the sky."

"Tell me what's going on," said George.

Chapter 16

On the South East coast, in winter, the sea could be tempestuous. Templeton Maudlin fidgeted, but nervousness was part of his makeup. His compact frame made him look like a tasered meerkat. Seagulls wheeled and dived, plucking out small fish and harassing other gulls, trying to steal their catch. His binoculars jerked, switching from one position to another, as birds caught his attention. His eye caught a lone skua, flying higher than the seagulls, and black terns. A skua dive bombed a seagull not nimble enough to devour its catch before the skua struck its head and stole it. Maudlin smiled and hummed with satisfaction as his hands shook with joy. Such determined ruthlessness.

Wind buffeted Templeton, and he adjusted his scarf inside his undertaker's overcoat. Standing on the deserted concrete walkway, a foot from the sandy beach, he forgot the world around him, sucked in the tangy sea air, snorted the bromine, and tasted the salty bitterness. A Sandwich Tern captured his attention. It dived, a glider cutting through a cloud, and slid into the water, to emerge with its catch. The wind, the crashing of the waves, and the squawking of the array of seabirds destroyed his quietness. And he loved it. This coastline and the seabirds were his second love.

Templeton almost dropped his binos as the wind caught his bowler hat and his hand went to catch it. A hand clamped on his shoulder from behind, and he jumped, turning. His face twitched; his eyes wide. His hand rose to protect his face.

"Good afternoon, Mr Maudlin, I hope you are well. What a dismal day, what?"

A rhetorical question.

Regaining his composure, Maudlin said, "Good Afternoon, Moss. I love this weather; marvellous. A day for bird spotting. The skua is quite a predator, don't you think? It attacks much larger birds. Quite fearless."

"Hmmm," said Moss.

"You cannot deny the beauty of such beasts?"

"Each to his own, Templeton."

"Are you a Philistine?" asked Templeton, turning to face Moss with a scowl.

Moss's smile didn't fade, and he showed no offence.

"Let's walk," he said, pointing to the path alongside the beach whilst taking out a pack of thin cigars. He lit one with a gold lighter, flicking the top open with practised ease. Templeton hadn't seen one of those in years. The smell of the smoke was pleasant, but it offended his temperament. He wondered what the seabirds made of cigar smoke.

Templeton Maudlin had examined thousands of faces in death, making it something of a study. Beyond pleasure, unlike birds. His vocation was more of a professional compulsion or hunger. He'd spoken to Moss on the phone, never face to face. From their phone conversations, Maudlin would have wagered the man was English and schooled at Eton. He had an affectation encouraged by public schools, one of inbred superiority, manifested by staring over the head of others with a bemused smile. Some would call it condescending, but it was more imperious.

They walked along the pebble incline. Templeton took a last glimpse at the seabirds, wanting nothing more than to stay and watch them feed. The two walked along the path next to the beach. The intensity of the rain increased, and Moss turned up his collar and pulled down the brim of his trilby hat.

"This," Moss swept his hand across the length of the sea, "and your little Funeral Parlour and Crematorium is your domain. Mine is a more demanding and a graver business, no pun intended. And that is what we must discuss."

"Who is to judge importance? You, despatching people from this world; or me, helping them make their last journey? Do you think you have the moral high ground?"

"You follow the philosophers, Templeton? Which school?"

"Yes. I find Plato the most rewarding of the ancient philosophers. I particularly like his work on 'Dialectic'."

"Ah yes, truth is the highest value, found through reason, logic, and discussion," Moss revelled in his rhetoric. "Each person should, primarily, seek truth to direct one's life. You like the idea?"

"Yes, I do. It has a symmetrical simplicity to it," said Templeton, feeling he was on home ground and within reach of wiping the smile off Moss's face.

To a casual observer, they were a couple of friends out for an afternoon stroll. However, the more observant might have noticed Templeton Maudlin gradually moving away from Moss, as if the other man was encroaching on his space, threatening him.

"In which case, you'll also understand Plato's ideas on society. Plato asserts, society is a tripartite class. On the one hand, as a Funeral Director, you are, in Plato's terms, a 'worker' a 'labourer', corresponding to the 'appetite' part of the soul. The men who do my bidding 'dispose of problems'. They are warriors, so to speak, and are the 'spirit'. Also, in Plato's terms, I am the governing class. I am a thinker, I am intelligent, and wise. My class is the 'reason' of the soul. We are few. So, my Funeral Director friend, may I suggest you keep quiet, follow my direction and all will be well. In which case you may continue to whet your appetite from the pickings I throw your way, and I may continue to govern. If, however, you decide you wish to discontinue our relationship, then I will have no choice but to resolve the situation by introducing you to a member of the warrior class. Do I make myself clear, Templeton?"

He turned to face Maudlin, peered down at his toothy, worried expression with a fixed 'risus sardonicus' gaze, which looked like an abnormal spasm of his facial muscles. Maudlin knew of his affliction and made the most of it. He liked to call it his 'Hippocratic smile'. To others, it made him look manic. He nodded, but remained silent and inched away from Moss. They walked on. The howling wind and the sea spray filled the pause, but Templeton didn't restart the conversation, which might end in his 'disposal'.

"There was an unexpected and unfortunate turn of events last week. We must bring the resulting fallout under control."

Templeton shivered, not from the cold, but from that awful memory of the sight of the girl racing down the stairs, lambasting him, and Bradley's appearance.

"Your son, Bradley, is now in police custody and charged with burglary, murder, and withholding evidence. I may have to dispose of the boy, but now, my reach is limited. However, I have taken certain steps to control him. He saw one of my men. But there was insufficient time to clean your mess. Is this boy of yours likely to remain silent?"

"It is unlikely he'll say anything to incriminate me, and he has no connection with you. He saw little," said Templeton.

"Whether he incriminates you, is not my concern, whether he compromises my operation, is. At the right time I may dispose of him, as a favour to you. In the meantime, it will be your job to maintain your son's silence in prison. In this way, we may continue our current arrangement to our mutual advantage, and you may continue with your sordid little foible. Do you agree?"

Templeton cleared his throat noisily and swallowed the resulting phlegm. The cacophony of the seabirds drowned out the noise. "Yes, I think so."

"You think so? The alternative would be unfortunate and may also result in your own demise. I hope my message is clear?"

"Yes, absolutely," said Templeton, his voice breaking. "About the girl who saw me?"

"A work in progress, Mr Maudlin, which may eventually be your concern. She is in a coma, and if she stays that way, all will be well. In the unlikely event of her recovering from the coma, we may have to address the problem. It may require your active participation to resolve the matter. If you decline, I will dispose of both you and the girl. It is not in your interest to disappoint me, Templeton. Do not become a stone in my shoe."

Maudlin thought hard, his attention straying. What could this man mean 'it may eventually be his concern'? What was Moss asking him to do? Did Moss want him to dispose of the girl in his cremator? In which case, it would be a pleasure. He was sure Bradley would say nothing, especially after Pinchin had visited him at the police station.

"I'll try not to, but with a son like Bradley, it's difficult," said Templeton.

"To try, and to fail, will effectuate your own reckoning, Templeton. I'm sure you understand."

Templeton stopped and pulled himself up to his five foot five inches, turned to Moss, and captured his gaze. "I recognise a fellow crazy, Moss. But in my case, I even scare the dead and you are obligated to me," he said, with a boldness he didn't feel.

Moss smiled and seemed to mellow. "Crazy? Possibly, but there are compensations. People like me have a rare but misunderstood intelligence. Neither of us would close both eyes in the other's presence. But I sympathise, Templeton, I wouldn't like to be in your head, I'm sure you have issues. You've heard the story, a man said to the Universe: 'Sir I exist!', 'However,' replied the Universe, 'That has not created in me a sense of obligation'. Neither do I feel an obligation toward you. Let me explain in the minute we have left. Whilst I find your mental meanderings interesting, they are to me, of little significance. Your ego Maudlin is your concern and your anchor, and you must find your own way through this. I will watch with interest, but encroach on my affairs and I will squash you like a beetle in the path of an elephant."

Moss smiled the warm smile of an accomplished sociopath, and Templeton Maudlin turned ashen. He was familiar with the dead and was sublimely happy in their presence, but transferring someone from one state to the other required something more than he possessed. But the alternative was unthinkable. He restrained his ego and remained silent. This man seemed bent on being circumferential.

"I've enjoyed our brief chat, Templeton. It's gratifying when one can have a mature discussion with a fellow, with an agreement on important issues. By the by, here is your reward for your humble service."

Moss slipped his leather-gloved hand into his inside pocket of his overcoat and withdrew a small sealed package, which he handed to Templeton. Someone watching from over fifty yards would have observed nothing amiss. Templeton furtively pocketed the package and glanced along the empty road.

A moment later, Moss increased his pace, leaving Templeton behind.

"Good day to you," said Moss, waving to Templeton without turning.

Dread and panic gripped Templeton when he realised Moss was as sane as Jack Nicholson without the lobotomy. Moss measured his words, and he knew the implied threats were a plan of action. He had the urge to distance himself from this man.

Chapter 17

Had Bradley told the police the full story, he wouldn't be sitting in a 'SECURE4US' van with blackened windows, on his way to Maidstone Prison. He kept his head low, bending over until his hair flopped in front of his face and almost brushed against his knees. The guard watched him, ready for problems. It needed backbone to survive prison, not something Bradley considered himself to have much of. He'd keep his head down until the trial, use the time to rethink, and above all, avoid attracting attention.

The van halted, and the double gates opened with a rasping drag, and thumped closed behind them. He was on remand, but it marked a finality to his old life. To the prison system, he was a criminal. Metal grating against metal was ubiquitous. Wherever he turned, metal grating against metal rattled in his brain. As the van door opened, the light caused him to blink, and he shaded his eyes from the winter sun.

"Out. Follow me. Move your felonious arses. I haven't got all day."

The guard used the word 'felonious' as if he'd practised it, giving his charges a cursory glance.

The hour-long 'reorientation' flew over his head without landing. A search, then cataloguing his personal effects; one Sekonda watch, one cheap ring, one shirt, jacket trousers, one pair of shoes, one comb plastic, one wallet containing fifteen pounds, a membership card for the local library, well used and one card for the fitness centre, never used. Issue of prison uniform, blue T-shirt and jeans and cheap trainers, and shower, safety briefing, 'dos and don'ts'. Bradley kept a neutral, sullen expression, even when he walked into his cell carrying a pile of blankets and a pillow.

"Shepherd, meet Bradley Maudlin," said the Prison Officer, in a voice which told of decades of shouting, cajoling with shift after shift of boredom and depraved criminals.

He said Bradley's name as if trying to get a fig seed out of his false teeth.

"Your cellmate and new best friend," said the Officer, pushing Bradley into the cell.

The Officer seemed impervious to the stink of urine, body odour, and halitosis, which hung in the cell like a rotting corpse. The ferocious assault on his senses made him gag. With a supreme effort, he suppressed it, leaving his face cold and wet, his body shaking. The Prison Officer stabbed a finger at Shepherd and wrinkled his nose.

"It is your job to sort him out. Make sure he knows the rules and sticks to them. Maudlin, Shepherd here may seem like a nice guy but don't let him deceive you, he's a convicted criminal like the rest of you. Clear?"

"Yes, Mr Brewer," they said together.

Bradley was on remand, and a court would find him innocent or guilty, but he held his tongue. He needed them more than they needed him. This would be his home, his punishment for months, until his trial, which was top of his thinking list.

"Bottom bunk," said Shepherd in a Glaswegian accent, pointing at the bottom bunk.

"What's your tally, mate?"

"Awaiting trial."

He preferred to remain unknown. He slumped onto the lower bunk and glanced around the cell. The dominant colour was grey, grey metal table and chair, dull grey walls, and even the blue prison clothes looked grey. He stared down at his prison-issue plastic trainers. A sigh escaped him.

"That's only a shit 'n' shave," Shepherd laughed, sitting next to Bradley on the bed.

"What was it? Don't tell me, let me guess, fraud, stolen library books, yeah? What are you charged with?"

"Breaking and entering and withholding evidence," said Bradley, glancing at Shepherd.

"Get away. You aren't the type," said Shepherd, with mocking respect.

"It'll be scoff time in half an hour. I'll introduce you to

a friend of mine. He'll enjoy meeting you."

He grinned at Bradley and squeezed his knee. Bradley pushed him off with an effort. He didn't enjoy the idea of being hawked like a prostitute, and a shiver ran down his back.

"No need to be unfriendly. Sometimes it's better to be someone's friend than the wing's bitch. Me and my friend can look after you."

He saw Shepherd sneering, and he realised the die was cast. Shepherd had marked him for abuse and intimidation. He could become accustomed to Shepherd's ways, but who was his 'friend'?

They joined the lunch queue at its busiest, and Shepherd pressed himself against Bradley from behind. Although tempted to confront Shepherd, he didn't resist the intrusion. He needed to trust him, for now. He had no option.

"Don't get the cottage pie. I know what they put in it. Get the toad in the hole," suggested Shepherd, slinging a shovel full of meaty slop onto his plate.

Bradley followed his suggestion, swallowing vomit. He'd either adapt or starve.

"Sit over there with that big bloke, his name's Josey. I'll introduce you," said Shepherd, pointing to a Con sitting on his own, hunched over his food, shovelling it in with a massive spoon.

He avoided cringing and held back; Shepherd pushed against him with his groin. Resistance would mark him as the enemy, and he had to share a cell with Shepherd; he also had to sleep sometime. Bradley was no hero, or even physically robust. Any fight with Shepherd would elicit Bradley stamping his feet and shouting for help. Josey Bingham stared at Bradley as a sewage engineer would examine a specimen from a septic tank.

"Who the rubber duck are you, and who gave you permission to sit?" he said. His voice high-pitched, barely masculine.

Bradley picked up his tray to leave when Shepherd intervened. He placed a hand on Bradley's arm and squeezed. If he meant it to be reassuring, it wasn't.

"Josey, I'd like to introduce you to Bradley. He's in my cell," said Shepherd, with enthusiasm.

The way he said 'Bradley' suggested Shepherd thought Bradley as either homosexual or prime for conversion. Josey grinned through broken teeth, placed his tattooed, dinner sized hands on the table and glowered. Bradley fought an urge to run, find a corner and come to terms with his slop.

"I'll find another table."

"Not likely, I want us to get acquainted." Josey's voice cackled and his lips smacked. "We can be friends. Sit next to me. Eat. We can do each other a favour."

Josey blew a kiss at Bradley. Within one hour, two prison inmates had humiliated and intimidated him. His bottom lip quivered. Bradley didn't trust himself to speak, his head hanging over his food. He tried not to catch Josey's eye as he wiped his own.

Chapter 18

Templeton sat in his study, waiting for the pallbearers to deliver the coffin to his Funerarium, as he called it. The coffin contained the remains of Mrs Julia Stone. A woman whose company he should have enjoyed earlier, except for the unplanned entry of the girl who'd attacked him like a devil.

A curl of cigar smoke wafted towards the yellowing ceiling. Cigars and whisky go together, but he'd leave the whisky until after his work. Tonight, he needed a clear head. It was too early, and except for emergencies, he didn't touch alcohol until the sun hit the horizon, and this wasn't an emergency. A pleasure, but not an emergency. Although it was mid-afternoon, the light was fading. He laid down his cigar and walked over to the window to draw the curtains. Whilst death was a friend, the night was a passive ally. As he turned away from the window, he caught his image in the mirror and scowled. Seeing himself in the mirror didn't frighten him, he simply found it unsettling; perhaps self-loathing or something deeper. He'd stopped self-analysis years ago. He found it unproductive and confusing. It wasn't superstition or fear of the unknown; there were no superstitious undertakers. They didn't survive long if they were. Nothing made Templeton happier than a night spent preparing a dead friend.

The police had asked him to deal with this case. He supposed at this time of the year, most Funeral Directors closed for the Christmas season. Didn't they realise Christmas is a busy time for the dead? To the rest of society, death at Christmas was a messy and inconvenient affair. To him, it was both business and pleasure. A bang on the door brought him out of his reverie. He recognised Michael's knock, his devoted helper.

"Yes," despite whispering, the door opened and Michael entered and stood in the doorway, as if walking on hallowed ground. His hands clenched and unclenched, but Templeton smiled.

"Yes, Michael. You've completed your work?"

Michael was the only living person with whom Templeton relaxed.

"Yes, Mr Maudlin. Our friend is in your workshop. Is there anything else I can do?"

He said 'our friend' as if taught to say it. It pleased Templeton.

"You may leave for the day, Michael. Unless…" Templeton Maudlin left it hanging.

"Right, Mr Maudlin. See you in the morning, unless."

Michael backed out of the room.

Templeton smiled at Michael's awkwardness, finished his cigar at a leisurely pace, and reflected on the night ahead. Delayed gratification. It would be a pleasure to meet a 'friend' again. He found it reassuring that Bradley had spent Christmas in remand at 'Her Majesty's Pleasure'. But most things had a good side to them, and at least Templeton had spent Christmas alone. He would have liked the body before Christmas. Her company would have been a treat.

Templeton Maudlin walked into the workshop, glancing down at the body recently brought into his funeral parlour, and smiled; the way one might greet a friend. He relaxed, Zen-like. Life vanished from the room; a wisp of smoke drawn under the door by wind.

The pathologist had finished his work, and in Templeton's opinion, he'd made a bloody mess of it, particularly in cutting the skull to examine the fracture. He inserted his finger under the skull section and pulled. The pathologist had sliced off the skull top and after inspection, replaced it badly, making a mess, which was unnecessary because the cause of death was obvious. He shrugged and sighed.

"Julia Stone, what's your story? Let me guess, raised in a posh part of London, an office job, local government?" he asked the corpse rhetorically. "By the look of your features and high cheekbones, you were someone. Pity I can't see your hairline."

"You are tall, aren't you? You must be what, five foot ten?"

He slid his fingers along Julia's arm and the hairs on the corpse stood on end like goose bumps. Templeton showed no surprise. Corpse frequently showed such a reaction to the touch of something warm. Still, it pleased him. His fingers continued down along her wrist to her hand and fingers, caressing them.

"You know, it's not true that fingernails continue to grow after death. You have such lovely, manicured hands."

Templeton let the corpse's fingers slide through his own and land back onto the white cotton sheet. He peered at them and noted the Embalmer had done a decent job. They look alive, almost.

"I wonder what you did to attract Moss's attention? I suspect yours is a long story."

He stood at the foot of the table, looking along her body, inspecting it for several minutes.

"You may have an English name, but you aren't originally from these shores, I would guess. Sturdy bone structure and fair complexion. Nordic or more likely from your dark hair, East European, I would say, somewhere in the Baltic States, or Poland? Julia Stone, is that your real name, married name, or is there something more mysterious about you? Have you been a naughty girl, hiding a past? I imagine the latter. Otherwise, the wrong people wouldn't have taken an interest in you."

He slid his hand along the elderly woman, from armpit to thigh.

"As I suspected, you had excellent muscle tone. An athletic woman at one point. Your physique reminds me of a gymnast in the 1960s. What was her name now, Lucie something? No stretch marks, childless, not sure. You are a most unusual person. I suspect whatever you had hidden in your skull, will now remain a secret. Moss made sure of that."

He took his time washing, bathing, cleaning, and closing her mouth and eyes. He cooed and sighed with closed eyes, enjoying the feel of her skin and the texture of embalmed muscles. Breathing in, he threw back his head. For Templeton, the smell of the living was unpleasant. It reminded him of the smell of an old person's sofa, which made him nauseous. The smell of decaying human flesh and embalming chemicals was as natural to him as death itself.

Some hours later, he'd completed his work. She was ready. He took each hand and foot between his hands and fingers, turning, squeezing the bones in the wrists and ankles as a doctor might check for broken bones. Finally, he took a set of pruning shears and snipped off a finger from Julia Stone's hand and placed it into a small copper container, which he deposited in his waistcoat pocket.

Satisfied, he sat back in a straight-backed chair and gazed at his handy work. Eventually retiring to his study, he glanced at the long-case clock. The family had passed it down, but he hated resetting the weights. He did it without fail, and to his knowledge, the clock had never missed a beat.

Easing into his armchair, and with practised hands, he rolled his left shirt sleeve past the elbow. He'd found that on these occasions, a small therapeutic helped him to appreciate his handy work, an appetiser. Templeton closed his eyes as he depressed the plunger on the hypodermic, and his breathing became shallow. His main course would come later.

To his knowledge, no one except Michael had seen him in this mental state, and had someone in authority done so, they would have committed him to an institution on suspicion of being a necrophile. He considered himself purely and precisely a necrophile, but his love of the dead was pure and filial, never carnal. He readjusted to the present, closed his eyes, and thought about the following day's events; the cremation of Julia Stone, and a visit to Bradley languishing in prison.

He felt no sympathy for his son. Even as a child, he was soft, a pushover. His mother often had to rescue him from trouble and fights. Bigger boys saw him as an easy target. His height and dark, good looks should have made him a natural for any woman, but his style, and manner gave men the wrong idea. Bradley didn't have his father's affinity with the dead. Despite his wife's repeated denials, he was far from sure that Bradley was his. They were as different as dead and alive. Templeton hoped one day Bradley would inherit the funeral business, but he must get himself some steel and sagacity if he was going to enjoy his work. Prison would toughen him up; maybe make him into a real man. By three o'clock in the morning, he'd worked for twelve hours. Twelve hours of sheer heaven, and his drugged mind was finely balanced, anticipating the main course.

A faint sound encroached on his thoughts. He thought he recognised the tune. He'd first heard it many years before. It must have been when he was watching the film 'The Pianist', Władysław Szpilman playing Chopin's 'Nocturne'. His wife used to play it whenever she had the chance, and in his opinion, she played it beautifully, even better than Szpilman. The notes slid off the keyboard, as a shroud caresses a body.

The sound may have come from the street, but to date he'd never heard so much as a bird singing. Templeton stood on shaking legs and held onto the chair. Julia Stone now forgotten as he walked towards the source of the music coming from his former wife's music room. The room had remained unoccupied since the last time she'd played the piano fifteen years ago. Well, it couldn't be a ghost. Ghosts don't play the piano. Perhaps a burglar, but would a burglar break in to play the piano? He'd heard his wife play the piece so often, he'd recognise it in his sleep. Regardless of his lack of superstition, as the volume rose, his throat constricted and his eyes bulged. He knew of only one person who could play Chopin's 'Nocturne' with such skill and passion.

He put his hand on the doorknob and jerked it away as if he'd received an electric shock. Gaining courage, he grasped the knob, turned the handle, and threw open the door. The music emanating from the piano overwhelmed his senses. The woman was dressed as she had at their last encounter, and looked not a day older. He stood, paralysed. This was impossible; he'd guaranteed that fifteen years before. It was several seconds before he could speak.

"Please, please, stop. Who are you?"

The music continued, but the woman turned her head to him smiling, a smile he recognised. A few moments later, she stopped, and her hands rested on the keys. She lowered the piano fallboard and faced him. A wet patch appeared at his groin and a pool formed between his feet.

"Hello, Templeton. It's so nice to see you. You need a drink, malt. You'll find relief in the decanter," she said, pointing to a dust-covered sideboard.

Templeton walked over, his body shaking like a shack in an earthquake, and poured himself a full glass. Holding onto the sideboard with one hand, he turned to his 'wife' sitting in the armchair she'd been so fond of.

"Come sit next to me, Templeton. We have much to discuss. She patted the armchair next to her. You're no doubt wondering what I'm doing here. And how could I possibly be here?"

Templeton recognised this woman, her clothes, even the way she smiled with her eyes. But her style and confidence differed from the woman to whom he was married for thirty years. Sitting with their knees a few inches apart, he gulped half the glass of whisky.

"Who are you?" he asked.

"It's a good start. At least you know I'm not your wife, Barbara Maudlin. You made sure, but your reaction and your face are priceless."

She laughed; her head thrown back; the way his wife laughed.

"So much for your lack of superstition regarding the dead. It amuses me to appear to you as your wife, or should I say former wife." She smiled, patting his leg. "Regained your composure? Come now, Templeton, how difficult is it to cast aside all you believed about the dead? If the dead could talk, what would they say about you, Templeton? Here stands Templeton Maudlin. He finds more solace in drugs and the decanter than in life. He cares more for a slab of decomposing flesh than the living. A man who relates to the dead but finds the living revolting. I'm pleased to be the one to enlighten you. The dead can talk, I'm proof."

Reason told him the woman sitting next to him was dead, like the corpse next door. Her smile might have been endearing to some, but to Templeton it could have frozen a blacksmith's forge.

The woman watched and waited, an eternity on her side. Sitting cross-legged, a shoe hung off one foot, the way his wife used to sit.

"Better? So, Templeton, your question, what do I want. You, Templeton. I'm here to negotiate the terms of your voluntary surrender to me. I'm a kind of negotiator. I negotiate passage to the next place. Oh, don't worry, I've not come for you right now. Your remaining time here will be part of our agreement. Silly man. Templeton, I've been watching you, and from a cast of billions, I've chosen you. You look sad and worried, but rejoice, it's a rare privilege."

She grinned, reached over, and patted Templeton's leg. He flinched, trying to withdraw. Her hand stayed on his leg, not reassuring, but leaching threat and foreboding through his trousers. It froze his marrow.

"So, what is there to negotiate?" asked Templeton, more composed, and his complexion returning.

"Some amongst the living call me 'The Ferryman' others 'Charon'. I have many names. But whatever they call me, I use my discretion, let's say, to ensure in every case, the newly departed from your world find their proper place in mine. I've been doing this job for an eternity; I've handled them all. For example, Julia Stone, such a charming woman, I've recently found the perfect place for her."

"But after millennia, I'm tired and wish to move on to other things. And you will be my successor, if you agree, of course."

Good luck for your
1 x Mon draw
on Mon 03 Oct 22
1 play x £1.50 for 1 draw
£1.50

| SET FOR LIFE®

1233-020301320-264779 011706

Your numbers

Life Ball

A 07 10 21 30 34 - 10

AMAZING THINGS HAPPEN WHEN A
LOT OF PEOPLE PLAY A LITTLE
SEARCH: DREAM BIG PLAY SMALL

CHECK IF YOU'RE A WINNER
▼ SCAN WITH THE NATIONAL LOTTERY APP ▼

1233-020301320-264779 011706 Term. 46211601

[. . . . .] Fill the box to void the ticket

THE NATIONAL LOTTERY®

For information visit the website at www.national-lottery.co.uk or call the National Lottery Line on **0333 234 50 50**. Calls cost no more than calls to 01 or 02 numbers. If your phone tariff offers inclusive calls to landlines, calls to 03 numbers will be included on the same basis. A separate MINICOM line for the hard of hearing is also available. A proportion of National Lottery sales goes to the Good Causes. For further information please refer to the Players' Guide.

GUIDANCE ON HOW TO PLAY

For how to play and prize structures see the Players' Guide (available from retailers), see the website, or call the National Lottery Line. Results can be found through recognised media channels, retailers, the National Lottery Line or the website. Tickets issued in error, illegible or incomplete can be cancelled if returned to the issuing terminal within 120 minutes of purchase and before close of ticket sales from that terminal on that day.

GUIDANCE ON HOW TO CLAIM A PRIZE

For details about how and where to claim prizes see the Players' Guide or visit www.national-lottery.co.uk/prize. If you hold a winning ticket you must claim your prize by post, or in person at a retailer, or Regional Centre as appropriate, within 180 days of the applicable draw date, or within this period notify the National Lottery Line of your intention to claim, and then claim within 187 days of that draw date. Claims over £50,000 must be made in person. **If you believe you have won over £50,000 telephone the National Lottery Line.** For all claims over £500 (over £5,000 if claiming by post) you will be required to complete a claim form and show proof of identity. For a claim form telephone the National Lottery Line.

To claim by post, please send your ticket (and completed claim form for prizes over £5,000), at your own risk to The National Lottery, PO Box 287, Watford WD18 9TT.

SIGN YOUR TICKET. MAKE IT YOURS.

Name _____

Address _____

_____ Post Code _____

Signature _____

Safe custody of your ticket is your responsibility. If your ticket is lost, stolen, damaged or destroyed, you can make a written claim to Camelot no later than 30 days after the winning draw date, but it will be at Camelot's discretion whether or not to investigate and to pay the claim.

THE OPERATOR OF THE NATIONAL LOTTERY

The National Lottery is operated by Camelot UK Lotteries Limited under licence granted by the Gambling Commission. The principal office of Camelot is Tolpits Lane, Watford WD18 9RN.

GAMES RULES AND PROCEDURES

National Lottery games are subject to the relevant Rules and Procedures which set out the contractual rights and obligations of the player and Camelot. Games Rules and Procedures are available to view at retailers or on the website, and copies can be obtained from the National Lottery Line. Camelot is entitled to treat a ticket as invalid if the data on it does not correspond with the entries on Camelot's central computer. Players must be 18 or over. Play responsibly.

If you are concerned about playing too much, call GamCare on 0808 8020 133 (freephone). www.gamcare.org.uk

THE NATIONAL LOTTERY®

For information visit the website at www.national-lottery.co.uk or call the National Lottery Line on **0333 234 50 50**. Calls cost no more than calls to 01 or 02 numbers. If your phone tariff offers

Good luck for your
1 x Wed draw
on Wed 05 Oct 22

|LOTTO

1233-013015286-089079 017861

GOOD LUCK!
This is your free Lucky Dip
for matching two Lotto numbers.

YOUR NUMBERS

A 07 10 22 24 42 43

AMAZING THINGS HAPPEN WHEN A
LOT OF PEOPLE PLAY A LITTLE
SEARCH: DREAM BIG PLAY SMALL

CHECK YOUR TICKET THE EASY WAY
SCAN WITH THE NATIONAL LOTTERY APP

1233-013015286-089079 017861 Term. 46211601

SIGN YOUR TICKET. MAKE IT YOURS.

Name _____
Address _____
_____ Post Code _____
Signature _____

Safe custody of your ticket is your responsibility. If your ticket is lost, stolen, damaged or destroyed, you can make a written claim to Camelot no later than 30 days after the winning draw date, but it will be at Camelot's discretion whether or not to investigate and to pay the claim.

THE OPERATOR OF THE NATIONAL LOTTERY
The National Lottery is operated by Camelot UK Lotteries Limited under licence granted by the Gambling Commission. The principal office of Camelot is Tolpits Lane, Watford WD18 9RN.

GAMES RULES AND PROCEDURES
National Lottery games are subject to the relevant Rules and Procedures which set out the contractual rights and obligations of the player and Camelot. Games Rules and Procedures are available to view at retailers or on the website, and copies can be obtained from the National Lottery Line. Camelot is entitled to treat a ticket as invalid if the data on it does not correspond with the entries on Camelot's central computer. Players must be 18 or over. Play responsibly.
If you are concerned about playing too much, call GamCare on 0808 8020 133 (freephone). www.gamcare.org.uk

TR14

THE NATIONAL LOTTERY®
For information visit the website at www.national-lottery.co.uk or call the National Lottery Line on **0333 234 50 50**. Calls cost no more than calls to 01 or 02 numbers. If your phone tariff offers inclusive calls to landlines, calls to 03 numbers will be included on the same basis. A separate MINICOM line for the hard of hearing is also available. A proportion of National Lottery sales goes to the Good Causes. For further information please refer to the Players' Guide.

GUIDANCE ON HOW TO PLAY
For how to play and prize structures see the Players' Guide (available from retailers), see the website, or call the National Lottery Line. Results can be found through recognised media channels, retailers, the National Lottery Line or the website. Tickets issued in error, illegible or incomplete can be cancelled if returned to the issuing terminal within 120 minutes of purchase and before close of ticket sales from that terminal on that day.

GUIDANCE ON HOW TO CLAIM A PRIZE
For details about how and where to claim prizes see the Players' Guide or visit www.national-lottery.co.uk/prize. If you hold a winning ticket you must claim your prize by post, or in person at a retailer, or Regional Centre as appropriate, within 180 days of the applicable draw date, or within this period notify the National Lottery Line of your intention to claim, and then claim within 187 days of that draw date. Claims over £50,000 must be made in person. **If you believe you have won over £50,000 telephone the National Lottery Line.** For all claims over £500 (over £5,000 if claiming by post) you will be required to complete a claim form and show proof of identity. For a claim form telephone the National Lottery Line.

To claim by post, please send your ticket (and completed claim form for prizes over £5,000), at your own risk to The National Lottery, PO Box 287, Watford WD18 9TT.

SIGN YOUR TICKET. MAKE IT YOURS.

Name _____
Address _____
_____ Post Code _____
Signature _____

Safe custody of your ticket is your responsibility. If your ticket is lost, stolen, damaged or destroyed, you can make a written claim to Camelot no later than 30 days after the winning draw date, but it will be at Camelot's discretion whether or not to investigate and to pay the claim.

THE OPERATOR OF THE NATIONAL LOTTERY
The National Lottery is operated by Camelot UK Lotteries Limited under licence granted by the Gambling Commission. The principal office of Camelot is Tolpits Lane, Watford WD18 9RN.

GAMES RULES AND PROCEDURES
National Lottery games are subject to the relevant Rules and Procedures

To rationalise the obvious, Templeton said, "I don't know how you've done it, but I don't believe you. Leave now, or I'll call the police."

Templeton stood, shaking. He pointed, his arm looking more like a question mark than a demand for 'The Ferryman' to leave.

"Let me see if I can convince you. The police can't help you. Now you've completed Julia Stone's preparations. Does this help?"

There was no puff of smoke, no strange lights, no smell of incense. A Julia Stone manifestation replaced the apparition of his wife, even though he knew Stone lay dead in the other room.

"Come now, Templeton, you'll catch flies, and cut out the cigars, they're unhealthy," she chastised, smiling.

Tears rolled down Templeton's face. He curled into a ball on the armchair, his legs pulled tucked beneath him. Julia Stone's voice drowned Templeton's whimpering.

"Would the traditional image of me help?" asked 'Julia Stone'.

A grinning skeleton replaced Julia Stone, covered by a greying, rotting shroud. Its legs crossed, it swung one leg, which reminded him of the way his wife hung one shoe off the end. The skeleton held a scythe. The smell of decay assaulted Templeton's nose and lungs, causing him to cough and retch.

The Ferryman stood over Templeton, swinging the scythe along a line where his legs had been a second before. He bent over Templeton, their faces an inch apart.

"You love the dead so much. How about this? This, Maudlin, is death, the thing you love so much. I can end your obnoxious, misdirected, insignificant life in an instant."

The Ferryman breathed on Templeton, who coughed and slid to his hands and knees, retching. Instantly, the Ferryman transformed back into Templeton's former wife. She sat in the armchair next to his prostrate form, sipping whisky; she smiled, as if nothing of any consequence had happened.

"Thank you, Templeton. I am pleased with our work tonight. I must leave now. You will hear from me. I will watch you and remember you are a heartbeat away from my tender mercies."

The Ferryman poured himself a glass of whisky and sipped it, swinging one leg over the other.

"What is it to be Templeton, your ignominious death now, or continue your useless life and eventually replace me?"

Templeton coughed, and a line of saliva hung from his mouth to the carpet.

"Did you say 'Yes', my friend? Say it, damn you. Tell me you agree, and I'll go."

"Yes," mumbled Templeton, snot dribbling from his nose.

"Good. Now, I have a gift for you to give to your son. Something which will help ensure his silence."

'Julia Stone' handed over an envelope and a ring. He recognised the ring as his wife's and the handwriting as hers. You must arrange delivery of these to your son via Pinchin, such a nice chap. I look forward to seeing Bradley's face when he sees them.

"In the meantime, Templeton, *Memento vivere, memento mori*. Remember to live, remember to die."

The apparition disappeared.

***

It was the fault of that woman. The bitch had made life a misery; the constant baiting and browbeating. Even his profession didn't escape her taunting. 'Not work for real men' was one of her favourites.

He might have been able to resist this 'Ferryman' thing if he hadn't used 'her'. A coughing fit brought on a bout of retching. His face pressed against the abrasive carpet; an outside force pressing his head into the floor. He could believe anything after meeting 'that thing'.

He lay still, his body and mind consumed, barely able to open his eyes and hardly wanting to. The clock striking returned him from his self-imposed misery, and he found himself unable to move, one arm trapped under him, the other too weak to push him to his knees.

With effort he rolled onto his back, his head resting in the pool of drool and vomit. If ever he needed care and attention, it was now.

He summoned the strength to shout 'Michael'. After the third asking, a door quietly opened. Through slit eyes, he saw a shadow moving. Without a word, Michael manhandled Templeton onto his side. He was now in expert hands.

Later, a flowery scent permeated the room, a sweet perfume with floral undertones and a thick richness. His body slumped and relaxed, anticipating the hit.

Like a film out of focus, Michael, his faithful servant's feet approached, unhurried. He placed a thick bamboo pipe near Templeton's mouth. Maudlin opened wide; a baby desperate to attach to its mother's nipple. But a baby's need is instinct, Templeton's, an addiction.

He drew on the pipe and the effect hit him. Feeling the opium smoke enter his lungs and sit there, promising the world, a world out of reach by the width of a dragon's hair. After the third hit, his desperation subsided. A warm pressure in his head took care of his hurt, and the dragon nullified his thoughts.

The familiar disorientating rush faded to a solid opiate high, and he smiled. The world wasn't so bad. Even 'The Ferryman' had his good side. He giggled, but didn't mean to. The elation felt perfect, encompassing. It took him to a summer place. He was lying in a field of wheat, the sun on his face, the pipe transformed into a straw, which he chewed and sucked. This place was peacefully warm. A warm cloud, with a softness crafted by the gods, covered him. A part of his brain registered reality, Michael covering him with a blanket. His mind said 'thank you', but his lips refused to leave the pipe.

Lying in an opium-induced euphoria, Michael would stay with him until he was safely in his own bed. In this place, neither Moss nor The Ferryman existed. He'd never met Moss; or were they best friends? He couldn't remember, and didn't care. Another pull and deeper he went. He glanced at Michael, sitting impassively in the armchair in the corner. He loved the boy.

Chapter 19

Leaving Captain Andrew Pritchard's flat, Melanie Syman smiled, satisfied. Since Robert Syman, her husband, had returned from the frontline in Iraq, she'd sought comfort from an alternative, suitable, and reliable source, and Andrew served her purposes adequately. Obviously, she loved Robert, and twenty years of marriage counted for something. Andrew was a traditional officer from a good Scots family, single and living off base. He ticked the boxes. Although he had other women, most single officers did, and she didn't care.

She wasn't into rough trade; officers and soldiers should stay apart. She couldn't stand other ranks. No breeding, no money, no class, above all, often terribly rude, and disrespectful. For example, that woman, Sergeant Stone, who did she think she was? Being shot in Afghanistan and losing her mother didn't entitle her to be so rude. Robert doted on her, but he was too close to the ranks. A 'Soldier's soldier', they called him. He should spend more time thinking of her needs and less time with 'them'. She suspected he knew about her social activities, but he either tacitly approved, or didn't care. Probably the latter.

She'd told Robert she'd spend the night out with a friend; no further explanation needed. Should she head back home and have a few tipples, or visit Daphne's? Although Daphne would want the sordid details. Melanie looked at herself in the mirror on the lift wall, retouched her lipstick, and smiled, delighted. Finally, a spray mouth freshener, which she used liberally. She didn't want Robert to smell Andrew on her breath. As it was, she insisted on Andrew showering before and desist from using fragrance.

She was careful, parking her car in Andrew's lockup garage. No evidence was the key to success. A two-year affair with Andrew had proved her right. Opening the car door, a gloved hand dropped onto hers. She yelped and dropped her key.

"Quiet, Mrs Syman, remain calm, and I won't hurt you," said a man with a coarse British accent.

Melanie Syman peered through the dark at the man, trying to see his face. "What do you want? You can have my purse, please don't hurt me. How do you know my name? I'll call the police," she said, her voice quivering, an octave higher than normal. She fumbled in her bag for her phone and pointed it at the man who stepped back, his hands folded in front of him.

"Mrs Syman, I wouldn't recommend it, if you don't want to explain to your husband why you're here?"

He knew her; her name, he'd researched her. This couldn't happen, it must be a nightmare. How did she find herself in such a sordid predicament? Who was this, if not the police?

"If you'd like to keep your arrangement with Pritchard private, come with me, quietly."

The man frogmarched her towards a waiting car. She sagged, letting him manhandle her into the back seat. He joined her.

"Where are we going, who are you?"

She couldn't place the accent; quite harsh, rough trade, no doubt. There was no way of escaping unscathed. Robert would want a divorce. Their two children would disown her. This was about blackmail; she'd bet her life on it. She'd fall apart and end penniless. She wept, not sorry for the wrong she'd done; it was her husband's fault; she was sorry for the pain she was going through.

They stopped outside a terraced house on the outskirts of South London. A posh house, but terraced all the same. She grimaced. She hadn't been tracking their route and vaguely knew where they were. The drive could have been thirty minutes or one hour.

The man led her into the house, along a corridor and into a study. A tall semi-bald man dressed in the style of a 1950s solicitor waited. He beckoned her to a seat, and sat next to her, too close for her comfort. A folder lay on a coffee table.

"Mrs Syman, nice to meet you. I apologise for your unseemly arrival. Can I get you something, tea, coffee, or something stronger?"

She shook her head. She must have looked like a refugee. Her body wouldn't behave, neither her hands nor her face muscles, and her stiff upper lip was now limp.

Adopting a lopsided, amused smirk, Pinchin said, "Sure?"

"Yes, I'd like whisky," she said. "Please," she added.

Pinchin nodded at the man standing behind Melanie, who poured a whisky.

"I'm Wilson Pinchin, Melanie, can I call you Melanie?"

"If it's money you want, I can get it." Her voice rose in tone and volume as she wrung her hands.

Pinchin smiled. "Calm, Melanie. Here is your whisky. Relax, drink, and I will explain."

He sipped his own whisky and watched her in silence, and waited. She looked away from Pinchin. Nothing more than a blackmailer and for what, a goose egg indiscretion? The Army could wreck your life for an indiscretion. The military way of life was Victorian. They lived as they fought, fifty years in the past. Her father had been proud of being a 'balcony pony', as her mother called it. She'd brazen it out, and this man Pinchin could do his worst. She glared at him, her nerves back where they belonged, under control, filled with self-righteous indignation.

"Better?" Pinchin smiled at her.

"Yes, do what the hell you want. Let me tell you, you jumped up opportunist, you won't cow me. Beat me if you must, so I'm having an affair, I don't care."

"Better, Melanie. I like spirit," he enthused, waiting.

"We won't have to resort to a beating. Unless you insist," he said, leering at her. "But before you decide," he said, his voice now serious.

"I have 'decided', and I want to leave, now!"

"You're free to leave, but this can be painless, there's an alternative; a potentially lucrative arrangement. I want us to work together, make this a profitable enterprise for us. But if you wish, I can show you many crisp, diaphanous photos, together with details of the last two years. It would make a real romp of a story, but I want to avoid it, if we can work together," said Pinchin, steepling his fingers.

He spread out a few of the photos and pointed.

"This one, for example, is nicely in focus, no mistake who the culprits are."

"Pressure from whom?" she asked, glancing at the two photos, then pushing them to one side.

"I'm not at liberty, but I can assure you, they can be generous, and ruthless. The choice is yours."

Generous, he'd said. This wasn't kidnapping. She had something he wanted, and vice versa. She should test his generosity. If she couldn't outsmart this pompous bank clerk, her name wasn't Melanie Syman.

"I want the photos and the originals, I want them deleted, all of them, or whatever," her words falling over themselves, and added, "and I'm not cheap. What is it you want?"

"Much better," he said, beaming. "I'm sure we'll work together nicely and our relationship could be fruitful, Melanie."

She resented the word 'relationship'. How could she possibly have a relationship with this horrid man? Still, she would cooperate for the sake of her reputation and the money. Their mammonism made Melanie smile; Pinchin returned her smile.

"I want what is in your husband's head," said Pinchin.

Chapter 20

George walked along the church aisle in dress uniform, wearing a black armband, her leather heeled shoes tapping on the stone floor, echoing, and reminding her of the solemnity of her mother's funeral. She walked faster to avoid it sounding like a dirge. Her Mum had discussed religion with her and Charlie. George decided she wanted to be a Methodist, Charlie was a fervent atheist and her Mum, Church of England. Julia Stone loved her God as much as she loved life.

Neither she nor Charlie had ever worn black, except for Charlie's short rebellious phase when she was a Goth. Mum told them to wear cheerful colours and be proud. One or two people glanced George's way, old people from Grain who'd known her Mum. Perhaps they thought it inappropriate to wear uniform to a funeral.

"Your Mum would be proud to see you in uniform, George," said Sheila, loud enough for a group of women to hear.

George turned, took Sheila's hand, and kissed her

cheek. "Want to escort me, Aunt Sheila?"

"Hmm. I'd be pleased to."

Sheila put her arm through George's, and they walked to the front seats. Silence broke out amongst the women as they passed. The closed coffin had wreaths laid upon it. Her Mum had few friends, she'd never been one to be over-friendly with the locals, and she had her reasons. Her one close friend was Sheila. George sat and prayed, prayed for Mum, and prayed for Charlie, and lastly prayed God would give her the strength and ability to do what she had to do, and his forgiveness for doing it.

A few people arrived and left. Whoever had killed her Mum would be at the funeral or the Crematorium. If George spotted suspicious faces, they'd be the first on her radar. Sheila occasionally squeezed George's hand, and George reciprocated.

She'd asked Sheila to read the eulogy, and whilst Sheila was at the pedestal, George sat alone and felt alone. Who would she confide in, moan to, express joy with, and above all, who could she trust?

Her Army friends were all too distant compared to her relationship with Charlie. Many of them she'd trusted with her life, but if you showed weakness, especially in front of the men, your reputation suffered. Frontline soldiers whose life was on the line knew they could count on their mates, but in barracks, most friendships were little more than banter.

Even in Afghanistan, she kept in touch with both her sister and Mum. They kept her on the straight and narrow. Charlie would say, "Oh, George, get a grip. It can't be that bad." Her Mum's voice was something to look forward to when tired, wet, cold, and stressed during training. "Remember, you're doing this for your country and for us."

She was big on loyalty to one's country. But to which country was her Mum loyal? Why had she spied for the Soviet Union, and why did they kill her? As she mulled it over, her fists clenched. George needed to come to terms with this new reality Sheila had talked about.

The service over, she followed her Mum's coffin through the church to the exit. George busied herself looking around for suspects, and Sheila hurried to catch her, but said nothing. Apart from Sarah Frolic, who promised to make the funeral, she spotted a few strange faces, one or two professional funeral-goers. A rather dapper early middle-aged man wearing a long black woollen coat nodded and smiled at George as she passed. She noticed he carried a trilby, which was unusual, athletic build under all those clothes. His whole face focussed, calculating eyes like snakes. She didn't like him.

Another man, late fifties, accompanied by a woman and a boy. She did a checklist of the man's features and clothes; average height, a 'British Warm' overcoat, the type worn by Army Officers, brown leather gloves, and brown shoes. She recognised ex-military when she saw it. His face was going to fat, hardness gone to seed sitting behind a desk. Although he wore his hair Boris Johnson style, it didn't look unkept. He stood in the far corner of the church, in the shadows. Anyone not expecting suspicious characters would have dismissed him as a local Tory Councillor. His hands hung loosely at his sides, zombie like. She'd look for him at the Crematorium.

Colonel Syman stood near the door, wearing mufti, his wife in tow, her arm looped through his. She didn't expect the Colonel, and his wife even less, but the fact he'd made the effort meant a lot to her. They smiled as she approached. He stuck out his hand to stop her saluting. She took it and gave him a firm grip, even with her injured side. Syman maintained eye contact, watching to see if she winced. She didn't.

"Hello George, you look well. Sorry to see you under such circumstances. I think you know Melanie."

"Hello, Sir. Yes, we met."

Did she spot a scowl from Melanie?

"This is Mrs Wallis, Mum's closest friend. Thanks for coming. Are you joining us at the Crematorium?"

"Yes, we will. Can we chat after?"

What did Colonel Syman want? Surely, the Assessment Board hadn't decided.

"Let's meet back at Mum's house after the cremation. We can talk there," George suggested.

The CO knew the address. She walked with Sheila, thinking.

She'd recognise both 'Snake Eyes' and Mr Ex-Military again. She took a photo of 'Snake Eyes' over her shoulder on her smartphone, on the pretext of checking her mail. Mr Ex-Military remained in the shadows. No chance of taking his photo.

She watched the workers in the Crematorium. The short guy in a 1930s black dress suit seemed in charge, probably the Funeral Director. As he opened the curtain for the coffin to disappear into the furnace, she noted he seemed animated, and wiped his hands along the side of his trousers, wet with sweat. She didn't know any Funeral Directors, but he looked weird.

Syman arrived at George's house a few minutes after her. He parked on the track near the gate. George let him and Melanie through the five-bar gate and walked them the hundred metres to the house.

'This should be confidential, not the subject of an officers' wife's forum,' she thought.

She'd changed into a tracksuit for her daily run and anyway, it did no harm to show the CO her determination to increase her fitness.

"Hello Colonel, Mrs Syman, welcome to 'Rose Court Farm'. A grand name for a family home, or it used to be," she said with a weak smile.

Smiling, she waved them into the house and into the living room. He sat in an armchair next to his wife; she sat on the sofa.

"What are the police doing?" he asked.

Strange question. She hadn't even asked him if he'd like a coffee.

"They're holding a suspect on remand who was at the scene, and they've charged him, but he called in the incident, so he's covering for someone else, and he'll probably do two years. It doesn't look right to me. Can I serve you coffee, or something stronger, Mrs Syman?"

"I don't drink on my own these days, but coffee would

be welcome," Syman said.

Melanie smiled.

George heard rumours of his hard-drinking in his early years, and his complexion and bags under his eyes betrayed his past. George disappeared into the kitchen. Syman walked around the living room and shouted through.

"I see your mother had a military connection, George. What did she do?"

He'd seen the group photo, a few wearing uniforms.

"She was an accountant with the Ministry of Defence. But she retired years ago."

Best to stick to the official truth. She trusted Syman, but he was part of the establishment and her Mum had been specific about whom she could trust. George returned with a tray of coffee. Melanie Syman hadn't said a word, but George guessed she was attentive.

"I'll pour the coffee, shall I?" asked Syman, rising from his chair.

He didn't stand on ceremony, and he never stood on his rank. She smiled but said nothing.

"What are you going to do?"

"There's not much I can do. The police will do what they can, then it'll be a cold case."

"So, you think it wasn't a simple burglary? You're not thinking of trying to find out the truth for yourself, are you, George?"

George looked down at her coffee, then held his gaze. "They murdered her for something other than the family silver. We aren't wealthy, and I'd like to dish out my own justice."

"I don't need to remind you how dangerous that could be. You could find yourself in trouble, even prison. Best leave it to the experts. I understand the National Crime Agency is investigating. They don't think it was a burglary either."

"Why the NCA?" Melanie almost blurted out.

"Usually because there's a bigger issue involved, organised crime, for example," said Syman, glancing at his wife.

His smile curled at one side. He was wasting his time telling her to let the police deal with it. He sat forward and leaned towards her.

"This is more than a social call. I'm sorry to raise this now, but I'm afraid it's the least bad opportunity we have, so let's get to business? How's your fitness? You've been keeping to the regime?"

"I'm slowly building up my strength, and I'm running a lot. I have occasional discomfort in my arm, but not much, and my leg is almost healed, apart from the occasional bleeding. Another month and I'll be ready."

He took a folder from a bag, placing it next to the armchair, glanced through it and laid it on the table. George knew it was for appearance's sake. He took his job seriously, and he'd read the file several times before seeing her.

"You've been at Stanford Hall for three months. I've asked for an assessment and impact statement, and I've spoken to the Chairman of the Assessment Board. They've still got to write their official conclusion, and maybe I can influence them a bit, but you know, once they've published their Assessment Report on you, it's a done deal. So, tell me how you'd like me to influence them? Tell me what you'd like to happen, George."

She took a gulp of coffee and placed the mug on the coffee table. What she'd like and what she knew must happen were different. She wanted things to return to before her injury. Soldiering was her life, action, adrenaline rush, and no-nonsense humour, which came with military life. She wanted an operational posting; the Army had trained her for it. George knew the CO wouldn't allow her anywhere near a war zone, especially with PTSD, but she wouldn't soldier at any price. She didn't want special treatment, because of her injuries. And she didn't want charity, or a cushy job.

She reached for her mug of coffee with her right hand, to show him she could, stifling a twinge and stalling. The weight of the mug and the angle pulled on her injured shoulder, but she gritted her teeth and smiled. Cold beads of sweat gathered on her forehead.

"Excellent coffee," he said, filling in the silence. George smiled, but remained quiet.

The CO sipped his coffee, glanced at her, and waited. He was on her side, but looks didn't deceive her. Colonel Syman was a part of the military system. He worked for the greater good not for her. He was also one of the busiest people on the base, and he'd travelled to see her.

The ticking mantel clock was the only sound. She glanced at it, trying to decide how to approach this. It was worse than visiting the doctor. Her brain screamed, 'For God's sake, tell me what they've decided.'

"I want to return to the frontline, Sir. But I guess you won't allow that, will you?"

It was both a statement and a 'have I won the lottery' question.

"No, I won't. What do you propose?" he asked, leaning back and folding his arms.

"Could I return to the Army Physical Training Corps as a trainer?" she asked, knowing she was grasping at straws.

"Let's review where we are," he said, putting down his cup and opening the file again.

"You were in hospital in Camp Shorabak and Kabul for two weeks. Had operations to save your shoulder. I'm sure it was tough. Then Birmingham, a few operations to insert a titanium plate in your shoulder to hold it together. You take medication for nightmares. Sometimes PTSD recedes. Are you still having nightmares?"

She looked at him and a bead of sweat ran down her face. She must look like a damp rag. It was in the file. "Sometimes."

"Hmm. I thought so. Realistically, you might take medication for years. I know what it's like. Rehab staff tells me you've got balls, George. You never give up, even when it hurts like hell. I know you used to go out in the morning doing extra training against my staff's advice. Don't deny it, I've seen you. George, you were lucky the bullet didn't go deeper and disintegrate when it entered your leg, otherwise, it might have been amputated. Keep training, but don't push it too hard," he said, pointing at her. His words were uncompromising, but his eyes betrayed his feelings. "You're almost back to full fitness."

And there lay the problem. 'Almost' in her profession didn't cut it. Despite his biting words, he delivered them with a smile and a hint of approval.

"Admirable. I wish half the soldiers with whom I've served had your determination and guts. But…,"

Nothing before 'But', mattered a toss, "… the frontline or even a war zone is not an option. You boxed for the Army I see, to a high standard as well. Combined Services over 65 kg Champion. Not bad. Almost professional standard. You transferred from the Adjutant General's Corps as a clerk to the Royal Army Physical Training Corps as an Assistant Physical Instructor. Your annual staff reports have been consistently 'Outstanding' since your transfer six years ago. You were an excellent Physical Instructor."

Again, he used 'were'. The CO leaned towards George, almost conspiratorially.

"Frankly, George, the Royal Army Physical Training Corps wants people who are at their peak, as you were. You were due for a promotion or even commissioning, but not now. There are young instructors coming up behind and pushing, and they are fit. You can't train people with a gammy arm and leg, and yes I know you'll work night and day to improve your fitness and strength, and you'll try to hide the pain and the nightmares, but I'd be doing you no favours if I allowed you to revert to your previous life."

"What's the options, Sir?"

"You have two options. You can return to clerking, or something more active, keep your rank, and look forward to a productive Army career. Or if you wish, you can leave on a medical discharge with a decent disability pension. I'll support you whichever you choose, and I think the Assessment Board would cooperate. It's time to decide. Call me and let me know. I've put you on indefinite compassionate leave to sort out your family affairs, but stay in contact."

Melanie nodded enthusiastically, glancing towards her husband.

"The Board will deliver their report within the next week. Afterwards, things will move fast. I can stall and keep you on the books for a further three months. More, and there'll be questions."

The CO had signalled the end of soldiering, as she knew it. George nodded in a daze, then looked at him. She slumped into her chair. "Sir, I've thought about it, and I've decided. Do you mind if we discuss this on our own?"

She'd been ill-mannered, but she disliked the woman who carried her husband's rank. The antipathy was mutual. Melanie stood to leave; George noticed the 'huff'. "I'll be in the car, Robert. I'll see myself out."

She slammed the door closed, and George waited a minute. She didn't care for the woman's lack of manners, but she didn't have to live with her.

"Sorry, Sir, but we need this discussion on our own."

Twenty minutes later, Colonel Syman gave George his card and his private phone number and waved as he left, but couldn't manage a smile as he headed towards his car. He waved as he drove away, but he wore a deep frown and shook his head; he knew how she felt. She'd eventually return for a medical and discharge. In the meantime, she'd take him at his word, use her leave to do what she had to do. She returned to the house, slammed the door, ran to the toilet, retched, and threw up. Looking in the mirror, a wretched, bedraggled woman stared back at her.

Chapter 21

"Come on Maudlin, the Governor is waiting," shouted Mr Lockhart, the Chief Warder, turning puce.

Regardless of Lockhart's attempt at coercion, Bradley Maudlin strolled unhurried, and shuffled along the corridor. There was a guardrail on his right, intended to stop the likes of him throwing themselves to the ground, thirty metres below. A maintenance team had rolled back the safety net for repair, and Maudlin wondered whether Lockhart might try to stop him. He thought not; he might even hold his jacket.

At the sound of Lockhart's voice, Josey Bingham and Shepherd looked up as Bradley Maudlin stared at his fellow prisoners. Lockhart prodded him with his pace stick. Mr Lockhart had been an RSM in the Military Detention Centre. His nickname was 'Lockjaw' or 'Lockhart the Tart', depending which gave the inmates more amusement.

Maudlin ignored the prod and stood, thinking. It had to be now. No hesitation. Right now. Left foot on the lower rail, right foot on the top rail and over. He looked down at the Con's upturned faces, twisted, like blackthorn branches, dark, dangerous, and painful if spiked.

"Did you enjoy last night's shower time, old son?" shouted Josey in a countertenor voice, grinning from ear to ear.

Encouraged by his boss's excited squeal, Shepherd slid the pool cue between his legs and made an obscene gesture.

"We'll be in the exercise yard, Bradley. We'll make beautiful music. It's a date." said Shepherd, imitating Bradley Maudlin's tone.

Shepherd gyrated his hips, using the pool cue to resemble a grotesque pole dancer. The inmates broke into fits of laughter. A few seconds later, Josey thumped Shepherd playfully and motioned for him to take his shot at the pool table. Maudlin amused them, a disposable memory, until tonight when he'd be a source of release from their hormonal tension.

Maudlin imagined himself falling thirty metres, spread eagle like Batman, descending onto an unsuspecting rogue. He may even land on both, and end their meaningless lives. If he didn't hit them, at least he'd land on the pool table and upset their game. But if they survived, they'd enjoy hours of fun in the retelling, and it would legitimise their game. In the countless telling, they'd exaggerate and embellish their story. Like a burlesque theatre production.

He looked at his hands, his knuckles white, bloodless, shaking. Lockhart shouted something, but he may well have been reciting Shakespeare for all Maudlin cared. He leaned further out, almost doubled over, a shock of black hair falling over his face. He was above the men, a bomb aimer. Maudlin focussed on Shepherd's comb-over bald patch. Josey, who was about to take a shot, reminded him of a squeezed doughnut. If he waited until Josey had taken his shot, he might land on both. The pool cue came back, then smacked a white ball with a crack, the noise ricocheting around the prison, like a gunshot, which spurred Maudlin into action. Left foot on the bottom rail and a firm grip on the top rail. The men below exchanged a few words, their heads a few inches apart. This was it, 'The End'. He put his weight on the rail and pushed, but a hand grasped his wrist with a firmness that would have shamed a Sumo wrestler. Looking at his hands still grasping the rail, he realised Lockhart must have guessed his plan and prepared to prevent him taking his life. He didn't want to hang by one wrist supported by Lockhart, and provide more hours of entertainment for the cons.

The opportunity to free himself from his living decomposition, and end those of his tormentors, passed. It was a winning lottery ticket except the 'valid until' date had passed. He couldn't even top himself.

"Not on my watch, sonny. My pension's due soon."

Now held firm by the Chief Warder, he forced himself to release the railing. He ambled along the corridor to the Governor's office, Lockhart's steel-tipped boots making tiny tip taps on the concrete floor. As they stood outside the office, Lockhart looked Maudlin top to bottom, inspecting him. He 'humphed' his dissatisfaction.

"Self-expiration, as we call it," he pointed along the corridor the way they'd come, "is too easy. I'm here to make sure society gets payback. You…you…girl," he whispered, spitting out the last word as if there was no greater insult, and Maudlin supposed for a man of his limited ability and bigoted disposition it was.

Lockhart released Maudlin who wiped his hand across his hair. Lockhart rapped once on the wooden door.

"Come," echoed from inside the room.

Lockhart pushed the door open, giving Maudlin a push in the back.

"510679, Maudlin Bradley, Governor, Sir," said Lockhart, standing to one side, his last mission accomplished, he'd saved the world, his chest the size of a buffalo's.

"Thank you, Mr Lockhart. You may leave us," said the Governor, dismissing Lockhart.

"Sir, this is most unusual. The rules are quite clear, 'Prisoners must not be left unattended in the presence of a Senior Officer', Governor, Sir."

"Oh, all right. But please don't interrupt us."

Maudlin imagined Lockhart's vexation. He kept his eyes downcast until he realised there were two voices unless the Governor was a practising ventriloquist. Pinchin sat next to him, tapping his pen against the folder, but showing no signs of recognition. His eyes fixed on Maudlin. Prison visiting unnerved some, but not Pinchin.

"Maudlin, please sit. I've sent for you because we have news and Mr Pinchin has asked to see you."

The tables were set out in the shape of a 'T'. Maudlin and the Chief Warder standing at the foot of the 'T', facing the Governor.

Maudlin considered this statement. 'Sit' and 'News'. Prisoners were rarely allowed to sit, suggesting bad news. He wondered, what bad news in his present circumstance? A transfer to another prison, maybe? Even the Governor couldn't be oblivious to Maudlin's torment. Solitary confinement? But what was Wilson Pinchin doing here? He hoped his father was ill, or on his deathbed, and had confessed to the murder of Julia Stone. Or even dead. What a wonderful thought. He laughed, his shoulders trembled, and he let out a soft mewing sound. His father dead, the old man dead. He thought of his father as eternal, always there to persecute him. No more of his incessant talk of the honourable profession of Funeral Directors, burials, and 'preparing'. No more 'Entombing' magazines to litter the house, and no father figure to despise. His ghost laid to rest. He'd finally be free to sell everything and blow the lot. His mind leapt, a butterfly dancing from buttercup to cornflower. All thoughts of the evening's planned abasement at the hands of Josey and Shepherd disappeared. The past pain would be a distant memory. He'd bide his time and smile as they accosted him. The feeble-minded scumbags could enjoy crushing his body. Given time he'd heal, but out of prison, he'd be a man of means. And if Templeton Maudlin could see him, he'd know the meaning of 'squander'; give him a lesson in having a good time. The Ritz would be his local, and a waiter, expecting him, would prepare Dom Pérignon on ice, which he'd brisk like water.

He laughed aloud. "Oh, please excuse me, Pinchin, I'm quite taken aback at the thought of Maudlin the elder kicking his clogs. When's his funeral?"

The Governor looked at him open-mouthed. "Nothing in this prison warrants you laughing like a baboon. I'm sure this is a serious matter and please remember you are an inmate and whatever the news Mr Pinchin has, you will serve your time in this prison. Am I clear?"

"Yes, I'm sorry. Pinchin, please continue," said Bradley, airily.

Pinchin's left eyebrow rose a full quarter inch, surprised at being called simply 'Pinchin'.

"Mr Maudlin, I'm pleased to report your father is in rude health. He asked me to convey his best wishes, and to give you these. Does this ring mean anything to you, Bradley?" asked Pinchin.

Pinchin showed Maudlin what appeared to be a gold wedding ring and pushed it towards him. Bradley picked it up, looked inside the band, recognising it as his mother's. He placed it on the desk and sat back. His face had lost its mirth and colour drain.

"And this," said Pinchin, pushing an envelope across the desk.

Bradley took the unsealed envelope and read the single page. It was his mother's handwriting. It told him to behave in prison and do as his father directed. She said she loved him. Bradley had resigned himself to his mother's death years ago. But this letter seemed to show otherwise.

Pinchin's employer had sent him a message. The warning couldn't be clearer. 'Behave yourself in prison and don't make an ill advised statement'. Bradley looked at Pinchin with a glazed stare. It was an effective threat. Behave yourself, keep your mouth shut or you and your mother will meet the same end as Julia Stone. They'd won, whoever 'they' were. Yes, he'd keep his mouth shut, he had to. In prison, he thought he'd be out of reach of his father. How wrong could he be? He'd underestimated old Templeton Maudlin.

"Yes, I'm familiar with this ring. It's my mother's, and the writing in the letter appears to be hers," said Bradley, his face ashen and his voice breaking.

If only Pinchin knew how close he'd been to removing himself from any threat. A few seconds earlier and Bradley's broken body would have landed on the two tormentors. Bradley barely heard the Governor talking.

"Governor, could you make an exception and allow Maudlin to keep this in his possession?" asked Pinchin, fawning.

"I'm afraid it is out of the question. There is no doubt of both material and sentimental value. I will have these stored with his other items. We'll return them on his release. I'm sorry, but prison rules are rules. I doubt if Maudlin could keep it in his possession for long, if you understand my meaning. However, I'm sure Maudlin would wish to return his mother's wishes."

Maudlin stood with mouth open, unable to utter a sound. No fortune, no good time. His thoughts returned to his fleeting plan to end his life, and he regretted his previous hesitation.

Chapter 22

George needed to get her head straight about what had happened and how she'd redress it. She took the hospital Sister's advice and left Charlie alone for a few days. She'd spend the time living out of a tent on the East coast near the Thames Estuary, enjoying the winter air. Now on the final leg, she'd be home by midnight. The family had visited this part of the country, and thoughts of those halcyon days returned. She knew the area but didn't treat it lightly. The weather could turn on a sixpence with disastrous results. There'd been several shipwrecks.

She was free of anyone telling her when and how to exercise, or asking how her night was and whether she wanted to talk about her experience, accompanied by sympathetic looks and soft touches. She mentally reprimanded herself for being bitter and vengeful. The keen wind blew against her face and dug into her eyes, stinging her, causing tears to roll down her cheeks.

She'd been one of the best Physical Training Instructors in the Army, a damn excellent instructor at the height of her physical and mental fitness. But 'was', cut like a knife. Now, she needed to return to fitness, and she needed a job. In a few weeks, she'd neither be in the Army nor a physical training instructor, which was both scary and liberating. She could pursue her mother's killer without restrictions on her movements. The Army embedded principles and a moral code, and she'd miss it. It was part of her. No doubt she'd either seek others with similar experiences or move on.

Her mother had left the house to her sister and her, which she'd keep until her sister was well, then they'd decide together. Also, Mum's life insurance. She didn't need to work for a while. But, in the long term, she'd find a physical occupation, something to stretch her, use her skills, and galvanise her. She could go to university, train to be a school physical education teacher, but the boredom might leave her suicidal. George decided she'd give herself three months to find her mother's killer and her sister's attacker. If she failed, she'd abandon the search and consider joining the police force. Not much of a plan. There's no loyalty greater than family loyalty, her Mum used to say, and George still believed that. Although she would have given her life for the Army, now she'd give her life to her new mission.

The nightmares remained a problem. She'd never get into the police force if she had PTSD. She couldn't hide it. But she hoped the nightmares would decrease over the next few months. A steady job would allow her to care for Charlie, her priority. Her feelings improved and her step quickened. As she walked along the North Kent coast and ran when she felt like it, things looked better. The physical skill and dexterity she needed to make and break camp in the rain, start fires, and lug thirty kilos felt great. Walking along the beach in good boots with her world on her back lifted her mood. She even forgot about her injuries. Even when it thrashed with rain, she didn't stop. She faced it head on, enjoying the sting of freezing rods and needles on her face and the wind whistling and roaring. When her right arm ached too much, she stopped, sat on her pack, and ate.

She recognised many species of seabird wheeling above her, although only the seagulls pestered her for food. She was glad to share. Two herring gulls squawked and squabbled over a fish, and she watched them for a minute until the challenger withdrew and the winner disappeared into the marshes with its catch.

Carrying your home and your bed on your back has advantages, freedom, self-sufficiency, it weighs over thirty kilos, and George loved it. Most of her military career seemed to have involved carrying heavy weights. If it wasn't her home in a rucksack, it was a fellow soldier, male or female. It didn't matter. Soldiers called it 'yomping'. She strode through the discomfort along the beach, sand hard as concrete under her feet, but good for walking. The arctic skuas called to her, and the cold gusts battered her face until rain and tears mixed and flowed down her cheeks. For the first time since Afghanistan, she was alive, and she sang to the birds. With her face lifted to the sky, and walking at a pace that would crumple most men, she resembled a demented seagull. A casual observer might have labelled her a lunatic. But to George, it was the most fragrant blossom of her thorny existence and the discomfort was worth the freedom, free from bullets, bombs, and the permanent vigilance to minimise the risk of death.

Although there were gathering clouds on the horizon, George thought little except she must make camp in the rain. Not a bad idea. It would bring a sense of urgency. Her waterproofs gave her excellent protection, so long as she kept moving and generated heat. Her tent would protect her from the elements, and she could make a mug of tea on the gas stove. The Welsh mountains were wetter, the Afghan deserts arid and harsher, but the English coast could be ferocious. She managed a thin smile and ignored the ache in her shoulder and leg.

Two opposing winds fought for dominance. The higher, darker clouds in the offing were swirling and broiling, the lower ones driving into her face. They seemed eager to throw a deluge at her and George welcomed it, digging in, and increasing her stride. The sea was angry and in accord with the clouds and waves crashing near her; she marched on in a straight line, challenging the elements to beat her. The wind and rain knew the mould of the waves, shaped the sand and dunes, and drove along their contours.

Biting winter rain lashed at her face as if tanning leather and blood vessels in her cheeks tightened as she laughed. The distant rumble of thunder sounded like a rumbling steel drum. The sky turned from white and fluffy to grey and threatening. She stared at the scene, and her elation grew. She'd seen storms in Northern Scandinavia, Europe, and the Middle East, but nothing beat the beauty and drama of a home-grown thunderstorm.

The electricity in the air smelt of scorched metal, and it tingled. She sensed streak lightning before seeing it. A memory of the fateful afternoon in Afghanistan flooded every neuron and fibre in her brain. It knocked her off her feet, lifted her and dumped her on her face in the sand. The thirty kilos on her back conspired to press her into the sand. Hard, uncompromising, a zap of thunder registered as the sound of a high-velocity round. A rush of adrenaline felt like a slither of ice slicing down her back. Again, she felt the first bullet drill through her shoulder with contempt, her hand felt the slimy substance of brain tissue and skull, and a few moments later a second bullet sliced along her lower thigh, finally exiting near her buttock. Blood from Brigadier Wyson drained into the sand and disappeared. Someone screamed, rumbling voices and helicopter blades.

"No, no more. Stop," she begged.

Another flash pierced its way through her sealed eyelids, and her imagination filled in the gaps to form another high-velocity 7.62 mm round, which found its way into her back. For George, every crash of thunder was a high-velocity round, zinging, breaking the sound barrier. She curled up, and murmured, her face pressed into the sand and seawater washed her lips. Her backpack dug in, making it as real as the first time. The pelting rain and howling wind drowned out her tears and sobs.

Minutes or hours later, she felt the slimy texture in her fingers and recognised it for what it was, seaweed. Her pack dug into her shoulder, giving her back a thrashing, and her legs ached. The storm had subsided, but with dusk, the temperature had dropped. The driving rain and wind reinforced the danger of freezing cold. Unless she got her act together, she'd die of hypothermia. Then she'd say goodbye to finding the killer.

How often had she lectured young recruits about the dangers of exposure and the elements? And here she was, sucker-punched by hiemal weather in her home county. She heaved herself into a sitting position and glanced at the waves. When she'd collapsed, the sea was coming in. It had washed over her, and the storm and freezing seawater had soaked her. She shivered and recognised the first signs of hypothermia. If she was lucky, she had fifteen minutes to get herself onto her feet, plan, and get to safety and warmth. Lights shone in the distance to the south. Too far.

Another light a mile away to the west and inland, probably a lone house. She'd head towards the house; maybe she'd be lucky. Shifting her pack to a more comfortable position, George headed off towards the light. The fading sky told her it would be black in half an hour. Hopefully, by then, she'd be at the house. She had a torch in her pack, but time was more important. If she didn't reach safety, she'd make camp and pitch her tent in the dunes.

If she slowed, she'd lose more body heat and collapse through exhaustion. George's will to survive drove her on through the sand dunes. The light in a cottage window, her single focus. As she stumbled from windswept ridges to damp hollows, she focussed on that tiny light and nothing else. When she fell, she grasped at the dense, grey-green tufts of Marram Grass and dragged herself along. This wasn't as hostile as many other places she'd known. But now it was more deadly.

Rolling down a sandbank, sand covered her face, and a dog barked. A minute later, she felt its breath on her cheek. She couldn't imagine a more welcome feeling. A moment later, a 'wuff' and growl. She rolled over to face the threat. Footsteps approached with firm, slow, confident strides.

"What you found, Jaws?" said a voice from the bottom of a well. A shadow leaned over her and a hand swept hair out of her face. George grasped the wrist and twisted inwards. But the effort was too feeble and the man's wrist too strong. A stench of whisky swept over her, and warm breath struck her neck. The thought of a drunken sex maniac rescuing her made her struggle to stand.

"Now then, lassie. Let's get you indoors," a Glaswegian accent.

Someone pried her fingers from their wrist, and she flopped back onto the sand. For now, she was at this man's mercy. She felt herself rolled over onto her side and her rucksack removed. If the man wanted to attack her, she'd have no defence. Someone pushed her rucksack to the side, and she felt herself hoisted and carried in a fireman's lift.

She woke to the smell of foetid, tuna breath on her face and opened her eyes, gasped, and pulled her head back from the black eyes and snout against her nose.

"Jaws, come away, leave her alone," slurred a voice out of her vision.

The Welsh Border Collie stepped back, whimpered, and lay near the sofa. George tried to lift herself to identify the voice. The dog's eyes never left her.

"Huh," she mumbled, rubbing her head, and shrugging off the blanket covering her. "My head hurts. I have to get away, sort out my kit."

"I'm not surprised. You are going nowhere; you're wet through and washed-out. People die walking in that shite."

She winced at his use of language but tried to focus on the man who may have been a well-worn sixty or younger, sitting in a beaten-up old leather armchair, nursing a glass of amber liquid. His knees seemed higher than his stomach, which must be his height, a sagging armchair, and his slumped posture. He was side on to her, and she had difficulty seeing his face, partly in shadow. He didn't look directly at her. His nose looked like a small beetroot growing on a clean-shaven face. She knew his strength, he'd carried her and her kit into the cottage, but he was thin and sinewy. He gave her a sideways look, and she wondered if he was blind.

"Want tea and an egg banjo?" he asked, rising from the chair.

She heaved herself to the sitting position and said, "Hmm, please."

He lurched, suggesting he'd been drinking for a while. George looked around the living room, with its old but good quality furniture. The placed stank of stale alcohol dampened by cleaning chemicals. The unmistakable smell of pipe tobacco; something she liked.

A bottle of malt sat on the shelf. He probably lived on his own. Old wooden beams in the ceiling and the walls looked original, whitewashed brick. A threadbare carpet covered the floor. Maybe he had a cleaner, and from experience most single men living on their own declined into a grubby collection of beer cans, cigarette buts, and stale curry. A wood fire roared. She supposed he'd stoked it for her. He'd removed her waterproof jacket, which hung on a chair, and her boots, now drying on the hearth. Her feet and hair steamed. Her fuzzy brain and thrashed out body felt like she'd been in a giant washing machine.

Looking around, she spotted photos covering the walls, black and white, and others with faded colours. The light prevented her from seeing details. He returned, holding a mug and a plate of doorstep sandwiches. She hadn't seen a thicker sandwich since her time on Salisbury Plain.

She grinned and gulped at the murky brown brew.

"What do I call you?" he asked.

"George. Look, thanks for bringing me here, but I was

okay, really. I'll finish this," she said, pointing to the tea and egg banjo, "then I'll be on my way. I don't want to bother you."

He looked at her from his armchair, his hands clasped, resting on his chest, no longer nursing the glass of whisky. She sensed a trust in him, but he might be a drunken recluse who preyed on people happening upon his cottage by accident. Despite her size and increasing fitness, even if she made a dash for it; he'd catch her. Anyway, if he'd meant her harm, he'd have done it when he brought her into his cottage and as far as she could see, she was unharmed, and he hadn't tampered with her clothes, except her outer garments. Did he like to play cat and mouse, play her along, feed her up, make her comfortable, delay her departure and keep her captive? But she was a soldier, for Christ's sake. The man had to sleep, and she could beat him to death.

"You can leave if you wish. But you'll not get far at night in this weather. What's your story and what's your association with the Army, or did you get your kit from the surplus Army and Navy store?"

His tone neutral, not accusing, a simple enquiry, and she detected no sarcasm, often found in drunks.

"You've been through my kit?" she said, her hackles rising.

"Enough to see you have an Army sleeping bag, a two-man tent, Army torch, and olive-green fleece, and your name is George Stone," he said, looking at her sideways.

She turned towards him, and he returned the look. The fire and subdued standard lamp illuminated his face. The side turned away from her shone, dancing flames making it difficult to see. George stared at her host's face, recognising the shine and the lack of lips on half of his face as major burn injuries. She'd seen similar injuries at Stanford Hall; soldiers caught in vehicle fires and bomb blasts. His injuries didn't disturb her. But a civilian meeting him might stare and turn away in shock. Her acceptance of his injuries caused him to smile, his mouth and eyes welcoming her to his cottage.

"So, who are you, George? What's your connection?"

"Sergeant Stone, RAPTC. Not long returned from Afghanistan. Yours?"

"Former Sergeant Major Ted Shields, Scots Guards. Northern Ireland, The Falklands, etc. Call me Ted."

"Was it The Falklands or Northern Ireland?" asked George, referring to Ted's scars. 'Best to be straight and get it out into the open,' thought George.

Ted laughed, half of his face creasing with crow's feet showing against his right eye, his left side hardly moving. George smiled, met by another chuckle from Ted.

"Northern Ireland. I escaped The Falklands without a scratch, went to Northern Ireland and got caught in a blast in a Snatch Land Rover. It removed my left foot and burnt the left side of my face. Could have been worse. I left the Service a while ago."

Ted picked up his stick lying alongside his chair and tapped it against his left foot prosthesis. Even through his trousers and sock, it gave off a dull metallic thud. George grinned and Ted broke into a fit of laughter, taking out a tin of tobacco, and taking his pipe from a small table at his side.

"Do you mind?"

"It's your house. Kill yourself with tobacco and whisky, if you wish." George shrugged. Ted grinned, filled the pipe bowl, tamped it down, and lit it with little ability, laughing, before coughing through the smoke.

"I used to smoke cigarettes, but I've changed to a pipe. If I can't get a hang of it, I'll give up. You're thinking I'm a drunk, no?" he grinned.

"It crossed my mind."

"I could give it up tomorrow if I wanted to," Ted retorted.

"Most drunks say that."

"Look, little lady," he said, sitting near the edge of his chair and poking a rigid finger in her direction. "The pills they gave me don't work anymore. The physical pain I can stand. It's part of the penalty. But this," he pointed to the glass on the table, "helps me sleep without dreaming, okay? It works most of the time. I would give it up now if I could get a decent night's sleep without it."

George sat back in her seat as if he'd slapped her. She didn't like alcohol and rarely drank. Within ten years, she may also do anything for a quiet night's sleep.

"Okay, sorry, Ted. Sorry, I understand. I have problems too."

"Enough, end of."

An awkward pause passed between them, and George

knew how stupid and insensitive she'd been.

Ted broke the silence. "So, what's your story?"

"I'm officially still at Stanford Hall, probably a medical discharge. I'm in good shape compared to a few weeks ago, and I feel much better. But the incident is having other effects. I also have dreams, but the medication helps a bit," said George, looking away.

"Were you the one protecting that one star in Helmand?" asked Ted.

"Yes, it was me. I failed; it was my fault."

She averted her eyes and tugged at her jumper. Despite the counselling, the advice, and behavioural therapy, she blamed herself and always would.

"Look, why don't you have a bath and wear one of my dressing gowns. I'll have a drink waiting for you, but no whisky for you. Top of the stairs, mind your head on the beams."

Her wide eyes must have given away her apprehension. Ted laughed; the first belly laugh she'd heard in ages. "Don't worry about me. You're safe, and I'm harmless, as far as that's concerned. The bomb took care of any urges I had. Mind you, before the bomb, I would have chased you," he laughed.

It was the best suggestion she'd heard in a while, and she accepted. She grinned at him, relieved and safe in his presence.

She turned to him. "Thanks for rescuing me. The lightning and thunder. I thought I might be over it. It caught me."

"You're welcome," he said, grinning.

An hour later, George emerged wearing Ted's dressing gown and a towel around her blond hair. Ted's eyes lit up when he saw her.

"Good. You scrub up well. I'll make a brew," said Ted.

"No, let me. Sit there."

Ted stood and faced her legs apart, humour gone. He hovered over her. He didn't threaten her, but his claw-like hands told her she'd hit a raw spot.

"Look, George," he said in his Glasgow brogue, "I'm as able-bodied as you or any other person. I don't want, or need, help, and I don't need sympathy. If I remember, it was me who dragged your rain-sodden arse in here, and I'm the host. Sit, for fuck's sake."

"Sorry, I didn't mean… But can I ask something?"

"Sure, what."

"Don't swear. Okay?"

"Right you are, Say no more."

Ted walked through to the kitchen and returned a minute later with two mugs. George gulped hers and relaxed into the sofa as Ted stoked the fire with more wood, the flames reflecting on the shiny side of his burnt face. His back looked strong; no fat, broad shoulders, and thick muscular arms.

"Who looks after your house?" asked George.

"I do. I'm capable, and I'm used to living on my own." He stared at George as if he was waiting for a fight.

"So why do you live here, miles from anywhere and anyone?" asked George.

"My marriage collapsed; I suppose my wife had enough of my cantankerousness. She didn't understand why I drink." Ted looked at George, searching for a reaction.

"Mind if I take my foot off? It gets sore if I wear it for too long?"

"Be my guest."

Ted raised his trouser leg, removed the bandage at the join at the top of his prosthesis, pulled off the foot, laid it down, and sighed with relief.

He sat back in his armchair, went to pick up his glass, which contained half an inch of whisky, paused, then left it.

"I got fed up with people staring and asking questions. So, I moved here. I enjoy my company. Out here, I disturb no one. I spend all the time I want with Jaws, on the beach and in the sea. It suits us," he grunted and reached to stroke Jaws' head.

George understood; but she'd met no one so reclusive or obstinate. Once he may have been the life of the party, but add Army life, a catastrophe resulting in his injuries, and there sat Ted, physically and mentally scarred for life. A soldier's backpack was never as burdensome as the chains binding the veteran. She didn't like what he'd become, but she wouldn't judge him. She yawned.

"And you? How do you deal with it?" he asked.

"The doc prescribed meds, but I want to get off them. Sometimes they help, but rarely. I stay focussed on doing things. Now, I'm focussed on my Mum's murderer and looking after my sister."

"Sorry to hear that. You from around here?"

"Grain, so yes. It was in the local paper. Someone broke in and killed Mum and attacked my twin sister. Police have one witness who isn't talking."

"Yes, I heard of it. Sad and mysterious."

An awkward pause. George wondered if this was getting too personal for Ted.

"I'm knackered. We should get some kip? I'll walk you along the beach tomorrow if you're up to it. I'm not giving you my bed, but you're welcome to the sofa," he offered, hopping towards the stairs.

George agreed and soon lay in her sleeping bag with Jaws lying next to her near the fire. For a minute, she thought of Ted, his career, his approach to life, and whether she'd follow the same path.

Chapter 23

George woke at 3 a.m. A low growling moan came from Ted's bedroom, and Jaws lying next to her, stirred, grumbled, then padded upstairs. She guessed Ted was having one of his dreams and Jaws went to Ted. He wouldn't understand PTSD, but he recognised his master in pain. George knew the bond between dog and master. Stories of military dogs employed in Iraq and Afghanistan bonding so closely with their master they would pine, sometimes for years.

She lay awake and half an hour later, Jaws traipsed in, but refused to settle. He grumbled, whined, and gave a low bark.

"What is it, Jaws, can't sleep?"

He heard things way beyond George's hearing range, but she caught it. An animal walking on the wooden terrace? Except it sounded like sand crunching underfoot, and it held a torch. George leapt off the sofa and pulled on her jeans and top. She tried to 'shush' Jaws, but excitement triumphed. He wanted to walk. Spurred by the remote possibility she might come face to face with a stalker, she mentally prepared herself.

As able as she was, she hadn't returned to full fitness. Nor had she recovered from her experience in the dunes. But what she lacked physically, she gained in motivation. By the light of the still glimmering fire, she looked around and spotted Ted's wooden walking stick standing by the fireplace. Seizing the weapon, she tapped her leg and Jaws went with her to the door. As she opened it, she lifted the door to avoid it scraping on the floor and eased it open. The rain had stopped, but the clouds obscured the stars and choked off moonlight.

The intruder had a ten-second start on her. He wore dark colours and ran away from the house into the dunes, which shrouded him. She wouldn't catch him. George noted his economical movements and running style, even in sand, an athlete or military trained. Although, if he was any good, she wouldn't have heard him. She watched for a while as he disappeared into the dark, then checked the area with Jaws, who stopped to sniff and lift his leg before catching up with her. Satisfied, she re-entered the house, now silent except for Ted's snoring. How long would it be before she lost the soldiering skill?

A few hours later Ted moved around upstairs, and she threw off the covers, washed in the downstairs toilet, and waited at the kitchen table for Ted.

"Morning, Ted. Sleep well?" she asked as he appeared on the stairs. He'd fitted his prosthesis, but unlike the previous evening, he limped. She supposed he'd put on his prosthesis for her benefit and imagined his usual routine was to hop down the stairs on one foot.

"Huhh," he grunted, rubbing his head. "Coffee later,"

he scowled, and sat on the other side of the kitchen table.

"It's fine outside. Good for a walk," he grumbled to himself. Ted pulled himself to his feet and stood awkwardly, like someone hungover too often. She gathered he was 'Not A Morning Person' or 'NAMP'. She wondered how he got on when he was serving, although soldiers accepted other soldiers' strange ways. He rubbed his scarred face and his backside simultaneously and reached for his stick.

She opened her mouth to speak.

"Jaws. Walk," he said, opening the door.

Jaws jumped to his feet and danced around Ted.

"Should I make you breakfast for when you get back?"

He didn't turn around. "Whatever. I'll be about an hour."

George had one hour to herself. She'd repacked her stuff ready for a fast exit after breakfast. She ran a short five kilometres across the sand dunes. A good day for a walk, or a run. Underfoot, the ground was vaporous, and the sky dappled. In contrast to the previous evening, the cool wind refreshed her, but clouds skidded across the sky, occasionally blocking out the sun. The previous evening's events had taken their toll, but she made the effort and did the five km in under twenty minutes. Not bad for an injured veteran carrying titanium plates. Her priority remained the same. She would visit Charlie later that afternoon.

As she walked at a brisk pace towards Ted's cottage with the sea and sun to her back, a glint of glass caught her attention. A single sparkle could have been someone holding a bottle, binos, or a badly concealed car behind trees. She'd seen it enough times in Afghanistan and was near certain it was the side window of a car two hundred metres away.

Considering the isolated position of Ted's cottage, the driver could only be there for one reason, either looking for Ted or following her. He'd told her to leave the door open if she left, but she'd closed it. Now it swung open. She let herself in, warily.

Ted busied himself in the kitchen, his foot lying on the floor.

"There's a car a few hundred metres away," said George. "I'll investigate."

"Ay, I saw it. All right, be careful."

"I'm a big girl."

Ted grinned at her. She couldn't tell whether he was sexist or careful.

Using the cover of bushes and the dunes, she made her way toward the glint on the glass she'd seen earlier. A man sat in the driver's seat smoking, his arm resting on the open window. He looked in his early thirties, dressed in a dark donkey jacket.

George stood at the rear window, watching the man read his newspaper. 'The Sun', a man of intellectual taste. A few inches from him, if he glanced in his side mirror, he'd see her.

"Do you want to come in for a chat, or are you going

to sit there admiring your girlfriend?"

The man looked up, shocked with embarrassment. "Fu"

"Shhhh…," said George, finger to her lips.

The man dropped his cigarette on his newspaper and spent the next few seconds avoiding setting fire to the paper.

She opened the car door. The man stumbled out. The newspaper and the cigarette now forgotten on the floor.

George stood back and scowled at the fiasco.

"What do you mean? I'm not going anywhere. I'm waiting for a friend," the man said with indignation, almost stamping his foot. His little asinine protest matched his appearance. She reached into the car, took the keys, and slammed the door.

"Look, Rupert, or whoever you are. My friend in the cottage you're watching has a short fuse, and a dog aching to make a meal of you."

She backed him against the bonnet of the car, leaning in close. He bent over backward to get away from her. She'd seen 'Ruperts' before, lots of them. They were par for the course in the better regiments, full of bravado, a Nanny, and a Public-school education. He probably worked in an official capacity. He didn't look like a cop.

She brought her face close to his, her blond hair hanging naturally and brushing against his cheek. A casual observer might have mistaken the liaison for seduction.

"How would you like to have your arse kicked by a woman, Rupert?" said George, her body pressed against his. "Because that will happen if you don't accept my invitation."

Rupert's mouth dropped, and his bottom lip trembled. George pushed her knee between his and raised it with enough force to make Rupert's eyes water, but not enough to disable him. He gasped, trying to disguise it as a cough, then nodded.

She stepped back and brushed her hair away from her face.

"After you, Rupert," said George, giving the man enough room.

She pushed 'Rupert' into Ted's cottage and pointed to a straight-backed chair. Rupert looked indignant, pouting. Ted stood over him, a walking stick in hand. Jaws sat by him, tongue lolling, full of enthusiasm. Rupert didn't know he was harmless.

"What's your mission? And don't give me old flannel either, else you'll get a stroke of my wee stick." Ted pointed his stick at Rupert and poked him in the chest.

"Bird watching and sightseeing," offered Rupert. "Nothing more. And here I am, accosted," he said, spluttering.

"In the words of the Virgin Mary, come again?" asked Ted.

"Perfectly innocent," blustered Rupert.

"Look sunshine, you don't do sightseeing with a pair of

binos focussed on my wee house." Ted raised his voice a few decibels, sounding like pebbles washing against a beach. "I saw you an hour ago, so one last time. What's going on?"

Ted thrust out a hand and caught Rupert in the chest, enough to send him and his chair crashing backwards with a thump as his head contacted the floor. Before he could regain his senses or composure, George pressed him back to the floor with one foot and kept it on his chest. Ted's mouth twisted into a grin.

"Son. I'm not as friendly as my friend here, and unless you cooperate, you could end up in the local hospital having my stick extracted from a place rarely exposed. Let's try again. I assume you're hired help, so who sent you? Are you recceing for a burglary?"

Ted knew the man was no burglar, any more than George was a vicar's wife.

Rupert sat up from his position on the floor. "I'm not at liberty to say. I have an ID card in my wallet. It will explain everything, and I'll bet you two will jolly well be in trouble."

He reminded George of Bertie Worcester, and she grinned. Ted glanced across at George and rolled his eyes.

"Look, pal. I'm not bothered if you've got a picture of the Queen Mother in your wallet. Let's see who we're dealing with?"

Rupert gingerly reached inside his jacket and took out his wallet and handed it to George. There were several credit cards in his wallet, and a Home Office ID card in a see-through wallet.

"So, Marcus Wetherby. You work for the Home Office. What's the Home Office to do with us?" asked Ted.

"Not you. Her," said Rupert, pointing at George. "Now may I get up? This is awfully uncomfortable."

George nodded and Rupert struggled to his feet, righted the chair, and sat. His reddening face showed annoyance.

"Alright, calm down, Rupert, explain," said George.

Marcus's anger piqued, and he'd taken umbrage to a woman dragging him in.

He jumped to his feet, confronting George, which didn't bother her.

Nose to nose, he shouted, spittle landing on her, "Now look here. My name's Marcus, and I'm MI…"

He never finished the sentence. George sensed the window behind Rupert splinter before she saw it. Too fast for her to react or avoid the contents of his head splattering her from a round designed to kill, even if it hit a limb or shoulder. It entered Rupert's head, remaining there to convert his blood and brain into a pinkish-grey smoothie. A dull, lumpy soup coated them. The front of Rupert's face bulged, and most of his skull exited through his mouth. He slumped forward onto George, forcing her back, landing on top of her, knocking her back and sideways, as a second round hit the back wall behind her.

George stayed on the floor, but pushed Rupert's corpse away as his feet rattled against the carpet. Ted dropped to the floor a moment later.

Rupert lay still, his sanguineous gore making a pool on the carpet. George shuffled away to avoid the dead man's bodily fluids.

She gestured for Ted to take the left side of the window whilst she went right. Either the gunman would remain undercover or have another crack. The shooter may have been anywhere from a hundred metres to five hundred, probably less in this terrain. Far enough away for the killer to get clean away. He'd probably left the scene and would plan another attempt. He had to succeed only once, as Rupert could testify.

She assumed she was the target. But the sniper may stay in place and take his chances on her leaving the house. A marksman could keep a platoon at bay for hours. Ted scowled. She had some explaining to do.

"A couple hundred metres, in yonder dune, I guess, but I think he's gone," said Ted.

"You got your mobile with you?" he asked.

"No, in the kitchen. You want to call the police?"

George heard another crack, and a round ricocheted, as Ted rose onto his knee and as George heard the next crack, she froze. It seemed to send her over the edge. A muck sweat broke out all over, and she shook. She knew what was happening to her, but couldn't counter it. The wind howling through the smashed window took on the character of a Chinook's rotor blades. Her shoulder felt as if a knife was twisting into her. She may have lain on the floor for a few seconds, but this affliction altered time, and the mental torture seemed like an eternity.

Someone lifted her, then dragged, her heels rattling on the wooden terrace surrounding the house.

Regaining her senses, she lay on Ted's kitchen floor, blood smeared on the floor tiles. She did a mental body check, from toes to head. No pain, and everything seemed to work. Ted's face came into view. He was naked from the waist up. The thought of him taking advantage of her flashed through her mind, then realised unless he'd lied the night before, he wasn't capable.

"Take it easy, lassie, you've had a bit of a turn. Can you get up?"

"Yeah, I think so. What happened?"

"The sniper seems to have had it on his toes, and I'm making a habit of dragging your buttocks out of the wet and smelly," he said with a hint of humour. She got to her feet to see Ted bleeding from a flesh wound on his arm.

"Is that bad?" she asked, seeing the trickle along the length of his arm, congealing. She estimated she'd been out for a couple of minutes.

"He was an inch away from missing me and plugging you. I'll live. But it stung like hell. Can you dress it for me?"

She could. "Stitches?"

"I'll live, had worse gardening. Dress it, and I'll be right as rain. Give me some medicinal whisky, will you?"

"First aid kit?"

"In the living room cupboard. There's a number on Rupert's ID Card. I called it. MI5 no less."

George dressed Ted's injury with a sterile dressing and poured a glass of whisky for its medicinal efficacy.

Ted slipped his shirt on. "Explain this. I'm the least informed and I don't like it. How about you?" said Ted, pointing to George.

The silence was palpable. George owed Ted an explanation. He was right, he'd pulled her arse out of the fire twice. After living alone for a decade with nothing more exciting than a low-flying seagull, eager to spoil his peace; to a half-dead woman, and a Rupert claiming to work at the Home Office. He'd seen more action than a squaddie could experience in his career, and she had to hand it to him, he was one calm and understanding guy. She owed him an explanation, but could she trust him with the whole truth?

She could phone Sarah, the NCA woman. She didn't know or trust her either, and had her suspicions about involving the police. For the moment, silence would be best.

Ted seemed callous, probably his survival mechanism. Now, she was the new target, so she had to take the initiative. One option was to leave this to the police, whether the NCA or the local plod, tell them everything, and sort her own career. Whoever killed her mother and put her sister in hospital now seemed determined to silence her.

"Someone will be here in less than half an hour," said Ted, "but we're hardly going to stomp around in his brains, and he smells awful."

Ted turned to George and whispered.

"You want to tell me what this bunfight is about?"

There was no anger in his voice, but George suspected it could change quickly if she lied to him. She owed him the truth. She'd try to get this mess cleared and get home. This was her problem, and Ted didn't have a dog in this fight.

"We should wait and see who turns up. I owe you an explanation, but this isn't your problem, Ted," George hissed.

"Not my problem, lassie? Not my problem? I'd say the moment I walked in here with you on my back I made it my problem. Wouldn't you say, sweety?"

George scowled. Ted had raised his voice above a whisper and his face was close to George's. She could see the tendons in his neck and the veins in his right cheek threatening to burst. The left side of his scarred face was drained of colour. One side was bright red and the other side white. It reminded her of the phantom of the opera.

"I'll tell you after our visitors have gone. Okay?"

Ted pointed a finger at George, and she prepared herself for a slap when several vehicles arrived, breaking the tension

Knocks on the door, and a thirty-something Asian man, tie, three-quarter length coat, and gloves entered. He'd taken out his MI5 identity card and waved it towards George and Ted, barely looking at them. The man looked for a minute at Ted, fascinated by his scarred face and his prosthetic foot on the floor. George noted the name 'Sam'.

"I'm Ted Shields and…"

"I know who you two are. I'll get this mess cleared up, and then we can talk," said Sam in clipped English with a touch of Essex.

Ted would need to calm himself before they talked again.

A team of three in white paper overalls and rubber gloves walked silently into the living room carrying holdalls, closing the living room door behind them.

Sam stood over Ted and George, his arms hanging loosely by his sides, gloved hands hanging limp, studying them, waiting. Ted fidgeted, then broke the silence.

"Sam what?" asked Ted.

"Sam," replied Sam.

"So, 'Sam', I assume you'll not involve the police. You know, forensics, scene of the crime, 'Police–Do not cross' tape, search the local area for evidence and so on?" asked Ted.

"Allow me to explain what I can," said Sam.

They sat on straight-back chairs around the dining table, Sam facing George and Ted.

"Marcus Wetherby works for the Home Office, MI5."

Ted interrupted. "Marcus Wetherby worked for MI5. By now he'll be lying inside several plastic bags."

George scowled at Ted. All she wanted was to hear Sam's story without Ted's facetious interruption.

"Quite," said Sam with a twisted smile in Ted's direction.

"I assigned him to watch you," said Sam, pointing at George. "We are aware of your family history. You may think you know the score, but you don't, so my boss wants to see you," he said, pointing at George.

"Here's his card and his number. Until tomorrow night, you can contact him at the guest house in Grain, 'The Lodge'. Please, meet him any time until he leaves. Believe me, we didn't want any of this to happen, and it's not Wetherby's fault. His mission was to watch you and report back. If you'd feel safer, I can assign someone to watch your home, but you don't want that, right?"

George shook her head, trying to subdue her anger. She'd play along with them for the moment. She needed to know what MI5 knew, hoping they'd reveal something, eventually.

"Okay, Sam. I'll give you the benefit of the doubt, for now. I need answers, and if Mr Chance can provide them, I'll listen. But I've been shot at, told a tale about my mother, and seen my family destroyed. However, if he gives me the 'guess which cup the ball is under' trick, neither him, nor you, will get in my way. Clear?"

Sam paused, assessing George's determination and ability to carry out the threat. But George sensed something else going on. Was he deciding if she was worth bothering with? Well, she'd let Chance work that out and she'd decide if she could trust him, but the one person she'd trust right now, was herself.

"Fine, see Mr Chance. My team will leave in an hour. We'll sweep the area. In the meantime, I know both of your backgrounds. Can I rely on you to keep this to yourselves? I can have you arrested, but I hope it won't be necessary," Sam said, looking at them for confirmation.

Ted chuckled, looked away, but remained silent. George disliked Ted's attitude. The sooner she left and returned to her own house, the better. She put a hand on Ted's thigh as a sign to keep quiet.

"Yes, we'll keep it to ourselves. I'll be at home. You know my address? I have to go see my sister today."

Sam nodded and left.

George turned to Ted. "Ted, I'm going home. I don't want to cause you any more trouble, and you've had enough excitement to last you a lifetime. Anyway, it's none of your concern. This is my number at Rose Cottage Farm in Grain. Call me if you wish, okay?"

George scribbled her mobile number on a shop receipt and handed it to him.

Ted took it, looked at her, but said nothing. She detected hurt. He thought he was being helpful. Perhaps it was his male ego, or he'd been living on his own for too long. He nodded, and George grabbed her rucksack and left.

Chapter 24

George arose early. She didn't regard the night as 'sleep'; more like an Escher maze. As soon as she had a grip on one part, another arose to complicate matters. Like grasping water and hoping to get a handful. How could anyone, let alone her own mother, hide her past from her own children for over two decades? Why did her mother not make a single mistake by revealing her true job as a government researcher? And what possessed her to turn on her country? Was that the reason her dad walked out, because he'd discovered her mother's dirty secret? If so, she had to reconcile that.

Dressing into her running kit was getting easier, and the ache in her thigh was only there when she thought about it. Even her arm felt stronger. She set off at a slow 8kph pace, loping along the beach, watching the weather, not wanting a repeat of two days ago. But it promised to be a decent day, with mist clearing, despite this being January early morning.

The feel of even hard sand under her feet and the sound of gulls surfing the sky lifted her. Her mind turned to training twelve years earlier; all she'd thought of was her career. Life was simple.

Her running speed increased. She was in the zone, mind wondering anywhere it wanted and her body taking care of itself. She forced herself to slow. At this stage in recovery, injuries came easy.

But her new reality still soured her thoughts. A mother with a background no doubt manufactured by a Soviet security agency, a father who she may have condemned wrongly, a sister still in a coma, with little chance of a complete recovery and little chance of her discovering the truth. Otherwise, everything looked rosy.

After running for forty minutes, she doubled back and stopped on the beach slipway, car park to the right. The beach was almost empty except for the diehards with flasks and dogs.

On the outskirts of Grain, she padded along the main street, towards Chance's guest house. She'd cleared her mind during the run, and now she wanted answers.

Slowing to a jog, she approached the Georgian guest house. She didn't imagine a mandarin in the Home Office would stay there. Too down market. Not spit and sawdust, but budget. Taking out a sweat rag, she mopped her face. She wouldn't look so unusual; she could be a guest out for a morning jog.

A man in his early fifties exited the hotel and walked across into the car park towards a Jaguar. She recognised those 'snake eyes' from the funeral. He carried an overnight bag and laid it by the driver's door. A cloud of cigar smoke followed him. He took the short thin cigar out of his mouth, flicking the ash from the end, then picked a speck of tobacco off his tongue. He stared at George, and she thought he might stop and ask her something, but he turned and leaned on the car door, studying her, one arm across his chest, the other crooked over it, holding the cigar. She returned his stare. He was lascivious; he looked the type. To see him twice in a week was no coincidence, and she considered asking him why he'd been at the funeral.

"Good morning," she said, passing close. He didn't answer, but nodded in her direction, his gaze steady.

As George entered the guest house, his car started, and she caught the registration number and stored it away, reminding herself to ask Sara, her new found NCA friend, to check on ownership. The Lodge guest house reception was open but empty, except for a barman.

"I'm meeting Mr Chance. Which room is he in, please?"

"Mr and Mrs Chance are at breakfast. Would you like to leave a message?"

Mr and Mrs, that surprised her. Did he have a girlfriend? She'd been around the Rupert class enough to know the possibilities.

"No, thanks. I'll wait for them to finish their breakfast. Can I have a coffee, please?"

The barman nodded, and she took a seat in reception.

The entrance to the dining room was opposite the bar. George glanced in and saw guests eating. Someone close to the entrance may have been Chance. He was also at the funeral; yet another coincidence. His wavy fair hair made him unmistakable. He leaned forward, speaking to someone. Then she heard Chance's voice. It was him; she'd recognise a 'plumb in the mouth' accent anywhere.

"Another spoonful, Patrick, down the hatch, there's a good boy."

Chance stretched to talk to someone, and George saw he was talking to a boy of about fifteen, sitting in a wheelchair, a blanket over his knees. The boy couldn't feed himself, but rocked back and forth to an unheard rhythm. Chance wiped the boy's chin, then offered another spoonful and smiled. A woman sat with them. If George imagined Chance's wife, she couldn't have been more different. Some may have considered the woman 'plain', dark hair, horn-rimmed glasses, and protruding teeth, but her smile when she looked from Chance to Patrick suggested profound affection. Younger than Chance, but she may have weathered well.

"I think Patrick's had enough, dear. Should we go?" said the woman.

Feeling guilty for staring, but fascinated by the scene, George blushed with embarrassment for intruding into this family's life. Chance saw her as he pushed the wheelchair into reception.

"Hello, Georgina. Did you come to see me?" he asked as his family approached. He seemed neither surprised nor discomfited, as if he'd known her all his life. "Helen, this is the lady I was telling you about, Georgina Stone."

Helen smiled as she greeted George. It could have melted ice. Helen Chance looked 'mousy', offering her hand, and pushing back her black fringe from her eyes. George took it and noticed it was firm, like a farmer's grip.

"This is Patrick, our son. Patrick, say hello to Georgina."

Patrick made a noise, sounding like 'hello'. She took his hand in hers, bending to be level with him.

"Hello Patrick, I'm George."

"Helen, would you take Patrick to our room? I'll see you in our room presently."

"Nice to meet you, Georgina," said Helen, pushing Patrick towards the lift.

"Now then, Georgina, I'm James Chance. But for the moment, please call me Mr Chance."

Stern sounding words, but Chance's voice was smooth and reassuring. George didn't take offence at the insistence on formality.

"Should we take a seat in a quiet corner?" said Chance, leading her to a corner table. "Wait here a few minutes, I have to get my briefcase from my room."

He returned carrying a briefcase. George recognised it as a military style security briefcase, impervious to anything less than a chainsaw.

As they sat at a ninety-degree angle to each other, she noticed the wrinkles and liver spots on his hands and reckoned James Chance was more like mid-sixties. George wondered where to start, so she sipped her coffee and waited.

Her surprise at seeing a normal, likeable wife, a family,

and a disabled son may have shown on her face. She'd expected Chance to live a watered-down James Bond lifestyle, a girlfriend or at least a trophy wife, a Range Rover, and a hotel reservation under an assumed name.

"What can I do for you, Georgina?"

"I'm so sorry to disturb you. I… I didn't know."

"I had a wife, and a disabled son? Why would you?" he asked, smiling. "I'm not a spy, Georgina. I'm a senior civil servant responsible for counter intelligence. The current security landscape rarely calls for my skills. My speciality is Russia, the Cold War and all that, not very sexy right now, I'm afraid. I work in MI5, but I report to the Home Secretary. If you were expecting something more, I'm sorry to disappoint you."

George warmed to this posh talking, seventies era, relic. She wondered if he lived in a fantasy world, reliving old battles.

"Please call me George, everyone does."

"I shall call you Georgina. I like the name, and I've always called you Georgina."

George sat open-mouthed. More surprises. "Explain… please," said George.

"You mother and I were old friends. Adversaries in the old days, friends later. She often talked about you and Charlie. She was so proud of you when you joined the Army, and worried sick after the shooting and the extent of your injuries."

"So, you know the story, about my mother spying for

the Soviets, etc?"

"Yes, I do, but it's not that simple; in the old days it never was. There, I sound like a fossil," he chuckled, reaching for his briefcase.

George listened, but as he spoke, information overload rolled over her.

"This is a great deal to accept. You've been through hell these last few months. I'm going to give you a short brief on the situation. It has all you need for now. You have attracted the attention of unsavoury relics, but if you're prepared for it, I'd like to use you."

He looked into George's eyes; this was familiar territory for him. He was weighing her up, assessing if he could trust her. The sheet had 'RESTRICTED' stamped across it. For what they were talking about, 'RESTRICTED' was tame.

"I know your background, so I don't need to remind you of the Official Secrets Act, do I?"

George shook her head without looking at Chance. She clasped the sheet and sighed. This could answer a few questions, or at least provide clues.

"I have a proposal for you. Read this tonight and meet me in London at this address tomorrow."

He handed George a card with an address in plain type. "I'll expect you at 1200 hours. We shall have lunch together."

George grinned, once the posh boy, always the posh boy. She left the guest house grinning. It was progress, a step towards getting even for her Mum and Charlie.

She ran back to Rose Cottage, clutching the sheet of paper. She welcomed her burning determination and optimism. A tiny light shone at the end of a long tunnel. The sheet she clutched gave her speed, but meeting Chance lightened her spirit enough to break into a sprint as she approached her house.

Chapter 25

George read the close typed Summary Sheet given to her by Chance then read it again. It swept away all thought of breakfast. She sat at the dining table, so used by her Mum, Charlie, and herself, nursing her coffee mug, enjoying the aroma wafting from it. Extracting her Mum's letter and photo, she laid the Summary Sheet next to them and read everything again. She'd sat for too long, dropped the sheet on the table, winced at the stiffness in her thigh, and struggled to unclench her fists. Chance's information confirmed what her Mum had said in the letter.

She struggled to understand how it all happened. From the moment she'd told Mum and Charlie she'd be joining the Army as a young girl, 'stubbornness', as her Mum called it, was her principal asset. Charlie called her 'pig headedness', but from her, it was a compliment.

How could her Mum become entangled in this without them knowing? Mum wanted her to trust Chance. But she wasn't naïve. He might also be the killer. Her favoured theory, Mum had been 'disposed of', like rubbish in a waste bin, MI5 clearing out former spies. Once the Soviet

Union collapsed in 1990, she worked for the UK as a double agent, passing to the Russians whatever MI5 told her, until she retired. So, had the Russians discovered her betrayal and disposed of her? George didn't like contradictions, they impeded truth.

She hadn't yet gone through any of her Mum's stuff, though she may find a little substantiation. Either way, she couldn't believe her mother could spy without keeping a record, leaving evidence or documentation. If Mum was a spy, she would have had a Russian 'Handler'. Who was her 'Handler', and did the Handler kill her?

The same photo Mum left inside the letter to her, lay on Julia Stone's bedside table in a gilt frame. A couple of hours later, George had looked through Mum's bedroom thread by thread, photo by photo. She'd even laid out hers and Charlie's baby bootees, and as she'd cried over them, sifted through love letters from her dad to her Mum and frowned over their divorce papers. She went through their holiday documents from fifteen years earlier, walking in Snowdonia, ballooning in Egypt, and skiing in Garmisch-Partenkirchen. Her Mum had kept their school books from primary school to 'A' Levels and even their school reports were intact.

> *'Georgina Stone is not short of effort, but can become bored. She excels at Physical Education, but needs to extend her range of academic discipline and show her erudite side.'*

George read between the lines and knew what it meant. The teachers had suggested she was thick but good for physical work. As a female, that was damning.

As she laid out her Mum's possessions, George's emotions were also laid bare; anger and determination to find the truth, fear, pity, sorrow and back to anger and determination. George stood over clothes, documents, and photos and gritted her teeth.

Hearing a sound, she recognised outside, a smile cracked her face. Jaws, so no doubt Ted was also visiting. She didn't want to see him, but she'd be courteous. As she opened the front door, Jaws rushed forward and danced around, followed by Ted walking along the track, his limp hardly showing.

"Hi Ted, come in. Were you passing, or do you have another mission?"

"No, I wasn't passing. We started a long walk and a think, and ended here," he said, in his broad Glaswegian accent.

He grinned sheepishly. She hadn't taken him for someone easily discomposed, but maybe there was more than a discontented former squaddie making a virtue of self-persecution.

"I have coffee going and I think I can rustle up cake."

Jaws headed into the house, making himself at home and sniffing the kitchen. She led Ted in and pointed to a chair in the kitchen.

"Take your weight off. Take your foot off if you like."

She grinned, and Ted chuckled, breaking the tension.

"I don't mind if I do."

As she busied herself making coffee, Ted fidgeted, grasping his hands to keep them still. George had no intention of making it easy. She watched and waited.

"Look, George…" said Ted, before she cut him off.

"Let me finish getting something for Jaws, then we'll talk, okay?"

"Hmm,"

Waiting and suffering made agreeable companions.

She placed a dish on the floor and Jaws sat and waited, looking expectantly at Ted. She should have known Ted had trained Jaws properly.

"Go get it, Jaws," said George, but he sat impatiently.

Ted nodded towards Jaws, who dived for the bowl. George scowled.

She put two mugs on the kitchen table, sipped hers, and waited.

"I'm not sure if I dare talk," said Ted. "Was I much of a twat?"

"Yeah."

"I've been alone too long. I see about three people a month and one of them is the Postman. This came as a shock, after more than ten years of nothing, except the odd seagull crapping on my windows."

She guessed it would be as close to an apology as she could expect, and George couldn't help but grin. At least he knew humility.

"So apart from saying sorry, why are you here, Ted?"

"I want to help."

"What? No, thanks, Ted. What I must do, I'll do on my own. Someone killed my Mum and put Charlie in hospital; I need justice, on my own and on my own terms."

"You'll get yourself killed is what. I'm not the most sociable person, or the most physically able, but I can handle myself. And I can watch your back, and you need help."

Ted's eyes pleaded, but it didn't change a thing; this was her mission, not Ted's. His behaviour the day before had disturbed her. She'd known him only two days and despite him being a veteran, trusting anyone was a problem. She stared into her mug, searching for inspiration. What would Charlie say?

"Come on, George, don't be as big an arse as me; I can help you. I'm prepared to dirty my hands, and I'll lay off the booze. Finished, cross my heart. Please."

"Who's the boss, Ted?"

He grinned and did a mock salute. "You are, ma'am."

"I'm sorting Mum's stuff upstairs. Read this and when I come down, I'll answer questions," she smirked, and handed Ted the Summary Sheet.

"Right you are," said Ted.

As George stood on the stairs, she hesitated. "This could get messy, and dangerous. Are you prepared for time in prison?"

"I know it'll get messy. For too many years, all I've done is walk my dog and look out to sea. I need to do something before I become a grumpy old pensioner; so, yes, I'm up for it."

***

George descended the stairs as Ted made more coffee.

"So?" she said.

"I've read nothing like it in my life. How much did you know?"

"Nothing, until a few days ago. Mrs Wallis at the Post Office gave me a letter from Mum explaining things from her point of view, and Mum told me I could trust Chance and to get more information from him. It seems Mrs Wallis knew everything and kept Mum's secret."

"The Summary talks about your Mum not being born in the UK, but doesn't say where. Any idea? And what did your Mum do for the Soviets?" asked Ted.

"No idea where she was born. Her birth certificate says Rainham. She told us, she worked as an accountant for the UK MOD. But Mrs Wallis tells me she was a government research assistant. Certainly, she spent time in London at meetings and Aunt Sheila baby sat us. We loved her, still do. Sheila said she was a sort of Soviet Quartermaster or Logistics Officer."

"Bloody hell. How long was she passing information to the Soviets?"

"Hard to tell, probably from the time she started working for the UK MOD, until the Soviet collapse. Then

MI5 capitalised on the collapse and turned her. Something strange, Mum's letter said to trust James Chance, the chap I went to see yesterday, and he arrives in this backwoods town. Nothing happens here. Also, as a spy for the Soviets, who killed her and why? It could have been the Russians, or our own side. But why?"

"Apparently, Grain is spy central. You showed me the summary, is there a complete file?"

"I'm sure there is. No doubt Chance is weighing up whether he can trust me. Are you in or out?" asked George.

Ted looked at his hands. A minute later, he looked up; the straight line of his lips and the stare gave her his answer.

"Look, Hen, I'm in. Meeting you, and the opportunity to help you is the best thing to happen to me since I retired from Her Majesty's Service. The question is, are you all in? I assume you're trying to get justice. What aren't you prepared to do and beyond what point won't you go? What won't you do to get even, hey? This is a big boys' game, and they won't play nice. We could both be killed."

"This isn't a game to me, and it isn't simple revenge, Ted, it's justice. I'll do what I must, and distance isn't something I recognise. I'll do whatever I have to, kill whoever I need to no more, no less. My mission is justice for my family, and if it means punishment and retaliation, so be it. And don't call me 'Hen', you one-legged wonk."

Ted rubbed his hand over his face and grinned, and George grinned back.

"Righteo. Deal," said Ted.

"Chance has invited me to see him in London tomorrow, which I hope will reveal more. Come to London with me, so long as you keep a safe distance and stay unseen."

"Give me the address where you'll be meeting, and we'll separate as soon as we arrive in London."

"How's your navigation?"

"Great. I passed my B3 map reading over thirty years ago."

Chapter 26

Templeton Maudlin's phone rang. He rarely received personal phone calls. So, this had to be business. He could count his friends on the fingers of a tightened fist, not counting the local Council, and even they gave him a wide berth. Some may have thought, if they associated with a Funeral Director, it would hasten their end. They'd made him a Council Alderman because his father had been one, but he looked on Council members as nothing more than business associates and busybodies. A mafia of the mediocre.

But Moss was increasingly calling on his services, frequently after midnight. But two calls in two weeks were rare. It never occurred to him to ask how the customer died, or the identity. Although when he inspected the body, it was usually obvious how life had ceased, and he admired Moss's handiwork. He glanced at the digital clock; 2 a.m. mid-January. Maudlin threw the bedcovers back and cursed. For all they knew, he could be worse for wear.

A part of his mind was preparing for a delivery. In the dark, he searched for his horn-rimmed glasses, and eventually put them on at a comical angle. He switched on the bedside light, and answered the phone with a curt, "Yes?"

The caller, blunt and to the point, informed Templeton he'd deliver a 'customer'. Customer description: 'male, 180 pounds, age thirty plus'. Delivery, three o'clock this morning, back door. Templeton tried to make a quip, hoping they'd done a better job than last time, but the click of the phone disconnecting showed the caller's indifference.

Fine, thought Templeton. Pity it's not a woman, but you can't have everything. He made a call to Michael who occupied the flat adjoining the Funerarium and directed him to meet him in the Crematorium, 500 metres along a track from the Funerarium. The warmth of his bedroom slippers, which he lined up before retiring to his bed, was welcome. He couldn't stand disorder, especially when he arose, and particularly when called to do a 'job'. His hand ran over his face to his tiny toothbrush moustache where it rested, as if counting the hairs with his fingers. He didn't switch on the overhead light, which hurt his eyes, he'd laid out his things in such a way to prepare himself in the semi-darkness.

He washed, shaved, and dressed quickly, his suit laid out on a hanger, with a white shirt and black tie. In his opinion, a gentleman should dress well, formal to the occasion, never casual. Michael had polished his shoes a few hours ago to prepare for the possibility of a premature day. Templeton examined himself in the full-length mirror, whilst shaving; a man should be clean-shaven, except for a moustache, appropriate to his occupation.

Did he need new glasses? He stepped back but had difficulty focussing, and momentarily, his reflection dimmed to a greyish tint. He brought his face close to the mirror, his breath fogging it, which defeated the object. All he could see was his nose, now a dim grey.

He walked over to switch on the light; returning to the mirror, he saw the strangest thing. He dressed in black and white, obviously; but the image of himself as he walked towards the mirror was smoky grey, even his complexion. He stared at it for several minutes until his phone rang. It was Michael telling him he was ready.

Templeton made a mental note to mention it to his optician.

"Yes, I'll meet you in the Crematorium Room."

"Right, Mr Maudlin."

Templeton twitched the corner of the curtain, to ensure the backyard was in darkness. He thought it best he didn't see the person making the delivery. He had no problem with the arrangement, he'd been doing it for years, and it was rewarding.

"Start the Cremator. Then stay in the Preparation Room, I'll see you there," said Templeton.

He made his way along the track to the Crematorium, as he'd done dozens of times before. The dark was his friend. Trees marked each side of the track at fifty-yard intervals; the dark, giving them a baleful look. The light through the Crematorium Preparation Room window revealed Michael working.

He saw him dressed in a dark blazer, a size too small and a flat cap. His tie, one short end hanging loose. He looked away without expression. His other employees would have elicited a spitting reprimand from Maudlin, but Michael was special, anomalous, and Maudlin patronised him. He tolerated Michael's lack of care in appearance, his natural ability compensated.

The long-case clock said 2:48 a.m. He glanced at it anyway and put on his black leather gloves. His father had taught him to take the same pride in his own attire as he did with dressing his friends. One affected the other, and he'd paid meticulous attention to preparing friends. On Templeton's eighth birthday, his father had introduced him to his workplace, allowing him into the Funerarium Preparation Room. On entering, the young Templeton sensed the calm of the place and his father's transformation, from being a fastidious, controlling little man to a confident artist, at ease with himself, his work, and his friends. Less than a year later, he drew Templeton to the body he was preparing.

"Come, Templeton, touch his hand, you'll find it's quite cool and not in the least frightening. It can't hurt you, and there's no such thing as ghosts."

His father grinned at Templeton with bleached teeth. "Take the hand. See?"

Templeton didn't 'see', but he took the dead hand in his. He noticed his father said to take 'the' hand, not 'his' hand. This dead person was a 'thing' to his father. The weight of the hand surprised him. He wasn't at all comfortable holding this dead hand. The bloated skin was rough against his eight-year-old fingers, even to his untrained eye. His father had cut and cleaned the dead man's nails, but Templeton felt this hand had orchestrated much sin. The distorted knuckles must have caused others pain. He slid his fingers across the areas where his father had applied Funeral Director's filler and make-up to disguise the collateral damage to the man's crimes.

For over a year, he avoided touching the dead, and his father seemed satisfied for Templeton to stand next to him whilst he performed the embalming, cleaning, and preparing. It didn't frighten him, even when a customer's dead nerves gave a last jerk.

Later, after first asking his father's permission, he took a woman's hand in his. He must have been ten. His father nodded and grinned, his extruding teeth showing his assent. Templeton gazed up at his father, hoping this experience would be better than the first. A shiver rattled him. His father's eyes sparkled, and it seemed to his innocent mind, his father was telling him he'd come of age. The woman's skin was cold and blanched, but not heavy. He slid his own finger along the dead woman's fingers, then took them in his boy fingers. His father had explained rigour mortise and after a day or so, the body became flexible again.

"It's different from the last time," said Templeton. "Because I haven't embalmed it yet."

Templeton again noticed his father called the dead woman 'it', not 'her'. He let the hand rest in his for several minutes and closed his eyes, feeling the coolness of her skin, the tiny flaws, and wrinkles brought on by decades of life. His fingers pressing into the soft flesh, he delighted in the soft texture of this dead woman's skin. He tried to recall her name, but after many years it eluded him. But he could check his records. He didn't like that aspect of his father's approach. A dead man is only an 'it', simply dead. But after death, a woman is 'her', a precious thing.

A tap on the door returned him to the present. The return to silence filled moments later by the three o'clock chime. Pressing the black leather gloves into the creases of his fingers, he glanced in the mirror; satisfied, he answered the door. Despite the lack of light, he recognised and smelt the black rubber of the body bag. The smell of the dead body permeated his senses, and he breathed deeply.

A person dressed all in black stood astride the body. A black baseball hat hid his face, but from the stance and the height he assumed it was a man.

"Place it in my Preparation Room, please," said Templeton.

The man lifted the body and dropped it inside the room.

"He's all yours," said the courier.

Maudlin detected an accent, but couldn't be sure. The man disappeared into the dark. People could be so inconsiderate, so disappointing. He called Michael to lift the body.

"Is the Cremator ready?"

"Almost. Another half hour," said Michael.

"I'll be in my study. Call me."

"Right, Mr Maudlin."

At 5 a.m., Templeton Maudlin looked through the Cremator's spy hole and saw glowing ash. His eyebrows creased in concentration and a twitch crossed his lips, which may also have been a smile. The temperature gauge read 750 degrees centigrade.

"Let it cool off, but monitor it until it's finished. Collect the remains in the collecting vessel and grind them with the cremulator," said Templeton.

Michael enjoyed using the steel vessel designed to reduce any remains bigger than a breadcrumb to unidentifiable ash using rotating steel balls.

He nodded, smiling, "Right you are, Mr Maudlin."

Templeton left the Crematorium and strolled along the tree lined path towards the Funerarium. Quite a picturesque place during the day, but visitors were few, usually joggers. Word got around. The Funeral Director was weird. He scowled, thinking about visitors, muttering to himself.

A few nights after preparing Julia Stone, he'd convinced himself the 'thing' had been in his imagination. When a caressing breeze touched his cheek, he gasped and hurried on. Every tree, bush, and pothole along the path were familiar. He'd welcome a return to his bed after this night's work had interrupted his sleep, and quickened his pace, feeling watched.

About to sink into bed, he turned the duvet down, and saw movement in the mirror. Enough to make him turn and stare, then squint. Templeton searched for an offending item causing the peculiarity. Nothing.

Regardless, he checked the window catch, and satisfied, finally sank into his bed.

Sleep usually came easily to Templeton. Within seconds of his eyes closing, sleep overcame him. His mind may have been overactive, even agitated. His late-night duties rarely disturbed him, but his meeting with Moss could disturb him. With Moss, an enquiring mind meant trouble. And he didn't need to know details, sordid or otherwise. Despite the rewarding nature of their arrangement, his last meeting with Moss caused him to consider a withdrawal plan.

"You may well reflect, Templeton," a silky voice murmured.

Was he dreaming? Maudlin sat up in bed and peered into the mirror. There it was again, a shadow, a simple illusion, nothing more. Reassured, he resettled, only for the shadow to renew his disarrangement. Bedclothes to his chin, he called out, his voice verging on the soprano.

"What is it, who are you?"

"Calm Templeton, this is a simple reminder, I'm still here. Why are you surprised? The Ferryman keeps his word and intends to ensure you keep yours."

"I've done nothing wrong. Please…"

He stared, squinting, but could distinguish only shadow. He recognised the voice; how could he not? They'd been married for decades.

"Others pass judgement on your nocturnal activities, but not I. To me, you are an amusement."

"This isn't real, and you aren't real. You're dead."

"Am I?" asked the apparition.

Grasping the bedside lamp, he hurled it at the mirror, which smashed but remained in its frame. The bedcovers flew back of their own volition. Eyes bulging, he gripped the digital clock with quivering hands, ripped it from the cord and smashed it against the full-length mirror. After several attempts, the mirror finally shattered, and with it the shadow fragmented into a thousand smaller images. After repeated blows with the clock, both it and the mirror lay on the bedroom carpet, destroyed. He shuffled over to the bed and curled into a ball, burying himself in his dishevelled bedclothes, and slept fitfully. The sleep of the disturbed.

Chapter 27

Ted and George travelled in different coaches on the train to St Pancras from Rochester. George looked at her watch: five minutes past ten, on time. She took a taxi to the South Bank of the Thames, far enough from her destination, but close enough to walk, and gave the taxi driver a tip, small enough to forget. George strolled along Salamanca Street, onto Vauxhall Walk to the crossroads like any other tourist. Except this was a cold and overcast January. Youths stood outside a bookies shop discussing the racing certainties for the afternoon and looked her way. She used the opportunity to look around, her eyes darting around, detecting no tail. She hated being late, or too early, and walked around the block, doubled back, sat on a park bench, and watched. A text from Ted.

"Embankment heading along Whitgift Street."

She texted him back, giving him her location.

She recognised the name of the street. It ran a hundred metres parallel to Black Prince Road. Ten minutes before her meeting, she stopped outside 'Charcoal Grill Easy

Chicken', a fast-food café, reeking of grease.

A couple waited to be served. The Asian man behind the counter glared at George and asked, "Clinnin?"

George squinted, a question mark on her face.

"You clinnin… clinnin gul?" he asked again, then rolled his eyes and pointed with his chin towards a door in the corner, a broom cupboard.

George nodded and opened the door, hoping this was part of the cover. Otherwise, she'd be scrubbing floors in the café. She stepped through and the door clicked closed behind her. A light came on, illuminating a windowless staircase, which led to a landing, with no discernible door. She examined the walls and door, and saw they joined the terraced block next door. Two flights and fifty stairs later, she realised the stairs must lead to the large Victorian three-story brick block, next door to the café. From the outside, she'd spotted the secondary double glazing, either a listed building or a security measure. A concealed door at the top opened and James Chance stood on the threshold, smiling down at her.

"Welcome, Georgina. Sorry for the subterfuge, but as you'll see, it was necessary. Come in."

The contrast with the grubby exterior and the café was stark. In the oversized office, a curtained window provided light onto an oversized desk. On the desk lay a single file and a laptop in the corner. On the inside of the grubby net curtains was a screen, which may have been a copper Faraday mesh. Velvet curtains were open. A table, for meetings, with six chairs. It could have been any senior bureaucrat's office in London.

"Have a seat," said Chance, pointing to one of two chairs facing the desk.

George sensed there was something wrong with this setup. Why hadn't Chance told her to meet him at MI5 HQ at Thames House? Why the deceit? And why the Indian takeaway downstairs? Intriguing, but it was only because of her mother's words she placed some limited trust in Chance.

"So, why didn't we meet at Thames House?"

He slumped behind the desk; exhaustion manifested, but sat back and smiled.

"I can trust *almost* everyone in MI5, hence our meeting here. MI5 doesn't know about this place. You may think you were the target at Ted's house, but you were not. I suspected for a while Marcus Wetherby was a weak link. I suspected him of working for the Russian underworld, but we couldn't prove it. His killing at Ted's house seems to reinforce that. He had a weakness; he liked girls too much, and the Russians exploited it. It may also have been a warning to you too, not to interfere. If you'd been the target, you wouldn't be sitting here now."

"Let's talk about Julia Stone, your mother. Later this afternoon, you may read the file on your mother and her activities. But it remains in this room."

"For the last fifteen years of her working life, your mother was a close friend, and valued asset. She passed to the Russians what we asked her to pass on. But prior to that, during the Cold War, she spied for the Soviets exclusively for many years. She was what we call an 'illegal', a Soviet citizen and a plant. Your Mum posed as English, but she most definitely was not. In your mother's case, she was born in Lithuania, which was part of the old Soviet Union."

Hearing her Mum wasn't even British, left George staring at Chance, almost open-mouthed, an expletive on her lips. She said nothing, she couldn't. So, she and her sister were half-Lithuanian. Chance paused and continued when he realised George wouldn't ask a question.

"Also, not on the Summary Sheet I gave you, was how the Soviets achieved this transformation. They sent across to England a gifted young lady and gave her a new identity. She applied for a British passport based on her British birth certificate and from then on, she was, for all intents and purposes, English. They didn't bother to take the identity of a dead girl; they created a person from birth, complete with British birth certificate, born in Rainham in Essex, genuine school records. Based on her 'A Levels', she attended Durham University, where she achieved a first-class degree in Mathematics. No doubt tutored before and during her studies by the Soviets. Remember, in the seventies, there were no computer records, but I'm sure it wouldn't have stopped them. But it made it easier."

"The Soviets went to a lot of trouble to ensure Julia Stone was genuine and able to pass rigorous vetting, which she did, many times. In the 1980s, she worked at the Military Research Centre in Grain and passed information to the Soviets. She had 'TOP SECRET' security clearance, and the information she had access to would have been invaluable to the Soviets. When the Soviet Union collapsed, she came to me. I encouraged her to continue to work for the Russian SVR, the successor to the KGB. From then on, she passed on to the Russian state what we gave her. She revealed almost nothing to us of her earlier work with the Soviets. She believed in the Soviet system and never quite trusted us."

This was too James Bond for George. Julia Stone was her mother, for Christ's sake. She remembered playing in a farmer's field and running towards a herd of cows to the horror of her mother who chased after her, rescued her and hugged her until George and Charlie stopped laughing.

"But what about her mother and father, brothers, and sisters, et cetera? There must have been records? She used to tell us she was raised in an orphanage after her parents died and stayed there until she was sixteen."

"Julia Little was your mother's maiden name and there are records of a Julia Little, which appear to be genuine. No parents listed. So, the authorities would have assumed her parents abandoned her. There are records of her presence in the orphanage, but little evidence of her actual presence. When we checked with surviving staff, three were dead, one was in a hospice with dementia and one swore she knew Julia Little, another agreed, after prompting and being shown a photograph."

George's thoughts skitted from one idea to another, trying to make sense of this. This was hard to accept. If her Mum had been alive, they'd have had an almighty argument. But George understood she was a Soviet citizen before the twins were born, and spying was her job. She tried to keep her composure, which contradicted how she felt. But she guessed Chance knew how to read these things. Given an opportunity, she'd blame Chance for all this, take her revenge and bear the consequences, but something said 'wait'. But why had he revealed this now? Why not leave well alone? It made little sense. What did he want from her? Did he know who killed her mother?

Chance sat back in his chair and waited, watching George. For now, George would not reveal her feelings to this stranger, who claimed to have known her mother.

"Why tell me this now?" George asked, staring at Chance.

"Because you deserve to know. And you need to know," he paused, "we can help each other."

"I'm listening."

"We have a leak in our department. Someone must have told the Russians your Mum was working for us, and she expressed her suspicion."

"And they killed her because she turned against her former masters?" surmised George.

Chance didn't meet George's look. Was he being elusive or lying? He glanced up and studied her, examining her features. He was a sharp character, this Chance; a former field Officer, maybe. The difference for her was whether loyalty went both ways. He hadn't done a good job of protecting her Mum, even though she was a useful 'asset' as he called her.

"Not exactly. Everything changed after the wall came down. The Soviet Union collapsed in 1991 with a change of regime. We'd known of her activities for some time before she approached us and volunteered to work for us. She didn't like the direction in which Russia was moving after 1991, she lost trust in them, anyway she was Lithuanian, not Russian, so no love lost there. She held information about the Soviets in the UK but refused to release it to us, even though we knew her job in the Soviet system. But all her previous Soviet related activities stopped when she retired. So why was she killed? That's still a mystery. She said you were putting your life in jeopardy every day in Afghanistan, and you never complained. You weren't a 'bewailer', as she called it. You are the bravest person she knew, and not because she was your Mum either. She said if you could fight for your country, at least she'd pay penance for spying for the Soviets. A mole in MI5 is almost part of the story. My guess is she held valuable information, and the Russian mob feared she would hand it over to us. Either they would have it or no one would have it. The Russians have long memories, and they don't like traitors, as they call them. They 'terminate' them, eventually."

George had difficulty working out how much was the truth and how much was horse-feathers, but if it got her closer to her Mum's killers, she'd cooperate. Chance had judged her, seen she hadn't fallen apart, and noted she may be useful. She had no choice, but who needed who the most?

"Okay, so what do you want from me?"

Chance sat straight, and he reminded her of Colonel Syman. Chance may also have been former military.

"I have a proposal for you, but first I promised you lunch."

He smiled, stood, and opened the door. The Indian café assistant from downstairs entered. A clean white coat replaced the decaying, food encrusted apron. The man laid the conference table in the opposite corner and turned to Chance.

"Would sir and madam be ready for lunch? I'll serve charred vegetable salad, followed by crispy Sichuan-spiced duck and a light sorbet for dessert," said the waiter. Gone was the pidgin English.

"This is Adam. He manages the café and the property."

He could have passed as Head Waiter in any restaurant.

Chance smiled. "Adam, is the finest chef this side of the river."

"Wait," said George, "Before we eat, tell me your proposal, if I agree we'll eat, if not I'm out of here. Okay?"

Chance raised an eyebrow. It was possible no one had spoken to him like this before.

"Your Mum said you'd be forthright. If you accept, we'll get on fine."

"Adam, please give us another ten minutes?"

She disliked mixing business with pleasure. She liked to attend to business, discuss, agree or otherwise, shake hands and leave. This lunch was a ploy to get her to agree.

"Your job will be to infiltrate the Russian mob. Find out what you can about their operations and report to me. I want to end their criminal activities in the UK," said Chance.

This was a 'feeler' in principle. If she agreed to this, they'd discuss details. If not, she'd leave and know little more than when she arrived. He hadn't yet shown her the file and that seemed conditional on her agreeing to work for him.

"My mission is to find Mum's killer and ensure Charlie's safety. But I'm still employed by the MOD and a serving NCO. What would be my status?"

"I can fix your status by requesting your secondment to us. Your status would be the same as any of our MI5 field officers, but Colonel Syman and I must arrange it, for obvious reasons. The last thing we want in my office is a paper trail. I've also seconded Sarah Frolic from the National Crime Agency, more to keep the NCA onside than anything else. I'll keep her informed of what's going on, and she'll act as a backup as and when needed."

He sat back, took a deep sigh, and his tone changed. Chance's suspiration meant he was about to talk to her as a subordinate. "You wouldn't have a licence to kill, George; this is not Afghanistan. We usually hand villains to the police."

George spotted the word 'usually', but let it pass. "I would have no power of self-defence then?" asked George.

"That's a different matter. I can't protect you from prosecution unless you use force in fulfilling your mission, and/or the lives of yourself or others are in danger. Come on George, if I can protect you, I will, unless you commit an execution, in which case you'll be charged. Unless you leave no evidence, then…"

She found his last comment strange. Was he inviting her to commit a crime, a killing, so long as she camouflaged it? But she didn't have a choice, and it was the best offer she'd have.

"I can accept that. If you can square it with Colonel Syman, I'm in."

"One more thing. Your insertion into the Russian mob will need careful handling. We must give you a legend of sorts. A motivation for turning, which means we will have to ensure our mole sees it and passes it on."

"What do you have in mind?" asked George. It needed to be convincing and genuine.

"Dishonourable discharge. After you've completed your mission, I can have it reversed to a medical discharge with a pension. The Home Secretary and his counterpart in the MOD will cooperate, I'm sure."

A double-decker bus had hit her head on and mowed her flat. Even a fake 'Dishonourable Discharge' would destroy a part of her; but it was necessary. The slightest nod gave her assent, but Chance had caught the doubt on her face.

"I want to visit Bradley Maudlin. He knows something, and I need to learn what he knows. Can you fix that?"

Chance rubbed his chin. "He won't give you the time if he knows who you are, I'll see what I can do." He scrutinised George. That assessment again. As if he was assessing her mental capacity, whether she was up to the quick-thinking required.

"George, this must be an appalling experience for you. And I know we're doing this too quickly, but I will support you."

He was right there.

"Okay. Let's get to details. I've asked Colonel Robert Syman to join us, we've been friends for years, and he was in London for a meeting. I see you've asked Ted to support you, he'll freeze out there watching your back. Is he part of the package?"

George nodded and grinned. Chance may sound and dress like an upper-class twit, but he was no soft-boiled thicko.

"So, you've spoken to Colonel Syman?"

Chance didn't answer. The door opened and Colonel Robert Syman and Ted entered, reliving the old days, Sarah Frolic brought up the rear.

Chapter 28

Prison Officers treated Bradley as a commodity, a piece of meat. Shepherd was a minnow picking scraps, a 'runner' for Josey. If Josey said run to another prison block and deliver a wrap of 'C' or 'A', Shepherd ran. If he said 'go get my meal', Shepherd said 'how many sausages', and if Josey said 'Maudlin is a piece of shit', Shepherd spat on Maudlin's shoes. Josey the terrible, Josey the hard man and the unofficial, but no less undisputed boss of 'A' Wing.

According to rumours, Josey had severed a man's head clean off. Both head and body now support the M1 motorway. All for a few quid. Now he was serving time for dealing in stolen goods. He'd serve two years tops, and one for good behaviour and time served.

Forget the Governor or Chief Warder, they were prisoners, like Bradley. If it wasn't for their status and their blue uniforms, they'd have been running tricks for Josey, like Shepherd.

Maudlin walked towards Shepherd with the Screw at his elbow. Despite trying to look casual, his hands shook and his body looked beaten, a coward hiding his fear. Ignoring the Screw, Shepherd slammed Bradley aside, bouncing him off the unforgiving brick wall. No point in complaining. He kept his head down, and a shock of hair fell into his eyes. His black hair, dark, almost black eyes, and his almost feminine good looks responsible for his pain and humiliation. A flash of silver green caught his eye. A gob of phlegm and spittle hit Maudlin's shoes like a protein guided missile of contempt. He imagined the expectorator smiling, an expert dart player making a clean score.

The Screw ignored the incident. It didn't happen. Prison officers were neutral and treated all prisoners the same. But for Maudlin, they were worse than inmates. At least inmates represented natural selection, the law of the jungle, the strongest at the top and Maudlin at the bottom. Josey and cons like him would beat and use Bradley until he was at the bottom and broken. He may even get a shank in the back, whilst Screws looked away.

He regretted agreeing to his father's visit. He'd received no visits in the two months, except Pinchin. At one time, Maudlin had hoped his natural charm, wit, and class might protect him, before realising those characteristics appeal to inmates' baser and libidinous instincts.

His father wasted no time. Bradley no sooner sat opposite his father than the sermon started in that whining, nasal voice.

"Hmmm," said Templeton Maudlin in greeting. "You got what you deserved, no more. If you engage in criminal activity, what more can you expect? You must bear the consequences. Society runs on order and discipline, and respect for one's place in the scheme of things. Where did you go wrong, Boy Scouts or that damnable overpriced private school?"

Bradley showed no surprise at his father's elastic memory. His reality had all the flexibility of bubble gum. His father didn't need to convince himself. To him these were the facts. He'd thrown Bradley under a bus, as casually as walking across the road.

Templeton didn't pause for breath, and Maudlin hoped one day this wizened old undertaker would run out of it. Maudlin looked across at him and smiled. A smile he'd learnt as a child annoyed his father.

"Although goodness knows, it should have been your making. You had all the privileges I could invest in you, and I had every expectation of you earning my approbation. There are morale and honest ways of earning a living, and even gaining substantial affluence, if one is prudent, hardworking, and ready to learn. I give one quarter of my net income to philanthropic causes, and I will increase it, and in a small way, it may compensate and make amends for your appalling behaviour, although I doubt redemption is appropriate in your case. My disappointment is beyond proof, you are an abscess plastered on a beautiful landmark."

Templeton Maudlin always spoke like a middle-class Charles Dickens character, unless it was practical, such as 'I'm going to the shop.' Even then he would say 'Maudlin, I'm walking out to make a purchase'. Reference to a charitable donation meant Bradley would receive less when his old man died. Please, God, make it soon. He thought about correcting his father on the abscess issue. An abscess on a landmark was impossible. There was more, much more. Bradley lost concentration and drifted away to a place where his father wasn't. His father rehearsed his arguments. Bradley had seen him do it. Eventually, he'd argue with his maker. Maudlin drifted towards his own 'safe room', a place so deep and isolated. A self-inflicted incarceration, where his father didn't exist. Isolation could be hell for some, but for Bradley it was sanctuary. Of the two prisons, one real and one of his own making, he preferred the latter.

"How are you, Bradley? And stop that cheese slime grin, I've told you before, it's rude and unnerves me."

Templeton took out a small box from his waistcoat pocket, and applied snuff to the back of his hand. The Screw stared at it, looking confused, his brow furrowed. Brolly carrying undertakers don't sniff illegal substances.

The Screw strolled across. "What's that substance, Sir?"

Before he could answer, Templeton Maudlin had vacuumed the snuff up his nose like a Dyson on turbo. With a mighty guffawing sneeze, he deposited a mucus covered rhinolith into a pure white handkerchief.

Satisfied, the Screw stepped back, likely to avoid drenching by further nasal projections. Bradley continued to smile. Templeton examined his deposits in his handkerchief, smiled, and braced his shoulders, folding the cloth and placing it into the top pocket of his jacket. Bradley suspected his father of saving soiled handkerchiefs. Even as a child, he didn't recall handkerchiefs being washed or disposed of, but his father sported a clean one each day.

"Is there anything else, father?"

"You should be ashamed. You had it all: looks, brains and money. My money, mind. No disadvantages. Now look at you. Straighten up and remove that silly grin off your face. I'm going."

His father stood, half turned, and pointed at Bradley.

"And don't telephone me to ask for help."

The Screw led Bradley to his cell. From then, Bradley Maudlin amused inmates. News of his encounter with his father was no doubt passed on by the Screws. The inmates took delight in mimicking his father's manner.

Chapter 29

George finished on the phone to Ted. Even late morning, he was a grumpy tight-lipped sod. He'd walk across in the early afternoon.

She planned to see Sheila for lunch, although she hadn't arranged it yet. Mail dropped onto the mat; she laid her toast on her plate, wiped her hands, and padded through to collect it. A brown envelope marked 'On Her Majesty's Service'. Even though she expected it, she stood on unsteady legs. The letter signed by the Military Secretary was short and to the point.

> *'The Disciplinary Investigation Board considered the evidence related to your relationship with a senior Officer during your recent tour of duty in Afghanistan. The Board concluded that your behaviour was inappropriate, fell below the standards required of a Senior Non-Commissioned Officer in Her Majesty's Armed Forces, bringing the Service into disrepute. I am directed to inform you that your services are no longer required. You are to be discharged from the Army at the earliest convenience and at the discretion of your Commanding Officer… blah.'*

> *'In coming to its conclusion, The Board acknowledged your dedication and commitment during your tours of duty and expressed its regret that you sustained serious injury (see note below)... blah... blah.'*
>
> *'Note: Your injuries will be assessed under The Armed Forces Compensation Scheme (AFCS), and The Armed Forces and Reserve Forces (Compensation Scheme) Order 2011 (SI 2011/517). The level of award will be determined by Claims Assessors, using a tariff of your injuries set out in the above legislation.'*

This so-called 'relationship' was false and part of her cover. Regardless, even this contrived fakery hurt. A low growl escaped her lips. She looked at the letter, seeing wetness, and realised silent tears were rolling down her cheeks. She leaned against the wall and slid to the floor until she was sitting with her back against the front door, clutching the letter ending George's Army career. Her tears weren't sham. No serving soldier wants to receive such a letter, regardless of the circumstances.

Minutes later, a knock on the door rattled around her head. Renewed knocking, louder, and on the third knock, she stood, wiped her face with the sleeve of her cardigan, glanced in the mirror, and opened the door.

George fell into Aunt Sheila's arms on the doorstep. Sheila pushed George inside, closed the door with her elbow, and hugged her former friend's daughter. They hugged for ten minutes. George pulled herself away from Sheila and smiled her thanks.

"I needed that, Sheila."

"Why don't we have a chat? I'm sure it'll not be as bad

if you share it."

George gave Sheila the letter in the brown envelope and beckoned her to go into the living room while she made tea.

As they sat across from each other, Sheila asked, "Is this true, George? Did you have an affair?"

George nodded and looked at her feet. She tried to see Sheila's face. She was studying George. Sheila had appeared exactly when the Postman would deliver the letter. They were playing a game, and she must be careful. Not something George excelled at. They sipped their tea in silence.

"Well, look, you'll get another job, love. With your skills and talents, there must be opportunities."

"What? When employers see how I left the Army, they won't touch me. It's unfair. After what I did in Afghanistan, and twelve years of Service, I'm finished. The other bloke will get a job. Do they expect me to work at Tesco? I'm a soldier, Aunt Sheila; a close-quarter protection operative, and a physical training instructor. I need local work to support Charlie, and she may need private care."

"Are you still seeing him?"

"No, it was a short-term entanglement. Pressures of a war zone, et cetera. He was available, and I fell for him. He's married with a kid. And anyway, it was hormones. You know how it is."

Sheila laughed. "Not really, dear. As you know, I never married, except to the job, my hormones never kicked in."

"Look, it's going to be hard, but your Mum was a survivor. She fought to raise you kids when your dad left, and you're made of the same stuff. Let's ruminate, see what we can think of."

George saw her in a new light. She was brighter than she'd given her credit for. George also needed to be careful. Too easy and she'd smell the proverbial.

"Well, the Army won't touch me. They'll no doubt pay me for a couple of months, but I doubt anyone will be ready with a job contract. And I won't ask. I've been a soldier for Christ's sake, Sheila, I won't beg."

"Look, why don't you wash your face and brush up. I'll set the table for lunch. I'll see what you have in the fridge. How does that sound?"

"Okay, Sheila. So long as we don't talk about it over lunch."

"A good idea."

George disappeared upstairs, but waited at the top and heard Sheila whispering on her mobile phone.

Chapter 30

As Bradley shuffled towards his second visit in as many months, his thoughts turned towards self-imposed mental isolation. Entering the visiting room, he saw other prisoners watching as they sat at tables, waiting for their visitors. Their smirks caused him to focus on the floor. He sat and after a minute of silence, glanced up to meet the smiling eyes of his visitor. She'd wanted to see him as part of her higher education studies. A professional visitor; but at least her smile would gain him a little respect amongst the inmates. She wiggled a pencil with a rubber on the end between her fingers, watching him.

"Good morning, Mr Maudlin. Can I call you Bradley?" she asked, with a sunny smile.

He smiled for the first time since he'd entered this quagmire of festering humanity.

"The Screws told me I had a visitor, something educational. I had two minds about whether to accept your visit. I can refuse, you know. So, who are you?"

He'd been too harsh. She could be an accomplice of Wilson Pinchin, or she might be genuine. She looked like a student, hair in a ponytail, glasses, notebook, and pen.

"My name's Susan Freeman. I'm doing a Master's Degree in Social Work."

She grinned, an overexcited teenager going on a first date. Bradley expected her to wrinkle her nose, pull her shoulders up, and clap her hands. She seemed like a typical excited student. He'd seen her type whilst at university. Her intentions were probably genuine.

He imagined her saying, 'Let's go on a march for the oppressed, especially those poor people in prison.'

"And what do you want?"

"Hmm… I've permission to choose one convict to study for my dissertation and write a report. You can say no, but I would be ever so grateful."

He didn't tell her he wasn't a convict, but on remand; what was the point?

"Why me?"

"The Governor suggested you." She leaned in, hand to mouth, and whispered. "He said you were unlike other prisoners, and I might obtain valuable material from you."

Was that a seductive smile? He smirked.

Then Susan's shoulders slumped, and she watched him with her pleading, puppy dog eyes. Tempted to tell her to shove it, he hesitated. He needed a minute to think about it, but visiting time was short. Something told him to seize the opportunity. Anyway, the alternative was to return to his cell and reread a five-year-old 'Mayfair' with sticky pages. She wasn't bad to look at if he ignored her face. At least she filled the blouse. She sat taller than him, with dark brown hair, NHS glasses. A sensible cardigan stretched over her blouse, and a chain with a crucifix dangling between her blouse buttons. Did she want to convert him?

"Look, Susan, isn't it?" She nodded, still smiling, ponytail bouncing. "I'm an inmate on remand, not a convict, I haven't been convicted, and I am innocent, and I'm a born-again atheist, so if you intend converting me, forget it, I'm happy the way I am. But if all you want is to visit and pass the time of day, I've got the next few months. But anything sounding like 'have you thought about God', I'm back in my cell. Deal?"

"Deal," she said with puppy enthusiasm. She stretched over to shake his hand, but Bradley shook his head, rolled his eyes, and looked across at the Prison Officer. Susan withdrew her hand, placing it in her lap, and looked down.

"So, do you want to know why I did it? What nick is like, the food, recreation, what we do in our spare time for amusement, apart from giving ourselves a hand shandy, or in my case used and abused by others? Or is it esoteric, like the philosophy of incarceration?"

"Golly, nothing like that." Susan said, giggling and covering her mouth. "I want to ask you…" she opened a folder and scanned it, adjusting her NHS specs. "Whether the justice system was too hard or too soft on you."

She looked at him, blinking.

"That's it?" said Bradley, almost ridiculing her. "What about guilt and innocence, the victims, life in this five-star establishment?"

"I'll tell you what's hard and soft, love. I'm hard, and he's soft," shouted a prisoner, pointing at Bradley, and eliciting a chuckle from around the room, which the Screw ignored.

Susan looked uneasy, squirmed on the straight-backed metal chair, then coughed, her cheeks turning red and carried on.

"We can discuss whatever you like. Should we talk about practicalities? How often can I see you, weekly? If they'll let me. Do you have other visitors?"

"No other visitors. You're the second in two months."

Susan made notes. "Do you mind?"

Bradley shrugged; it was all the same to him.

"I'd like to ask about your first visitor. Was it a friend or family?"

"My father."

Bradley smirked in disgust, as if he'd tasted a piece of old tripe. He thought it best not to mention Wilson Pinchin's visit. Even he wasn't sure what to make of that, except Pinchin had defended him badly and suggested his mother may be alive but in danger. He wanted to explain more. After all, she wasn't so bad looking when you ignored the zits on her chin, the squint, the glasses, and the 1950s clothes.

"My father is Templeton Maudlin. He's the only family I have."

How much should he tell her, and would it look like complaining?

"Bring me a packet of fags," said Bradley, wanting a reward for his time.

"You know I can't, Bradley, it's illegal, and it would get us both into trouble."

She hunched her shoulders and squirmed again.

"And smoking is bad for you."

"So is prison. I don't smoke them, but I can sell them. Slip them across when the Screws aren't looking. They know the score."

"Depends. Tell me about your father and his visit."

"A couple of weeks ago. He said how ashamed he was of me and how he'd exclude me from his will. There's an irony."

Susan scribbled something into her folder. "So, you weren't happy with his visit. Why is that ironic?"

"He has a way of twisting things. Nothing is ever his fault."

"Many people do that."

"Not like Templeton Maudlin. He carries it to extremes. He's a work of art. His mind is so warped, whole star systems divert to avoid him."

"What does he do?"

"He's an Undertaker and Cremator and enjoys every second of his job. In fact, he loves the job. He hopes I'll take it on when he dies, which I hope won't be long."

"And will you?"

Bradley scoffed and slouched in his chair.

"I'd like the money, but not the business."

"Time's up. Please finish. Visitors, please exit from the rear door," barked the Prison Officer.

"Well, Bradley. Thank you, very interesting. I'll see you next week if you're willing?"

"If you bring the fags."

"We'll see. Thank you," said Susan, closing her folder.

Susan Freeman walked off with the other visitors. He watched her go, paying attention to the knee-length skirt and trainers. He smiled at her walk, which to Bradley, resembled a donkey. She was almost as tall as him and from the back, not a bad sight. Seeing her again might be rewarding.

Chapter 31

In the week following the receipt of the letter telling George her 'services are no longer required', she'd visited Bradley Maudlin in prison, hoping she might get a clue as to her mother's killer, but little came of it. She'd visit Bradley again in a few days. He was no pilchard, although naïve and a soft touch in prison for bully boys and deviants. But he'd be no good to her dead. She had no sympathy for him, he'd seen the killer but he'd remained silent. A coward.

A visit from Sarah from the NCA was unexpected. Ostensibly, she was calling to check on George, but she suspected she wanted to talk. Something was on her mind. They exchanged pleasantries, then an awkward silence.

"Doug's gone missing," said Frolic, pouring it out.

"Two days ago, he aimed to visit you, to see if you could recall anything new. Did he?"

"No, but I was out all yesterday with Charlie and seeing Bradley Maudlin."

Sarah's eyes glazed over and her mouth turned down, bottom lip quivering.

"Are you and Dougie an item?"

George stared at Sarah. It was blunt, but she wasn't uncomfortable asking; better than tiptoeing around it.

"Yeah, something like that." Sarah peered at her hands in her lap.

She had a responsibility to womankind to be ashamed, especially gallivanting with a dork like Dougie. From George's assessment, he was a Mr Bean.

"He's probably following a lead. Fancies himself, does Dougie. How did you land Dougie? Is he married?"

"Stupidity, love, and yes."

"So why don't you phone him at home? His wife will know where he is."

George knew the answer before Sarah spoke; she'd seen enough soldiers in a similar predicament. George groaned and gave Sarah a 'how could you' look.

"His wife knows. She kicked him out. He rented a bedsit. I've been there. He hasn't returned for two days. I've reported him missing to the NCA, but him and me aren't the flavour of the month at the NCA, so I received the usual 'why are you asking us, he's your boyfriend, sort out your own shit'."

Sometimes the brightest fall for the most unlikely characters. George had her share of flirtations, but she drew the line at attached men.

"I'm sure he'll turn up, Sarah; they usually do. Then you can give him his papers."

They laughed, but George saw Dougie had besotted Sarah. If he reappeared, she'd take him back like a long-lost child. They deserved each other. She also had a hunch Dougie may have got himself into trouble and gone missing permanently.

Sarah left, promising to stay in contact. George asked her to keep her updated. As she closed the door, George noticed a plain white card on the front door mat, obviously slipped through the letter box as they were talking. Handwritten in blue fountain pen, a mobile phone number. Neat handwriting, the '*7*' written continental style.

A simple message: "Call this number, Georgina."

She smiled, hoping they'd seized the bait. But would she be the main meal?

Sheila would visit George later in the day, so she left the card on the mantelpiece for Sheila to see. Sheila took an interest in it, which was enough to raise George's suspicions.

She sent the card to Chance, hoping he may pull something from it, fingerprint, maker, origin of the paper, fish, and chip marks, DNA, traceable phone number, whatever. Nothing, not a dent, or fibre from a glove, and the mobile number was a 'throw away'. Someone had taken care.

She waited a couple of days before calling the number. A man answered on the second ring with a curt "Hello."

She gained little from the one word except the lack of accent.

"Hello, this is George Stone, who's speaking?"

"Good afternoon, Miss Stone. Thank you for calling. My name is Moss. I would like to meet you at your convenience."

"Who are you, and why?"

"I will explain when we meet and depending on how it goes, I have a proposition."

There was no point in getting windy. They both knew the game.

"Please be at the seafront in Grain, near the visitors' car park tomorrow, thirteen hundred hours. There's a path to the beach," said Moss.

"Right," said George.

They disconnected at the same time. On the surface, Moss was succinct, even clipped. A businessman, crook, or spy, or all three?

She called Ted, who knocked on her door an hour later.

He left his prosthesis in the hall and hopped into the living room followed by Jaws.

"Right, George, how can I help?"

"Fancy spending the morning in a hide near the beach,

where you can observe the path leading to the sea and the car park?"

Ted didn't even need to think. He was former Infantry, this was his bread and butter, and he knew the terrain.

"Aye, I know a place. Brambles to the right of the track. He may have someone monitoring, I'll get cosy, ready by first light. I'll be able to see who comes and goes; take a few pictures. It's my hobby, so maybe I'll get a few snaps of the sea and the bird life."

George arrived on time for the meeting. Both her Mum and the military had drilled it into her. Her sister failed every time; Charlie was rarely on time or well-prepared. It exasperated both her Mum and her.

George recognised Moss walking along the path two hundred metres away. And if she'd been less diligent, he'd have approached her without her knowledge. Dressed in a dark windcheater, floppy hat, a small rucksack on his back and wearing hiking boots, he could have been any walker. The weather was atrocious with howling winds and drizzle, but this part of the coast attracted winter walkers. She'd dressed the same.

She could surmise he hadn't entered from the car park but by a roundabout route on a secondary path. She ignored him until he stood on the steps to the beach. He puffed on a cheroot, causing a small cloud to develop. The wind blew from the north towards her, and the smell of the cigar enveloped her. As he approached, his smile never reached his eyes, which were as cold as a reptile in winter. Sure enough, it was the same man she'd seen in the car park and at the funeral. As tall as George, fiftyish, handsomely rugged, he carried himself like a man who'd been active all his life. In a different time and place, despite the eyes, George might have found him charming, in an old school way. His smile showed too many teeth, but she imagined him verbally tearing an adversary apart. Hard beyond his looks.

He lifted his hat. "Good afternoon, Miss Stone. I've heard good things about you."

"Good afternoon, Mr Moss. From whom, and what have you heard?"

He fell into step beside her, and they walked south along the path.

She wanted it in the open. She didn't trust 'a nod is as good as a wink', and someone I know knows you.

"A mutual friend. My company deals on confidentiality and personal recommendations."

Her initial attraction towards him faded. His tight-lipped approach didn't impress her.

"I'll accept that for the moment. What's your proposition, and why the skulduggery?"

"My, you are prickly. I hope you're as good at your job as you are brusque. My sources tell me you are. Tell me about your military experience."

He pulled on his small cigar, leaving a cloud of smoke. George didn't like smoking and usually expected others to ask if they could smoke in her presence. Still, she needed to progress this contact, so said nothing. As her Mum had said, looks may capture the eyes, but personality captures the heart. And so far, Moss wasn't scoring high on the latter.

"Mr Moss, you know my military career and what you don't know you don't need to know. Is this a job interview?"

"Yes, sort of. I work for an international company, and I'm looking for someone with your skills for a job. The world is a dangerous place, especially in the UK, where handguns are illegal. Large companies sometimes feel the need to hire insurance."

"Who are you, head of Human Resources, a head hunter for a third party, or someone looking for cheap labour?"

"None of those, Miss Stone. Let's call me the senior executive? Much of our work can attract unwanted attention, and we have use for someone who is not afraid to protect her assets."

"I suspect you know enough about me. The last asset I protected tragically died. What's the company, and what's the job?"

"Actually, you'd be working for me. I'm aware of your previous altercation, hardly your fault. It's difficult to protect the principal against a well-concealed sniper from over four hundred metres, especially in Hermand."

They walked in silence for a few seconds. She mustn't appear too eager. He'd called Helmand by its old name, 'Hermand'. Either he'd received a classical education or he'd served in Afghanistan in the 70s and 80s. Did he intend her to notice such an obvious error?

"I'll consider it. I have your number, and I'll call you."

He stopped, turned towards her, and beamed. That smile would have caused many women to swoon, but she'd seen killers before and he was a killer.

"Come, Miss Stone, what is there to think about? I like you. We can both keep secrets, and I've given you the essentials, nothing to worry you, or for you to research. Your Army career is over, you have a sister lying in a hospital bed, and you have bills to pay. So, you need the work. The rewards could be considerable. So, shall we stop playing games and talk as one adult to another? I'm sure you'll enjoy the work."

Only a madman is sure. And Moss was, in her opinion, a psycho. It seemed to George he could be as blunt as her, which she liked.

"I'll think about it, Mr Moss, and call you, midday tomorrow. Please be ready to explain the 'rewards' package, a date for starting and a location."

She was pushing her luck, but she guessed Moss wanted something from her. What and why? But she was one step nearer to finding out.

"As you wish, Miss Stone." His smile remained fixed.

He marched on, waving dismissively. George watched him walk along the path. He had a long walk to the next exit to the village. She supposed he'd call one of his Russian friends to collect him. She watched him until he was a speck.

George doubted she could provide any additional information to Chance, and suspected Chance knew Moss. She wanted to play her cards close to her chest and let Chance tell her all he knew. Now she sat in her kitchen,

Ted sitting across from her, discussing the previous day's work. She'd provided the pictures taken by Ted to Chance, who after twenty-four hours, contacted George by secure mobile. George put him on speaker.

"George, I have some interesting information. It's best you know with whom you are dealing. Stephen Moss is a native of Russia, real name Sergei Mosin, aged fifty. In his twenties, he served in Afghanistan with the Soviet Special Forces, the Spetsnaz. He last saw combat in Chechnya in 2002. Stephen Moss is the son of Anatoly Mosin, who was a Russian Cabinet Minister and former politburo member with links to the KGB, now called the SVR or '*Sluzhba Vneshney Razvedki Rossiyskoy Federatsii*', otherwise known as the Russian Foreign Intelligence Service. Mosin's area of responsibility in the Soviet Union remains a mystery. During this period, your mother was in direct contact with the father, Anatoly Mosin, and I discussed this with her several times. They met frequently. But, after 1991 and the collapse of the Soviet Union, Anatoly Mosin came into disfavour during the Yeltsin era and consequently demoted to 'Minister'. The United Russia Party tried to 're-educate' him, without a great deal of success. Anatoly Mosin was, and perhaps still is, an ageing oligarch."

"1991 Yeltsin encouraged 'privatisation', which quickly led to power and wealth for a few. In Mosin's case, in payment for his valuable contribution to Mother Russia, they gifted him the privatised 'entertainment' sector, instead of a pension. Few thought Mosin could make a living in the world of gambling and vice. If he used his old KGB methods, so be it. It kept crime in Moscow and St. Petersburg under control. However, after his illustrious past, entertainment wasn't his thing, and he took a low profile."

"In 1999 Putin engaged in a power-struggle with a

group of oligarchs, including Mosin, and reached a 'grand bargain'. It allowed the oligarchs to keep their power, in exchange for their support for the United Russia Party and Putin's government. Putin didn't like Mosin, which can end in disposal. Mosin saw Putin as too shrewd, too powerful, too popular, and too intelligent. Mosin represented the new guard but paid nodding respect to the party and the Russian Government, and quickly became persona non grata with the party. Anatoly Mosin's current whereabouts and status are unknown, but if the old Cold War warrior isn't dead, his days are few. He must be over eighty by now."

"His son Sergei has an ego the size of a London bus. He came to the UK for education in 2010 when the British government let in anyone with the right amount of money. In his case, his father's fortune. He is obsessed with taking British citizenship but also exploiting his father's skills, contacts and growing his dad's modest entertainment empire. Sergei Mosin changed his name to Stephen Moss, and changed his style. On the surface, he is the epitome of an Englishman, but he is not a gentleman."

"There you have it, Georgina. Stephen Moss is a gangster, a thug with pretensions of legitimacy. Make no mistake, he would sell his mother for a Russian Ruble. He has a weakness. He fancies himself as a 'swordsman' with the ladies, and he has a vile temper. A sombre anecdote. Back in Russia he invited a rival and so-called friend to his izba for a weekend break. Whilst there, he locked his rival inside his concrete dry sauna, turned the temperature to high, and left. A week later, his rival's desiccated body was disposed of. Frankly, Georgina, I'm sorry I asked you to get involved in this. Withdraw, if you wish, I can fix it. And eventually I can row back on the 'Services no longer required' thing."

George listened carefully and gave Ted a question mark look. Words were important, and Chance didn't use them lightly. The words, 'eventually I can row back…', disturbed her. So, she either took the job and made it her opportunity to find her mother's killers, or she'd be hung out to dry.

"What is Stephen Moss's track record in the UK? How much is he involved in organised crime?"

"We don't know. If I were to guess, I'd say up to his neck. But to date, we can prove nothing."

George sat for a few moments, deep in thought. Stephen Moss wanted something from her. Whether she could take on both an ex-Spetsnaz soldier, and his criminal empire was another matter.

"Mr Chance, I'm still in. I'll need and appreciate your support."

"That's a given, Georgina. Good luck."

George made the call to Moss, accepted the job, haggled over the 'rewards' package and offered to join him at his residence outside London in one week. The job was residential, she packed. Stephen Moss tried to commit her to an earlier arrival, but she resisted.

She sensed Moss's pique. She smiled to herself and waited on the silent phone line.

"Fine. One week, Miss Stone, and yes, time off every three days to visit your sister."

"Good. I look forward to seeing you then."

"Good day to you," said Moss.

George looked forward to seeing Moss and to getting something done, resulting in requital, even though it scared the living hell out of her.

Chapter 32

Susan Freeman was becoming a regular at the prison. What was this, her third or fourth visit? Bradley's mood improved when he found out Susan Freeman, the higher education student, would visit again. He'd become a fifteen-minute celebrity last time she'd visited. Shepherd escorted him to Josey's malodorous, testosterone fuelled rat's nest called a cell. Josey wanted details, a cheap thrill. He suggested if Bradley gave him details, prison might not be a hellhole. Shepherd stood in the corner, eyes flitting between Josey and Bradley, waiting for Josey to do or say something 'smart' or amusing. Bradley might even give Josey an excuse to start something 'fleshy'.

"Describe her figure to me, exactly. Details, I want details," Josey said, wiping his hands across his uniform tunic after eating a sausage. Shepherd grinned and salivated in the corner.

Bradley did his best, most from his imagination. He doubted Josey cared whether it was fact or fiction. If he told Josey he'd enjoyed foreplay with a bisexual gorilla, he'd get excited. At the end of a demeaning, but from

Josey's viewpoint, and from trouser evidence, momentarily satisfying experience, Bradley looked forward to escaping Josey's cell.

"Next time I want more detail and colour, what's wrong with you? Pay attention, how difficult can it be, and you know the alternative?" Josey scowled, and Shepherd joined in.

"Now leave, and give me value for money, you tosser."

***

Susan Freeman's wish to see him put a smile on his face and quickened his step. Unlike Josey, his keenness stopped there. She didn't compare to the girls he'd known at university. Susan was too immature, and an airhead for his liking; a pencil sucking giggly school girl. Too young for him by a long way, but if he ignored her acne, glasses and lowered his standards, she'd be okay. But behind her facade she might be bright. No one at university could have a global lack of intellectual function.

Hushed voices made the visiting area buzz like a half-tuned radio, decreasing as Bradley entered, as if someone had suddenly slammed a window shut. One or two prisoners looked his way, a few sneered their contempt, and a few watched him. He sensed a minute decrease in hostility. After all, from a captive audience of thousands, she'd chosen him.

She waited for him at a table. He recognised her back, her head on one side, as if she was thinking, her brown shoulder-length hair in a ponytail. Good posture, her back pressed against the chair back. He glanced underneath the chair and saw her legs crossed at the ankles. The last time she'd visited, he'd noticed she tended to concave her chest to hide her assets. Embarrassed perhaps, especially with so many men. She was studying something, probably notes from the last visit or questions she wanted to ask him.

"What are you studying?" he asked.

Susan flinched, then gasped, looking at him, her hand going to her chest. Her eyes widened. She stared at him. He smiled.

"I'm sorry, Susan, I didn't mean to startle you."

"Oh, that's okay, I'm a nervous sort and I scare easily."

She grinned, looking over her glasses, then repositioned them by screwing up her nose. "How have you been, Bradley?" she asked, grasping his hand.

Bradley took the packet of twenty cigarettes from her and pocketed them.

"No physical contact with the prisoners," yelled a Screw. Susan looked across at him and mouthed, 'sorry'.

"I've been okay. Normal stuff. Like a holiday camp. As much slop as you can eat; and sex whether you like it or not. I'm not complaining. What did you want to ask me? What was the subject again, I forgot?"

Susan leafed through her folder, embarrassed. "Erm, it's 'whether the justice system was too hard or too soft on you'. So, is it?"

He leaned back and thought. "Look, Susan. This place is full of innocent victims, but in my case, I am. In answer to your question, yes, the justice system is too hard. My crime is stupidity."

Susan looked at him quizzically, squinting. He interested her. The first since his incarceration. Stupidity or innocence, he couldn't determine.

"What do you mean? I mean, do you want to explain? I mean, can you explain for me? Please," she said in a tremulously excited voice.

His first thought must have been correct. It reinforced his idea she was clueless, but Bradley gave her a condescending smile; an adult to a child. They must have low standards in university these days. Still, there's no harm in telling her a few home truths. Not that she'd understand. The nearest she'd ever been to prison and the criminal fraternity was 'Eastenders'.

"Can I explain? Sure. Will I explain? Depends."

She didn't answer, concern wrinkling her brow. Did she think he wanted something salty?

He broke the second of silence, laughing. "Not that. I have my pride, even in here, and anyway, you're not my type. I like mine more mature and cerebral. No offence, mind."

"None taken." She frowned.

"More fags, another packet, and we'll take it from there."

Her face and shoulders drooped. He thought tears were possible. She wasn't bright enough to think of bringing a spare pack. Never mind more for next time. He smiled; disappointment written across his face, sorry for her limited mental state.

"Next time, three packs. Okay?"

"Two."

He nodded. Where to start. He could tell her his life story; the victim, his father's insistence on precision, controlling everything, even reality itself. His reality was reality; there was no such thing as fantasy. If his father said a fantasy was real, it was his reality for all those in his orbit. Or his obsession with the dead. How weird was that? A round peg in a round hole. But he doubted this middle-class girl, with a privileged upbringing, had the experience, and in her case, the intelligence to understand pain, real pain that turned your skull inside out. She'd never even broken a fingernail. Probably a 'snowflake'.

"You should talk to my father. He'd tell you I did it, my fault. That's his version of reality, not mine."

Bradley sat back in his chair, one arm over the back, not to impress the airhead sitting across from him, but because it looked 'cage' as they called it in prison. She stared at him, her face a mask of anxiety, as if he'd told her he wanted to take her over the table.

"So, who did it? If you didn't?"

"I honestly don't know, even though I saw him; every crease, penetrating stare on his face, and I heard his croaky migrant tone. If the police hadn't come, he'd have killed me too. Big chap, Polish, maybe Eastern European. He could handle himself. The police saved me, and probably the girl too, but I didn't do it. Answering your question, is the justice system too hard on me? Yes. But it would have been easier if I'd told the truth. But my lawyer stopped me."

Susan looked focussed, her mouth ajar, tongue touching her bottom lip. He couldn't have done better if he'd read Roald Dahl to her.

"Why didn't your lawyer save you; tell them you were a victim, a hero, why didn't he tell the police?"

He watched the excitement in her face, her changing body language. She probably wanted to start a protest on his behalf.

"Because Mr Wilson Pinchin was interested in putting me away. A street lawyer would've been better. And who hired him anyway? It wasn't Templeton Maudlin. His usual solicitor friend is a different kettle of fish altogether, and this Pinchin character is in a class of his own."

"Are you saying Pinchin is an accessory to the crime?"

"Well done." He grinned, leaning back, clapping. "I think even the judge who remanded me questioned Wilson Pinchin's ability and or motives. I was a patsy. You know what one of those is, don't you?"

"Yes, a victim. Why didn't the judge act? I'll see the police, or the Governor. We can get your charges dropped or something."

He admired her indignation and enthusiasm for his injustice. She was a drone, revving up, close to taking off, her voice rising until Screws looked across, and even prisoners glanced in her direction, as if the noise disturbed them.

Jesus, not much style, but one hundred per cent for enthusiasm. Bradley could imagine Susan in a fight, she'd be a poodle fighting a Rottweiler, all fur and yap, and nothing more than a meal for the bigger dog, like in prison.

"Calm down." He pointed a finger at her. "You can't do anything. Anyway, what can a student do that I can't? You wanted to know the truth."

Her face returned to a more normal colour from the crimson glow a minute before, but her lips quivered and her teeth clenched.

"Times up, visitors. One minute, then please leave in an orderly manner from the rear door. Do not have physical contact with the person you've been visiting. Thank you," bawled the Screw.

"I'll come to see you next week," said Susan, rising and collecting her papers, which she held across her chest. She was someone searching for a shin to kick.

"Okay, but I want three packs."

"We'll see, Bradley," she said, a stiff smile holding his stare.

For a fleeting moment, she showed something new; focus, backbone, and there was a difference in the way she walked; not like a donkey, more like a predator.

As she left, a couple of prisoners sitting closer to the door stared at her and one of them turned, grinned at Bradley, and blew him a kiss.

"Enjoy your time with Bradley? He's a talker, ain't he, love? He'll be taking his meals through a straw soon, or worse, so this'll be your last visit with him. He won't be here next time, see? But don't worry, Josey Bingham will see you next time. Ask for him by name, he can't wait, and don't forget the fags, Ogfot. And next time wear lipstick, Josey likes lipstick."

***

Safely out of the prison, she met Ted in his Land Rover, George removed the wig and glasses, wiped off the make-up and blew a sigh of relief. Despite his cynicism and disillusionment, Bradley was a good person. He wasn't capable of murder, or anything illegal, except lying under oath. But he'd seen who'd killed her Mum, and he was ripe for turning, if she could find the trigger. Bradley mentioned his father, who he didn't get on with. What was Templeton Maudlin's role in this, and what was his hold over Bradley?

"So, verdict?" asked Ted.

"Good. I'm getting somewhere."

She filled Ted in on the details, and they sat in silence as Ted drove to Grain.

"You'll be starting your new job in a day or so. You need to talk to Chance," said Ted.

George took out the phone given to her by Chance and switched it on, pressed keys two at a time, and it bleeped, showing it was in secure mode. She tapped in Chance's number, and Sam answered on the first ring. Sam had a closer relationship with Chance than she'd originally thought.

"Yes."

"Hello Sam, George here."

"Good afternoon, what can I do for you?"

Sam was the gatekeeper, first line of defence for Chance, also his fixer.

"I'd like to speak to Mr Chance, please. Is he available?"

"Yes, I'll put you through."

A moment later, Chance spoke. It sounded as if he was in another office. Chance could be anywhere, even watching her.

"Good afternoon, Georgina, how was the visit?"

She was eager to make sure Bradley Maudlin remained safe. If the other prisoners broke him, he'd be useless as an informer and a witness.

"Okay. But Bradley is under threat. It's something more sinister than simple natural selection. A lag mentioned Josey Bingham, could you have him checked? We've got to keep him safe, for the moment. Can you do something, Mr Chance?"

She sensed his hesitation. Either his reach didn't extend as far as influencing the prison system, or he didn't see the value. Surely, the prison service could place him in solitary.

"I'm reluctant to do that, Georgina, because it may expose one of my assets in the prison, working on a different job."

"Do it for me, please. If Bradley dies, I'll be annoyed.

He knows far more than he's revealed so far."

Would Chance do it? He needed her.

"I'll see what I can do. Anything else?"

"No. Thanks. I'll be on the job tomorrow. Ted will monitor. He'll give you a bell if he or I need anything."

She clicked off.

"Ted, what does 'Ogfot' mean?"

He laughed, "You impressed them, Ogfot means, 'Only good for one thing'. Your cover is holding."

George and Ted grinned.

Chapter 33

Despite the warm spring morning, Templeton sat shivering on the bench facing the sea. Moss wanted to see him again. Payment was welcome, but he suspected bad news. Knowing you are part of a bigger arrangement but dispensable didn't ease his anxiety. Over the years, the arrangement had been convenient. Moss paid in medicinal prescriptive and Maudlin received bodies. Some were women, but death is an unforgiving master. In return, Maudlin disposed of dead bodies. Neither his disposition nor his appetite suit disposing of life ones.

He watched a gannet wheel high above the waves, circling and performing its characteristic fishing dive. He turned his attention to a Kittiwake, one of his favourites and a gentleman of the bird world. For Templeton, it was the nicest of the gulls. He picked up his binos, thought better of it, laid them next to him and turned his mind to the present burdensomeness.

He was sure Bradley, even with his myriad flaws, would keep his silence. Templeton had convinced himself, his grip on Bradley was unshakeable. But in case of 'force majeure', Moss and his organisation had a long reach, and Moss could ensure Bradley's silence. Even as his son, Bradley was even less important than a hair on Templeton's Maudlin's head. He had always been a problem. Even Templeton's father, Bradley Maudlin's grandfather, had warned Templeton about Bradley. 'He's far too deep thinking is that one, you'd better watch him'.

To date, Bradley Maudlin had been useful to Templeton, but that was his duty, his calling. A select few served the dead, some fulfilled a service to their fathers, and Bradley was the latter. Everyone had foibles, Bradley had an unhealthy interest in 'doing the right thing' regardless of the repercussions for others, especially him. How selfish. Templeton's foible harmed no one and performed a service.

Then there were the two women. He stood and paced, glanced along the promenade, empty except for the occasional dog walker.

"Enjoying the seabirds again, I see, Maudlin," said a voice behind him. His tone suggested Maudlin should spend his time more productively.

How did he do that? Templeton had looked there only seconds ago, and he'd seen nothing.

"Good morning, Mr Moss. I enjoy mornings, when the birds are waking with no one to disturb the peace. Especially when we've had a successful evening in the Crematorium, and the Cremator is cooling. It's so satisfying."

He sucked the air in, self-satisfied.

Moss grimaced. It seemed he had no time for

pleasantries.

"Perhaps. Let's walk. Two men sitting on a seaside bench gazing out to sea looks strange," said Moss, looking down at Maudlin.

Maudlin shivered.

Templeton wondered whether it was less strange to be strolling along the seafront dressed as an undertaker.

Moss said, "My father used to say one can avoid any manner of detection so long as one is beyond suspicion, or devoid of presence. When one is unseen and unseeable, then we are invulnerable. My father was neither the wisest nor the most successful of men. Not someone I regarded as a role model whom I wished to emulate."

Maudlin nodded sagely, barely understanding. "What did your father do?"

"He worked for the government. Not this one, of course."

Maudlin wrinkled his forehead, confused, but remained quiet. He hoped Moss would get to the point. At the last meeting, Maudlin thought about Moss's words for several days.

"It's almost always our wish to remain below the radar, to appear anonymous, harmless. Once we draw attention to ourselves, our effectiveness and therefore, our mission is under threat. Do you see?"

Templeton thought it was a rhetorical question and remained silent. He was unfamiliar with Moss's reasoning, which confused and obfuscated. But he was the boss, as he'd clarified during their last meeting. All Maudlin wanted to know was Moss's plan, but discretion stopped him from asking, and Moss paid him handsomely, and Moss fed Templeton's 'special need' adequately.

"To remain innominate and unhonoured is reward enough in our profession. It is desirable, and positively essential. I'm sure you understand, hmm?"

Templeton supposed he was right, but creases wrinkled his forehead. Did he mean, 'don't draw attention to yourself and don't get caught?'

"Do you recall the last woman you prepared and disposed of?"

A jogger ran past; not a health freak, too heavy. Probably someone who made a new year's resolution. A scrawny dog trotted a few paces behind. Moss remained silent until the man ran out of earshot. The sky was clearing, and they saw the sun rising at their nine o'clock. The reds and yellows scattered amongst the clouds, a sprinkling of sherbet colours.

"What a glorious sight; you see those suns left and right? They're false suns called sun dogs, created by light interacting with atmospheric ice crystals. It may appear God has given us a gift. However, it's mainly man's pollution, and illustrates an important point. All is not what it seems. When we don't know all the facts, we jump to conclusions. Because something is beautiful, it doesn't mean that good accompanies it."

Templeton grasped the basic point but wondered what Moss was blathering about?

"Yes, I recall the woman. I thought she wasn't what she

at first seemed. She may have been East European."

Moss pointed at the sunrise. "And there is my point, exactly. You have neither the full facts nor the intellect to appreciate our mission. Here, the false sunrise is the daughter of the woman you prepared for despatch; her name is 'Georgina'. She will soon be in my pocket and useful, but at the correct time I will deal with her. Your son, Bradley, you don't seem too fond of him, am I right, Maudlin?"

"He cannot escape his punishment. If you're thinking of having him released, I do not agree. I'm happy to see him permanently incarcerated. He must be tried, found guilty, and locked away."

"Dear me, no. I'm not about to allow his release, Maudlin. I'm thinking of something more permanent than that. Do you have any sentimental attachment to him?"

Templeton Maudlin gulped. Whilst he wasn't fond of Bradley, and happy to see the back of him, he would not endorse his expiration. The boy had been an encumbrance. He saw no use for him. But it would have to be conducted with care, to remove any evidence that may point to him.

"No, Mr Moss, Bradley is nothing to me. I assume the closure would seem 'natural'?"

Moss huffed, "There would be no link to you, or me. Are you content?"

Maudlin nodded.

"A 'Yes' or a 'No' will suffice."

"Yes, damn it. Yes!"

"Good, that's final. However, I offer this simple instruction; the other girl, the one in hospital, is an easier customer. I shall want you to attend to that issue, so start planning, but do nothing, yet."

Maudlin stared at Moss in disbelief. Was he suggesting that Maudlin terminate the girl? That was out of the question. He needed to avoid that eventuality.

Moss marched on at a faster pace, leaving Templeton Maudlin in his wake, waving back at Maudlin in silence.

Chapter 34

For Bradley, prison life meant routine drudgery, constant vigilance, to see if the inmates wanted a laugh at his expense or worse, and use him for their pleasure, physical or mental. There were no friends in prison, only accomplices or fellow prisoners, harmless, but prepared to fend for themselves. Prison, like most institutions, works. The weakest at the bottom, received the most aggro, the majority in the middle operated mainly below the radar, a few at the top abused those at the bottom. If a prisoner resisted intimidation, most cons moved on to a weaker mark.

Despite attempting to keep a low profile, Bradley was that weaker mark, to cons and prison staff alike. For the Screws, it made life easy. They knew who to target when trouble brewed, which was rare; unless there was a challenge to the established order. Because of his 'on remand' status, Bradley Maudlin was 'low risk' and laundry work was easy and normally harmless.

"Maudlin," shouted the Screw, so the whole laundry heard him. "Visit tomorrow, fifteen hundred hours. Same visitor as last time, if you're a good boy and get this stinking lot finished tonight. You can work late with Bingham and Shepherd. If you don't finish it, the visit's cancelled, clear?"

"Clear," said Bradley.

Sniggering infiltrated the prisoners' chat and banter. Bingham, otherwise known as Josey, strolled towards Bradley, as if he was walking in the park.

Bradley loathed his Northern abrasiveness. "So Bradders, tonight's the night, it's you and me, alone amongst these lovely soft sheets. Can't wait."

As Josey turned away, he blew Bradley a kiss.

Shepherd laughed, but pretended to hide it, and looked at the others, amused or deaf, relieved they were off the hook.

***

After the evening meal, which Bradley ate alone, he passed through the gate to the laundry. The Screw made a cursory search, but everyone knew Bradley was 'clean' and least expected to have snout, a weapon, or illicit material. A second search; the Screw yawned, barely acknowledged Bradley's presence, ran his hand along his arm and let him pass, never breaking his chewing gum rhythm.

"Bingham's in the laundry. Enjoy yourselves, but try to keep the squealing to a dull scream."

Bradley ignored him and walked the twenty metres round a corner, to where the industrial washers thrashed the prisoners' washing to a lighter shade of grey. Screws couldn't see them, which was good for what Josey had in mind. With no chance of a Screw hearing a scream, let alone a squeal over the noise of the machines, Bradley's guts loosened. A screw usually supervised the laundry work, but staff shortages and a payoff ensured he'd be on other duties.

Shepherd kept watch and announced Bradley's arrival.

"She's arrived, Josey. Fun time."

With nothing to say, Bradley stood silently, running his palms down his trousers to dry them. All three knew the game plan. Josey would punch Bradley to the ground, enough to call it an 'industrial accident'. He should defend himself, but what was the point against even one? Early in his prison career, he'd realised, he'd best take the punishment and whatever else they wanted and not complain. His constitution and bearing suggested 'weakling' and someone else's plaything.

With Josey's permission and under his supervision, Shepherd took his share. A beating provided pleasure, but tonight a beating wouldn't be enough. Bradley doubted he'd be in a fit state to meet his visitor tomorrow.

Sweat ran off Bradley's face, and he shook. He wouldn't blubber and give them even more gratification, and more to brag about later to their devotees, disciples, and subordinates. Bradley stood, his back to a dryer to distance himself from Josey. The machine's vibrations ran the length of his spine, and the heat from the dryer caused sweat to run between the cheeks of his buttocks. Josey took two strides towards him and pushed him against the curved steel surface, bending him over backwards. Grabbing hold of Bradley's shirt and jacket at the neck, he raised Bradley onto his toes. Bradley saw the blackened, broken skin on Josey's hands, his filthy fingernails digging under his chin, and Bradley attempted to push Josey away.

"Please… ," said Bradley.

He'd promised himself he wouldn't blubber, and blubbering what he was doing.

"Please?" said Josey, giggling.

"She wants more. Manners as well. She even says 'Please', Josey. Give her more, why don't you?"

"Come on, Bradders, it's better when I have to fight for it," said Josey in Bradley's ear. His lips almost touched him and a gob of spittle ran into his ear.

"You were a naughty boy on the outside. I've special permission tonight, and paid well to make this your last time. So, who's a lucky boy?"

Gobs of saliva dripped from Bradley's chin; his eyes pleaded. He'd heard of contracts carried out inside. So, this was his finale.

"Please, no, don't kill me, please."

Bradley felt something else trickle down his leg and realised his bladder had surrendered to fear. Josey lowered his gaze, scowled, hardened his strangling grip, and pressed Bradley's head against the warm steel of the dryer. With his right hand, Josey punched him below the rib cage. Bradley let out a grunt and gasped, and tried to double up with pain, but Josey kept a tight hold on his neck and repeatedly punched him in short jabs, drawing back his right fist and hitting the same point. With each punch, Bradley felt himself deflating, air expelled, sure he'd never breathe again. He wanted this to end, painlessly and quickly.

Josey released Bradley, who slumped to the ground, gasping, and dribbling saliva until a pool formed on the ground beneath his chin, the fluorescent light making it sparkle. He curled into a foetal position, his face pressed against the filthy concrete floor, his knees drawn to his chest to ease the pain. A boot found his kidney, and he rolled onto his side. Josey stood over him, Shepherd waiting for his turn. It couldn't come soon enough for Shepherd. He looked at Josey's rotten toothed grin, Shepherd stood two paces behind him, salivating in anticipation. Bradley pushed his forehead into the ground to ease the chest pain, barely able to breathe but reflexes forced him to gulp air into his burning lungs. Josey's boot touched his face. He waited, expecting a kick in the face, or a demand for Bradley to clean his boots with his tongue. If they planned to kill him, he'd die on the floor, no boot licking, no more pleading, simply death's timely release.

The screws left the laundry lit day and night; ideal for extracurricular activity. Sometimes prisoners paid screws to let them use the laundry for drugs or smoking pot. He'd smelt the same thing at home. He'd even seen Templeton comatose in his study, a blanket laid over him and the place stinking of sickly-sweet flowers, like an old lady's parlour, his opium pipe by his side.

Had Josey kicked him in the head? Had he lost an eye? The dryers had stopped.

Josey grunted, and Shepherd shouted. "Lights! Switch on the truckin' lights."

"We're sharkin' in here and I can't see a bloody thing," shrieked Josey, referring to the colloquial term for having a good time at another inmate's expense. But a slight shudder broke into his voice. The lack of windows in the laundry magnified the darkness as black as his father's drugged out heart.

The discrete sounds of the three inmates. Bradley still wheezing, Josey rasping from a lifetime of smoking, and Shepherd's fear of the dark betrayed by his short, harsh breaths. Bradley considered crawling into a corner to die, but they'd find him when the lights came on. He crawled a few feet and lay still, trying to control his breathing.

Something invaded his senses; a dull thud, a body, or head against the metal dryer. Bradley jerked in surprise, pressing a hand over his mouth to control an outcry. A grunt, another dull thud, same as the first but less intense. Josey's rasping stopped. He recognised Josey's grunt, but a grunt not of pleasure, but pain. The man was being beaten. Bradley shuffled further away to another dryer and clung to a steel pipe.

"Let me out. Truckin' hell, someone's trying to kill us!" screeched Shepherd, running blind toward the gate. A curse, a tumble, then silence.

Bradley thought about the possibilities; a grab for power to change the order of things or someone settling a score. The latter could be vicious, someone would receive a fractured skull by slipping in the shower, or a wannabe losing an eye by having his face slammed against the inside of a sink. But Bradley threatened no one, least of all the cons at the top of the pile. He'd keep quiet and wait for the lights to come back on. Would the new boss want what Josey used to get? He had no way of knowing, but silence was his best defence.

The sound of Shepherd's voice returned him to the

cold concrete, and the smell of soiled laundry. "No, please. It wasn't me. I didn't do it. I'm not part of Josey's gang. Honest!"

He heard dragging and imagined Shepherd dragged backwards by his collar.

"Please, please. No," said Shepherd, pleading.

A dull thud followed by a grinding crunch of a blunt weapon on skull. A specialist in his craft. He imagined Shepherd's head collapsing and reshaped under someone's oversized fist. If the attacker could silence Josey, Bradley had no chance. A soft 'plump', something hitting the ground a few metres away, then silence descending, broken only by Bradley's heavy breathing.

"Get up," said the attacker.

Bradley clung to the pipe, praying for the man to leave. The last thing he wanted was Josey and Shepherd's punishment.

"Now!"

The tone didn't ask for subservience; he expected it. Bradley guessed it wasn't the man's first time. The attacker knew where to find him. If he wanted to kill him, Bradley had no defence and no hope of a Screw coming to his rescue. Not the usual power grab, but maybe a debt paid off or a contract. He scurried onto all fours and scrambled to his feet. He reached out to touch whoever talked to him, but his hand fell on emptiness. A hand grabbed hold of his shoulder and spun him. Bradley faced the man. A sharp light caught him, probably a LED torch. He raised an arm to protect his eyes. After a few seconds, he lowered his arm and squinted. He saw a shape. Despite Bradley's height, the man was taller and broader than him.

"Listen, squirrel head. I'm going to hurt you, not kill you. Okay?"

Bradley nodded, and the man grunted. He tried to place the accent but failed. Not an inmate from his wing. It wasn't posh, but neither was it a working dialect.

"This is how it was," said his saviour. "Josey climbed inside the dryer to get stuff out and Shepherd attacked you, the lights went out, you slammed the dryer door shut and the machine started. You don't know how. You sucker punched Shepherd and beat him to a pulp? Josey, an accident, and Shepherd, self-defence. Okay? Tell me the story."

"Josey, an accident, got stuck in the dryer and I beat Shepherd in self-defence," mumbled Bradley.

"Why?" asked Bradley with a shaking voice.

"Someone's looking out for you. You've got a visit tomorrow. Cooperate. Got it?"

Bradley nodded.

Bradley had heard what the man could do. No threat was necessary. His lifesaver shone the light on Josey first, then Shepherd. He grimaced at the blood oozing from Josey's head wound, and one arm probably broken. Shepherd's injuries appeared superficial, but Bradley wasn't so sure. Despite having seen more than a few dead bodies, and peering through the LED light, he thought Josey and Shepherd may live.

"They'll be out for a while," said the man. "Get Josey

in a tumble dryer, close it and lock it."

Josey was bulky, like moving a huge sack of potatoes, but given a supreme effort and time, he could inch him towards the dryer. His hands fumbled with the locking mechanism, and the door swung open. A torch shone on Josey, and Bradley took Josey's arms and dragged. The man watched as Bradley struggled and swore, finally getting Josey's head and upper body into the dryer. The rescuer lifted Josey's legs, bent him double, and pushed until Josey was nothing more than a pile of washing. He slammed the door and locked the mechanism.

"When the lights come on, the dryer will start; lie still and wait for the Screws to find you. Do not raise the alarm. When they find you, look worried, frightened, as if you're traumatised. That won't be too difficult. Listen numbnuts, your strength is in here." he wrapped Bradley on the head with his knuckles. "So, use your brain and stop acting like a tart. Now, put both hands flat on the floor."

Without warning, he stamped on Bradley's hands, then slammed a fist into his ribs. Prepared for neither, Bradley slumped to the ground, trying to breathe. The punch made Josey's assault feel like a fairy kiss. Bradley felt a rib break. A boot to Bradley's chest, a second rib broke. He tried to cough, wishing he hadn't, and darkness descended on him.

***

Bradley felt himself lifted and carried, whispery voices, sometimes resembling echoes. He mumbled, then realised it might be more expedient to feign unconsciousness. That was easy; the pain made it difficult to open his eyes or move a muscle, and he was scared. Easier to close his eyes, relax and let others do the work. He found he could learn a good deal using this minor deception. Several voices, but he could not identify any except Lockhart's. All seemed frenetic, concerned for their own well-being and above all, redirecting blame. Their blathering attempted to justify their way out of trouble. What happened and how to limit the damage to them. Violence and injury in the prison were normal, but death because of a Prison Officer's negligence would lead to prosecution and prison for the warders concerned. Bradley listened to their discussion of his demise, and panic momentarily washed over him. They suggested suffocation, death by traumatic injury or even throwing him down a staircase, to resolve the 'Maudlin Problem', as they called it. After asking if Maudlin was unconscious and being reassured he was, Lockhart argued that a second death would elicit an inquiry and police investigation. So he vetoed Bradley's murder, not through any humane motive but simple self-preservation. The doctor's arrival set the course of action in concrete. He pronounced Josey Bingham dead at the scene, and treated Shepherd's critical injuries before ordering paramedics to take him away to the hospital.

The doctor demanded space to work on Bradley, shooing the prison officers out of the corridor where Bradley had been deposited. Bradley guessed the doctor knew he was faking unconsciousness, and he talked to Bradley in a conversational tone.

"Now how did this happen, Maudlin? Quite minor head injuries, but two broken ribs and crushed hands. But I'd guess, not because you beat those two cons to within an inch of their lives. So how? Let me guess; you didn't get these hand injuries in a fight. Am I right? As for your ribs, enough to break them, but not enough to cause complications. Interesting, inflicted by an expert. You fared better than Shepherd. He will survive, but he'll spend weeks in hospital and traction and I doubt you'll ever see him again. Your head injuries are slight and wouldn't cause a coma or unconsciousness, but enough to cause amnesia; if that is what you want, Bradley. If you understand me, flutter your eyes." The doctor waited. "Good, so we understand each other. I don't know what happened in the laundry, and I'm not bothered but, if carried out to its conclusion, it would not have benefited your health. I know your predicament because of prison gossip, and I don't like it. But I'm feeling magnanimous today, and I wish to give you a fighting chance. So, when you leave my nurse's tender mercies tomorrow, your life could go one of two ways: either carry on as you are, and someone takes over from Bingham and he and his friends use you as their personal whore. Or, if you decide you don't like that option, I can let it be known that you have the constitution of a horse, but are as crazy as a gorilla with a 'Trinidad Moruga Scorpion Pepper' in its anus. One twitch for option one and two twitches for option two. Good, that's settled. Now, I'm going to inject you with something soothing and leave you to my nurse. I will discharge you tomorrow from the prison Health Centre. And remember, Bradley, tomorrow you will be a changed man. Goodnight."

Bradley drifted into a drugged sleep, to a world where many respected him but a few loved him. Above all, his mother visited his new Dali-esque world. He asked about his father and the pledge he'd given. She was adamant; he was free of his pledge and must rid himself of the ogre, Templeton Maudlin. They talked. She regretted she hadn't been around to teach him self-respect, probity, courage, and inner strength. His dream persisted. When he weakened, she insisted, when he doubted, she shook him and reinforced, and when she was satisfied, she handed him over to a specialist in 'crazy', who gave him a master class in surviving in a world inhabited by 'normals'. Only then did she let him sleep the dreamless repose of a man at ease with himself. At midday, he surfaced to the smell of cleaning fluid and food, and the Health Centre nurse asking how he felt. Finally, in a state of equanimity, he was ready to face the world.

Chapter 35

The drive to Moss's address took one hour. Charlie's condition filled her mind; she hadn't deteriorated, but neither had she improved. The doctor's original limited optimism was now ambivalent. The police's interest in Charlie had waned, and George worried about Charlie's safety. She could ask Chance for a favour, but even he couldn't give Charlie twenty-four-hour protection. Ted and George visited Charlie as frequently as they could, and she'd convinced herself Charlie would be fine in a hospital. Ted had also agreed to visit Charlie each day she was away. Despite being in a coma, George explained to Charlie she could trust Ted.

Moss's Georgian house, gated and guarded, was twenty miles south of London. An out-of-place bloke in a dark suit and anorak stood at the gate.

Another guard stood on the steps to the front door. The guard waved her through the gates at the side of the house leading onto a path, then to an underground car park where several cars were parked. As she parked her Ford Focus, removing her rolling suitcase, rucksack, and holdall, a man arrived with a 'couldn't give a toss' attitude. Shorter than George, probably overdosed on steroids, his suit jacket bulging at the arms.

George loaded herself with luggage as the man approached, his feet slapping against the concrete.

"Come with me, Miss Georgina Stone," he said in a heavy Russian accent.

"Let me take case," he said, chin pointing towards the rolling case.

George pulled away and shrugged off the man's offer of help. She needed to prove her worth right away.

The man shrugged and muttered, "Lesbian."

He walked a pace in front of George and despite a grinding ache in her arm; she kept pace with him as they entered the lift, where they stood in silence. The bodybuilder stared at himself in the mirror, flexing his upper arms. As the lift door opened, he turned and smiled.

"Your room on top floor, no lift, you need help?"

His self-satisfied grin gave her strength. George imagined the bodybuilder's plan; she'd cave in to his charms, thank him for looking after her, swoon, and invite him to her room.

"No, thanks, I can manage."

She gave him a British Airways smile and didn't slow her pace until the third floor, when she was sure he was out of sight and earshot.

"Boss will see you in lounge when freshened up, lady," he bellowed up the stairs.

Moss waited in the lounge, whisky in one hand, thin cigar in the other, leaning on the mantelpiece, his foot resting on the polished brass fireplace surround, and a fire blazed in the hearth. As Chance had warned her, Moss resembled a foreigner's idea of an English aristocrat. Prints of hunting and coastal scenes hung on the walls.

In contrast to when they'd met on the beach, Moss wore a dark blue lounge suit, looking like a well-heeled politician. He approached George, guiding her to an easy chair. He sat close to her, their knees almost touching, and gave her his smile, accompanied by those crocodile eyes.

"I apologise for the secrecy surrounding my business and around my work, but until I know you're on board, it's a necessary precaution. Now let me fill you in on the job."

George smiled. "Call me George, everyone else does."

"I shall call you Georgina. I like that name. A drink? What's your poison?"

George prickled and froze; Chance had said the same thing.

"Water, please, fizzy."

His eyes narrowed, and he frowned, but didn't serve the drink.

"You are no doubt wondering why I need you. This is my primary residence; I also have one on the coast. You may have gathered, most of my employees are East European. As much as I love this country and respect the inhabitants, I use the best, most able employees I can hire. Also, I must like them, if there's no chemistry it doesn't work for me and I rarely, if ever, make a mistake with my employees, but if I do, I discontinue their services. I do not tolerate failure."

How many had seen their 'services discontinued'? She understood his threat, but this was 21st Century England, and even a Russian gangster couldn't kill without consequences. Her mind turned to Alexander Litvinenko, and her own mother. It was possible this man, sitting not a metre from her, had ordered her mother's death. She could try to kill Moss where he sat, but it was doubtful she'd succeed. She also needed to know the person who had executed her mother and why. His background as ex-Soviet and Russian Spetsnaz meant he wouldn't be a pushover, even though he was past his prime. Moss could wait.

George nodded, not so much to agree, but to show Moss she was on board.

"Your job, I have a demanding and attractive wife, who leads a full and active life. You will look after her, keep her out of harm's way, ensure she does not associate with or is seduced by the wrong company, and she must not attract attention towards me or my business. You understand?"

George understood all right, Moss had hooked a trophy wife, a spoilt brat, half his age, with a mouth the size of the Dartford Tunnel who could be mischievous. George's job was to babysit his wife, whilst pandering to her needs. George accepted that, so long as it didn't interfere with her own mission. The wife was a means to an end.

"And where is your wife now, and when will I meet her?"

"She is away for two weeks."

George detected a change in his voice, bitterness, even though he didn't break off eye contact. Moss hardly ever blinked when he talked. Most people glanced away occasionally, but Moss didn't. He fixed his victim with his stare.

"She's in the south of France, taking the sun, so learn who my staff are, get to know them, and acquaint yourself with the working routine and practises. I demand absolute loyalty to me and my enterprise and complete discretion. Whatever happens within these walls or indeed within my organisation stays here. Are you clear, Georgina?"

George said, "Clear and yes."

"Good." He stared at George, weighing her up. Satisfied, he asked, "Do you have a problem carrying a concealed weapon?"

She gasped in mock surprise, but she didn't mind; she expected it, but he expected her to react.

"Mr Moss, you know British law, handguns, concealed or otherwise, are illegal in Britain."

They waited, George with a neutral, unblinking stare, Moss with a fixed grin. She broke the impasse. "But I have no objections, and I'd like to handle one again."

"Good. Oleg, the person who met you, handles the armoury and ammunition, and we have a firing range beneath the car park. Use it at your discretion. It is soundproof. You will carry a weapon when you are on duty for me. Do you have questions?"

"So, I'm employed as your wife's minder, troubleshooter, and fixer. What am I supposed to do until then, and why the rush for me to be here now?"

Moss grinned, "How refreshingly blunt and charming."

'Patronising bastard,' thought George.

"I have activities ongoing, and I will shortly be one man down. Tonight, you will accompany me on one such activity. Today, meet your fellow operatives. See Oleg, he will brief you, give you a weapon, et cetera."

There was a solid knock on the door and a five-thousand-dollar suit, silk shirt and crocodile shoes walked in; 'Sunset Strip' pimp written all over him. He ignored George and walked over to Moss, grinning. Moss rose from his seat to greet the newcomer. They shook hands like old friends, but George sensed the fondness was one way. Moss turned his smile towards George to introduce her.

"Tony, this is Georgina, she's joining us."

George stood and shook a slender hand with a firm grip. "Nice to see you."

"I'm sure we'll get to know each other, Georgina, I look forward to it."

He held onto George's hand, resisting her attempt to pull away; he was propositioning her. His gaze said 'when and where'. She fixed her smile and wrenched her hand away. She didn't want enemies this soon, but in the twenty seconds she'd known him, she disliked him.

"So, you'll be working for me in the club, Georgina, I can't wait."

"Not in the club, she'll work for me, although I'll bring her along tonight to see how you operate."

Moss gave Tony a warning look. Did he consider George his property? That's the way it seemed.

"It will be my pleasure," said Tony.

"Tell me, Tony, how was the action last night, no trouble? I see the takings were down again."

Moss's gaze never left Tony's; his grin fixed.

"Action was slow, no trouble. We're going through a lean patch, but it will pick up, I assure you."

"Good, I know it will."

"Georgina, I won't keep you, please see Oleg."

She left the room, thinking about the staff. So far, a bodybuilder, a pimp, and Moss.

Oleg sat in the kitchen, eating with two men and a woman; they glanced her way without acknowledging her. A short woman speaking Russian threw out a comment at her expense; two men laughed. A third man, tall, athletic, permanent grin, sat apart and took no part in the conversation.

George needed to get on with her fellow 'operatives' and put out her hand.

"Hi, I'm George Stone. New in today. Call me

George."

A Geordie voice answered. "Hello, George. I'm Tom, I'm new too, I arrived a few weeks ago."

Oleg pointed a Cumberland sausage sized finger at her. "Never mind chat. Come with, and I fix you up. We take stairs, make legs strong."

They descended a flight of concrete stairs to the car park level. A lockable metal door between each floor. He led her through to the lower floor and locked the door behind them. She assumed this was the firing range, armoury, and ammunition store. It wasn't the best practice to have all three in one place, but the Russian mafia worked to their own rules. A sharp crack of a handgun firing, and for a moment she thought she'd have a flashback. A searing pain streaked through her still weak shoulder, and her head spun. Another crack, and her legs buckled. This was the last thing she wanted. Glancing at Oleg, he was in front of her and wasn't aware of her distress. Pull yourself together, girl, was all she thought and forced her legs to walk, keeping contact with the cold concrete of the wall.

Oleg turned to her. She forced a smile. "Are you okay, lady?"

"Fine, Oleg, lead on."

Oleg sneered, "Sound of gunfire can do that to you, but not me. I from Norilsk. Much below freezing, tough. Here is armoury. I select weapon for you. Lady's gun."

"I'll select my own, Mr Moss's orders."

Oleg's eyebrows met in the middle, and he squeezed

them together, scowling. Despite Moss and Oleg being Russian, she'd bet there was history or mistrust between them.

"Okay. You select."

He opened a metal cabinet and showed George the selection.

She was familiar with three main handguns. Browning Hi-Power, SIG Sauer P226, Glock 17 Generation 4. They all used the same ammunition, the 9×19 mm Parabellum. But she'd also used the Smith & Wesson SW9VE, used by the Afghan National Army (AFN). A Browning Hi-Power, heavy and almost impossible to conceal. The Glock 17 was lightest and a Makarov pistol, a Russian semi-automatic 9 x18mm, reliable but non-standard ammunition, and a Glock 19 Modular Optic System with the possibility of attaching a specialised laser sighting mechanism. She took a Glock 17. It held 17 rounds in a witness sighting magazine. Light, one inch thick, essential if she was to conceal it. She noticed the weapon had the Internal Locking System (ILS), which was the bane of most soldiers' lives, but the dimple safety keys prevented it firing or being stripped.

Oleg smiled. "Okay, choice for lady; I get ammunition, you have practice."

He gave her a box of fifty rounds, and she went into the range. Three targets were set at twenty-five metres. They were on manual pulleys and lit by overhead fluorescent lighting. Behind the targets was the Primary Impact Berm, a sandbank, to catch the spent rounds. The firer on the range looked like another minder, muscular, tall, dark hair, thirties, athletic, but she'd bet not a druggie. He finished firing, made safe, looked her way, and removed his ear defenders.

"Hi, I'm Andrei, are you the new wife minder?" he asked in accented English. He had a warm, open face. No attempt at sarcasm.

"That's me. I'm George. How many of us are here?"

"Five. Mr Moss, Oleg, Tom, me and now you. Those outside the house are British hired help. They don't live here. Unarmed."

"The woman?" asked George.

"Admin staff."

"I'm finishing, but I'd like to watch, if you don't mind?" asked Andrei.

"Sure. Getting my hand in."

"Afghanistan?"

"Yes. You?"

"Russian military service. Afghanistan and Syria, finally private. I've worked for Stephen for a while."

"And?"

"He's hard but straight. Employment is brief if you screw him over or don't measure up."

George stripped the weapon, wiped it down, reassembled it, and prepared four times ten round magazines. She fired off ten rounds at the head and ten at the centre of the target, wheeled it in and studied it for a minute, calculating the change. Not bad, considering she hadn't fired a weapon in months. She was firing right, which she could adjust. Andrei stood behind her, watching; Moss would get a report soon enough. Changing out the second empty magazine, she noticed Oleg watching, but talking to Andrei animatedly.

She fired off the remaining thirty rounds, the last ten rapid fire, cleared the weapon, showed the open breach to Andrei, and wound in her target.

She'd made several 3-inch groupings from twenty-five yards. Not bad. Taking the paper target, she folded it, and replaced it with a new target. Oleg clapped a slow clap and scowled.

"Annie Oakley, let's see what you like with real target."

He walked off until Andrei yanked him around by the shoulder and pushed his face into Oleg's, his back to the wall. Andrei was taller, and he looked down at Oleg, speaking slowly, quietly. There was history between the two, with Andrei using it as a face-off with the bodybuilder. The latter remained silent until Andrei let him go. Oleg straightened his clothes, glanced at George, clenched his fist, gave her a middle finger, and hunching his back, slunk away.

"Sorry, George. Some of my fellow Russians are uncivilised, especially those from Siberia, where it's cold and their women don't know how to handle their men."

George rolled her eyes, she'd heard it all before from squaddies, who could teach this Russian all about mockery and worse.

"Or like most men, his brains are in his balls. Thanks,

but I can take care of myself, and I'll fight that fight on my own."

She holstered the weapon in the small of her back and put two full magazines in her rucksack. But she needed an ally whilst she was on enemy territory, and she guessed Andrei was more civilised than most.

Andrei shook his head. "Okay, I understand. Are you women's lib or a lesbian?"

"No, to both. And what is it with Russian men and lesbians? I must prove myself. Do me a favour, keep out of my way."

Andrei laughed and shook his head. "British women."

She liked him, but hoped she wouldn't have to kill him.

Chapter 36

George glanced at herself in the mirror. Not vanity, but checking she was up to snuff. She wore a dark trouser suit with a longish jacket to hide the holster but didn't expect to use the weapon this early. She hoped tonight would be a 'look-see'.

Oleg waited in the foyer. He eyed her up, grimaced, and turned his back on her.

"You sit in front of the car, with the driver, I sit with Mr Moss."

She answered without looking at him. "I'm the newbie. I'll do as I'm told."

The car drew up to the front of the house. Moss ignored them, walked past, and got into the back of the BMW.

"George, in the back with me," he shouted as the rear door slammed shut.

She quickened her pace and climbed into the car beside Moss. They set off in awkward silence until Oleg spoke in Russian and Moss answered in English, "Speak English, you Siberian oaf."

Oleg sat in silence, sulking. That answered a question about Moss's relationship with Oleg.

It rained as they passed Darent Valley Hospital and an Ambulance swept past them, ejecting spray. Ambulances were common, even on a Sunday night, but she hoped they wouldn't need one tonight. They headed towards Dartford town centre, which was hotting up, but swept on towards Fawkham and stopped at locked gates.

"This is the Moon Dance Club, run by Tony Daglio, who you met this morning. It's a private club and tonight it will be quiet. Keep out of trouble, watch, and learn. If you don't like what you see tonight, I've made a mistake," he scowled, staring out of the window. She nodded, but if he saw her, he didn't acknowledge it, his scowl said enough.

Inside the club, George fell in behind Moss with Oleg on his other side. Several rooms led off from the foyer. Heavy metal music assaulted her hearing. A 'heavy' gave them entry to a side room. Escape, if needed, could be a problem. She took a few seconds to see through the disco lights. Slow music took over. The floor had a central sunken area and there appeared to be several couples dancing. A pole dancer on the stage made a half-hearted attempt to interest the few punters without success. Cheap perfume, tobacco, and testosterone pervaded the club. George recognised the stench; she'd been in enough barracks. They made their way around the walkway surrounding the sunken floor, Moss leading. A spiral stairway led onto a balcony used to view activity below.

Along a corridor, Moss walked into Tony's office without knocking. Tony Daglio sat behind a desk, sipping from a whisky tumbler, a phone to his ear, chewing the cud about women. Daglio waved to Moss, who sat opposite him with Oleg and George standing either side of Moss.

Tony sat back, taking his time, speaking excitedly, eyes wide. George guessed he was using cocaine. Moss lifted a finger towards Oleg and pointed at the phone. Oleg walked around the desk, snatched the phone out of Tony's grasp, slammed it on the desk, and resumed his place. Tony's eyebrows squeezed together. He growled, stared at Moss, his eyes bulging, mouth hanging open. He looked at Moss for a few seconds and his demeanour changed.

"Stephen, what do I owe this pleasure?" he said, his speech tripping over itself, his arms open in a welcoming gesture. "Let me get you and your colleagues a drink. What will it be?"

"Scotch. My associates don't drink."

Tony went to the bar and poured Moss's drink.

"This is a fine malt, twenty years old from the Isle of West Linga, Shetland, peaty but nice. I get it shipped. Can I interest you in dinner, Stephen?"

Daglio's pupils dilated. Drugs, fear, and drink controlled his body language. He stood in front of Moss like a naughty schoolboy. Moss sipped his drink and waited a few moments. "Sit," said Moss.

Tony tumbled into this chair behind the desk.

"Or one of my girls. I have a new one. Your type."

Moss waited.

"What, Stephen?"

Daglio slumped, running out of energy and ideas.

"I want to know why, Tony?"

Tony opened his hands, palms up and shrugged his shoulders. "Why, what? I've done nothing. On my children's lives."

"Tell me everything, Tony, from the beginning, you'll feel better."

"God help me, I couldn't help it, I needed money."

His head dropped, and he looked at the floor between his feet, sobbing. Either an excellent actor, or guilty as hell.

"Money for what, drugs? You know how I feel about that, Tony, and women, too. You can screw club girls."

Tony nodded his head and sat back in the chair, tears, and snot dripping down his chin.

"Please, Stephen, last time, a last chance, I won't screw up again."

George watched Moss in her peripheral vision. He looked at Tony almost benevolently.

"Okay, Tony. I'm not a cruel man, I'm fair, this is your last time."

He took a handkerchief from his top pocket, gave it to Oleg and waved towards Tony Daglio.

Oleg stood beside Tony and handed him the handkerchief. He blew his nose. Oleg removed his jacket and dropped it on the floor. He grabbed Tony's hair and slammed his face into the desktop. A crunch and a spray of blood evidenced his nose's destruction. Oleg wrenched him back over the chair, straddled him, and landed roundhouse punches to his head until his face resembled a car crash.

George watched, but didn't believe even these Russian thugs would kill him. Oleg studied his handiwork, grunted, and looked at Moss.

"Tony, that was for skimming twenty-five per cent off the top. I am in a good mood. For that crime, I'll let you keep your miserable life. But for screwing my wife for the past year," Moss raised his voice, which George suspected was for effect. "The woman I hired you to protect, look after, guard like a precious jewel, but you took her and abused my trust. You had more girls than you could ever use, but you used my personal property. I cannot forgive that. Oleg."

Oleg studied the beaten form and set about Tony's body. He was still conscious, probably from the cocaine. He grinned, even as a boot contacted his kidneys. Tony rolled himself into a ball to lessen the punishment. A sound came from Tony's mouth, bubbles. He was trying to say something.

"What are you saying, Tony? Did I hear 'sorry'?"

Tony grinned, his eyes wide with the effects of the drugs.

"She begged for it, Stephen, wanted it, begged for more. I did you a favour, you Russian prick."

Moss walked around the desk and stood over Tony, surveying Oleg's handiwork. He pushed Oleg away.

"Remember this Tony and remember who spared your life, this once."

Moss kicked Tony in the head, silencing him. Oleg smirked, but lost interest and set about cleaning himself and putting his jacket on. George watched closely as Tony pulled his legs into him and tucked them up, as if in pain. The glint of a chiv, which Tony removed from inside his sock. He gripped the weapon in his fist, reached up and expertly sliced into Moss's thigh with the makeshift knife, like a master butcher carving beef, his target, to cut the femoral artery. He pulled the knife back, preparing to deliver a second cut.

George removed her Glock from her holster, chambered a round, and put a single bullet into the centre of Tony's head. Tony's body dropped flat on the floor, the weapon dropping from his hand. When Tony was no longer a threat, and the chiv was out of reach, she holstered her weapon and knelt beside Moss. The wound to his thigh was deep, Tony didn't have the perfect angle or the strength, but Moss's blood poured. She guessed he'd hit a vein, but he'd live.

"Oleg, Get the car to the back. We'll carry him down. Phone a doctor to be at the house in one hour. Move!"

Her tone brought Oleg out of his shock and paralysis. He nodded and left the room.

Moss, conscious but shocked, lay alongside Tony.

She removed Tony's waist belt and secured it above Moss's wound, which was now a steady trickle, ripped a strip off Tony's shirt and bandaged Moss's wound as she'd seen done often before.

"Stay with me, Mr Moss. We need to get you to a doctor; you'll need a stitch or two."

"I can walk, Georgina. Don't fuss."

His words said one thing, his tone another. He was in shock and looked pale.

"Pen, paper," gasped Moss.

George gave him a piece of paper and pen from the desk, and he scribbled.

"Phone this number, tell him we have a customer, give him this address. Need him now. He'll understand."

She phoned the number. A curt voice said, "Hello."

"Who's speaking?" she asked.

"The Funerarium, Templeton Maudlin speaking," came the reply.

Hearing his voice drained George's face. After a pause, she passed on the message. She'd found another rat in this disgusting nest.

She sat with Moss in the car. He slumped against the car door, eyes closed. The sound of her single 9 mm Parabellum round rang in her ears like tinnitus. Her hands shook, and she clenched them. Besides Moss's occasional twitch, he slept. Blood soaked his trouser leg, but she'd seen worse. She needed to keep him alive until he'd given her answers.

The Glock pressing into her back, reminding her she'd shot a man, and for what, so she could later execute Moss? Although she'd fired many rounds on operations, she'd never killed a person as far as she knew. Even in Afghanistan, she couldn't be certain she'd hit her targets, but that was the nature of war, and this was close and personal, almost an execution. Had she become a hired killer, nothing more than a thug?

She'd told Ted she'd do whatever it took to avenge her family, but they were words and this was real. It shocked her. George needed to talk to Charlie and Ted, friendly faces, but above all, she needed to harden herself to achieve her mission and stop thinking like a wimp. It irritated her to think she was fallible.

Chapter 37

"Trouble at the club last night?" asked Tom the Geordie, at breakfast, "Oleg's got a right strop."

George poured herself a coffee and sat opposite Tom in the workers' restroom and dining room.

"Yeah, we had some hassle. Oleg took his eye off the ball for a minute. No big deal."

No one needed to know she'd killed someone.

"I'd appreciate you keeping anything you hear to yourself. I'm new in the job and I don't want Mr Moss thinking I'm a liability."

"Sure, I get it, lass. Watch yourself, with Oleg. He's like a bear with a sore head, and he's not reluctant to throw his weight around. If that happens, his male pride will kick in, never mind what Moss says. Anyway, Moss believes in natural hierarchy, so if Oleg clips you one, Moss won't rescue you unless he has a spark for you; if you know what I mean."

"Thanks for the advice, but I'm a big girl."

"If you say so," said Tom.

Despite Tom's tendency to talk, they sat in silence as she drank her coffee.

"Does Mr Moss often go out to clubs?"

"Yeah. He likes girls. I've been with him twice. He sometimes has a few bevvies and maybe stays out if he fancies a piece, but he's selective. He sometimes stays over at his apartment in Rochester, especially if he pulls."

She needed to keep Tom talking. Anything she could learn about Moss was useful. She nodded and smiled, although inside she loathed his misogyny.

Tom looked at her from under hooded eyes and muttered. "Bloody hypocrite."

"Why?" George asked.

Tom carried on whispering and took hold of her arm across the table. "It wouldn't be the first time old Stephen has taken a liking to one of the club's boss's wife or a girlfriend, he's famous for it. And we all knew Tony was screwing Moss's missus. It must have been someone on the staff who grassed him up. He's as sharp as a razor, but he has an issue with his trousers."

Oleg came in dressed in a tracksuit, sweating like a galley-slave, and stinking of testosterone.

"Boss wants to see you, in the bedroom, now," he said, looking at George.

She finished her coffee and looked at Tom. "Thanks for the company."

Tom grinned at her and frowned at Oleg.

"Chop, chop," said Oleg.

George smirked at Oleg's macho turn of phrase. There'd been no word from Moss since the doctor had attended him.

She knocked on the door, 'Enter' from Moss. Sitting in an armchair in a dressing gown, his leg bandaged, resting on a footstool, his mouth in a beaming grin, but no hint of kindness or empathy in his eyes.

"Come in, Georgina, I want to chat, sit here."

He pointed to a chair next to him. So, a proposition or another job?

"Thank you, Georgina. You did well last night. Oleg would have panicked if you hadn't acted, and I might be dead. Impressive, and I reward loyalty. You passed the test last night."

"It could have been worse, and I'm glad you weren't seriously hurt. How does it feel?"

"Fine. You didn't panic, and I like that, you reacted without hesitation, good. How would you like to work for me, instead of my wife? Oleg bores me and is becoming a millstone. Don't worry, Tom or Andrei can handle the rough work. Muscle is easy to resource, Russia, and the Baltic States have plenty, but a real thinker, that's different. I can use your talents and initiative."

It could lead to her getting closer to Moss and the truth. She was up for it. "Okay, Mr Moss, fine by me, but how will you square it away with Oleg?"

"I won't, you will. Your first task is to tell Oleg, and sort out the fallout. Can you do that?"

"Yes. Is that all?"

"For the moment, Georgina."

"I need to take tomorrow off, to see my sister."

"Fine, but don't make it a habit. Send in Andrei and Oleg right now; I have a job for them today, so I need you here all day, okay? Enjoy your day with Charlie tomorrow."

Moss waved her away, but grimaced.

She nodded, fine by her. Closing the door behind her, thinking, she walked along the upper corridor leading to the bedrooms as Oleg opened a door to a side room and followed her, keeping a dozen steps behind. She ignored him. As she approached the top of the stairs, he ran at her, grabbed her by the back of her jeans and hair, lifted her from the ground, and threw her down the stairs. As she sailed halfway down towards the landing, Oleg stood laughing at the top. No excuse; she should have readied herself. As she thumped onto her injured shoulder on first impact, she rolled into a ball and bounced from step to step, her head tucked in. She rolled to the landing, grasping a stair rail to stop herself from rolling further. No broken bones. Rising to her feet, she faced Oleg as he sauntered down the stairs. Despite her shoulder hurting like hell, she descended the stairs and turned to face Oleg who stood on the landing. She didn't have her Glock with her, but she had to face Oleg blow for blow. As she prepared herself to confront him in the foyer, she looked around for weapons, but saw nothing of use; paintings on the walls, a coat stand, a round table with a vase of flowers and a chaise longue. She doubted Mr Moss would appreciate having his house used as a Close Combat training ground. Oleg stood a few steps up from George, his arms by his side. He looked at her and grinned, relishing her destruction. Could she beat him in a straightforward punching match? She doubted it, he needed to hit her with one uppercut, and she'd be out, but she'd need a dozen jabs to make any impact. She had speed on her side and she was one of the best. Tom entered from the staff restroom, wiping his mouth on his sleeve. Oleg descended to the last step.

"Away, there, Pet, what's the noise?"

Tom looked about, weighing up the situation.

"Stay out of this, Tom, it's not your fight. I will deal with the lady."

"Well, Oleg, mate, I'm making it my fight. I won't have you," he pointed a stubby finger at Oleg, "interrupting my breakfast, so unless you back off, I'm going to put a 9 mm in your kneecap." Tom reached around and withdrew his Sig, pointing it in the general direction of Oleg's groin.

"This time of day my aim's not good, especially with a moving target, so I might hit your knackers, okay, Oleg?"

He chambered a round, stood his ground, and took up a two-handed stance.

"I can handle this, Tom. Stay out of it."

George pushed her hair back and faced Oleg on the bottom step, hands in a boxing stance to defend herself.

"Now then, bonny lass. No one interrupts my breakfast. So, Oleg, back off mate; or should I call an ambulance? Your call, son."

Oleg pointed a stubby finger at George and spat through gritted teeth. "You won't always have Tom to fight corner. I enjoy wringing your neck, like chicken. Brits are pussycats."

He made a wringing gesture with his hands and walked past Tom and George.

George smiled. "Oh, Oleg. Mr Moss wants to see you and Andrei now. Chop, chop."

Tom grinned but blew out a breath. "You were lucky, pet. Oleg's a tough nut. Watch him. I heard you come clattering down the stairs from the restroom."

"Tom, thanks, but I can look after myself. It wasn't a problem. Eventually, I must confront Oleg, and one of us will need medical attention, and I don't plan on it being me."

She ached everywhere, and her shoulder was killing her. She'd pick her battleground with Oleg, but either way, it would be messy.

Chapter 38

Ted sat talking to Charlie, telling her how he'd met George. She'd mentioned Ted to her, but a strange bloke could frighten her, even in a coma. He promised to look out for George and to visit Charlie. Ted didn't expect a reply, but if Charlie was like George, she wouldn't mind.

He massaged his injured foot to stimulate the circulation. The nurses and admin staff knew him, they'd seen him several times and accepted his presence like a part of the furniture. After visiting Charlie, he sat in the waiting area, watching the routine of the ward. He stayed away from George whilst she was on the job, in case Moss became suspicious.

A man sitting opposite Ted looked rough, tramp-like but well fed. Unwashed, he reeked of alcohol and growled as he played with the single flower drooping in his hand. He'd soon be a patient if he carried on as he was. He pulled the filthy overcoat around him, like a prized possession. Ted pitied him. What a life.

Through the glass-panelled door, five people

approached from a patient's room. An older woman sobbed, and a girl in the group hugged her. He'd seen similar sites whilst visiting, and in his military career, but he'd never become accustomed to it. Probably the husband had died. Ted fidgeted, thinking of the suffering, and all eyes turned to the grieving group. The tramp staggered along the corridor past the group. He wasn't too steady on his feet, but Ted had seen soldiers faking drink, and this tramp was faking, but no one saw it except Ted. The man disappeared; the single flower discarded. Something was wrong. The tramp slipped into a side room, and Ted hoped it wasn't Charlie's.

He didn't want to cause alarm for no reason and marched along the corridor and entered Charlie's room. The man had entered Charlie's room less than a minute before. Charlie's hand hung alongside the bed, above a pool of blood on the floor.

The tramp, leaning over Charlie, pressed a pillow across her face. He looked up, fixing Ted's stare. Gone was the tramp's growling expression and, in its place, a focussed, killer.

"You, get off her," shouted Ted, causing the attacker to pause, and alerting others along the corridor.

Seeing Ted, he left the pillow over Charlie's face and faced Ted, who grabbed hold of him by the collar of his coat, dragging him away. Although the attacker was shorter, the man was younger, much stronger, and fitter. The killer swung a blow to Ted's abdomen with a hammer of a fist, below his rib cage, forcing Ted to keel over, but keeping hold of the man's jacket. As Ted tried to wrestle him to the ground, the attacker lifted him in a bear hug, his arms trapped by his sides. He lifted Ted off his feet, squeezing the life out of him, Ted's stomach against the killer's chest, his arms trapped. Ted tried to shout, but a wheezing sound came out. The tramp stretched and looked into Ted's eyes. There was a professional's disrespect and annoyance that Ted had disturbed him. Ted brought his head back and butted him across the bridge of his nose, with a satisfying crunch, which resonated through Ted's forehead. It forced the man to stagger back and let go of him. Blood sprayed the man's coat and along the floor, joining Charlie's blood, where her assailant had severed a finger. A nurse rushed into the room.

"What the…," said the nurse.

The attacker backhanded the nurse, knocking her against the now closing door, trapping it open.

Ted grabbed the tramp's filthy overcoat as he scrambled to escape. The tramp shrugged out of the coat and stepped over the nurse. Ted followed. The attacker raced for the fire escape, Ted a few metres behind. The attacker would escape, he'd exited the fire door on the ground floor whilst Ted stood at the top of the stairs, no point in chasing after him. But he'd remember the tramp with the broken nose.

As another nurse ran the length of the corridor, Ted doubled over, catching his breath, and pointing to Charlie's room. An alarm sounded, and a doctor rushed into the room shouting instructions to the nurse. The nurse led Ted away to recover.

A hospital security guard wobbled along the corridor and approached Ted, as if he'd been the aggressor, until a nurse told him to phone the police. Ted looked in to check on Charlie. A nurse was with her.

"Charlie's okay; you saved her," said the nurse. "Any

longer, and we'd have lost her."

Ted texted George with the bad and good news, and assured George that Charlie was fine, which the nurse confirmed.

"Is she okay now? Is she stable? Who was it?" asked George.

Later, Ted phoned her again and described the assailant.

"A professional. Muscular. He knew what he was doing," said Ted.

"What did he sound like? Did he speak?"

"No, nothing. Any idea who he was?"

"I have an idea," said George, her voice turning to a throaty growl.

The police questioned Ted, but after answering a few questions, he referred them to James Chance. For the next twenty-four hours, a police officer guarded Charlie from the ward waiting room.

***

A nurse waited for George and Ted at the entrance to the ward, worry creasing her face, and she looked hunched, reducing her size, as if the incident had reduced her physically and mentally. She spotted George and cast her eyes down.

"I'm so sorry, it's our fault. We shouldn't have left Charlie alone," said the nurse through watery eyes.

"It's not your fault. He would have entered no matter what we did. Now we know the lengths he'll go to. How is Charlie?"

"She seems comfortable, and she's quiet, no reaction so far. A police officer is with her. The attacker would have killed her if Ted hadn't intervened."

George wished they'd stop apologising and care for her sister. She admired the doctors' and the nurses' dedication. Without them, Charlie would be dead, but it still annoyed the hell out of her. George and Ted entered Charlie's room silently. An armed police officer sitting in the corner watching Charlie stood as they entered.

"I'm sorry about what happened, Miss. Who's this?" he asked, pointing at Ted.

Finally, the police were taking an interest.

"This is Ted, a family friend," said George, her eyes fixed on Charlie.

"Was there any other evidence left?"

"Yes, an overcoat, forensics is examining it."

"Do you want time alone with your sister? I'll wait outside,"

"Yes, please, Ted can keep you company, and if you ask nicely, he'll show you his war wound," said George to the police officer.

Ted and the police officer left, chatting outside. She took Charlie's hand and sat at her side.

"You've been in the war," she said, trying to hide the croak in her voice. She dropped the forced smile, and a storm cloud of doubt and fear surrounded her. Taking Charlie's bandaged hand, she laid it in the palm of her own, feeling the warmth and comfort of her twin.

"I'm sorry, Charlie, I failed you, and I can't protect you against these criminals. All I seem able to do is exact revenge. At least I can do that. Remember when Mum used to say 'behave like a lady, fight like a tiger'? It's time to remove the gloves. I'm done with being a lady, and I'm not bothered about the law or going to prison, I couldn't care less about sending these butchers to justice who kill and maim women, they're going to taste my kind of justice."

"I'll try to guard you, Charlie. I'll ask for Chance's help. He was Mum's friend, and works for MI5. Did I tell you Mum also worked for MI5? Yes, it shocked me too. I thought I'd be able to tell you this when you woke up. But the time isn't right."

She took Mum's letter, holding it as if Charlie could see it. "This letter is from Mum to me, and she left one for you. I expect yours says the same."

She read; the words breaking her voice. She felt her Mum writing them, could hear her voice and feel Mum's tears rolling onto the page. They'd seen their Mum cry twice, when dad had deserted them, and when she joined the Army. The former was tears of sorrow, the latter tears of joy and pride. An unspoken family rule; tears were for family and never in front of outsiders. She waited for a reaction but received none. Neither a flicker of an eyelash, nor pressure from her hand.

"Yeah, I thought it'd shock you, me too. Mum, a spy, and for the Soviets. Maybe you suspected something, Charlie, you're always asking questions and I listen to the answers. Chance gave me some information with details. She was one hell of a career spy, was our Mum, but she paid the price. Now, it's my job to protect the family, and you are my only family."

She sat for a few minutes in silence, and said a silent prayer. Not something Charlie would entertain. George prayed for an edge to help her succeed.

"I guess I'd better go, but I'll see you tomorrow, okay?"

George kissed Charlie on the forehead, kissed her unbandaged hand, and left. Ted, still talking to the police officer in the corridor, handed her a coffee.

"George, if you agree, they can move Charlie to a more secure room, with live video feed and sound monitors. The police will guard Charlie for another two days, after that it's for us to keep her safe."

"Seems sensible. We don't want him returning, but I don't think they will, it's too risky. When can we move her?"

"I'll ask the Sister to move her straight away."

George stood as tall as the armed police officer and made eye contact with him. "You look after my sister. If harm comes to her, I'll hold you responsible. Am I making myself clear, or should I rephrase it?"

"I'm here to protect her, and I'll do my job, Miss, you aren't threatening a police officer are you?"

"It's Sergeant, not miss. Arrest me if you must, but I don't recommend it. I'll be back tomorrow and my sister had better be alive and well. Clear?"

The police officer felt for his handcuffs, but Ted placed a restraining hand over his. "I wouldn't do that, son. Relax," whispered Ted.

They locked eyes, and George maintained eye contact. Ten seconds later, the police officer removed his hand from the handcuffs and relaxed. Maybe he thought he understood George's state of mind, but he didn't. How could he?

"Yes, clear, I'll report this incident to my superiors."

"Good, remember my name."

She turned and walked along the corridor. Ted smiled and raised an eyebrow to the Officer.

***

As they sat in Ted's Landrover, George pondered and Ted let her.

"Why do you think he tried to kill Charlie?"

"I don't know, who do you think authorised the attack?" asked Ted.

"I'm sure Moss decided, but why, she's no threat to him?"

"I doubt it was a strategic decision. He sounds like a selfish bastard, and he has a problem with you taking time to see Charlie? Never underestimate the male ego and his trouser problem. He not only wants something from you, he probably wants you. Charlie will be safe for now, but she needs to be moved to a secure location. He may have an interest in Charlie not recovering from the coma," said Ted.

George took out her secure mobile phone, tapped in the encryption code, and entered Chance's number. She recognised Sam's voice.

"Sam, there's been an attempt on Charlie's life. Can we move her to a secure facility? Maybe a military hospital?"

"I heard via the local police. Most unfortunate. What else do you have?"

George knew she had to keep it together, keep a cool head. 'Most unfortunate' annoyed the hell out of her. Ted glanced sideways at her, expecting a barbed reaction.

There was a pause. Sam may have been reflecting on it, or referring to someone.

A click, and Chance spoke. "Chance here, Georgina. We can't interfere with the local police, I'm afraid, except to emphasise Charlie's safety."

"Look, Mr Chance, if you can't guarantee her safety, my job for you is over and with it our cooperation. We'll struggle, but we'll manage without help. I'll cooperate so long as I can count on you, and your support, and don't give me the line about you're a simple Cold War spy. Please, sort out her safety or our deal is off."

"Threats go both ways, George. I could have you arrested within the hour, but I won't, so let's not make petty threats. I'll do what I can, I can't say fairer. What else?"

"Fair enough. I also need to visit Bradley Maudlin within the next couple of days. He is the key to all this. Can you fix it?"

"You're outside the hospital. I'll call you at your home. I assume Ted is with you, so have him with you when I call."

A click marked the disconnection then silence, and Ted grinned at her.

He was not only tracking her phone, but Chance knew she was with Ted. How did he know?

Chapter 39

George boxed better than most men, equally skilled with orthodox and southpaw. But with Oleg she'd need an equaliser. Before dawn, she walked down to the firing range, took a chair, and sat opposite the lift door, waiting. Oleg often fired off a few rounds and lifted weights before breakfast. The indicator showed the lift was on its way. As the doors slid open, she stepped into full view and faced him, less than two metres apart. Her eyes remained on target, but she feigned high. Oleg drew his hand to protect his face, and she smashed him across his leading leg at the kneecap with her baseball bat. The leg crumbled, but he sagged onto his injured side, supporting himself with one arm and his hand. The baseball bat found its mark again at the elbow, and he collapsed, but quickly raised himself onto his hands and knees. If he'd imbibed with steroids and coke, he'd likely not feel too much pain. As he rose, George smashed the weapon across his lower back with a double handed blow. He momentarily settled face down, but rose and stared at the floor, getting his focus. She whacked him again to keep him down, and struck his left kidney. Again, he fell flat, heaving, and cursing in Russian.

"You want some? I kill you with one hand," he said, spitting out the words and getting to his knees, pain etched on his face and body.

She dropped the bat, which clattered on the concrete floor, and faced him. The damaged leg didn't bother him too much, as he raised his hand to punch her. He couldn't grab her, so she had the advantage. She punched him with two right jabs. He staggered. George stood her ground, letting him come to her. She had height on her side, not underestimating the power of his fist on her own guard. As he approached, she kicked at his knee she'd injured earlier. It didn't seem to trouble him, and he showed a slight limp, rushing her hippo like. If he caught her with his good arm, she'd be in trouble. She waited until the last moment, let him aim a cross at her head, then ducked underneath to plant a few punches into his kidney as he sagged. As he lay on his back trying to get his breath, she brought her heel down on his nose, feeling the crunch, and knowing for a normal person it would be over. But with Oleg, nothing was certain.

She leaned over him, foot on his throat, and smashed a couple of jabs into his face with a gloved hand. His nose now resembled a large smashed strawberry. He wasn't getting up. He wheezed. She hadn't killed him, which was good enough.

She lifted his head by his hair and slammed it onto the concrete. George hissed into his face, his malodorous breath making her gag.

"You so much as glance my way again, I'll kill you. You understand, you Siberian pig?"

Even through the blood, Oleg grinned at her and she realised she hadn't beaten him.

"It will be my pleasure to execute you."

She shouldn't, but he left her no option. Grasping the baseball bat, she slammed it on his hand, lying flat on the floor, then repeated the treatment, smashing his other hand. In Oleg's case, the crunching sensation was a pleasure. He wouldn't be able to use his hands for a while.

George knelt next to Oleg; her mouth close to his ear. "You reek like a rancid septic tank, take a shower and clean your mess, now. Chop, chop."

As she entered the lift carrying the baseball bat, Andrei emerged from the shadows, a plaster across his nose. So, he was the culprit at the hospital, but he'd keep for later. One fight in a day was enough. He hadn't come to Oleg's aid, so there was no love lost between them.

She stared at him, then at Oleg lying on the floor, until the lift doors slid closed, hoping he would reflect and absorb the lesson.

A message waited for her to see Mr Moss in his study, but she retired to her room to clean up. Ready, she knocked and entered. He gestured for her to take a seat next to him on the sofa.

"Come sit with me. George, good to see you. I hope you are well. How is your sister?"

Their knees touched. Moss's eyes were as dead as roadkill, and she read nothing.

"She's fine. No change, I'll see her again soon."

His grin remained fixed.

"Good, good. I hope you've spoken to Oleg and addressed that issue?"

"Yes, I've talked to him, it's settled. You won't hear from him for a while."

"Hmm. I like equilibrium and natural selection. You've earned your place." he paused, angling his head.

"My synopsis of our activities today. I shall pay a visit and go shopping. You will accompany me, all right?"

George wanted to stare at Moss, give him the same treatment she'd dished out to Oleg, but for the moment she needed him. She nodded and shrugged. "When do you wish to leave?"

"We'll be out tonight, so bring an overnight bag. Please meet me in one hour in the foyer."

George passed Tom in the corridor, on the way to her room.

"Hey, all okay, pet? So, you sorted out your problem with Oleg."

"Sort of. How did you find out?"

"I saw the doctor attending him. He looked in pieces. I underestimated you, you made a mess of him. What will Moss make of it?"

She had a job to do, and no one would get in her way.

"I got lucky. Oleg is history, and I'm sure Mr Moss will understand. In fact, he may appreciate it."

George moved on whilst Tom muttered to himself. She'd riled him, but didn't care, he'd live with it. George changed into loose trousers, blue blouse, and a long jacket, slid the Glock into her back holster and wore flat shoes. She couldn't wear high heels and do a decent job of minding. Turning an ankle whilst chasing a mugger would be unforgivable and unprofessional.

Moss met her in the foyer, inspected her and frowned. She felt for her trousers zip, but all seemed in order.

"Georgina, change into a dress. I need you to look like a lady, not a minder."

She said nothing and bit her tongue. "Any preference?" asked George.

Moss didn't understand George's sarcasm. "Something nice, not too flamboyant, classy. I want class, not slapper."

She returned to her room, sent a text to Chance on her encrypted phone, changed into a skirt, slipped her Glock into her shoulder bag, and pulled a jersey over her blouse and finally fixed a set of pearls around her neck.

Moss scanned her as she approached the car. "Okay, but on our way, we'll go to a lady's shop and buy you clothes I prefer."

George sat in the back with Moss and turned towards him. He grinned at her.

"Mr Moss, I didn't accept the job to be eye candy for you. I'm here as hired help, to be your fixer and minder. I can't look both pretty and do my job."

Moss laughed, not a snigger but an unrestrained guffaw.

"Oh, how the ice queen melteth," he teased.

She turned back, stared out of the car window, and grinned. Moss's reflection in the window told her his humour hadn't waned. Maybe she'd underestimated this villain. He had a well-hidden sense of humour, and he seemed relaxed in her company. George did not reciprocate. She'd saved his life, and despite her loathing for male chauvinist pigs, her dislike of Moss showed the slightest sign of abating. She reminded herself of her mission, and this man's capabilities, and what she must ultimately do.

"Where are we going?" she asked as they drove towards her home town of Grain.

"We're going to visit someone, you'll see."

They entered the grounds of the Medway Maritime Hospital in Gillingham, the hospital treating Charlie. George glanced at Moss, who was grinning but stared straight ahead. She feared Moss's intentions. George needed backup, and that meant Ted. She took out her phone and sent him a text. If Moss noticed, he didn't care. George's humour turned to dread, and blood drained from her face.

"What's going on?" asked George, ready to confront Moss. She'd need to contain her temper for the sake of the job, and not least for Charlie. If she had a face like thunder, she risked blowing it.

"I thought I'd repay you for saving my life by taking you to visit Charlie. You don't mind, do you, and it's the least I can do?" said Moss.

His voice said 'Innocent', but his eyes said 'Treachery' and 'Megalomania'. The car dropped them, and they walked through the hospital, like any couple visiting a sick relative. She spotted Ted standing outside Charlie's room and made eye contact. George walked behind Moss and nodded to Ted, who opened the door for her. She walked around Moss who tried to follow her, but Ted placed a hand in the middle of Moss's chest.

"Where are you going, sunshine? And who are you, the Queen Mum?" asked Ted.

"Who are you to stop me? I'm with her and if you don't move your hand, I'll have someone remove it," said Moss.

"I'm Ted. You won't get through me, but phone a friend if you like."

Ted pushed the door open and shouted in a whisper to George. "Hey, George. This 'gentleman' desires admission, all right?"

George needed Moss to understand the difference between family and employer.

"No, I want to talk to Charlie first."

George turned her attention to her sister, sat at her bedside, and took her hand. "So, recovered from your ordeal, Charlie? You look much better. No, that's daft, you're the same, Charlie. I'm sorry you had to go through the ordeal, but whatever I do, I'll keep you safe. They'll have to kill me and overpower Ted before they harm you again."

George put her face next to Charlie's and whispered. "I'm going to let Mr Moss in to see you. Try to remember his voice. If my guess is right, he's at the heart of our problem. This will be the only time I'll let him near you. Okay?"

"Okay, Ted, Mr Moss can come in now," said George towards the door.

Moss walked in and stood on the opposite side of the bed to George.

"I'm sorry, George. I should have been more sensitive; you were close."

"Twin sister," corrected George. "And yes."

"You are identical twins."

"Yes."

He was being nice. Why? Was she missing something?

"I heard about the incident. What a pity. It should never have happened. If there's anything I can do, please tell me. It would be such a shame if anything were to happen to Charlie."

'A pity! Such a shame,' what a thing to say, especially now.

That was a veiled threat, but what was he hoping to achieve by it? Psychological advantage, or simply securing her acquiescence?

"I'll kill whoever attacked Charlie, and I'll enjoy doing

it. And whoever ordered it.," said George, through gritted teeth.

"We shall all have to try our best to ensure nothing happens then, won't we?"

His hand reached for Charlie's cheek as if to stroke it, and George reached across with a speed that seemed to surprise Moss. She grasped his wrist and lifted it from Charlie. She didn't want this man touching her sister.

"Don't touch her… please."

She tried to force a smile, defensively. "I'm sensitive after the last attack, and I don't want anyone who she doesn't know near her."

"In that case, I'm privileged."

"Don't be. I work for you, Mr Moss, but Charlie is my only family, and you came here uninvited, remember?"

"And the ape?"

He pointed with his thumb towards the door.

"That ape is a close and trusted family friend."

Moss lowered his voice to a growl. "George. I'm sure between us, we can keep your twin sister safe. Don't you think?"

"Should we leave? After you," said George.

Moss had targeted George with his equivocal threat. But the threat was clear, 'Play ball with me, and I'll make sure there's no more attempts on Charlie's life.'

Moss looked at this as a game, cat and mouse, or chess. The chess pieces were in place. Moss simply had to manipulate them to win. But a win for Moss was acquiring whatever Julia Stone once had, and which he hoped George now held. For George, playing chess was fine until someone came along, kicked over the board and shot the opponent. Now, she was the mouse to Moss's cat, he'd soon discover this pussy could turn into a tiger.

The drizzly rain thrashed them and penetrated their clothes. By the time they reached the car, the rain had soaked them to the skin. George suspected Moss had asked the driver to meet them a couple of hundred yards away from the entrance to the hospital so that they'd get drenched. She'd been wetter and colder and usually enjoyed it. But her blouse stuck to her, and Moss gawked.

"Shall we go shopping? I have a couple of items to purchase, and I can treat you."

So that was Moss's game; buy her a new wardrobe, strip her out of her wet rags.

"Don't mind me, this is par for the course, especially in England."

She was playing a dangerous game. George relied on Moss needing her more than she needed him. But it would get her closer to him, and she needed his admission of guilt before killing him.

"Yevgeni, stop at my club in Fawkham."

"The Moon Dance?" asked the driver.

"No, 'The Red Flag'. Wait outside."

Minutes later, they halted outside the club where an old Soviet Union flag flew on the roof.

"I'll be a few minutes. Stay here until I come out. Get a taxi home and leave me the car."

Yevgeni looked in the mirror at George, sucked on his bottom lip and raised his eyes. She'd never seen that before, but the meaning was obvious. It told her all she needed to know.

Moss went into the club as George used the opportunity to check her secure texts from Chance, who confirmed her visit to Bradley Maudlin the following day. She gave a quick update, watching the club door. Sensing the driver staring at her, she glanced at him. He studied her through the rear-view mirror.

"Anything you want to say?"

He looked down, silent, thinking. "I like you, Miss Stone, you not like the other women. There's a bone in your nose, so I tell you this, watch yourself, all is not what it seems with Mr Mosin."

"Thanks, I'll bear that in mind."

The driver had used Moss's Russian name. He was not always popular amongst his staff.

A taxi stopped alongside them and Yevgeni left the car and waited for Moss to return.

A text from Chance. "Can you stop Moss returning to South London tonight?" asked Chance.

"Why?"

"Activity at his residence starting at midnight. Occupy him for the night, inform me when he returns. It's in both our interests."

It confused and intrigued her. What was this 'activity', what was Chance planning for Moss's house; and why, 'in both their interests'? She hesitated, not wanting to commit herself. Was Chance another piece on Moss's chessboard, or was he playing his own game? Moss left the club and headed towards the car, a few seconds away.

"If I must, but you owe me," she texted.

She'd visit Bradley Maudlin on her day off. She couldn't afford to miss it, and getting closer to Moss might work to her advantage, even if she had to swallow her pride and morals and sleep with the enemy.

Moss got in the driver's side and invited George to sit with him in the front.

"So, we're going to make you beautiful, my little minder friend. Off we go to Romans in Chatham," said Moss.

"I told you, I choose my own clothes, even for work, but I have no objection to you paying. And I'm happy the way I am, you Russian pike."

"So, you've done your homework on me, so now we know where we stand, I think we can start again. New clothes, change out of those wet things, then lunch. Okay?"

Moss laughed as he drove off. George gave him a

sideways glance and grinned, then turned to the side window and scowled.

***

Moss pulled into his parking space outside his garage.

"Leave your parcels in the car, you can collect them tomorrow when I drop you off," said Moss, grinning. His movements were nervous, jerky. He seemed eager to slake his arousal.

"Okay, but this one, I want to try it on for you," said George, smiling.

Clothes shopping, a romantic dinner for two, up to his apartment for coffee, or champagne, and from Moss's body language and fleeting hands, seduction. Worth it if he implicated himself in her family's disaster, and it brought her closer to unravelling this mystery. She glanced at her watch; 9 p.m. He put an arm around George's shoulder as they walked together to the lift. Inside the lift, he made his first pass at her. She responded as she must. But had to admit, he wasn't a terrible kisser. As they approached the fifth floor, and his penthouse apartment, they separated, and she cast her eyes down, coy.

"Are you okay?" he asked.

"Yes, I'm not so experienced, but I'll be okay."

Her cheeks flushed with both dread and excitement. Could she have made a dreadful mistake, and Moss was guilty of nothing greater than a parking ticket?

He grinned at her. "Good."

She didn't know if he meant 'good' that she was inexperienced, or that she'd be fine. She guessed the former. They walked hand in hand to his apartment and before he switched on the light, she'd attacked him, pressing him against the closed door, kissing him fiercely. She relished his smell, not a fragrance she recognised but designed to stimulate. Conflicted, she had to admit she enjoyed it, but told herself it was an act he'd mistake for passion.

Later, as he fumbled with her clothes, she broke away. "Coffee, please?" she asked.

"Or champagne?"

"Yes, champagne would be nice. Can we talk?"

"Sure, we can talk for a while, but after, I want to show you what it's like to be a Russian woman."

"Can't wait," responded George.

They half sat, half lay on the floor, their backs to the sofa. He poured the first glass and George filled his glass at regular intervals. They talked about Afghanistan, politics, and the great composers of the twentieth century. He said she could hardly describe herself as educated if she hadn't listened to Mikhail Ippolitov-Ivanov. He unfolded her from his arms, wobbled to his feet, and walked on unsteady feet to an old record player.

"Listen to this, it is Caucasian Sketches Suite No. 1, Procession of the Sardar. Quite beautiful and sublimely romantic." He grinned at her. She half opened her eyes and smiled back.

"I'm more Vaughn Williams 'The Lark Ascending'."

Moss belly laughed. "That is pop music. This Russian composer is real romantic, majestic music and shows the true character of Russia, strong, proud and heroic."

He attempted to stand straight, clipped his heels together, laughing, reaching for her hand, and she rose on unsteady feet, glancing at her watch as she did so. One a.m. As they danced to the music of Ippolitov-Ivanov, Moss's landline rang. He ignored it, and George nuzzled into his shoulder, even though she was as tall as Moss. The phone persisted, joined by his mobile. He cursed in Russian, "*ty chop ohuel?!*"

George first heard that phrase in Afghanistan from Afghan tribesmen who'd picked it up from the Russian military. The polite version translates as, 'Who the hell is that?'. He disentangled himself from George, who stood on the spot swaying to the music as Moss answered the phone. Despite the drink, he waved his arms.

"Come back to me, Stephen, please," said George. Desire dripped from her voice.

He waved at her for silence, turning his back. Moss spoke in Russian for five minutes, then threw the handset onto the sofa.

"We have to return to London. There's been an incident outside, a disturbance. Maybe a demonstration. Don't the unwashed have better things to do?"

"What sort of incident, darling?" asked George.

"That's all I know. Make coffee. Now, quick," said Moss. "And sober up. I need you."

Moss's change in tone surprised even George. This was Moss, the sociopath. In less than five minutes, he'd changed from a vibrant, educated lover into a monster. George redressed in the bathroom. They drank instant coffee whilst preparing to leave, the powerful aroma and the adrenaline reviving them.

In less than ten minutes, they stood in the lift in silence and made their way to Moss's car.

"Should I drive?" asked George.

"No, get in. I'll drive."

George expected the road out of Rochester to be quiet at 1:30 a.m. The police car that pulled out behind them didn't surprise her. Although quiet, this was an urban area and 30 mph zone. Moss didn't even slow when he saw twos and blues but swore as he topped 80 mph, then skidded to a halt spitting and cursing. He opened the window and adopted his British Airways smile.

"Good morning, Officer. Can I help you?"

"Morning, Sir. Do you know what speed you were travelling? Can I see your licence, please?"

The Officer bent so he was in line with the window and able to smell Moss's breath.

"I may have driven a little over the limit, not much."

Moss handed over his British driving licence.

"Have you been drinking, Sir? Would you get out of the car?"

Moss took out his wallet and removed two fifty-pound notes.

"It's a dark night, Officer, and you could have been mistaken. Why don't you get yourself a drink?"

The Officer inspected the driving licence and stared at Moss. "Stephen Moss, I am arresting you for dangerous driving and attempting to bribe a police officer. You do not have to say anything…"

"Impudent prick. My house in London is being wrecked, and I must go there now. The least you can do is escort me. Don't you have any real criminals to arrest in this bloody country?"

"There's no need for that aggressive tone, Sir. You must accompany me to the police station where you will be breathalysed, and processed."

A second unmarked car appeared behind the police car, two men got out, one walked to the police car and shot the police officer sitting in the driving seat. The other walked to Moss's car and approached the police officer facing Moss, punched him to the ground, then shot him in the head.

"Get in our car, Mr Moss," said Tom. "Get in the back, George. I'll take care of the Jaguar."

This plan was falling apart. Chance had arranged for the police to hold Moss in the police station overnight. This was an imbroglio worthy of an Italian tragedy. Moss and George sat in the car. Behind them, the Jaguar burst into flames. They sat in silence for a few miles as they drove within the speed limit towards Moss's South London house. George took out her phone, surreptitiously selecting secure mode. A message waited for her. She ignored it. Turning away from Moss towards the window, she composed a new message to Chance to warn him there were two dead police officers. Moss moved, and she turned back towards him.

"Give me the phone, George," said Moss.

Backspacing, she deleted the unsent message before Moss snatched it from her, throwing it into the lap of the front passenger.

"We'll chat on our arrival."

George grasped her bag, reached for her Glock, but found only space. Moss had removed it from her bag in his flat, whilst she was in the bathroom.

"Lost this Georgina?" said Moss, holding her Glock.

She showed no surprise and resigned herself to doing this the hard way. The passenger unclipped his seat belt, knelt on the seat to face her, and pointed an automatic at her neck.

"I've played this game longer than you could imagine. How could you, Sergeant George Stone, hope to beat me?"

They approached the house; the front was damaged, windows and doors wrecked. There were no police officers around, perhaps they were in the house. Could they help her? Chance would know something had gone wrong. As they approached the barrier to the underground car park, George weighed the odds of successfully making a break and running, but no doubt the driver had locked the car doors. With Tom on one side and the passenger who'd taken her weapon on the other, they marched her upstairs to Moss's study, shoved her into an armchair and waited for Moss. She still had fight in her.

In this game of chess, both she and Chance had been out manoeuvred and outplayed. But it was only 'Check', not 'Checkmate'.

Chapter 40

There'd been a ruckus in the house since they'd arrived. The guy who'd killed the police officer stood behind her as they waited, a firm hand on her shoulder. No doubt someone was sucking the brains out of her secure phone and giving it to Moss. A raised voice expressing a view about why drunks could throw missiles at the house, and what were the police doing? Someone else said it wouldn't be a good idea to involve the police. Could she take advantage of the chaos in the house? She might take down the bloke holding her. Then what? This was her opportunity for fact finding. She suspected Moss's disappointment and consequent punishment for her treachery would involve a severe beating at least, or worse. She'd wait. She had little option.

Oleg stood on his injured legs, broken nose, and wore heavy gloves. No doubt a liberal use of painkillers and Oleg's recreational drugs of choice would do wonders. He grinned at her, and she wondered if she'd been promised to him. Overall, he didn't look too bad, considering what he'd been through at her hands. How did he even stand?

Moss entered the room and sat behind his desk.

"Georgina," Moss leaned back and shook his head. "How did it come to this? And we were getting on so well."

"What do you want?" asked George.

"We've had a look at your phone. Thanks for unlocking it for us. James Chance is such a nice chap, but he's sentimental and weak."

"Your mother worked for my father, way back. The Cold War was a different world. She worked tirelessly for the greater good of Soviet socialism, trained for it from childhood, but you know this."

He waved his hand as if swatting away the past. His ruminations were for his own benefit rather than hers.

"Three months ago, she declined my generous offer of employment. Sad; she would have been useful to me. I suppose she suspected that the socialist ideal was not my motivation. Being sentimentally attached to my father was foolish."

"Who gave you my mother, was it your father?" George asked.

He ignored her, talking to justify himself and caring nothing for George's questions.

"They were besotted, and he declared her 'protected'. However, my father is old, weak, walking dead, but I am the future. So, his protection is no protection at all, and so it transpired. Your mother came courtesy of another source."

Another source, names ran through her mind. The mole that Chance mentioned? Sheila?

"Did you kill her?" George asked, her heart thrashing a heavy drumbeat in her chest.

"Me? No. My days of killing are over, I simply gave the order."

That told her enough. He'd as good as killed her, and now he was on top of the list.

"Who did? Who went to her house and killed my mother and put my sister in a coma?" she said, her voice a whisper.

Moss ignored her.

"After the collapse of the Soviet Union, she turned to the British Secret Service. I wanted what she had, in here," he tapped his head, "and her records. She held the complete list of assets and resources from the Soviet era in the UK and at the height of her career she called on them for the 'greater good' to great effect. She was almost genius-like, and my father was smitten with her."

"Why did you have to kill her?" asked George.

"Her death was symbolic and marked the end of an era. Above all, it sent a message to my father. Not only is he useless, he is powerless," he said, grinning.

"What does one do with a faulty and errant child? I threatened to have you executed in Afghanistan, but she still wouldn't accede." He raised his voice and Tom's hand on her shoulder tensed.

"Was I the target in Afghanistan?"

Moss smiled. He looked demented, and she reminded herself, that less than 6 hours ago she'd been prepared to give herself to him? What did that say about her?

"Your mother was a genuine Cold War warrior and trained to resist interrogation, so I cut my losses with her and her kind. They tired me. I arranged for her disposal. My source suggested she'd trust only you and Charlie with this information. So, Georgina Stone, here we are."

Moss had, in his own words, 'disposed' of her mother. That was all the confession she needed. She also needed to know who wielded the sword?

"She left me a letter," said George.

The landline phone rang, but Moss ignored it.

"I've seen the letter and my people have been over it, a fruitless exercise. Either you hand over what your mother had, or I will kill you and your sister within the next few hours. And to amuse me and hurt you, I will kill your sister first. I suppose the only thing you can influence now, Georgina, is how you die and whether Charlie will die. If you cooperate, I'll spare Charlie, how's that?"

Her Mum had left nothing except the letter and the USB stick. The scales slipped from her mind. The USB stick!

"Many people would give their right arm for that information. Once you've handed over the information, as you certainly will, you will be presented to our friend the undertaker, so there's no harm in telling you."

"You'll have no more success with me than you had with my mother."

"Yes, I know, but Georgina, you have a weakness, your sister. I believe you when you say you don't know where the information is. So, here's your opportunity, you rack your brain, find the information and in return, I won't kill your sister. Should we say twenty-four hours? Once this unpleasantness is over, you and I can continue what we started."

He was contradicting himself. A few minutes ago, her disposal was imminent. Now he wanted to restart their relationship. George didn't doubt, even if she found the information and handed it over, he would dispose of her and Charlie as he had their mother.

"I've told you; I don't know."

"And I believe you, and now you have an incentive to find the information."

The phone persisted, and Moss's mobile joined in. He rejected the call without looking at it and nodded to one of his men to answer the fixed phone. Andrei picked it up. "*Da. Kto eto?*" (Yes, who is it?).

His tone changed as he recognised the voice. He stood to attention, then handed the phone to Moss. The voice evoked a similar but less pronounced reaction in Moss; a one-way conversation. Moss gently replaced the handset and sat back for a full minute before looking at George.

"It looks as if the old Cold War Warriors have joined ranks and returned from the dead. That was my father, he's still someone in Russia, it seems. You have an ally somewhere who has direct contact with my father and my father wants you released with a stay of execution of five days, after which time you hand over the package, or you will become a target and no one will save you, neither my father, nor Chance. No one. So, Georgina, you have five days, then you are mine. My father guaranteed your life, but not the quality of it. So, think hard, find what I want and hand it over. Then I may reconsider your future."

He grinned at Oleg. "Take her to the garage to collect her car and take Tom with you. And Oleg? Hurt her a little. Nothing serious. Make sure she can still drive her car. Georgina, enjoy your five days of freedom."

Oleg grinned and grunted. Tom dragged George to her feet and out of the room. Oleg followed.

She could take a few slaps. It would do nothing to dent her determination, and if she was lucky, she'd get a few punches in herself.

The garage sounded hollow, and no one would hear her or see her pain. Tom pushed George against the car door and Oleg used all the force in his one good arm and gloved hand to lay a punch into George's stomach. She dropped to the floor, heaving as Oleg kicked her in the side. She made it look worse than it was, and lay gasping for air. Tom stood back, arms folded, but didn't interfere.

She looked at the feet in front of her, and another pair of feet silently approached from behind the two thugs. A dull thud and Tom dropped in a heap. She recognised Ted's faulty gait. How had he got into the garage? She looked up to see Ted standing over Oleg who gripped Ted's throat and pushed him over the bonnet of another car. Ted struck out at Oleg, but with insufficient force. She opened the side door to her car and took out a steering lock, which had a long straight bar with a hook on the end. She pulled herself to her feet and brought the weapon down on Oleg's skull. He released Ted and looked at her. Using both hands, she swung the weapon at his knees, where she'd hit him previously. He screamed, and she followed it with a bone breaking crack across his broken nose. From the sound and the blood, she doubted doctors would ever rebuild it. Oleg was down, but not out. She looked across at Tom as Ted stamped on Oleg's chest with his prosthesis. A few broken ribs, she guessed. Tom rose to his feet, shaking his head.

She knelt next to him and gripped his throat. "And I thought you were one of the good guys, Tom."

"In it for the money, Pet. Fire away, beat me unconscious, and I'll pretend I've been beaten by a girl, okay?"

She laid two jabs at his head and he lay still; grateful for small mercies. Oleg was another matter, and she guessed, with all the steroids, he hardly felt the pain of a broken nose, broken ribs, and broken hands.

Ted made a valiant effort at holding off Oleg, who raged like an errant gorilla. Despite Ted's punches, the man remained upright. She doubted she could do a better job. She struck Oleg with the steering lock along the side of his face. He let go of Ted, turned and grinned, waving his hands for George to give him another to show he was unhurt. Ted stood back and heaved against the side of the car as George repeated her attack on Oleg's head. Oleg dropped to his knees, still groaning. Ted took the crook lock from George and brought it across Oleg's throat, a knee at the back of Oleg's neck, and heaved until he lay limp, and posed no further problem.

She pulled Ted towards the car and into the passenger seat, and George drove. Ted threw the crook lock onto the back seat of the car and George noted to clean it later. The guards were expecting her to leave on her own, and she hoped he'd let her pass.

"Head down," said George through clenched teeth as they waited for the guard to open the barrier. As they headed out into the traffic, she looked in her rear-view mirror and saw the guard talking animatedly on his walkie-talkie.

Driving to Grain, she updated Ted but resisted calling Chance. Moss had her secure mobile. She'd call from home.

"I have a five-day stay of execution, but not you, or Charlie. This is war, and I need to speak to Chance ASAP."

***

Ted rubbed his wounds, but with a broad grin.

"Can I offer you a mint humbug, I swear by them? It gives me something to do, calms my nerves and gives me a sugar rush, all in one perfect sweet," said Ted, grinning.

He seemed to have discovered his forte, and was enjoying himself. But she hoped he wouldn't pay for this flirtation with danger.

He produced an old-fashioned sweet bag, shook the bottom to loosen its contents, and offered George the bag. George broke into fits of laughter.

"Next you'll ask if I want to see your puppy."

Ted grinned, but his eyebrows met. "I'm not like that, and you've seen Jaws. But if you're offering, you can massage my stump."

George placed a hand on his arm and took a mint humbug from his bag. "I'm joking, Ted."

"I know, and I'd never take advantage of a nice girl, even if she were partial to my mint humbugs and even if I could be naughty, which I can't."

"Do you play chess?" asked Ted.

"I used to play with my sister. Our Mum taught us. She said it was part of our upbringing, but I didn't understand, but now I do."

"Do you think we killed Oleg?" asked George.

"I don't know, and it wouldn't upset me if we did. He tried to kill you, and would have in a heartbeat, so I won't be grieving for him, and it was self-defence."

"Still, it's a life."

"George, you know what you said; 'Whatever it takes'. Oleg was a sick bastard. Sorry for my French, but he'd grin as he killed us both, so I don't want to hear any more, and Moss will clean his own bodies. You'll hear nothing on the tele."

It was different for Ted; he didn't have a personal stake, as she did, but she admired his composure. He'd committed himself, and she trusted him. Ted was old school, plain speaking, never said 'awesome', 'cool', 'outstanding' or 'reach out' and she couldn't imagine him doing a 'high five', unless on the end of his fist.

Chance waited for them near the five-bar gate at George's house, which he opened for her, then walked along the path after the car.

In the house Ted asked, "Should we have tea? I'll make it."

George nodded, but her face sagged. The operation had failed; she'd failed to get information from Moss for Chance, lost her secure mobile, and didn't keep him out all night. Chance sat opposite George, meeting her stare. His look accused George, but she wouldn't admit defeat, yet. Chance's face softened.

"It's not your fault, Georgina, and it wasn't a waste of time, but tell me what you know. We may have achieved something."

Ted carried the tea-tray. She related her experience, giving an edited version of the events and those involved; the police incident and how they let her go. She left out Oleg's killing. He didn't need to know.

Chance said. "We inserted two people inside the house during the demonstration; Ted at his insistence, to support you and Sam to open Moss's safe, take copies of anything he found and return them. It was not a waste of time."

George sat up straight. "So where is Sam now?"

"He'll be a minute once he's extracting himself from your car boot."

A knock on the door, and George greeted Sam with a grin. He'd been in her car boot for several hours, but looked unruffled.

"Good morning, George, I apologise for my entrance, but I had no choice. I assume Mr Chance is here?"

"Please come in, Sam. Yes, he's here. Please, go into the living room. We have tea and cake."

"Marvellous."

He straightened his tie and joined the others with a smile. A permanent fixture.

"Sam, good to see you, you look fresh. How did it go?" asked Chance.

Sam grinned. "I opened the safe without too much fuss, but unfortunately, the 'mark' returned and interrupted my work, so I took the lot, including Moss's laptop. It's in this bag."

He handed a holdall to Chance. "I may get a great deal of information from this lot. Well done, Sam, but he now knows I have it."

George noted Chance said, 'I' not 'we'.

"Mr Chance, I'd be happier if we could move Charlie to a safer location. A secure hospital somewhere close? Can you fix that?"

"Yes, I can; I thought you'd ask. We can move her to a military medical facility in a barracks. How does that sound?"

"Local?"

"South East of London, Gillingham, I can have her taken by unmarked ambulance tomorrow if that suits you?"

"Good, yes. Can you also arrange a safe house for us nearby?"

"There's a few houses owned by the MOD, near the barracks; you can use one of those. It's basic but the best I can do at short notice, but I guess you're used to Army basic."

Chance gave Ted the address, Ted knew the place, and nodded to George.

"The housing manager will meet you at the house, and he won't ask questions. I've arranged for you to see Bradley Maudlin tomorrow afternoon. Anything else?"

"Also, a lawyer called Wilson Pinchin, Bradley Maudlin mentioned him and I plan on seeing him. He visited Bradley in prison, and he's linked to Moss. Can you find out anything?"

Chance nodded. "Will do."

Chapter 41

Bradley ambled from his cell. He expected catcalls, snide remarks, and smirks, but there were none. The occasional whisper broke the silence. Over the last few days, the prison rumour mill had worked overtime; half-truths, exaggerations, and embellishments were prison fuel for their twisted imaginings, their sense of titillation and exaggerated intrigue. Rumours provided a catalyst for prison myths and legends. The prison was coming to terms with the incident, but the repercussions weren't his problem.

He clenched his teeth, cast his gaze down and looked through his hooded eyes. But, from the prisoners' reaction, he looked like a crazy. He tried to walk normally, but with every step, a barbed harpoon pierced his chest. Bandaged hands close to his chest to avoid banging them, he resembled a boxer returning from a bruising fight. Word had spread, Bradley Maudlin was bat shit crazy and had given Josey and his mate a pasting, killing Josey and transforming Shepherd into a vegetable. Craziness alone was no guarantee of a peaceful existence. But being hard and with a craziness orientated towards destruction at any cost; that was a guarantee. A US President with nuclear weapons wasn't so scary; but a North Korean leader with a history of mental illness and the same number of nuclear weapons would scare the hell out of anyone fancying a quiet life.

Someone had put out the word, Bradley was on remand for murder, and when he went off on one, best get out of his way. Someone suggested he was a 'face in the smoke'. He grinned. It fed his sense of humour, so he perfected a Jack Nicholson look, staring into the face of anyone who dared look at him. Most didn't. Bradley's focus had to be so intense, prisoners thought him unhinged. They must also believe that his every move, look, sound, and gesture was a potential nuclear button. There are two types of cons to avoid; the bad and the crazy, and of the two, a reputation for crazy, with evidence of violence, guaranteed a quiet life. In prison, even the biggest and hardest nutter gave way to a homicidal lunatic.

Two inmates stepped out of his way and he sat at a table awaiting Susan Freeman's arrival; the last thing he wanted now was a nerdy student study. The stranger said to cooperate. Bradley understood; his saviour could do to him what he'd done to Josey and Shepherd. Bradley waited, calm, inspecting his bandaged hands on the table, almost touching. A few prisoners whispered amongst themselves, others waiting for their own visitors. He kept the crazy grin, holding out his hands. When Bradley looked at inmates, they either looked away or found something interesting on their hands.

She entered the visitor's room first. The Prison Officer said something to her and pointed towards Bradley. He didn't recognise her, not at first. Almost everything about her was different, except she was female. A woman had replaced the girl. She strode towards him wearing a business suit and confidence, with a commanding presence. Gone the cardigan, trainers, glasses, hunched posture, blackheads, pustules, and nerdy clothes.

"Jesus," he said.

She scowled and pointed at him. "Don't swear and don't blaspheme."

She sat, he nodded.

"What happened to you?" she asked without a hint of disdain.

"I got into a fight. What happened to Susan?"

She ignored the question.

"Right, Bradley Maudlin, I'm not here to socialise, I'm George Stone, and if I look familiar, I should; you are on remand for breaking and entering my mother's house, and attacking my twin sister, so tell me what happened."

"I didn't attack anyone."

Jesus, he thought again, but stopped himself from saying it. His mouth open, he remained silent.

"We haven't got time for the strong, silent type. Talk," she said.

"What happened?" he repeated.

"I haven't got time to play games. Tell me what happened, from the start," George said, looking round at other prisoners, all focussed on their own business.

Bradley understood the threat, and he could only surmise she had a link to his rescuer, who he assumed could 'unrescue' him.

She took hold of his hands and squeezed until blood oozed through the bandages. He squeezed his eyebrows together, but kept the grin, didn't flinch, and held George's stare. This was nothing compared to last night. His mind was elsewhere.

"Was Charlie your sister?" he asked quietly.

"No touching," said the Prison Officer.

She let go of his hands and sat back.

George wiped her hands on a tissue that turned red.

"No, Charlie is my sister. I didn't come here to answer questions, talk."

He talked, telling her everything about the incident. She listened.

"It was the East European man. My father's not capable of killing, I don't think. But this man held a piece of wood, so he may have struck your sister. It may have been self-defence if she was like you."

Bradley, head lowered but looking at her through hooded eyes, feared her reaction to his barbed comment.

"Describe this East European."

"Tall, athletic, short thick black hair, thirties, or early forties, maybe military, enjoys his work. Dark trousers and jacket, smooth strong hands. Not a worker or hard man, like some of these," he nodded towards one of the biggest prisoners. "More refined."

"An assassin? How tall, my height? Heavy accent?" she asked.

"I don't know, could be. About your height, accent, not heavy."

"Complexion, eyes, body language?" asked George.

"White, no idea on his eyes, an athlete I'd say; a soldier maybe."

He sensed her relaxing with a sigh and a sad look.

"So, did your father take part in the attack?"

"No, I don't think so."

"Why was your father there?"

"He helps clear up, after."

"You mean the bodies?"

"He's an undertaker, so he can get rid of bodies easy enough, and he enjoys it, but Templeton Maudlin's not right up here."

Bradley tapped his forehead with his bandaged hand and imitated his father. "He told me he has a special relationship with the dead and enjoys their company."

"How often does he do this, and how long has he been making these trips?"

"He often works at night."

He thought for almost a minute, thinking back to the start.

"Go on," prompted George.

"He does night excursions a few times a year, at least for the last ten years. Templeton Maudlin's been out like that lots of times, and on those nights he works late."

What a transformation. Bradley liked this woman she'd become, strong, straightforward, and probably unforgiving.

Even without the threat from the previous night, he'd cooperate. It occurred to him she might reach across and give him a slap.

"Why didn't you tell the truth at your trial?"

"Pinchin, my lawyer. He swore I'd get a suspended sentence, then screwed me over. I promised my Mum I'd look after dad. Templeton Maudlin's unusual, wouldn't survive in prison. But my mother freed me from that promise."

She looked at him. "Explain."

"I can't. She told me."

Bradley couldn't describe what happened last night. How could he explain the visitation? That his mother and something else had tutored him? Or was it his imagination and the doctor's drug? Either way, it would take all afternoon to expand on what happened. Best to keep quiet and let her guess.

"She's still alive?"

"No, but she told me. My father may have disposed of her body. She didn't tell me."

She didn't miss a beat. No quizzical look, no question on that point, she listened and moved on.

"Explain about your father. You said he's weird. How and why?" asked George.

"He has this habit; it helps keep him…" Bradley searched for the word. "Untroubled and level." He settled on that. It wasn't quite right, but would suffice.

"Habit. What kind?"

"Drugs. Something like opium, he smokes it."

"So, someone is paying him in drugs, feeding his habit, what does he do in return?"

"He gets rid of bodies."

It dawned on George, an organisation wanting to dispose of someone's services, would use a Funeral Director to dispose of a body.

"So, whoever killed my mother also called on your father's services to dispose of her body, right?"

"Something like that," said Bradley.

"Does he do illegal cremations at night?"

"Yeah, he spends nights preparing the bodies, then gets

Michael, his labourer, to help him?"

"What's your role in this? You pleaded guilty to the charges because Pinchin told you to?" asked George, maintaining eye contact.

"Pinchin showed me a picture of an old friend, Stella, a special friend. He threatened to kill them unless I cooperated."

Bradley stopped momentarily, considering other reasons he'd volunteered for prison. He sensed her reading his face. Would she understand a parent controlling a child to the point of torture? And the child doing anything to avoid displeasing that parent? How could she know?

"Tell me," said George.

"Dad's the dominant type and I fell under his influence, but he did the same to my mother. He's never explained what happened to her. She walked out when I was a kid. I heard the rows and accusations; I know what he was like. Before she left, she made me promise to look out for him. He attracted trouble, but she loved him anyway. I'd assumed she was dead until Pinchin visited me in prison and showed me a piece of Mum's jewellery. As a sort of threat, it gave me hope. I don't think dad could kill, but if someone else did it, he might have cremated her. I suppose you want me to testify against my father?"

"No, I want information. What I do with it does not concern you. But I assure you, your father will get what he deserves. He will pay for my mother and my sister, and if you've lied, so will you," she said, pointing at him.

"Two minutes," shouted the Prison Officer standing near the door. Visitors prepared to leave.

George looked at him without a smile, but also without malice. "Bradley, I appreciate this information and that you called the police after the attack. If this information proves useful, it may help you get out of here. If not, you'll stay and rot, and no one will help. Okay?"

He fixed her gaze and nodded. He was changing allegiances, but he was in control. At last, he could cooperate with this woman and break free of his father's hold. George Stone strode towards the exit without glancing back at Bradley. Things might get better. One thing he was sure of, George Stone was no Susan Freeman. How did she manage such a shape shifting transformation?

Off-loading the burden of the attack on Georgina's mother and sister was cathartic. Like a confession to a priest, although he didn't consider himself religious. He squeezed his eyes closed, to stop an emotional tear escaping and sat for a few minutes, his head lowered. He'd embroiled himself in this mess unnecessarily. The time was past when he could tell the police everything and his father would be in prison. But a cleansing washed over him, a cleansing

. She'd been easy to confess to, an authority figure, judgemental, but with a mature fairness.

"What are you grinning about, Bradders?" asked a Screw. "Did she promise you something?"

For the first time, a Screw had called him Bradders instead of a derogatory term related to him being a wimp. Bradley grinned, looked at the Screw through hooded eyes, his lunatic grin. It suited his temperament.

"Yeah, something like that."

The screw led him out, the last to leave the visitors' room. He was calm, not threatened or intimidated or even imprisoned by false pretences. A sense of veracity descended. His ribs, back, and hands hurt like hell, but he walked with the gait of a man who'd engaged in a battle, and returned the victor not the victim. He sensed belonging, acceptance, and inclusion. His Jack Nicholson smile turned to a genuine smile as he dismissed the thought of the three packs of smokes he'd expected at the start of the visit.

Chapter 42

Templeton fidgeted and shivered. It got into his bones, his fibre. Even the sound of gulls and the wash of the sea couldn't stem his dread. He'd expected to hear something from the prison authorities, something to the effect of, 'We're sorry, Mr Maudlin, but I'm afraid we found your son hanging from a light fitting in his cell. He committed suicide, but there were no suspicious circumstances. We are sorry for your loss.' But nothing, Bradley remained alive and well, and living a life of ease at Her Majesty's Pleasure, idle sod. He looked at his shoes and kicked a stone. Not something he would normally do, but recent disturbances had taken their toll. He needed his special prescriptive and hoped Moss would supplement his supplies. For once, Maudlin heard Moss approaching, a slight limp, arthritis, or an injury. Moss beamed at him, causing Maudlin to chill.

"Maudlin, it is imperative we remove the cause of our meetings, as much as our little discussions give you so much pleasure, not least because you believe you are my intellectual equal, which amuses me."

They strolled along the concrete path for a few minutes until Maudlin could contain himself no longer.

"Was the Bradley issue resolved?" asked Maudlin, the words falling over themselves. He turned towards Moss, looking into his eyes, willing the answer he wanted.

"Do you like the Russian philosophers, Maudlin?" asked Moss, ignoring his question.

"Not particularly. I find Solzhenitsyn so obvious. Why?"

"Oh, never mind Solzhenitsyn. Alexander Suvorov was a pragmatic military philosopher and the finest soldier and general this side of Attila the Hun. He lived in the 18th century, took part in many campaigns, and never lost a battle. Ponder this and tell me what it means to you. Suvorov once said, 'No battle can be won in the study. Theory without practice is dead'."

They walked for a few moments and Maudlin wondered if Moss had forgotten the question. He hoped so, and would therefore move on to something else. Another of Moss's mind games.

"Well?" asked Moss, his voice stressing the urgency.

"I suppose it means one must do and study."

"Bravo, Templeton. Or in Boris Yeltsin's words, 'A man cannot fight a battle from his armchair.' You, my little Cremator and Funeral Director, will join us in the battle. You understand what I am saying, Maudlin?"

Templeton nodded without understanding.

"Ha, we're agreed then. Within a few days, you will end the girl in a coma. Can you manage that? I will, of course, provide support. I will not send you into battle naked; that would be madness. I know of someone who will recognise your customer, or at least her identical twin. She will confirm your customer." Moss smiled down at Maudlin.

Moss laughed at his expense, and Templeton gulped air, gasping, his throat constricting. Seeing and handling the dead was one thing, but despatching them was a different, and for him an altogether impossible matter. People don't die easily; he could tell from the bodies he'd attended. His training wasn't despatch, it was care of the dead. How should he do it? What would he need? A knife, a noose, or drugs? He knew the effects of his drugs on the dead, but on the living, they would not be efficacious. His mind raced. If he could have spoken, he would have pleaded with Moss.

"But… how," Templeton hissed.

"I will direct you. But you must do the deed. Set free your inner, creative child," said Moss, waving away Maudlin's question and smiling at him.

"But be sure and do it; she must go, no excuses. Her coma must be a full stop, not a comma. Am I being obtuse, or am I being simple and unambiguous?"

Templeton nodded, open-mouthed.

"But why now, why me?"

"Now, because I have thus decided, and you do not need to know more. Why you? Because you have potential and may be of more use to me in the future. You will end someone, prove your credentials, earn your colours. So, open the caged maniac, which we know is yearning to emerge."

"Was Bradley Maudlin, 'finalised'?" asked Maudlin, unable to use 'son' or 'killed'. His voice quivered. He looked up at Moss.

"Bradley Maudlin is 'Work on the Anvil', as they say. That work is yet to be concluded."

Maudlin was no wiser, except to conclude that nothing had been concluded and had to assume, 'Work on the Anvil', meant it was in progress and imminent.

"One last thing; get caught and no one will come to your aid. Fail and you will transition from an 'asset' to a 'customer'."

Moss beamed at Templeton as if he'd congratulated him on his birthday.

"Come now, Templeton. Look at this as an opportunity. It's settled, marvellous. I will arrange for someone to call on you, to coordinate details, but please don't call me."

Moss paused, removing a package from his inside pocket, but held onto it as if in two minds whether Maudlin deserved it. He handed the package to Maudlin who grasped it to his body. Moss marched off as silently as he'd arrived, even with the limp, leaving Templeton standing alone on the seafront, sky, and sunrise forgotten, sobbing.

"Why?" he asked rhetorically.

Templeton Maudlin's steps skittered as he returned via

the town from meeting Moss. He considered breakfast at the café, but his mental state fed off nervous energy and an empty stomach. He knew he wouldn't be able to eat until he'd formed a plan to dispose of the girl.

Should he walk into the girl's private room and smother her? How difficult could it be? He'd find out if she was faking, she'd wake for a few seconds before her last curtain call. Too risky. He liked to do things correctly, precisely, and risk-free. He needed to deliberate further.

On his arrival at the Funerarium, Michael served Templeton his afternoon tea; two digestive biscuits, and Earl Grey tea. Templeton grunted his acknowledgement. His tea and biscuits remained untouched. He worked longhand, using a foolscap pad. Feverish writing and scribbling filled most of his day, his writing getting faster and as he sketched, listed, discarded, but failed to craft a risk-free method to despatch the girl. It would need to be 'natural causes', no mean feat, but a solution evaded him. Even as he prepared his mind for bed, he mulled over possibilities, but knew he would have a sleepless, turbulent night. A 'white night', as he called it.

His usual routine was to smoke a cigar and drink a single malt in his Library. Recently, Templeton questioned his arrival at this predicament. Bradley had contributed. Was Bradley a 'Maudlin'? A good question. A Maudlin would have supported him, taken care of him, entered the family business and appreciated the beauty of his vocation, as he'd done with his own father.

He sat in his study, caressed his glass of whisky, and stroked a wooden box sent to him by Moss, lying in his lap. The silkiness of the wood reflecting the priceless contents.

His thoughts returned to his early days in the profession. From the moment his father had invited him to touch, then hold the hands of his 'dead friends' as he called them, he relished death's beauty, longevity, permanence, and loyalty. This contrasted with his former wife, where there had been no loyalty. The thought of her causing him to grind his teeth. His father, Justin Templeton, explained the purity of death and its permanence, in contrast to life. He also explained how important hands were, which during life, encounter more earthly experiences than any other part of the body. People with the skill and sensitivity could sense a deceased person's life, experiences, and ordeals. Justin Maudlin explained; they both had this sensitivity and were born into the work. His father hadn't objected when he'd prepared a body in the coffin to discover a finger missing. He looked at Templeton, raised an eyebrow, but his eyes smiled. With his father's tacit blessing, he indulged his pleasure and amassed a collection, remembering each one, and when he touched the piece; he established a connection.

At nineteen, Templeton decided he had surpassed his father in the fine art of Funeral Directorship and unilaterally assumed management of the business, retiring his father to his studies, and suggesting he visit the Far East, to indulge in the pleasures of the flesh.

On his father's return, Templeton observed Justin Maudlin's enthusiasm for opium. Visitors sniffing the flowery, cloying fetor, attributed it to the peculiarities of the funeral industry, Templeton sought it out and finally ventured to sample then surrender himself to it.

Templeton delayed opening the box on his lap until properly prepared. He feverishly prepared his equipment and fifteen minutes later, and with a little help from Michael, took his first draw of the foot long pipe, crooked in one arm, the wooden box cradled in the other. Inside the box lay Charlie's finger and a single sheet of instructions from Moss, which he read and cast aside. His narcotised mind drifted as he slid his fingers along Charlie's severed digit, her presence palpable, before finally drifting off into a place familiar to him. An unseen visitor showed him the enjoyment awaiting him. He savoured thoughts of the girl's descent from coma to eventual rest.

Usually, Templeton's last act before bedding was to examine his reflection in the mirror wearing his flannelette pyjamas, not through vanity but to ensure his proper attire, otherwise it disturbed his sleep. He'd broken the habit after his ordeal with the manifestation, but finally convinced himself that an overactive imagination was at work, with no chance of a recurrence.

Templeton relished cold bedclothes and an open window, knowing that within fifteen minutes he'd be warm and comfortable in a drug induced oblivion. He grinned at his former timorousness towards his forthcoming task. The drug energised him towards finding a solution, and convinced him a plan would emerge as clear as the celestial heavens on a cloudless night.

He awoke a few hours later; the dark enshrouding him. He shivered, the cold boring into him. Far removed from his usual joyous experience, the hairs on his body stood erect and brushing uncomfortable against the sheets. He shucked down into his bedclothes, striving to stop shaking and calm his mind.

"You're wasting your time."

Yes, he knew that; but he had to try. He snuggled and took to deep breathing, even soft snoring. And an hour before dawn, he neither slept, nor was he closer to solving his problem, which rose like a serpent.

"Tell Moss you can't do it. He'll understand, won't he?" said a voice with a hint of derision.

There was that soulless voice again, caused by the medication. He'd thought of confronting Moss, but the prospect of becoming a 'customer' was less appealing. Would he understand? No, he would not. He knew from first-hand experience what Moss and his organisation were capable of. Despite his expectation that he'd warm up, he froze and arose to close the window, catching his reflection in the new mirror as he crossed the room. A wisp of smoke behind his image, nothing more. He'd looked death in the face, so illusion combined with his own active imagination couldn't scare him. He'd seen her face in the smoky mirror, but he also saw faces in clouds and Santa in snow. Scoffing to convince himself and not wanting to accept what his brain told him, he took a towel from the chair and draped it over the mirror.

If Charon or any other ethereal character wanted to watch him, they'd do it through a towel. He perched on the bed, but the cold seeped through the cotton sheet into his buttocks. Templeton took his whisky glass and sipped a last drop. His feet froze, and he slid his legs under the covers, pulling them around him.

"Is that better," asked the wraith lying next to him.

"Jesus!" he squealed, recognising both the face and the voice.

"What the hell are you doing here?" he asked as she took his hand, placing it next to her face.

"No, not Jesus, it's me. Calm, my darling, calm," she

said, her voice sliding like oil on ice.

Despite his effort to resist and pull away, he succumbed. Her coldness seeped into his hands like a cut-throat razor through the carotid artery. Unlike in life, he had no will to resist her in death, and he welcomed her embrace.

"Like this, place your hands here and here."

She took his hands, enwrapping them around her smoke grey neck. A simper of encouragement escaped her lips. He knelt across her chest, both hands around her neck. As he gripped her throat, she pouted until his fingers squeezed and touched. Her neck was as real and as responsive as any woman's, but unlike any corpse he'd attended. As he gripped, the trachea crushed, blood vessels collapsed and her skin enfolded. His fingers sensed a pulse feather, then cease.

"That, Templeton, answers your dilemma," said the thing.

"Now lay next to me awhile and disencumber yourself," she said.

Shaking, dripping, and groaning, Maudlin collapsed onto the bed beside her, and he spooned his body with hers.

He lay uncovered until daybreak, when Michael came to wake him. As he sipped his morning coffee in bed, his mind was as clear as a breezy, cloudless sky. His remaining problem, how to reconcile the instructions from Moss with the solution his night visitor had presented.

Chapter 43

Chance had directed George and Sarah to meet him at his office in South London. Nothing smelt right and both Ted and George decided a recce was vital. As they walked along a deserted road towards the Asian café and Chance's office, George pondered the time and location. 9 p.m. on Saturday night? Bad time, bad place. She suspected Ted thought the same. South London late at night in January could be a dismal, soulless place. They walked on the opposite side to the café. George glanced across at Chance's office window. No lights in his office, unless he'd drawn the heavy curtains. The Asian café was preparing to close but still lit.

George's brain itched. Chance had been short with her under pressure but reliable so far. Strange, but these were strange times. But the time and location were 'off'. Why not visit the house or phone? A grassy bank opposite the café, and a hundred metres down the road a 1960s style block of flats overlooked the area.

The block of flats showed that time and a lack of care could turn white plastic and concrete into a grey wart.

Someone in an upper flat facing Chance's office could see into the café and except for the curtains, also see into Chance's office. With the proper equipment, they could listen to conversations.

"Something's wrong," mused Ted.

The door to the Asian café remained open. An Asian man cleaned the tables, but no sign of Sarah. George would wait a minute, then go on her own and leave Ted outside to wait for her. The man looked at her but paid her no heed. Die Hard 4 was playing on the TV. He nodded to her as she entered via the cupboard door. He'd set the sound so high it spilled out for the entire street to hear. She doubted a fire alarm would punctuate his enjoyment.

Some guys on night shift in Camp Bastion, Lashkar Gah, Afghanistan, watched the film repeatedly. The film war was underlaid by genuine small arms fire, a C17 landing or the 'whup whup' of a Chinook or Westland Merlin taking off, flying injured to safety or the dying for 'processing'. All soldiers in Camp Bastion lived on edge. Even newbies recognised the difference between the Hollywood produced 'rat-a-tat-tat' of a make-believe Uzi, and the sharp 'dum' of a real AK47, or the lighter 'tat' of an SA80. They also came to their feet within a second of 'stand to', followed by the shouted 'SITREP'. In under a minute, buckled and ready to risk their lives. The film had amused George the first time, but coarse language and the light-hearted way actors portrayed action was not to her taste. Now she never watched that sort of thing, but she recalled the scene:

> *'I know I'm not as smart as you guys at all this computer shit. But, hey... I'm still alive, ain't I? I mean, you've GOT to be running out of bad guys by now, right? Huh? Gabriel? Honestly, you can tell me. I mean, how does that work? Got*

some kind of service or something? Some kind of 800 number? 1-800-HENCHMEN?'

She looked at her watch and made her way to Chance's office. Sarah could follow her. She texted Ted, then took the stairs as she'd done on the previous occasion. Unlike before, Chance wasn't there to meet her. The door to Chance's office was closed. She cracked it open. No light escaped onto the stairs from the room. Again, her brain tingled, and her scalp contracted. She checked the minute and second hand on her watch. Ted would wait for Sarah. Chance must have left the door open. George's pulse raced, and her hand went to the reassuring bulge of her Glock. As they'd both suspected, either Chance was playing John le Carré, or something was wrong. But she'd play the cards she'd been dealt.

Ready, she entered the darkened room at a crouch. The room hadn't changed, except no Chance, and no light except the street light penetrating the net curtains. She pushed the door closed behind her, laid her bag near the door and waited, listening, smelling, and sensing something, anything. A noise. There was someone else in the room, Chance? A rank smell of body odour, fear, and ammonia.

That noise, again. Someone whispering? Except she had excellent hearing and couldn't make out the words. A mumble, then banging, something thumping against a wall or furniture. She waited for her eyes to adjust and her night vision to give her a clue.

Bang, thump, bang, then more mumbling, urgent but irregular. George crept further into the room. A shape occupied the end of the room near the window, Chance's desk. The conference table and chairs two metres away looked to be unoccupied. She tried to make sense of the shape through the glimmer of light escaping from the streetlight outside. The corners of the lace curtains allowed a little light to enter the room, but light coming from the stairs created shadow. Perfect for someone watching the room from the street. She now had her night vision. A figure sat in a straight-backed chair, hands on the table, unmoving. Either Chance or Sarah. The dark shape told her it was Sarah, who was likely bound into position, and gagged. That answered George's question, why Sarah hadn't met her downstairs. Boy, Sarah got the thin end of this deal; first, her partner disappeared, now this. In a distant sort of way, she'd become fond of the woman. She needed to free Sarah. But everything suggested a booby trap. The ping of the pin released from a grenade, a shot through the window, or someone breaking down the door. These people didn't mess about, they'd made that clear.

"It's me, Sarah. Don't worry, I'll get you out."

Sarah mumbled and shook her head, then fell silent, and George felt Sarah's eyes bore into hers. George edged around the room, her back to the wall. She lifted the edge of the curtain, letting in more light. She peeked above the low windowsill but saw nothing.

Sarah now had her back to George. She no longer moved. No sound, no movement. The smell of cigarette smoke from the curtains invaded George's sense of smell. She gripped the bottom of the heavy cloth curtains and dragged them closed across the window. They shut off the sparse light coming into the room and bathed it in darkness. She waited to regain her night vision and used the time to consider her options.

Sarah looked like bait. Someone was trying to get George, Sarah, and perhaps Chance, into a killing zone.

George guessed the plan was for a Russian to enter with his silenced automatic. Two shots to the heart, one to the head. Kill George and Sarah and leave; quick and easy. So much for five days' stay of execution. On the way out, kill Ted. She could sit in the corner and wait for her executioner to show. George reached behind her and pulled out her MI5 issued Glock 17, drawing the slide back under control, to put one in the chamber. She feathered the trigger safety with a finger but applied no pressure to it.

George sat in the corner watching the door and window, aiming her weapon at the most likely entry point, the door.

Fifteen minutes passed, and she settled, scanning the window and door. Sarah remained silent. They might be here all night. This looked like a waiting game. Not her style, but she'd cope. On stiff legs, she stood, then crept over to the table and stood in front of Sarah, her Glock ready. Sarah's hands were splayed in front of her, flat on the table.

Sarah didn't seem bound, but she shook her head. The enemy had used superglue instead of ropes and tape, even her lips were glued together and hands glued to the table, no doubt her feet were glued to the floor, and her back glued to the chair. Simple but effective. One finger had been amputated, and the end sealed with superglue.

An unlit angle poise lamp stood on the desk, and a piece of paper lay in front of Sarah, ready for someone facing her to read. The two women's eyes met, and Sarah's tears mixed with pleading. There was no painless way to release Sarah, it would take solvent.

The main curtains were drawn, and George reached for

the switch on the lamp. As she flicked it on, she realised it was a stupid and fatal mistake.

Sarah lifted the table with her glued hands, turning it to form a barrier between the two women, and between George and the window. The lamp fell onto the floor, illuminating the ceiling. The table lay between her and Sarah; her glued hands taking the weight of the table. Too late, George realised what the plan had been. Sarah's action aimed to help protect her friend.

The window shattered, and the curtain twitched, confirming her suspicion. A sharp thud of a high-velocity round came a microsecond later. The table now rested on its side, George between the legs. The sound of wood splintering suggested the table had taken a round. George crouched behind the table, pointing her weapon at the window. It was pointless. Moss had outplayed and out manoeuvred her. The coppery smell of blood hit her nostrils.

George wasn't hit, and that left one possibility. She lowered her weapon and reached over, switching off the lamp, and crawled around the table to where Sarah lay. A second round sliced through the curtain and embedded itself in the upturned table. A chance shot, George guessed.

The killer had staged the scene to kill someone reading the note. Even with the curtains closed, using the right ammunition, if he hit, he'd kill. George expected he'd marked the window beforehand. The sniper didn't need a target. He'd waited for the desk light to come on, and fired at a mark he'd placed on the window and certain to kill whoever switched on the light. This sniper prided himself on being a perfectionist, but he hadn't bet on Sarah lifting the table and taking the bullet. They'd disturbed the sniper's stage. He couldn't know what Sarah would do, and he no longer knew George's location.

George produced a tiny LED torch from her pocket, and shone it on Sarah, lying on her side. She'd seen horrors throughout her military career, but few could prepare her for this. One of Sarah's hands, minus a finger, lay with its back to the floor a bloody mess. Although she'd wrenched her hands free of the table, her skin was ripped off, but remained stuck to the table. Shining the torch on Sarah's face, her sealed lips told her why she hadn't warned George or cried out, and George suppressed her nausea. There was no point in seeing if she could help Sarah. The bullet had entered her neck at the back and exited her throat, a soft-nosed bullet from the exit damage. Sarah's eyelids quivered open and George took her in her arms, held her and rocked gently, pressing her face against the stricken woman's. Their tears mingled, like rain drops merging on a window. Tear drops of life and death.

"I'm so sorry, Sarah. So sorry. Thank you for saving me. I'm so sorry."

Sarah's eyes remained open, but all life had disappeared. A pool of red and white matter splattered across the floor and the table. George lay Sarah on the floor and ripped the note stuck to the table. It said, 'YOUR FINGER NEXT'. She folded it and slipped it into her pocket.

She needed to move and confront Chance. Unless he was dead. George searched through Sarah's pockets for anything that could identify her or help George. A gold chain and locket hung around what remained of her neck, covered in gore. She unclasped and pocketed it and looked through the darkness towards the door. The sniper's bullets had torn holes in the curtains, allowing light in. A line of light also escaped under the closed door. If she headed to the door, light would enter from the corridor and they'd receive another bullet.

As she prepared to keep low and cat crawl towards the door, a knock caught her attention. George sat with her back to the wall and texted Ted to stay away. The door handle moved, and the door scraped along the carpet. Someone with manners was trying to get her attention. The door swung open and an arc of light spread across the floor. An oversized man, another Russian bear, stood silhouetted in the doorway, expressionless. He reeked of alcohol, adrenaline, and an overexcited bowel movement. A zombie waiting to be chopped down. A thud from the corridor told her someone had obliged. The man staggered into the room but remained upright. A shot came through the curtained windows and hit the bear in the chest. Another followed and caught him in his left shoulder, spinning him around. He landed on his back in the open doorway. Another shot went through the doorway and hit the corridor wall opposite. The Russian lay still but blew blood bubbles. A stream of bright red ran along his cheeks, pooling at the side of his head.

He mumbled something, and George cat crawled to his side. The room returned to silence. Ted sat to one side of the doorway, refitting his prosthesis, which George assumed he'd used as a weapon on the Russian. An automatic weapon lay by Ted's side.

"I saw him outside waiting. He entered the café when he heard the first shot, to make sure you were dead, but I persuaded him to accompany me."

The man was dying, and she thought about sitting with him to the end. She deserved to see him die, and he also deserved that much. But the Russian smiled and tried to speak but managed a watery whisper. Although she didn't want to hear the Russian's deathbed confessions, she hoped he might reveal something about others on the team. She bent and put her ear to his bloodied lips.

"Your sister is as good as dead, and you too will die. What's the time?" he said in an Essex accent.

She looked at her watch. Why was the time so important?

"Eleven o'clock," said George.

The Russian coughed and laughed. She thought it took a certain callousness to take pleasure in someone's death, even her enemy's. But if what she was guessing was right, she'd enjoy this enemy's death.

She knelt next to him and stared into his face; a proxy for the killer.

"George?" Ted said, sneaking a look around the door. "We have to go. Now."

"Yeah, coming. You go ahead, I'll be a minute. Leave me the man's automatic."

George dragged the Russian into the room, and pushed the door closed, returning it to darkness. The man left a dark, wet trail along the floor.

She'd seen soldiers die on the battlefield, never a pretty sight, and never easy, she'd been close to it herself.

"This is more than you deserve. What's your name?"

"Jack." Black bubbles frothed from his mouth. "You can call me Jack."

"Your full name? You work for Russian intelligence? Or do you work for Moss?"

"I have no other name. I've lived here in this forsaken place for so long my Russian name doesn't matter."

He coughed and grinned.

"In the old days I worked for the KGB, now I work for Mosin."

He used Moss's Russian name. His breathing was shallow and laboured, his blood running down his cheek in rivulets.

"It doesn't matter now, you're marked for termination, and Mosin won't stop. You may as well give up."

He smiled, giving him a clownish appearance. Blood spread around his mouth in an obscene grin.

"How many of you. Who are they?"

"Too many for you. It makes no difference."

He laughed until fluid gurgled up, which forced him to swallow.

"How did you know about the meeting?" asked George.

The dying man said, "We asked Chance."

The way the man said 'asked' suggested torture. It

stung George. Had Chance sold them out? Had they threatened his family or kidnapped his son? She couldn't believe that Chance would betray them, even if Moss threatened his family.

"He won't stop, you know, the sniper, Andrei." The man stared at the window. "He will come after you until either you or he is dead."

Taking the man's Russian made automatic, she crept over to the curtains, ripped a net from the curtain pole and wrapped it around the weapon and her wrist. She turned to where the Russian knelt, blood pouring from his mouth and chest wound. The man held out a hand, pleading. As she approached, he lunged, catching her in the side of her left calf with a penknife. She grunted in agony, dropped to her knees, and freed the knife from her leg.

"Let's die together. You, too, are a soldier. What do you say, George Stone?"

He lunged again, but she'd regained her feet, landing a kick to his head, which caught him under the chin, knocking him back. He lay still, head against the door.

"I'm nothing like you. I'm doing this because I have to," she said, kicking him again.

He was finally silent but stared at her, resigned to his fate. She could even admire that about him.

"What's the matter, cat got your tongue?"

She pushed the barrel of her automatic into his mouth, knocking teeth out, angled it towards his palate and squeezed the trigger. The dull thud from the silenced weapon would hardly carry to the street. His head lifted, then flopped back onto the carpet. Her hands were still, and her mind clear and calm. Killing was never good for the soul, but this was her job. If there was a God, he would forgive her; for this killing, and every other killing. She knelt over Sarah and reflected on the woman who she'd berated and pushed away and sacrificed her life for her. Sarah had family and friends who would miss her. George wasn't becoming soft, but she'd been too quick to judge the woman. George would make an anonymous call to the NCA, to collect her body. A search of the Russian's body revealed a pair of secateurs and a small plastic bag containing one severed finger. She pocketed both and promised herself to at least give that a decent burial.

She wiped the weapon on the curtain and laid it next to the body and, glancing around the room, retrieved her blood-covered bag and limped into the corridor. A shock for the cleaners in the morning.

Ted waited on the stairs but didn't ask about Sarah, the Russian, or her, and she didn't tell him. He helped her down the stairs, she with a knife wound, him limping. They descended the stairs together, each supporting the other. Reaching the bottom floor, she glanced around. The café was empty. Die Hard 4 still playing. The sound turned to maximum.

"That's gonna wake the neighbours," said John McClane.

"Another day in paradise," replied Ted in his Glaswegian brogue.

He led them around the counter, through the kitchen, and out the back door.

It occurred to George that the sniper could have killed

George in the street before they entered the café. The message wasn't lost on her. 'This is what we can do. No hiding place. No escape'.

George had parked her car a short walk from Chance's office. Their minds focussed on getting away and supporting each other through the pain and the trauma they'd seen.

At the car, Ted tried to tend to George's wound. She wouldn't have it and brushed him off with a wave.

"Get in the car, damn it," she said.

Ted got in the car, maybe thinking it better to leave her alone for a while. She leaned on the car; her fists clenched on the roof. Was it too much for her? Moss had outsmarted her from the start, and except for Sarah's martyrdom, she'd be dead now. Because of her own stupidity, someone, a friend, and ally had died. She slapped her hands on the roof of the car and bellowed, an animal in pain. Looking into the clear night sky, she roared. "Why? Why Me? Why My Family? What Do You Want From Me? Why Sarah? She didn't hurt you. She didn't hurt anyone!"

She didn't know who she was talking to, but at that moment she doubted anyone was listening.

Her hands hammered on the car. A couple passing pointed to her and 'tutted', thinking she was having a tantrum over a date, or other trivial matter. George ignored them.

Blood dribbled down her leg where she'd been clenching her leg muscles, but she felt nothing. She stood there for a time, eyes squeezed tight, teeth gritted, even questioning her existence.

She forced herself to relax. Ted exited the car and stood on the opposite side.

"Get in," said George, her eyes blazing into his.

"I'll drive. You're in no fit state," said Ted.

He didn't grin, frown, show anger, or sorrow and George realised Ted would always be reliable and loyal. All he wanted was to help her, as she'd helped him find meaning. And he'd follow her towards his own demise, if that's what she needed. Ted had become her new family.

She limped around to the passenger side, and Ted drove out of London towards Gillingham.

***

As George and Ted left Chance's office via the back door, they didn't see the white van with 'Stone Cold Air Conditioning' emblazoned on the side. The two men inside waited for the signal to retrieve the bodies for disposal.

Chapter 44

As George prepared to fight for her life in Chance's office, Templeton Maudlin made final preparations to conclude Charlie's life. A black military staff car with darkened rear windows met him in the Funerarium courtyard at 9 p.m. The uniformed Corporal driver said nothing and remained in the car. Templeton had all he needed in his bag, a bible, a phial marked 'Holy Water', a large metal crucifix, the book of common prayer and a khaki Army Officer's hat. As he walked to the car, wind whipped around him and Templeton protected his face against the rain, and shivered.

Maudlin didn't expect, nor invite, conversation. He had enough to think of and to rehearse, as his visitor had encouraged during his drugged state the previous evening. The sign for Gillingham reminded him to prepare himself. Satisfied, he relaxed, but fidgeted with his clerical collar.

The miles ticked off until a red and white sign showed directions to the barracks. They were within a few miles of the camp. He withdrew a credit card size military identity card from his pocket and squeezed it in his hands.

He whispered, "Padre Lucas West, HQ Southern District, to visit Miss Stone in the Medical Centre."

The driver caught Templeton's eye in the rear-view mirror.

"Put the hat on. And remember, I'll identify and confirm your target."

He reacted with a start. The driver was a woman, her black hair cropped short and tucked under a beret. He nodded, confirming he understood.

Templeton took his hat and pushed it onto his head. The Cpl glanced in the rear-view mirror, presumably to ensure that he didn't wear it back to front. But Templeton knew how to wear it. He had not only practised wearing it using a mirror, he'd practised saluting, so it looked natural. 'Casual, be casual,' he muttered to himself. His ethereal visitor had shown him how to do it, and he felt confident, adjusting his dog collar, running a finger between it and his neck, then sat back.

He glanced at the military houses and saw light coming from some. He supposed they were soldiers' married quarters, sterile and soulless. A ten-foot-high fence and barbed wire suggested they were approaching the barrier and entrance to the camp.

The driver slowed in the narrow road, towards the barracks ahead. The road was wide enough for two cars with barely a shoe's width to spare. Through the windscreen he saw unlit, concrete bollards, only a few metres apart. They formed a chicane, slowing the car, but nothing could slow Templeton Maudlin from his destiny. The dodgem track twisted and turned, making Templeton queasy. By the time they reached the red and white barrier, the car had slowed to a walking pace.

A military guard manned the hut on the left, its windows darkened. The guard looked at the tarmac to keep his night vision. The driver lowered both the side windows and switched to sidelights to avoid dazzling the guard.

Templeton recognised the guard's weapon from news reports from Afghanistan. The SA80 assault rifle pointed down; but he noticed the guard kept his right hand on his weapon and used his left hand to check passes. A spotlight fixed atop the hut shone into the car, blinding Templeton.

"Cpl Jessica Harvey, taking Major West to the Medical Centre. How is everything tonight?" she asked.

"Quiet, and that's the way I like it," he said.

She showed her ID card. The guard said nothing, satisfied. He walked to the rear of the car and looked through the open window.

"Light, please, Sir."

Templeton stared at the guard and froze, mouth open, until the driver pushed a switch illuminating the rear. Templeton remained mouth open. The driver coughed, dragging him from his trance. The guard's challenge threatened to derail his train.

"ID card please, Sir."

"Oh yes," said Templeton "Padre Lucas West, HQ Southern District, to see Miss Stone in the Medical Centre."

"ID card, Sir."

Templeton held his ID card in both shaking hands.

The guard took the card, examined it under the spotlight, then examined Templeton before returning it. He didn't salute, but satisfied, went into the hut, and raised the barrier. The car windows slid closed and Templeton blew out a breath. They entered the camp and Templeton flopped back into the seat; his bottom lip stuck out in a sulk.

"Take it easy. We're in. Follow the script," she said.

She knew the camp layout, which had myriad signs. He wondered how anyone could navigate the camp. A circuit designed to confuse visitors, and the mentally challenged. Despite the street lights, the camp was threateningly desolate. A branch swept under the car, but the driver didn't slow, and it rattled underneath, which jangled Maudlin's nerves still further. He put a pipe in his mouth and sucked, taking slow breaths. Less than five minutes later, they stopped outside 'The Garrison Medical Centre', where lights suggested the place was occupied. But at night manning would be reduced. They parked in a VIP space.

"This is it. I'll be right behind you. Relax and don't forget to salute if you see someone."

"That guard should have saluted me. I have the insignia of a Major. I'd practised," said Templeton.

The Cpl ignored him.

They walked into the Medical Centre, Templeton carried his bag as if it contained the crown jewels, and again ran his finger under his dog collar. The drizzle dashed against his face, and he hoped his makeup would hold. He used it on his friends. What could go wrong?

The Medical Centre's reception was little bigger than a town Health Centre. A smell of disinfectant permeated the air, evoking thoughts of illness and death. A Medical Orderly manning reception busied himself behind the counter. He looked at the Padre and Cpl. His look questioned why they'd interrupted his quiet night.

"Good evening, I'm Major West, Chaplains Department. Southern District informed you I was coming to see Charlie Stone."

The Medical Orderly put down his pen with finality and a huff.

"Yes, Sir, I received a call. But I don't think it's a good idea. You know she's comatose, right?"

"Even the sleeping need God's counsel. If her soul will listen, she will hear my ministrations. I will be a few minutes. I want to share a prayer with her and hold her hand."

Templeton had added to the script, and felt the Cpl scowl.

"I don't doubt you, Sir, but can I see your ID cards? And I must inspect the contents of your bag, please. There was a threat to her life; we're being careful. Sorry," said the Orderly.

"Yes, of course. Here's my ID card and please inspect my bag."

The Medical Orderly squinted at their ID cards and brought his face closer to Templeton's. Satisfied, he took the bag, placed its contents onto the desk and laid out the bible, crucifix, book of common prayer and phial.

"What's this for, Sir?" said the Orderly, holding the phial. "What does it contain?"

"As it says, Holy Water, my son. I don't go anywhere without it."

The Orderly returned the items and gave the bag to Templeton.

"You can stay for a little while. However, I need time alone with Charlie. Confidentiality, you understand," said Templeton.

The Orderly's face wrinkled, his eyes squinting, his mouth a straight line. Templeton registered the Orderly's suspicion. He nodded and led them along the corridor.

Templeton neither saw nor heard anyone else in the Centre, and their footsteps on the rubber coated flooring gave a 'tic-tac' sound.

"How many patients are here?" asked the driver.

"Only Charlie. We receive soldiers involved in training accidents, but we're quiet now. A doctor called earlier, he said he'd check her later."

They entered Charlie's room; the driver making way for Templeton, who clasped his hands together and frowned.

"My child, what an unholy mess. God wants us to pray together."

"I don't think you'll get much reaction."

The Cpl stared at Charlie as if trying to recall her face. Seemingly satisfied, she looked at Maudlin and nodded. He returned her look with a smile.

The girl's hands lay under the cover. A drip attached to the crux of her arm, and a monitor registered a steady heartbeat. Another tone registered her breathing. To Templeton, she was as serene as his friends in his Funerarium, and he looked forward to this time together.

He laid his bag on the floor and took out the bible and crucifix. He mumbled a few words he hoped sounded like a brief prayer, made the sign of the cross over the bed, sat, bowed his head, and squeezed his eyes closed.

"Let's leave them," said the driver.

The Medical Orderly looked around. "Alright. How long will you need, Padre?"

Templeton opened his eyes as if startled out of a trance. "Fifteen minutes, I should think. Twenty at most."

"I'll wait outside, and we'll see you before we leave," said the driver, flashing her eyes at the Orderly.

"I'll be in reception. Okay?" said the Orderly.

They disappeared, leaving Templeton Maudlin and Charlie alone.

His eyes flitted. He felt under the bedsheet for her hand, pulling it out and placing it on top of the cover to examine it. Yes, this was Charlie. Her index finger was missing, the stump stitched and dressed. Proof enough, he had the right girl.

Templeton placed the phial of Holy Water on a table, then levered the back from the crucifix using a small penknife and removed a tiny hypodermic syringe, which he laid next to the Holy Water.

The procedure was no stranger, and occasionally he'd used this method on himself. He pieced the phial and extracted a concoction of formaldehyde and opium into the syringe.

Meticulous in his movements, Templeton tended his new friend. The difference between Charlie and his usual customers being about ten minutes.

He pierced the drip tube to Charlie's arm with the syringe, depressed the plunger, and watched clear liquid mix with the drug in the drip.

"All will be fine now. Stay calm and meet my other friends."

Templeton knew he should collect his paraphernalia immediately and leave, as directed by the script, but he hesitated, then sat, smiling at the dying girl. Both heart rate and breathing monitor's recorded slowing rates. Taking her hand, he caressed it. Charlie, now a cherished friend. He wished he'd saved an amount of opium for himself. It would have been beautiful.

A minute or twenty passed. A phone ringing brought him back to his senses and a muffled voice answered, presumably the Orderly. Charlie's monitor made a last bleep, announcing Charlie's last heartbeat, followed by a shrill buzz, intended to bring help.

He'd stayed too long. Now he scrambled to throw items into his bag before rushing for the door. The driver stood in the corridor. One hand behind her back holding a weapon. The Orderly, twenty metres away, sprinted along the corridor, face flushed, eyes protruding, flatulence following him.

"Out of the way," he screamed.

The driver held the door open for the Orderly, who charged in, lent over his patient, and worked feverishly to check Charlie's pulse and breathing. Pointing her weapon at the man, she shot him in the back of the head. The weapon made almost no noise. He'd seen many dead bodies, but besides Charlie, none during this beautiful transition from one state to the other. Templeton gazed at Charlie and the Orderly, fascinated by the drama. Seeing the Orderly spread obscenely across Charlie, he gasped and stepped back. To Templeton, it was a grotesque work of art.

The Orderly flopped over Charlie like a dead fish with its head sliced off. The entrance wound was small, but his face had disintegrated. Brain, blood, and connective tissue sprayed over the bed and Charlie. Her lifeless face caught most of the fallout and gave it a mottled, red-grey colour, with a moonscape texture. The Orderly twitched and lay still, arms hanging on either side of the bed, a clownish actor playing dead. Charlie's eyes were wide open, but her monitor confirmed death. Charlie and the Orderly resembled actors in an exotic scene from the 1968 film 'Barbarella'.

Templeton had seen murder victims, but he'd never seen death brought about with such orchestrated callousness. The Medical Orderly's execution was as precise as a surgeon wielding a sledgehammer to perform brain surgery. The driver's mouth moved, but no sound escaped. She pointed to the monitor. He assumed she wanted him to turn it off. Templeton thought she might shoot him and shivered. He unplugged the machine, but as his hearing returned, so did the monitor noise.

"I can't stop it," said Templeton, forced to raise his voice.

"Leave it, we're going."

The assassin's last act before leaving was to point her weapon at Charlie's face and fire one silent shot. Charlie's eyes were still open. Her head lifted, then rested. Its contents spreading over the pillow.

As they passed the reception desk, the phone lay on the desk, as if dropped mid call by the Orderly. He followed the driver out of the Medical Centre to the car. She pushed her weapon inside her uniform. Templeton saw her staring at him and imagined she'd blame him for this little problem. She didn't understand. Moss thrust this temptation at him. He pouted, regretting involvement with such an unprofessional group.

Chapter 45

George clicked off her mobile phone. "I called the Medical Centre where Charlie is, but there was no reply. Something's wrong, I can feel it. Do you know the Guard Room number?"

"No, but I'll call a Senior NCO I know in the camp," Ted said.

A few seconds later, Ted spoke to the Sergeant. "Hey mate, it's Ted. There's something wrong at the Medical Centre, Charlie may be in danger. Can you send the guard there now? Ask the Guard Commander to check if anyone's visited the Medical Centre tonight. And if so, stop vehicles leaving the camp. We'll be there in less than thirty minutes. Tell him to let us in. We don't want an overzealous recruit stopping us. We'll go straight to the Medical Centre. Thanks, mate."

Ted drove along the A2 towards Gillingham. Part of it was dual carriageway. Ignoring the speed limit, he occasionally leant on the horn and flashed the car's lights to move traffic. Something was wrong; not only the phone call, but George sensed it. She hadn't had this feeling since the attack on Charlie, but this was colder, a chilling emptiness which neither the car's heater nor her coat could banish.

Ted pushed the Ford as fast as it was able, and the traffic allowed. Some drivers sounded their annoyance, and a Jaguar gave chase, no doubt in a road rage. Ted didn't have time for that. When it went bumper to bumper, he applied his brakes and let the tow hook make a hole in the Jags radiator. Ted floored the accelerator.

Ted's phone rang. "Yes?"

Ted listened for a minute.

"Stop that staff car with the Padre. We'll be there in a minute."

He clicked the phone off and glanced at George. "There's been trouble at the Medical Centre."

George looked down, mumbled a prayer to herself; or an appeal to anyone or anything that might help. Ted starred, focussed but calm. She rarely bothered God. People made their own luck and managed their own fate, but at this moment she needed something.

"What was that call about?" asked George.

Ted stopped the car and stared through the windscreen and took a deep breath.

"I was hoping you wouldn't ask right now." He turned to her. "I'm sorry, but Charlie's dead. Steve, my mate, is at the Medical Centre now. There's a search for a fake Padre and his driver. They may have poisoned or suffocated

Charlie. They also killed the Orderly."

Chance's meeting was a diversion. A cold chill ran the length of her spine, which numbed her brain. She couldn't think. Charlie couldn't be dead; she'd survived one attempt on her life, and this place was supposed to be secure. The question, 'How could it happen?' her brain screamed. How could anyone kill a comatose woman, in the Medical Centre, in a military barracks? What animal would have the iniquity to do that? She stared at Ted, who leaned over to hold her, but she pushed him away.

"I'm okay. I must move on, for Charlie's sake. This isn't finished."

She turned and stared out of the Ford's filthy window. "Let's get to the barracks, catch that Padre. Come on, step on it," she said.

Ted started the car and sent a text message as he was driving off. Tree lined woods on one side and a playing field on the other. The moonlight lit the puddles on the road.

Before they reached the chicane, Ted flashed his main beam to warn the guard, and the barrier rose. He didn't slow. They were a hundred yards from the barrier, another car, a black staff car, sped out of the camp and under the barrier towards them. Its engine screaming. Headlights blazing, they had no intention of slowing for the chicane. It negotiated the first concrete bollard but scraped the driver's side, sparks flying. For George, it was enough to convince her it had to be the Padre and his driver.

"Block the chicane," said George, pushing a switch to ensure the Ford's inside lights wouldn't come on.

Ted crept forward and entered the chicane. There was room for one car alongside the bollard. He didn't stop, but drove around the bollard. The staff car slowed to negotiate the second bollard as the staff car and George's Ford faced off. This was the worst case of chicken, an Army staff car versus a twelve year old Ford Focus. As the staff car scraped along the second bollard and straddled the road, Ted floored the accelerator and aimed to immobilise the staff car by wedging it against the first bollard and the Ford.

"Brace," shouted Ted.

George kept her feet out of the well of the car to avoid trapping them and braced against the passenger seat. The Ford impacted the staff car's front wheel and pushed the front of the car into the first bollard. Ted didn't break, and despite the sound of shearing metal, the Ford pushed the staff car against the bollard. The Ford jolted to a halt and the staff car driver's door sprung open; the driver looking dazed but conscious. Although the Ford's headlights had smashed, the staff car's lights blazed, lighting the woods.

George unclipped her seat belt, pushed open her passenger door, and rolled out onto the road. The collision had shaken her, and the news of Charlie's death and the stress and adrenaline from the earlier events heightened her senses and her reactions. Ted had difficulty getting out of the driver's side.

Movement in the back of the staff car revealed a uniformed figure staggering out. He looked around, then crawled towards the woods. George's hand went to the small of her back for her weapon, empty. Dislodged in the crash. She got to her feet and prepared to slide across the Ford's bonnet towards the staff car's driver. The driver emerged wearing an Army uniform and bearing a

Corporal's chevrons. Her movements were frenetic, shaken, but dangerous.

The 'Corporal' reached into her jacket and withdrew an automatic. George couldn't identify it, but a weapon was a weapon. Ted struggled to extract himself from the wreck but stood behind his driver's door, only two metres from the driver. The Cpl would see Ted as the main threat and therefore her primary target. The small automatic kicked but made no noise and George knew it had a silencer, or a Russian silent weapon. The round struck the door frame and ricocheted into the side window. The window shattering made more noise than the weapon itself. Ted flinched, but grabbed the car door. George saw why he couldn't move; his foot was jammed on the accelerator. George looked across at the Cpl and gasped. The last time she'd seen Cpl Faiza Mirza was in Afghanistan. Who better to identify Charlie than someone who'd worked with George? It fitted now. She'd been the target in Afghanistan, not Brigadier Wyson, and Mirza had ensured George had been in the firing line, a simple switch to ensure George was assigned to protect Wyson instead of Mirza.

However, the Cpl walked towards Ted and raised her weapon. George leapt across the Ford's bonnet, slid, and landed behind the assassin, who raised her weapon in Ted's direction. George brought her right arm around Mirza's neck and jammed the side of her wrist and forearm into the woman's windpipe. The assassin gasped and fired a second shot. George lifted the woman by her head and the shot went high. Her left hand locked behind the smaller woman's head, her right forearm across her throat, and right hand locked onto her left. George embraced Mirza in a python's grip. The woman's hand raised to relieve the pressure on her neck, then went behind her head to pry her fingers away without success. George stepped back to avoid Mirza's kicking feet, then dragged her back and down, wrenching her head forward. The woman held onto the weapon and clawed at George's arm. George pressed her body against her victim's back and twisted her arms up toward her right shoulder. A crack marked the woman's neck splitting, like a piece of wood cracking along its length before finally breaking in two. A last twist and snap, and George felt the strain, and Mirza's spine stretch and break. Mirza gave a final jerk and relaxed. The Russian made automatic dropped to the ground and clattered on the tarmac. George kicked the Russian PSS-2 silent weapon away but held tight onto the woman until her heels had stopped kicking. She let the woman flop to the ground, her head at a broken lollipop stick angle.

She looked at Ted, who'd extricated himself from the car. He now stood on one leg, near the dead assassin.

"Thanks George, I knew you'd be useful for something," said Ted.

"My pleasure. Now where's that Padre?"

They looked around, peering into the wood, seeing only inky darkness.

"I guess we can leave the search to the real squaddies," said Ted.

"I need to make a call. Can I use your phone?"

"Sure, who?" asked Ted.

"Colonel Syman. I don't know if we can trust Chance, but Syman has clout with the Army brass."

George's weapon would be on the passenger seat or

foot well; MI5 had authorised her to carry the weapon, but said a silent "Thank You". She hadn't fired it earlier in Chance's office, which would have complicated matters.

As the guard and other soldiers ran to the scene, illuminated by the lights of a Land Rover coming from the guardroom, Syman answered George's call. Both she and Ted raised their hands to show they were unarmed, but Colonel Syman's voice was on speaker.

"Colonel, we're in trouble, at the barracks in Gillingham. We need your help."

"Down, now! On the ground," yelled the military guard. "Flat on the ground. Now."

Both she and Ted lay on the ground, her phone lay next to her, George shouted a short version to Syman. Two squaddies approached with SA80s as a police car shrieked towards the barrier.

"I'll make a call to the police tonight via the liaison Officer here and get an MOD solicitor on the case, someone I can trust. If they don't release you tonight, use your one phone call to contact me. Otherwise, I'll see you tomorrow, George, at the safe house," said Syman.

George risked being shot by pocketing the phone but remained on the ground. Her arms and legs spread.

The squaddie was experienced; probably seen service in Afghanistan. Maybe at the same time as George. One guard stayed ten metres back and covered the first one who aimed his weapon midway between Ted and George. George wondered what the guard would make of Ted's missing leg.

George saw no point explaining who she was, they'd discover soon enough. The squaddie would have bragging rights. She lay flat. The cold and wet seeped through her cloth jacket and her front soaked in the contents of a puddle. Her shoulder hurt, and she made a mental note to keep doing the stretching exercises.

A second voice, deeper, more authoritative, "We'll take it from here, son. Thanks."

***

The local police arrived on the scene and charged Ted with driving without due care and attention and conspiracy to commit a crime, George with accessory, but the Police Officer said he'd like to charge her with manslaughter. They sat in an interview room in the guardroom. An Inspector arrived in plain clothes and took over. Judging by the coloured top underneath his jacket, he was wearing pyjamas.

"Right, Mr Ted Shields and Ms Georgina Stone you are being interviewed under the Police and Criminal Evidence Act. The time is," he glanced at his watch, "3 a.m. on Sunday 30 January."

A smirk twitched George's lip. He sat on a straight-back chair and leaned over towards George.

"I have better things to do on a Saturday night than ponce around with you two killing members of the public."

The Inspector held George's steady gaze across the table. "I suspect you wilfully broke the Russian woman's neck and that would amount to manslaughter at least, or murder," said the police Inspector without humour or compassion.

The solicitor intervened before George could answer. "The Russian fired at least two shots, both at Mr Shields, and the second would probably have led to his demise if Ms Stone hadn't intervened."

The Inspector snorted. George wanted to tell him she'd intended to kill the Russian, which was the whole point of that neck lock, to either asphyxiate, leading to death or to break her neck, bringing a quicker death than she deserved. She wanted to explain; alive, the Russian would have been a threat, and assassins don't give up. If they do, they don't last long. George expressed no remorse or regret. She did her job, and the woman was one less. She remained silent and let the solicitor speak.

"Why were no shots heard from the woman's gun?" asked the Inspector, staring at George.

"It was a silent weapon," said George, with a straight face, returning his stare.

The Inspector smirked and rolled his eyes. He pointed a finger at her chest. "Forensics will determine that, unless you're giving an expert opinion. Why did you kill the Russian? You are bigger than her; why didn't you overpower her? Jump on her, warn her to drop her weapon?"

George kept a straight face. She glanced at the clock on the wall, intending the Inspector to see it.

"You are going nowhere, so don't give me attitude, right?"

George fixed his stare. A warning to stop digging.

"The woman was armed, she'd killed, and she was a professional. If I hadn't killed her, she would have killed both me and Ted, and right now you'd be searching for her. How many officers would that take? Now, if there's nothing else, I'd like to go to the Medical Centre and see my sister, who, I remind you, was killed by either the Padre or the so-called victim."

The police Inspector ignored her request. "So, you confess to killing a woman of smaller stature. Where and why did you learn to kill like that? Are you a fanatic, where did you get your training, Afghanistan? Did you train, so you can go out and kill?"

He scoffed, glancing at the Constable to reinforce his humour.

"I'm a patriot and a fanatic for justice and defending my country. Yes, I served tours in Afghanistan, with the British Army, and I can kill, when I must. The British Army trained me to kill. It also trained me to protect life, and I've done both. I serve my country Inspector, what do you serve, your monthly pay packet?"

George could have slapped the Inspector, but Ted squeezed her knee. She needed to see her sister.

"I sympathise with your loss Ms Stone, but a crime is a crime, no matter who commits it. And I'll charge you with obstruction unless you pipe down, young lady."

Again, the solicitor defused the situation.

George pushed back her chair to stand. The solicitor put out his hand and lowered it, suggesting George remain calm and sit.

"Inspector, my client's sister lies dead in the Medical Centre. If the Russian woman didn't kill Charlie Stone, she was an accessory. Your family, I assume, are at home in bed?" he didn't wait for an answer. "My client is Sergeant Stone in the Royal Army Physical Training Corps assigned to MI5. Sgt Stone trained in close protection, close-quarter battle, and countering killers such as the one she met. She's completed multiple tours in Afghanistan, and senior officers have trusted their lives to her. She can act on her own initiative and the evidence points to her being right on each count. This was self-defence, or in defence of someone it was her responsibility to protect."

"Why didn't Ted Shields tackle the woman? He's bigger and stronger than her," he asked the solicitor.

George put back her head and laughed, but the solicitor kept a straight face. "Have you searched Ted, Inspector?"

"Not personally, no. The Constable did. Does that matter?"

Straight-faced, Ted lifted his leg onto the desk and removed the prosthesis, to expose his stump.

"I lost a foot on duty in Northern Ireland. This is a prosthetic foot."

He left his prosthesis on the table and lowered his own leg. The toe of the prosthetic pointing at the Inspector. "I was trapped, and I removed it to extricate myself from the crashed Ford. If I'd tried to tackle the woman, she would have shot me, and I'd have fallen over."

The solicitor smiled. "My client explained; the woman shot at Ted twice before George intervened. Both my clients testified to this. The guard heard no shots. And again, my client has explained this. Neither of my clients was armed, nor did they handle weapons. The only weapon Sgt Stone used was her own physical skills for which she is trained, and her own initiative. This was a case of self-defence. She saved Ted Shields's life."

Ted knew she'd been carrying a weapon. What had happened to it?

The Inspector wrinkled his nose as if a fish smell was offending his nostrils. He tried to extricate it by wrinkling his nose.

The Solicitor continued. "I don't think there's the least doubt. Despite being threatened, Georgina Stone saved Ted's life…."

"These MI5 officers work for me. They are authorised to carry personal firearms. Have they explained everything to your satisfaction?" asked Sam, entering the room.

"I'm Sam Ghosh," said Sam, smiling and taking out his MI5 warrant card to show the Inspector. The Inspector looked at the warrant card, then at Sam. He wrinkled his nose again and scrunched his eyes.

"If you say so, Mr Ghosh."

"Why are you holding these two officers?" asked Sam, with an accent straight out of grammar school with a hint of wide boy Essex, and the posture of someone used to taking charge.

"Why didn't they show their MI5 IDs?"

"They are both undercover. Are they under caution?"

"We have charged Mr Shields with dangerous driving. But we haven't charged Ms Stone, yet. But, there's insufficient evidence to charge them with murder. We found only one weapon and Ms Stone tells me it's a Russian made firearm. It looks like an amateur's pea shooter, but I'm no firearms expert. A firearms specialist and a more thorough search at dawn may reveal something."

George showed no surprise at the Inspector's lack of expertise.

"The weapon is a Russian made PSS-2. An assassin's weapon, silent. Hence, the guard didn't hear the two shots, but I'm sure your search will reveal two shell cases with Russian markings, which means she intended to kill with that weapon. That's the only reason she carried it. And she may have killed my sister with it. This weapon fires engineered 7.62 mm wedge ammunition and has an effective range of 25 metres. It can penetrate light body armour and will kill you as dead as a Glock or a Colt. I assume you've heard of them, Inspector?"

The Inspector screwed his mouth as if he was chewing gristle. "In the meantime, I'll release them on police bail, so long as you don't move out of the area. You can leave now, but we may want to interview you later."

"Inspector, unless there's evidence, I require you to release them unconditionally. I have spoken to the Home Secretary, but please call your Chief Constable. He's expecting it. And destroy the tape." said Sam, pointing to the PACE equipment.

The police officer grunted and waved the two away. "You can go."

"Inspector, did you follow the footprints of the man who fled into the woods?" asked Ted.

"As far as we could, but we lost the track. We'll continue in the morning."

They made their way out of the makeshift interview room.

George turned to Sam. "I'd like to see my sister for the last time."

"Yes. I'll phone Colonel Syman and keep him abreast of the situation. I'll drive you to the Medical Centre."

As they left the guardroom, Ted collected George's Glock from the Guard Commander and handed it to her. The Guard Commander smiled at them both and winked.

George grabbed Sam's arm as they walked to the car. "The woman in the car, the Cpl. I knew her as Cpl Faiza Mirza. We served together in Afghanistan. She no doubt identified Charlie and targeted her. I'm not sorry I killed her, but I acted to remove a threat not to settle a score."

Sam gave George a tight-lipped look and nodded.

Chapter 46

A solemn female Sergeant met George at the Medical Centre. She put out a hand to touch her arm, George withdrew. It hadn't quite hit her yet. The last of her family, dead. Apart from a few friends, she'd be alone. But she still had a job to finish and wouldn't rest until Andrei, Moss, and Templeton Maudlin were dead; her justice. Sarah died in the most brutal way; they will also pay for that. George accepted she'd probably be killed, or imprisoned for murder, but it didn't matter. This was war, a personal war.

"I'm George Stone, this is Ted. Come to see my sister."

"Hello George. This way, please. The police are finishing her room, so we've moved her."

The police and military staff carried out their tasks with quiet efficiency. Activity in the opposite corridor, where her sister had a room, caught her attention. The corridor had 'Police' tape across it. A police woman led along the opposite corridor to a private room.

"Wait outside will you Ted. I want to talk to Charlie."

He smiled, found a chair in the corridor, took out his bag and sucked on a boiled sweet. The room didn't smell of death or hospital. No tubes connected Charlie, no drips, nor monitors. She looked peaceful and beautiful. Charlie was in a clean room and now she looked 'normal'. The pillow hid the exit wound, and a dressing covered the entry wound. Someone had brushed her hair and cleaned her. But for the lack of life, she might have been sleeping. George had been told of Charlie's injuries, but she told herself it was a mistake. Her hair lay on the pillow and touched the sheets. One hand lay on top of the other, bandaged to hide her missing digit. The shape of her sister was clear under the sheet, her feet touching the bottom of the bed.

George stood at the foot of the bed, watching her sister, hoping she'd move. Not for the first time, she prayed someone had made a mistake. If there was mercy, someone had messed up, mistaken identity, anything would do. She watched for five minutes until the silence intruded on her mental turmoil. Her eyes glazed and threatened to spill, but she needed to restrain herself, keep it together until the end. No one understood death until they'd seen a loved one lying dead, where hours before, life coursed.

She leaned over and kissed her sister's lips then her forehead where the dressing covered the wound. It felt cool but not cold; room temperature she realised. George sat next to her, unable to contain herself, and tears welled, but she fought them back and laid her hands over her sister's.

"What did he do to you, Charlie? What happened? Did you recognise him? Was it the Padre? I'm sorry, Charlie, I should have protected you; I'm sorry. You must be so lonely now, wherever you are. I know you weren't religious, but I hope someone or something is looking after you. You deserve that. Say hello to Mum for us. Tell her I love her. I love you both and tell her I now understand."

George unwrapped the bandages and inspected Charlie's wound, not for sentimental reasons, but to see exactly where the perpetrator had amputated Charlie's finger, which was now dark red, with congealed blood. She needed to identify them with certainty. She took out her smartphone and took several photos of her hands and the wound, including the exact cut. Finally, she replaced the bandages and placed one hand on top of the other, and laid her own hands over her sister's.

"Don't argue with Mum wherever you are. I always had to come between you and Mum when it was school time. You were brighter than me and never did your homework, but always excelled. You graduated; what a waste of talent. Mum was proud of you. We all were, and I still am. I wanted to find dad, but you stopped me. You said no good would come of it, and you were right. But if dad is there, say hello, and I love him. Not sure how I'll cope alone, but I'll find a way. I'll make you proud of me. Next, I'll wipe the slate clean. I have a friend, Ted, but you know him, I expect. I trust him. Chance may be dead, and Sheila is probably working for Moss. If so, I'll finish her, and you'll meet her again, I'm sure."

George gritted her teeth and stared at Charlie, as if for agreement and support. She squeezed Charlie's hands. "Oh, sorry, Charlie," she said, realising her sister was past feeling pain.

"I promise you I'll finish this. The woman with the

Padre is dead. The murderers are still out there. I'll kill them. I'll do it, for our family and because that's justice, and it's what I must do. The undertaker must meet his end and anyone who gets in the way. I will hunt them down."

"I will stop him. Look out for him when he gets there and give him a hard time."

She whispered to her sister, and she believed that if Charlie could hear, she'd listen. That was enough for her. Her sister would laugh at her.

"I won't have you cremated, Charlie. That's not right somehow. I want to visit you, somewhere I can always say hello and talk to you. I can't do that if you're cremated. Silly. Don't worry I won't give you a religious service, you'll have a humanitarian ceremony. I'll bring Ted, he's a good friend, you'd like him. It's not like that though, he's too old for me, and he's got one leg. He lost the other in Northern Ireland."

She stood and leaned over her sister again and kissed her cheek, lingering there. The last time she'd see another member of her family.

"Bye for now, Charlie. I love you and I'll live for you. I couldn't stop this happening, but I can decide the ending and I won't waste a single moment. See I didn't cry," she said, as tears rolled down her cheek and dripped onto her sister's cheeks and ran towards her lips. A casual observer may have thought Charlie herself was crying. George wiped her tears on her sleeve, but left those on Charlie to dry by themselves. She turned, left the room, and walked out briskly.

Chapter 47

A road running along the front gardens of the row of houses led to the Guard Room 400 metres away, so the guard was close by. A 'safe house' had been assigned to George and Ted, in a row of ten houses, each identical, a path leading from the road to the front door, a grassed area, perennial shrubs under the front window. The back was similar, a back garden, used to dry clothes, have barbecues, etc., and a two-metre brick wall at the end, leading onto playing fields outside the camp. On the first night, the camp provided a guard outside the house, and Chance also assigned a minder outside who seemed happy to stay in his car. Now Ted and George were alone. They hadn't heard a peep from Chance, although Sam had covered for him, saying he was on urgent business elsewhere.

They entered through the front door, making no pretence of hiding their presence. Ted closed the curtains from prying eyes from the road. A standard lamp shone downstairs in the only house occupied. The lowest bidder had built the 1960s houses, which were used as overspill for troops returning from operations, or rehabilitation.

George had a hunch the night wasn't over, unlike her amnesty. They were fair game and vulnerable.

They went to the hallway upstairs, and George jumped to lift the loft hatch. She heaved herself up and reached down to help Ted. Replacing the loft hatch behind them, they crawled less than one hundred metres along the rafters to the house next to the end, taking care not to disturb their work in the loft. They dropped into the upper hallway, identical to the one they'd left and went into the front bedroom, furnished as a bed/sitting room.

"Drink?" asked Ted.

"Tea from the flask would be good. You can take a real drink, if you have any stashed away," laughed George.

"Tonight, I need all my faculties. Anyway, I've told you, my drinking days are over. Although, I may have a wee dram, when this is over. Right?"

"Alright. Keep your foot on," George said, still grinning.

Ted returned with two mugs of black tea, and they sat in the dark opposite each other, Ted in an armchair and George on the sofa. He took off his prosthetic leg, and the sock he used to make it comfortable and massaged his stump. They'd both worked on preparing for the coming attack. It wouldn't be pretty. Ted sagged into the chair; exhaustion obvious.

"I'll go get your cream, you stay there," said George, rising. She collected the cream from Ted's kit without switching on the light. She glanced out of the window. The road was empty.

"Here you go, enjoy," said George, smiling at Ted in the dark.

He spread the cream on his stump. "So, what happened to Chance? Did you get anything out of the guy in Chance's office?" asked Ted.

"Not much. He laughed when I mentioned Chance, which made me think Chance had been played."

"But I've been thinking," said Ted. "He could be dead, or being held. We'll need to check with Sam and Colonel Syman tomorrow. Chance has delivered on several things; the safe house and watching out for Bradley Maudlin. Only Chance and Sarah knew Charlie's location. They also knew the meeting place. I don't think Sarah would have revealed anything."

"You didn't see what they did to her. Anyone would have told them anything, and I don't blame her or Chance. Although it must have been obvious to her, she was a stalking horse, disposable. It was you and me they were after."

"This is tough on you, G. Can you cope with all this? What's your Plan of Action? Hand it over to the police?"

"Are you taking the proverbial, Ted? Be serious, the police have done nothing. They've even jailed the wrong guy. Not a good track record."

"Have you thought about what Moss wants? He said you had information he wanted."

"I have. Mum left a USB stick, it's blank. But Mum also left one for Charlie. It'll wait until we get out of here. This fight can't be delayed."

"How's the leg? He stabbed you?"

"I'd forgotten about it," she said, raising her trouser leg and felt congealed blood on the bandage.

"You need antibiotics. First thing tomorrow, Medical Centre," said Ted.

George frowned and sat in silence.

"Sorry, I didn't mean to remind you."

"I'll reflect on Charlie's life when this is over. Who do you think we should visit first, Moss, or Templeton Maudlin?" asked George.

"It's tempting to say Maudlin, but there's also Pinchin. For now, Pinchin is an unknown. Sam can get his address in London. I also have Templeton Maudlin's phone number."

George had a problem with that. Visiting Pinchin was fine, but she disliked violence for violence's sake. They could torture him, force him to confess, but it might not be worth a can of beans. Even worse, they'd never met. He might be as hard to penetrate as a Kevlar vest. It needed a more indirect approach, and maybe Bradley was the key.

"Enough, I'll discuss it with Colonel Syman. I'll take the first stag and wake you in three hours," said George

***

George watched from the front bedroom window.

Gingham curtains were drawn, but she'd fixed the edge so a sliver of night light shone into the room from yellow sodium lighting outside. These houses, like many owned by the MOD, were single glazed. The windows had a thick layer of grime and dust, but she left it dirty. Not ideal, but it would do.

She'd heard people wax lyrical about sodium light, saying it gave everything a golden glow, but that was for poets and dreamers. In the back streets of Iraq, it cast too many shadows and hid features; in Northern Ireland you could freeze to death despite its imagined 'golden glow'. For soldiers, sodium light was a menace. A black scarf covered her face, leaving only her eyes showing. She could see movement in her peripheral vision, but if she remained still, she'd be concealed. If the enemy had night vision goggles or a night site, they may spot her.

She scanned the road twenty-five metres in front of her and the woods at fifty metres distant. A fox trotted along the edge of the wood, stopped, looked around, focussed on something in the wood then continued its scavenging. She focussed on the area which drew the fox's attention, but saw nothing. Had the fox seen or smelt something, a human being, or gun oil? She wouldn't expect a professional to be sloppy. The angle from the wood to their assigned house, a hundred metres to her left, was right for sniping.

They'd been lucky with the Russian woman in the car. Her determination and resources were significant. They were fortunate. She said a prayer and a few words to Charlie. But her eyes never left the road. She remained motionless, and even though part of her senses remained alert, her mind settled and calmed as she prayed. She asked Charlie how she was doing. No reply, but she didn't expect one. She supposed her sister would be busy. 'In processing' must be a devil, wherever she was.

The street lighting switched off at 3 a.m., coinciding with the time an enemy might attack. There'd be two. If they couldn't use the sniper, they'd have to attack directly. One man would break into the house, climb the stairs, and deliver a single shot to the head of each sleeping victim. The other would keep watch. But he'd know they're soldiers, and at least one of them would be awake and alert. He'd wait for a light to come on in the house, perhaps one of them visiting the bathroom. That would be an easy shot with a silenced sniper rifle at one hundred metres. Then he'd discard the weapon in a prepared hide, run across the road, shoulder the door open and kill the other victim silently if possible, with a silenced automatic or a knife. What weapon would a Russian use? She'd seen a Russian sniper weapon, the *Vintovka Snayperskaya Specialness*, used by Russian Special Forces in Syria. Made for this type of hit, and likely the weapon used at Chance's office. The silencer surrounded the barrel, suppressing the sound and 'crack', which could be mistaken for a branch breaking. The subsonic 9 mm armour piercing round left no sonic boom but limited its range to about three hundred metres. If the sniper had a night site, he'd wait for the streetlight to extinguish and watch for a twitching curtain. If he had both targets in roughly the same area, he could even switch to automatic and fire through the brick wall, job done. He'd pack his weapon in four parts into a case weighing less than three kilos, and be away through the woods and onto the road to a waiting vehicle. She took a risk standing at the window, but he was expecting them to be in a different house. He wouldn't see her unless he scanned the whole row of houses with the night site, and even then, he couldn't be sure it was his target at the window.

Wisps of haze formed and drifted along the road,

forming natural camouflage for anyone crossing from the woods. It was cold enough, and the white mist reflected yellow light, challenging it to penetrate its impermeable cloak. A hoar frost formed on the road, its white feathery fingers creeping closer. It was colder there, a natural phenomenon, like a living shroud. She wasn't sure if the enemy was the Russian Secret Service or Moss's gangsters. It was academic. Moss employed the best and seemed as ruthless as the *Sluzhba Vneshney Razvedki Rossiyskoy Federatsii*, the SVR. In an organisation like the SVR, with its almost unlimited resources, they could insert a new member at short notice, especially if he wanted a quick resolution.

She surmised that if he didn't acquire a sniper target, they'd either get close and personal, or postpone for the night. George relied on his sense of urgency. The yellow sodium lights went out, casting the road into near full moonlight greyness. She became accustomed to the new light level and watched the wood, fences, and the road.

George risked a glance at her watch. In ten minutes, it would be Ted's turn at the window, and finally she could catch up on sleep. Perhaps tonight wouldn't be the night. A cat slinked across the road, stopped at the same place as the fox, turned, and sprinted away.

A figure emerged from the tree line, a dark shadow. No mistake. Dressed in black from head to foot, he carried no obvious weapon, but at that distance, nothing could be certain. As the figure moved, George didn't recognise the body language, but she recognised the type. From the way he stalked across the road, he was a professional. But so were George and Ted. This man didn't scare her; she relished their meeting.

As clouds obscured the moon, he slipped out of the

wood, and she lost him briefly then saw him walk across the road separating the wood from the houses. He went to the house assigned to them in the middle of the row. She lost sight of him, but knew he'd be picking the lock or using another method to gain entry.

She inched back from the curtain to where Ted slept on the cot and nudged his foot. This was it, the time of reckoning. "Up. We got action," she said.

Ted lifted his head, "Right," and rose to his foot. He'd loosely attached his prosthetic leg. Now he jammed it in place and replaced her at the window.

"Thirty seconds ago, one man, from the woods, entered the other house. I suspect there's a backup."

George switched on an LED torch on the floor below the loft hatch and left it on the floor, shining upwards towards the hatch. She jumped up, caught the rim, hoisted herself up and partially closed the hatch, leaving a slither of light visible from the LED torch. She was banking on the intruder seeing it. A loft wasn't the best place for close-quarter fighting, but she hoped it wouldn't come to that. She heaved herself to a sitting position on a makeshift wooden seat a metre above and behind the loft hatch. Anyone intending to crawl from house to house through the linked lofts would have to crawl beneath her, so long as they didn't spot her as they approached. George pulled her legs underneath her, to a kneeling position on the seat. Little more than a minute passed, George assumed he'd opened the door to the house. Head bowed, mouth open, breathing controlled, eyes closed in the darkness, her senses diverted to sound and vibrations. A sound like distant glass crunching underfoot made her fingers tingle. Had Ted heard it? She hoped so. Their lives might depend on it.

She remained still, breathing silently. If the man used even a silenced weapon, she'd hear the telltale slider as he cocked it, and if he fired, she'd hear the crack of metal on wood of even a silenced handgun. But he was unlikely to fire in the loft without a target.

The intruder had to limit the noise he made. The military guardroom was less than four hundred metres away, and alerting them would be a disaster. Her bet would be a holstered automatic, a PSS, and either bare hands or a blade, perhaps a spike. Excellent at night if he needs to stab, and doesn't expect resistance.

The killer would find the house assigned to them and search it. Tracking his progress in her mind, she counted the seconds, remaining still and not looking back to watch him crawling towards her. He'd be careful, but he didn't have time to squander. In two hours, it would be first light. After the killings, the intruders would aim to leave unnoticed. She was comfortable, but not moving a muscle except eyelids was difficult. Any movement would disturb dust and show as dust motes in the light.

She waited for the telltale shuffle of someone inching along from rafter to rafter. If he looked up, he'd spot someone perched above him. It was a risk, but professionals left little to chance. They could mitigate risks by skill and experience. George closed her eyes and waited, her muscles screaming to move, and she wanted to scratch her nose, and her thigh throbbed. Her calf muscle ached where she'd been stabbed earlier. She struggled to accept the discomfort, blank it from her mind and concentrate on sound and movements around her. The minutes ticked away, and she thought she'd misjudged this. Perhaps the assassin wouldn't take the bait.

There was a scratch, a rodent maybe. Except it wasn't. It was manmade. She listened for breathing and heard nothing, not even a disturbance in the air. Eyes open now, George changed her gaze towards the hatch and concentrated on listening for breathing.

A shadow of the intruder appeared a metre below her. She admired the killer's skill; he was controlling his breathing and slid along without a sound. George watched one hand slide under the hatch and lift. She hoped that would alert Ted, and it was her cue. The man crawled over the open hatchway, his back less than a metre from her feet. He held a dark object in his right hand, which she took to be a knife, holding it in a downward stabbing hold. It could be a problem, but she hoped she could deal with it.

She launched herself from her position and dropped onto his back. Her knees caught him in the small of his back, and the combined weight of the two caused weakened rafters to creak. Ted and George had sawn through them, leaving only a quarter of the thickness remaining. They sagged, and the assassin reached behind for George as she tried to get an arm around his neck. He was hurt, not disabled. If the rafters held much longer, he'd turn over and face her.

The thin supporting wood creaked and finally relented. The two dropped over two metres to the ground, landing in front of Ted, a cloud of plaster and dust surrounding them. She had to give the assassin credit. He held onto his knife, even though he grunted as he landed, suggesting it wasn't a landing he'd walk away from. A curse escaped the man's lips, and George recognised a Russian obscenity. For the second time, she landed with a jolt on the back of the killer, winding her. The intruder turned his head and stared at the feet inches from his face and sunk his knife into Ted's outstretched foot.

He looked up at Ted, confusion etched across his face. Ted smiled, pulled back a bony fist, and punched him on the left side of his head, snapping it right and down. That punch would have floored most men. The Russian was down, but not out. A splash of blood landed on Ted's shoes, and George felt the man's body jar with the impact of the punch. She tried to get a neck lock on the man, but despite Ted's assault he bucked her off his back and rose onto his hands and knees, head shaking, and gore dripping from his mouth. George fell to the side, and Ted kicked him in the stomach, eliciting a cursed and grunt from the Russian. Ted let fly another kick to the man's face, which was decisive, snapping his head back at an awkward angle. The killer's body rose to his knees. His nose would need extensive surgery, and his front teeth had pierced his lower lip and seemed to stick to the gums by threads of connective tissue. More blood splashed across Ted's legs and the man slumped unconscious onto his back. Ted bent and pulled the black ceramic knife out of his prosthetic foot.

George checked his pulse. The man was alive, his pulse steady. She wouldn't have lost sleep if he'd expired, but he was more useful alive than dead. They said nothing. George opened a holdall and took out a handful of industrial plastic cable ties, Ted working on his hands and George on his feet. Ted slipped a plastic tie over the man's two thumbs and pulled it tight. It was near impossible to remove the ties, and Ted took no chances, also securing his wrists. After removing his shoes and socks, George secured his two big toes together, then his ankles. This Russian was going nowhere, and they had questions for him.

Some might have relished this moment, but the action

wasn't over until the enemy was dead or neutralised. George stood at the window. Quiet outside, and dull rays of day highlighted a piece of clear ground in the distance. The second man would be impatient to finish the job before daylight prevented further action. George and Ted's problem now was to consider the enemy's next move. A frontal attack on the house? Wait and watch for them leaving the house or something more devious? One thing was for sure, it was inconceivable he'd leave without a result. The backup would use a different method of attack to avoid a similar fate. When the intruder didn't report, he'd act. He'd have to be deaf not to hear the commotion. He'd conclude the first attacker had been neutralised. Ted stood on a chair and looked along the line of loft spaces.

"Nothing, except a light from the first loft hatch. Let's see what this chap knows," he said, pointing a thumb over his shoulder at the unconscious assassin.

Ted dragged his victim into the bathroom. Water gushed, and George guessed Ted had pushed the man's head under the cold water in the bath. Torture didn't work… unless time wasn't on your side. Some excused torture by calling it extended, intensive, prolonged, or rigorous interrogation techniques. She didn't believe in calling a spade a 'spatulous device for abrading soil'. Now, her family was dead, and it was time for extremes. She'd explain to God later.

A struggle and thrashing from the man, so he was conscious. Ted could deal with it. He dragged the man by both feet back into the main bedroom. Despite his cuffs, the man rose, until Ted smashed his fist into the man's broken nose, and he flopped back.

Ted draped a wet towel over the man's face and, holding the man's jaw, poured cold water over his nose and mouth from a flower jug. Neither Ted nor George spoke. Ted wanted to get the man's attention and after ten seconds the man gagged, gasped, struggled, and tried to sit up. Ted held him firm, but he remained silent.

During the third session of simulated drowning, the man panted, and a gurgling sound emanated from deep in his chest. The man shook, the icy water dripping from him, but he remained silent.

"I want the name of the man who killed Julia Stone," said Ted.

The man remained silent, and Ted went to fill the jug in the bathroom. Time was running out and George didn't care if they killed him. The fourth session lasted longer, and the man retched. Vomit arose from the man's oesophagus, and the man was forced to breathe it in. He struggled, but with hands and feet bound, death seemed inevitable.

Ted took the cloth from the man's face, and his eyes bulged. Death was close.

"A name," said Ted.

"Andrei. Andrei killed woman. Please," he spluttered and pleaded.

No surprise there. Although Andrei was a professional, killing women and civilians didn't sit well with them. But now she had Moss, the undertaker, and Andrei in the frame.

"Why, why did you kill her?" asked Ted.

"She has something Moss wants." He stopped to spew

water from his stomach. "Information, she was a traitor, had to die. I've answered questions. Please. Moss will kill you."

The man gasped, his chest heaved, and water bubbled from his mouth. Ted placed the soaking wet cloth over the man's face again for twenty seconds. The man screwed himself like a mangled towel and slumped back. Ted seemed calm and unafraid of killing the man, but George wanted the man alive to answer questions.

Ted hauled the man onto his front and heaved his legs in the air and over Ted's shoulder. Water poured from the man's mouth. Satisfied, Ted dropped the man's dead weight, and placed a foot on his back, compressing to get rid of the remaining water. The man coughed, gagged, and spewed the remaining water from his lungs and lay on his front, heaving.

"The second man crossed from the woods to the house. He left a bag and disappeared. Can't imagine he's given up, and why would he leave his bag? Anything more from our friend down there? A location for Moss?" asked George.

"Give me a second, I'll ask him."

Ted rolled the man onto his back and re-laid the cloth over his face, leaving his eyes uncovered.

"Final time, sunshine, then it's curtains for you," said Ted.

"Curtains for all," the man gurgled. It sounded like a black laugh.

"Never mind the philosophy lesson. Where is Moss

right now? An address."

Ted lifted the jug of water and poured a few drops onto the cloth covering his nose and mouth.

"Fortress, Grain," the dying killer spluttered.

George screwed her face up. She knew the place, a disused concrete structure from the second world war, an old coastal defence fortress. No one had used it for years, decades even. No one went there, except youths in summer to smoke pot. About 600 metres off the coast of Grain, accessible by boat. Ideal for a night approach without lights. A plan formed in her mind.

The man collapsed as if he'd accepted death, and a shiver went along George's spine.

"Who killed Charlie Stone?" asked George of the man.

The man coughed and spluttered, but his reply was clear enough. "The undertaker."

George simply nodded. The sky revealed a new day. George glanced at her watch. Before 5 a.m., a shimmering haze brim covered the ground, like something from a James Herbert novel. A shroud of mist covered the distant barrier to the barracks and since midnight, not a single vehicle had passed on the road. She lost focus for a second and cursed. If soldiers hoped to stay alive, they didn't lose focus.

She peered into the dismal early dawn and realised they'd missed a trick. The backup must know that his primary was dead or caught. He wouldn't try the same thing. Even now, she could smell gas and understood the plan. The second man had opened the gas outlet in each house. No doubt he'd also left a candle or some other ignition device in an adjoining house. When the gas concentration increased to a critical level, it would kill anyone in the row of houses. How long would that take? It had been ten minutes since they'd seen the killer cross the first house. Another ten minutes to open the gas pipes and another ten minutes for it to reach a critical state. He'd be waiting in the woods for the explosion.

George whispered. "Gas. We must leave. Now!"

She grabbed her stuff, packed into a holdall. "The backup has left the building; I don't think he intends to confront us. That's too risky. I'll help you."

If they left the house via the back, the killer could wait for them there. She climbed the wreckage to the loft, leaned over the edge and grabbed Ted's hand. Despite his foot problem, and his age, he proved to be agile and heaved himself into the loft to follow George along the loft to the final house in the row. They dropped into the bedroom, and both ran to the back window. It seemed clear, but George doubted Ted's ability to jump from the window and land without injury.

She opened the window, hung from the windowsill, and dropped. Ted's artificial foot dropped to the ground, followed by Ted who landed on his side and rolled. An explosion blew out a house a hundred metres away, and George shielded against the wall at the bottom of the garden. The fire was spreading and consuming the row of houses. The shock wave from another explosion blew her against the wall. Ted lay on his front only three metres from the blazing building. He looked unconscious and although the fire hadn't reached him, if there was a secondary explosion, he'd be 'Tango Uniform'.

As George ran to Ted, the heat engulfed her. She glanced over her shoulder to see the raging inferno behind her with at least four of the houses engulfed. Grabbing Ted's false leg, she threw it to the wall. Glass surrounded Ted and even as she dragged him by his jacket, a jagged piece of glass protruded from his back. But under the circumstances, that was secondary. Before she'd dragged Ted three metres, he groaned and peered at her.

"Can you hop?" she asked without a hint of humour. "Come on, hang on to me."

Between them, they made it to the wall. Ted with one arm around George's neck and hopping on one foot.

"Get your foot on, we're going over. I can hear the fire engine. We can disappear in the chaos."

A mile from the barracks, George phoned Sam and arranged a collection. Sam would meet them at George's house. An hour later, they sat in George's house, a medic extracting glass from Ted's back and treating the wound. Ted winced as the glass came free.

"Don't start complaining, Stumpy. I dragged your butt out of the fire," said George with a grin.

"A man can whine and whinge a bit amongst friends. I could have been warming my foot against an open fire in my place instead of being abused by you."

She gave Sam an edited version of the events of the past forty-eight hours. George had given him a brief of events in Chance's office, and she expanded on that incident; how Sarah had died, and the dead Russian, who she'd killed in self-defence. At the barracks, she explained their stay by telling him they'd been making plans for

Charlie's funeral. He'd find out soon enough about the dead Russian once they'd sifted through the remains of the fire. The damage they'd caused was academic. But she intimated that they'd seen men in the woods. Ted and George had escaped by the skin of their teeth. But she needed to see Chance; he needed to explain himself.

"What about Chance, I'd have thought he'd be here?" asked George.

"I'm afraid we have bad news on that front. We've not seen him for the last 48 hours. My department is investigating. However, we've had communication with Moss, or Mosin to use his Russian name. He communicated via a friend at the Russian Embassy that he will release Chance and his family if you hand over the information he has requested. So, tell me about this information."

George opened her arms and sighed. "I don't know. Mum gave me a letter and a blank USB stick. She wasn't good with technology, so I'm not surprised. Happy to give you a copy of both if you wish?"

Sam nodded.

"I'll get copies of both for you, so long as you share whatever information you find."

"I agree," said Sam who seemed preoccupied.

"Off the record, and considering Chance thought they had a traitor in their midst, what do you think happened to him?"

"I don't know, and Moss gave no clue where they are holding him. Also, I've never heard of him speak of a traitor in MI5. That's news to me."

George dropped the smile and turned to face Sam. "And you, Sam, are you friend or enemy?"

Chapter 48

George visited Sheila at the Post Office to collect her Mum's letter to Charlie, and the chance it might provide a clue to what Moss wanted. Sheila met her at the door, hugged her, and asked about her and Charlie. George realised Sheila didn't know Charlie was dead, she hadn't spoken to her for a few days. She should have called, explained. This would be a shock.

"Sheila, sit with me, let's talk," said George.

"Tea first, then talk," Sheila countered. She carried on chatting as George listened, wondering whether she could trust her.

Sheila walked in with a tray; the silence and tension conveyed the gravity of George's news. Sheila sat next to George on the sofa and took her hands.

"What is it, George? What happened?"

George could hardly speak, and her eyes watered.

"It's Charlie, Sheila. They killed her," she croaked.

"Who, why, tell me," said Sheila.

She didn't give Sheila the gory details; it was enough to know she'd died.

"Probably Moss. He threatened Charlie and said he'd come after me. My time expired two days ago. He wants something, Sheila, and I don't have a clue what it is. I'm desperate, but I don't know. You remember Chance?"

Sheila nodded. "Your Mum talked about him and I thought she liked him at one point, you know, but he's married."

"Moss has Chance, and he wants what Mum had; information or something, in exchange for Chance and his family. What should I do?"

Sheila disentangled herself from George and stood. "Look, your Mum was not daft, she knew this day may come. She didn't tell me everything, but enough. Your Mum did nothing without a reason. The letter and photo are part of the puzzle, and I'm sure Moss wants everything."

"Can I have the letter to Charlie, please?"

"I'll get it, it's in my lost letters safe."

She returned, wiping her eyes, and carrying the letter. George studied Sheila; was she faking it? She looked genuine enough, but George's mind wasn't straight, still unsure who she could trust.

"Here's the letter to Charlie."

George opened it and read. It was similar, but not identical to her own letter. Her Mum asked Charlie to look out for George, included a photo, the same as the one she'd given to George and wrote 'that precious family moment'. Again, a credit card size USB stick, but no reference in the letter to the stick. Surely Charlie's stick contained the information Moss wanted. Why else would her Mum give them each a USB stick if they were blank? George looked at Sheila.

"I think I've got it, Sheila. This is what Moss wants. My USB stick is blank, but Charlie's may contain something."

Sheila sat close to George until their knees touched, Sheila's mouth a few inches away from George's ear.

Her voice a whisper, she said, "Your Mum, told me this may happen. She said if it's your life or this information you must give Moss the USBs, nothing else. You understand, George, nothing else?"

George gave Sheila a slight nod.

"She said it will buy you a few days, that's all. Your Mum wasn't daft, George, she was the best. Do what you must do. But don't waste time. Make sure you make them pay for what they did."

She pushed George away from her, stood and almost shouted. "Come on, young lady. Give them what they want, for your own sake."

George kissed Sheila on the cheek, put Charlie's envelope in her pocket, and hurried home.

Chapter 49

George lay in bed staring into the dark, wondering how to tackle this meeting with Pinchin. Over the past couple of months, death had been a constant. Her mother, Sarah the NCA Officer and probably her colleague in the NCA, now Chance's wife, and the three people she'd killed. More action than in her whole Army career.

She could go to his office, brush aside the gatekeeper, and demand to see him. Then what? What was she going to do, kill him, get arrested? Why did she need to see him? Lawyers knew where the bodies were buried. He would have information to clear Bradley Maudlin. Pinchin wasn't above dodgy legal practises, coercion of Bradley was a case in point, but if she beat it out of him, she'd be no better than Moss. She was an accessory the moment she didn't stop Ted from torturing the Russian in the safe house. Sam could help, she'd call him first thing in the morning.

Whilst she was in London Ted could do a little job for her. Not too late, so she phoned him. He answered on the first ring.

"Stumpy, you're going to a funeral tomorrow. I want you to visit Templeton Maudlin's place. Both his workplace and his home. See what his routine is. See who else is there. Okay? How's your leg?"

They disconnected, and satisfied she'd done all she could for the moment, exhaustion took over, and she fell into a nightmare sleep of death and dying.

***

A beggar sat on the ground outside the Costa café, a blanket around his knees and a Styrofoam cup to receive offerings. He mumbled to himself. She ignored him, but a few people dropped a few coins in his cup.

She sat in the Costa café opposite Pinchin's office to watch the comings and goings through the grimy window. From the photo Sam gave her, Pinchin was distinctive; tall, slim, almost bald, a model for a 1950s advert. Wilson Pinchin walked into the offices of Pinchin and partners at 9 a.m. As she finished her coffee and prepared to leave, Pinchin left the building opposite and walked across to the Costa cafe. The enemy was coming to her.

Pinchin dropped a coin into the tramp's cup and entered the Costa. She watched him order coffee, then glance around for a table. The place was quiet. Pinchin sat in the corner, his back to the door, hunched over the table, his eyes flitting around. By habit or nervousness, she couldn't tell. He leafed through a folder, looking for an entry in the documents.

A woman George had seen before entered the café; someone who wouldn't normally be seen dead in a Costa. George hunched into her jacket and hid her face. Melanie Syman paid for a coffee and joined Pinchin, sitting opposite him. This was London, and their meeting was no coincidence. George turned her back on them, hiding behind a magazine. She could see them in her peripheral vision.

George finished a coffee, went to the counter, ordered another then sat closer to the pair, with a free newspaper and her back to Pinchin and Melanie Syman. There was only artificial greenery separating them. Their heads were close but not touching. A muttered conversation ensued between the pair, so what was she doing talking to the lawyer? Pinchin talked in a loud whisper, his face animated.

"Bob may know, not sure," said Melanie Syman.

"Find out where she is and what she's got planned, and damn quick. I need to know what he knows tonight. What do I pay you for, because I like your company? Now on your bike and get on with it. Tonight, call me."

It didn't sound like a house sale, and Melanie Syman couldn't leave the Costa fast enough. A comedown since she'd last seen her. Melanie Syman stood with as much dignity as her humiliation would allow and, slipping on dark glasses, walked past George and left the café. George noticed she stuffed an envelope inside her quilted jacket. Melanie Syman turned right out of the café towards the underground. George waited, sent a text message to Sam, and the tramp hurriedly packed his things into a shopping bag, left his money on the street and walked in the same direction as Melanie Syman. She'd call Colonel Syman from home. George decided not to follow, but she was sure the tramp was Sam's man. Melanie Syman was compromised.

Chapter 50

Sam watched as a doctor attended to Ted's back wound. Chance had authorised the work 'off the books', so Sam was reluctant to escalate the operation, or call for backup. But George had doubts about how she and Ted could tackle this on their own. Sam didn't look the type to mix it with thugs, so George resigned herself to finishing a fight with Moss alone, even if she ended bust like a melon at a firing range, that's how it had to be. She couldn't ask Stumpy to do more than he had. He'd taken enough risks.

She came out of her reverie. Ted stared at her and barked. "Forget it. I'll be fine after the quack sorts me out. No offence, doctor."

Ted grinned, the doctor grinned back and finished dressing Ted's back.

"Take two of these twice a day. You'll be fine. I'd like to redress your wound every couple of days."

"See, doc says I'm fine, and anyway, we've had this conversation, so don't plan on doing this on your own."

George nodded, guilt fighting with gratitude came to the fore.

"What do you know about the Grain Tower, Sam?"

"The Fortress, or 'No. 1 The Thames', is its official name, purchased by a Russian some years ago and partially renovated before they shelved the project. He may have quite a strong position there. However, there are fishermen out at night fishing for mussels. They know of any Russian movement."

"Okay, Sam. Can you get us a plan of Grain Fortress and a map showing the coastline?"

Sam rubbed his chin. "Not something I would sanction, George. Chance had a tracker on him. I've accessed it. Last known location was Tower Battery, but it's stopped transmitting, it may have been destroyed. Moss may think his main residence has been compromised and gone to the Tower until this blows over. He will not abandon the fight altogether. Remember, he may still have assets working for him from the Cold War days. People like your mother. He needs to keep them active and paid. I'd advise waiting a few days. He can't stay there forever, and local plod will pick him up when he comes ashore. Heaven knows what he's doing with Chance."

"Hopefully, he'll hand him over once I've provided the information he needs," said George.

She didn't enjoy waiting and was impatient to confront Moss and Andrei on their own turf. Plod couldn't be trusted with this.

"Moss and his cronies would be out of jail within

hours. Pinchin, the lawyer, will see to that. It wouldn't surprise me if he doesn't have a judge on his payroll. Can you watch the Tower? Give me a warning if they leave? Is his Chance's wife and boy with him?" asked George.

"They were. But a woman's body washed up in the Thames Estuary near Gravesend. We haven't identified it, but it fits Helen Chance's description. The police have no leads and no one to identify the body. Mrs Chance had been in the water for two days and died from drowning. Police think it could have been suicide. Time of death was about the time you went to Chance's office. She may have fought, like your sister. Between us, this was not suicide. However, they still have Chance and his disabled son, and Chance may not know his wife is dead. So, we may have a hostage situation. For the moment, I assume Chance and his son are unharmed."

George mourned the loss of an innocent life. She was risking people's lives, not only her own and Ted's. It showed the lengths to which Moss would go. She'd been lucky so far, but Charlie had paid the price. Like all narcissists, Moss was impatient and wanted immediate gratification. Now Chance was also paying the price, and for what? When would they use Chance's disabled son as a pawn in this game of chess? She had to move this forward and fast. And she had to save Chance if she could, even though he knew the risks. One more reason to kill Moss and Andrei. She couldn't deny she'd enjoy it. Ted looked solemn, and his gaze drilled into her brain. She'd do what soldiers did at these times, store it for later and crack on.

Sam looked from George to Ted, a Deputy Director talking to subordinates. "Now Chance is temporarily unavailable, I'm acting Director, so any move you make, has to be cleared with me. I hope you don't object to that? But, if you're suggesting you and Ted go over to the

Tower and offer a swap; you for Chance and his son, the answer is 'No'. You'll be killed. Anyway, there's no saying Moss would accept it. I can't and won't go to my superiors with a half-baked plan."

"Last time I looked, Ted and I were both bona fide MI5 officers, albeit seconded. We'll do as we're told. But if it comes to it, we can handle it, but we'd do better with your help." George took a deep breath and remained calm. "I can understand your reservations, Sam. But please, get me the plans for Grain Fortress, and we'll talk about it again tomorrow."

Sam frowned and nodded, "Okay, but do nothing I haven't approved. George, you are not Bruce Willis. Any plan along the lines you're suggesting would have to have the Home Secretary's approval, and I can't take a half-baked plan like this to him. Do nothing until I see you tomorrow and if you have a viable plan, brief it to me first. Okay?"

George nodded, but had no intention of complying.

Sam looked at Ted. "Don't grin at me, you're old enough to know better. I expect you to talk some sense into her."

Ted's grin remained. "Old enough? I stopped maturing at eighteen, so no chance. Anyway, she'd kick my arse; excuse my French."

Sam said nothing, but shook his finger at them both.

Ted relaxed. He'd come to the same conclusion as George. He rubbed his stump and looked over at George.

"Foot's still sore, no chance of a stump massage

tonight I don't suppose?" asked Ted with a fake, salacious grin.

George responded with a spluttering burst of laughter. "Don't be a wimp. If you're lucky, I'll hand you the cream."

Sam shook his head as if he'd never understand a soldier's sense of humour. He looked at his shoes then inspected a piece of carpet. "I'll leave you two to it. You've had a rough time, and you need rest. I've contacted the local police, and they'll have a man in a car on the track monitoring you. If you see movement, don't shoot first. I'll be in contact tomorrow evening at 6 p.m."

As Sam closed the door behind him, George thought about their next task.

***

George needed to know what information she was exchanging for Chance. She took her USB stick left by her Mum.

"Let's look, see what we can learn," said George. "I won't hand them to Moss without knowing what's on them. I'll get my laptop."

They stared at the screen, which displayed the lack of contents on her USB. A blank Windows Explorer screen stared at them, defying them to contradict it.

"How good was your Mum with computers, George?"

"Okay, officially Mum was an accountant; but really, a Research Technician, she knew as much as there was to know. Why?"

"I'm not only a one-legged, pretty face. I spent years on my own messing around with computers. It's amazing what you can learn, with time on your hands. Self-educated, but there's not much I don't know about magic machines. Let me look at the raw filing system, bypassing the operating system, and we can access the other USB stick."

Both sticks contained random data, as if someone had overwritten them. Another hour passed and despite Ted's efforts, both sticks were blank.

"How many USB slots do you have?"

"Two, oh, I see, let's plug them in together."

Tiny LED lights flashed on both USB sticks, as if they were talking to each other and moments later the laptop screen blanked, a command prompt, and a new window appeared detailing files that looked like spreadsheets. Opening a file revealed lists of names, addresses, locations, their uses, and inventories of weapons and logistics, and thousands of records.

"Devious," George said, inspecting the data. "Now I know why Moss would kill for this. I've seen nothing like it."

George sat and pondered until Ted studied her. "What is it, what's troubling you, G?"

"Sheila was specific about handing over the USBs and nothing more. That was Mum's orders. There's more to this. We're amateurs, and it took us only two hours to crack this."

"We need to know if this data is real."

Some data made sense, but not all. A few locations were real, but most were fake, a few even in the North Sea.

"So, this is a false trail, otherwise the data would reveal real locations. It's a time waster."

They sat on the floor for another hour, knocking ideas back and forth. Perhaps there was still hidden data. George went to her Mum's bedroom, returned with the same photograph Mum had given to her two daughters and a magnifying glass. The glass from the photo frame was smashed, probably when the killer had searched the house. She showed Ted.

"This is Mum's copy of the photo she left for me and Charlie. The three are the same, yes? Final gifts from Mum to Charlie and me."

Ted examined the photos and nodded.

"Except they aren't the same. How's your eyesight?"

"So, so."

"Here, look through this." She handed Ted the magnifying glass. He looked at the three photos where George and Charlie were pointing, and rubbed his jaw. "Look identical to me, G. But my eyesight is none too good."

George looked again to check if she'd succumbed to 'pareidolia', seeing something that wasn't there? The dots on the three photos were in the same place on each, and the number of dots were the same, but the shape of the dots was different. But these were old photos, and anything could have corrupted them.

"They're microdots. How would Mum get so much information onto tiny dots?"

Ted brightened. "These days, with Extended Scalable Vector Graphics, she wouldn't have a problem so long as she had the right equipment and from the sounds of it, she did. During the Cold War, when microdots were in fashion, 2000 lines of information would fit on one microdot. That's tripled since 1990. But it'll be a job and a half to extract it. I may know a bloke who knows a bloke who can do it. But it's a long shot."

George's mother had intended the information for her and Charlie, and no one else. Her Mum would have left instructions on how to view the information. How would her Mum's mind have worked? George and Charlie often finished each other's sentences, even thoughts. They also played a word game where one word from George would lead to another from Charlie, then her Mum would take the next word etc. until they finished with a nonsense sentence. What if she'd done it with their letters? Their Mum also showed them how to play a game using only consonants from innocent looking text and juggling the consonants until a message appeared. The first to read the message won. Now she realised her Mum had been training them for this eventuality. What a smart woman.

"I have to get Mum's letters to me and Charlie, they're key. Stay there, I need your brain."

Hours later, they placed the letters side by side, juggled the words and letters, as they'd done as children. Finally, the rearranged consonants from the two letters revealed a set of instructions and a whole different story. It told of how Julia Stone had made the microdots, using her 60s

Cold War training by Lucien Nikolai from the NKVD, the predecessor to the KGB. Only Charlie and George would know where to find those dots.

"Mum used to have equipment at home. She has an old microscope in her bedroom. She said the Russian Bagulnik microscope was the best. I'll get it."

An hour later, both Ted and George saw the dots and lines of data. The information would take time to extract, but her mother had left instructions.

"I'm willing to bet this data makes no sense unless we superimpose the dots from the three photos. So, now we know why Mum said I should hand over the USB sticks."

"Okay, let's leave this until after I've been to the Tower. We'll have time then. If I don't come back, it won't matter," she told Ted.

Chapter 51

George and Ted had a 6 p.m. 'prayers meeting' with Sam. Jaws lay at Ted's feet, waiting for his evening walk, and occasionally grumbled.

Ted briefed them on his visit to the funeral he'd attended. Templeton Maudlin was also present and in Ted's inexpert opinion, Templeton Maudlin was a control freak, an anal tentative, scared of failure and as batty as a Chinese cave.

"But there was something else about him. He not only liked his job, and let's face it, you'd have to enjoy your job to be a Funeral Director, Mortician, and Cremator, he revelled in it. He loves his work."

The funeral was for a middle-aged woman who'd died of natural causes. Ted had seen him in the background, sliding his fingers down the sides of his trousers, smirking with a turned down smile. Ted interpreted this as meaning he had a secret he shared with the dead woman.

"He gave me the shakes," said Ted.

It confirmed what Bradley told her. George left out the Pinchin and Melanie Syman liaison; she still didn't know if she could trust Sam, but guessed the beggar who'd followed the woman worked for Sam. Sam ended the update and looked from George to Ted. Mouth open, on the verge of speaking.

"I spoke informally to the Home Secretary last night, sounded him out about your plan of doing a two-man assault on the Grain Fortress to rescue Chance. The answer was 'No'. Not only 'No', but if you try it on your own, you'll be arrested and charged. Now, I'm telling you, you're still seconded MI5 officers, and I'm ordering you to stay clear."

He watched George and Ted's faces; they remained passive. George twitched but controlled herself and waited. There was more.

"The SBS plan to assault the Fortress Tower the morning after tomorrow at 4:30 a.m. There's no moon, so the conditions are ideal. It's in hand, let it go. Okay? You both have emotional baggage and you know it. They also think they can do it with no innocents being killed. If Moss or any of the others resist, they'll bear the consequences. Likewise, anyone in the way will get hurt. Clear?"

"Clear," said George and Ted together.

For George, this was the last and best chance to kill both Moss and Andrei, but the SBS taking Moss and Andrei prisoner didn't cut it. She'd suppressed her hate and Moss's reckoning was not negotiable. George had changed in the last months. She hadn't joined the Army to kill people; she joined to help them get fit, to explore her own limitations. Achieving the former made her family proud, but it wasn't enough. Exploring her limitations was a work in progress. If she didn't take this opportunity, she'd never forgive herself because she owed it to her family. Her Mum was no traitor, she'd been faithful to the Soviet Union, but she hadn't tainted the twins with her own ideology.

Their mother had taught George and Charlie loyalty to the country they'd taken as their own, and for George, Great Britain was her home and she was English, and she'd die fighting for what she believed in. She believed in justice and living by the standards handed down by her Mum. Going to the Tower alone was suicidal. But she was an opportunist and resourceful, she'd find a way. There could be only one of three outcomes: she'd die trying, she'd kill Moss, or they'd both die.

The possibility of being killed didn't worry her, but dying without settling the injustice did. She'd come too far now to worry about dying. She glanced at Ted; his face was grim. Had he read her thoughts? Was he having second thoughts?

"Stay here and wait for my call to tell you it's over," said Sam.

George interpreted it as a warning to stay put and don't interfere.

"Sure, but I'd appreciate it if you could keep me informed, especially if they change the timings," said George.

Sam collected his papers and bag. "I have to leave now. Stay out of trouble, and I'll update you when this situation is resolved. Stay by the phone and behave."

Sam left, and George and Ted exchanged a look.

"Are you thinking what I'm thinking?"

"Maybe," said Ted.

"I'll make the call to Moss now, arrange a meeting and a swap at midnight tomorrow night. I'll swap Chance for the USB sticks, I can be away with Chance and his son by let's say 2 a.m., well clear by 4 a.m."

"Okay. At least it might give us an acceptable plan. I know a fisherman who'll take us across. He'll wait two hours," said Ted.

"Not 'us', Ted, 'me'," said George.

Ted scowled, they'd come this far together, and he didn't look happy. George sensed it, brushed his arm, and shook her head. She felt for him, he'd become a close friend, and he wanted to help, but she had to protect him. She was also aware he was somewhere between late fifties and sixty, no longer a young squaddie running round the bundu, and with only one foot. There was no doubt he was one hard bugger, he'd proved himself, and he'd die on the job before he'd fail. That was the problem for George. She didn't want another innocent death. There'd been killing, with more to come. Her job now was to cut out and destroy the disease.

"I have to do this alone." She grinned at him. "Anyway, if you come along, you'll cramp my style," she said, trying to lighten the mood.

Ted shrugged his acceptance and rubbed his neck. "I'll stay in the boat. If it gets to 2:30 a.m., I'll come to get you. Don't argue."

"If you can get a rowing or even a quiet motorised boat, it'll be mistaken for a fishing boat. That'll get me on board, although they'll have lookouts, but I'll have to deal with that. What's the tide like tomorrow night?"

"Rising tide at 10 p.m., ideal for a small boat. High tide at 3 p.m. Leaving the fortress before then will be fine by boat. At dawn, it'll be on foot via the walkway between the Tower and the shore, but in the dark, it's treacherous. One other thing, the boatman will return to the fortress once, to collect you. If you're late, he won't wait."

"Okay, noted. Thanks."

He looked into George's eyes, to emphasise the point. He must have known he was talking to the deaf.

"So, don't be late and no second bites."

"I'll be at the Tower with the boat at 2:30 a.m. Clear?"

"I'll make the call to Moss," said George.

"And I'll walk Jaws."

Jaws leapt to his feet and ran in circles at the door.

"You can take Charlie's room. We'll complete plans in the morning."

Chapter 52

George and Ted discussed the plan until they both had the same plan in their minds. Ted paced, rubbing his chin. It had weighed on him overnight; he wanted to be in the action. George estimated her chances of survival were slim, but she'd bear the consequences, however it turned out. She explained to Ted; he gave a morning grunt, which was as much as she could hope for.

They discussed the worst case. If it turned into a 'cluster foxtrot', he would contact Colonel Syman, and tell him everything, including Pinchin's relationship with Melanie Syman. The question they needed to know, could they trust Colonel Syman? She knew Syman from her time at Stanford Hall, and Ted said he'd trust him with his life. But George knew his wife was passing on information gained from Syman. She shared her lingering doubts with Ted, who nodded but remained silent.

By 10 p.m., she'd dressed in dark waterproof trousers and jacket. She slipped her mobile into her jacket pocket but knew she'd be searched. The USB sticks were in a waterproof pouch in an inner pocket.

An hour later, George boarded the boat and sat opposite Ted, her back to the stern. The boat had an outboard motor, but the boatman set his oars in the water. Ted had told him to keep it quiet. She reminded herself that fishermen did this for a living. Only the sound of lapping water and occasional scraping of the bottom of the boat on a gravel sea bed disturbed her silence. Even noise from the pub, 'The Hogarth Inn', didn't disturb her. With no moon, if she turned, she'd be able to see the town's lights. She didn't doubt the 'why' or 'what' of this mission. But part of her wanted a normal life, to live normally, do normal things, meet normal people, laugh with family, have a few drinks, meet with friends.

'But not tonight, Georgie girl,' she said to herself. 'Tonight, it's kill or die.'

She'd never been a good sailor; Charlie called her a wimp. The short sea trip made her queasy, not helped by the rotting seaweed, and she closed her eyes and relaxed and concentrated on the details of the next couple of hours. The night air was cold against her face, the wind taking her ponytail, lifting it and dropped it back onto her jacket. She wished she'd bought a beanie hat to cover it. They would spot her from the Tower. What was she thinking? It didn't matter if the men working for Moss spotted them. They were expecting her, and she'd get to see Moss again. Last time she aimed to win his confidence at whatever cost, this time she'd kill him, even if it meant her own death. The short trip was over in fifteen minutes, their arrival marked by a bump of the wooden side against the concrete leg of the Tower Battery. The place was once a wartime fortress and base for coastal defence. In recent years, an entrepreneur had purchased the Fortress for a 'goose egg'. There were rumours; a hotel, even a pirate radio station, but the locals considered them crazy. It would cost more to make it habitable than it was worth. Unless your name was Moss, with father's money, and a plan to use it for crime. Then it was the perfect place to carry out nefarious activities. It was local gossip that a body weighed down in the soft sand would disappear. A body dropped into quick sand would usually reappear days or weeks later. Regardless, a shiver went down her spine.

The tower loomed above, silhouetted against the night sky. It stared down at her stoically, scoffing at her audacious boldness. Would she be able to jump from the Tower and swim back? She'd die of the cold before she reached land.

The fisherman stood to help her climb the metal ladder leading to the first stage of the Tower. A landmark for decades, time and rust had taken its toll, and clumps of dark corrosion tore at her leather gloves until they were in shreds. A light shone down on her as she ascended the ladder and climbed onto the Fortress. The man dressed in a windcheater stepped back. He was, like many of Moss's men, over muscled. She guessed they injected as they worked out. It didn't mean they were fit, but for a short fight, it gave them the advantage. She recalled when she'd boxed a Welsh woman, the same weight as George but four inches shorter and built like a male weight lifter. After six rounds, her opponent's arms were so heavy, she couldn't even hold them up. By round seven, her opponent's corner had no more fight.

A second man kept a distance, guarding the first and covering George. He carried a Heckler & Koch MP5 as if he'd used one before. The man grabbed George by her arm, and frogmarched her along a railed gantry, opened a steel door, pushed her through and closed it with two locking arms. The inside cast shadows from a low-wattage bulb set into the wall. Even Ted couldn't help her now.

She was on her own, 'Lone Ranger'; without her 'Tonto'.

"Against the wall and spread your legs," the man said in good, accented English.

Normally, George would have replied with a witty response, but not tonight. Tonight, she'd behave, until the right time. 'Behave like a lady, fight like a tiger', she remembered her Mum's saying.

The man ran his hands along George's legs. He was brisk, no smiles or smirks, but overzealous.

"You want me to strip? You know you want to," said George with a twinkle in her eye.

To his credit, he didn't react, but kept a straight face and carried on, until he came to her jacket when he became a little too familiar. She shouldn't provoke him; it was unprofessional, but she was still learning.

"Okay, strip off your jacket and your top."

She guessed she was being hard on him. She took off her jacket and stripped to her bra, and dropped her clothes to the floor.

"Lift arms," he said.

The number of times she'd stripped off in front of soldiers were countless, but she'd drawn a line at stripping in front of Afghan locals. Russians usually took every opportunity to prove their manhood. But not tonight, Moss must have them on a short reign.

Tonight, she'd draw the line at taking off her bra. He'd have to do it himself if he wanted that. She held her breath. He looked at her without comment. Simply another piece of meat.

"Put clothes on, come with me."

George and her escort walked along a concrete corridor. Lights every few metres cast shadows, and their boots slapped on the hard, damp floor. The damp and mould invaded her nostrils, and even the smell of the sea didn't mask the aged smell. A flight of steel stairs to an upper level, a walkway, and a balustrade. It reminded her of Bradley Maudlin in prison.

She faced a set of wooden double doors, which would have been appropriate in a stately home and contrast with the metal doors she'd seen so far. Fitted into the concrete walls, they looked surreal and clashed with the dank grey concrete, reminding her of a 1960s black and white war film set in Norway, 'The Heroes of Telemark'.

As a goon opened a door, light flooded into the corridor and dazzled her. This time, she'd go willingly into the lion's den. A memory of her first parachute jump, a momentary fear pulling her back from the aircraft doors and the 15,000-foot drop. Like that drop, she rallied her strength and courage, and walked into the room, a few more steps towards vengeance.

Moss sat behind a desk and didn't look up. Two arm chairs were set before the desk, but she stood and faced him. The room contrasted with the outside corridor, warm and well lit, a chandelier hanging from the centre of the whitewashed concrete ceiling. It looked like a larger version of his office in South London. Moss looked like a pimp in a Las Vegas palace.

She waited. Moss was one for the dramatic. Tired of

waiting, she sat, facing him.

"Please sit, Georgina," said Moss without looking up.

He couldn't even stand to look at her. On the top of his head, he may as well have etched 'Hate'. But it wasn't unexpected; a narcissist either loves or hates. Those who are useful to him, he loves; those who are not, or fall from grace, he hates.

The goon with the Heckler & Koch MP5 stood behind her within arm's reach. Russians manned the Fortress; presumably the foreign heavies had left. That was unfortunate. She hoped Tom the Geordie might help her. He'd supported her in the house and hadn't resisted in the car park. She thought she might use that. No chance now.

Moments later, Moss looked up and gave a reptilian smile.

"How nice of you to come and visit me. I've looked forward to it. Should we get down to business?"

It surprised George, she'd reckoned he'd want to talk. To give her the benefit of his twisted logic and why he'd fallen for her charms. He'd say he was leading her on. She knew better. His opportunist hormones had spoken, but he could discard his feelings as easily as he changed his clothes. As unpalatable as it was, she'd been more affected by their encounter than him. It drove her even more to a reckoning with him. She had a job to do; free Chance and his son, kill Moss and Andrei, and anyone who got in her way.

"You have something for me, Georgina." he barely looked at her but held out his hand, waiting for the package.

She would not hand over the package unless he released Chance. They both knew what this was about.

"Let's talk about Chance and his son. I want to see them before I hand it over."

"Okay, we'll do it your way."

Mind composed, hands steady, her breathing slow. She'd been shot in Afghanistan, bombed in Iraq, had the urine taken out of her by countless squaddies, and she'd kept her composure. She stood and leaned over his desk, both hands flat on top. Moss nodded at a goon. A moment later, as she turned towards her attacker, a bone crunching blow to the side of her head reverberated like a grenade inside her skull. She'd taken many punches, but not from a MP5. A fuzzy outline of the goon filled her fuddled brain, and her legs buckled.

Chapter 53

The cold concrete seeped into her muscles, and her shoulder ached. The titanium seemed to conduct the damp cold into her body, and to add to her discomfort, her face rested in a pool of something wet; she guessed vomit. Not unusual after sedation with the butt of an MP5. She was in a mess.

Something brushed against her face and despite feeling like crap, she dared to move her head towards the softness. Shaking her head, hurt, and her focus took a minute to fix the source of the contact. Someone had their back to her, and as her eyes focussed and adjusted to the dim light, she saw someone sitting near her. Something again touched her face, and she withdrew, bringing up her hands to ward off the 'threat'. With distance between herself and 'something', she found it easier and less painful to focus. They'd taken her jacket, and she shivered.

A slurred grunt, and she recognised the sound, Patrick, Chance's son. A finger poked her cheek again. More noises from Patrick.

"You awake, Georgina?" asked Chance.

She grunted and lay still, focussing through the gloom towards Patrick. Slowly moving her muscles, she did a system's check to see if everything worked. It did. They hadn't trussed her, unlike Chance. Moss's men probably thought she no longer presented a threat, and that suited her. She stood, stretched, and looked around. A single bulb hung from a shielded wall light. Chance lay on his side on the floor. The smart suit was gone, and with it his refined looks. He looked as bad as George felt. He wore jeans and a T-shirt, and plastic ties bound his feet and wrists. But he looked around and gave a feeble smile.

"Welcome, Georgina. It doesn't surprise me to see you. But you may yet get us all killed. I can't imagine that the Firm sanctioned your presence here."

"Nice to see you too, Mr Chance. The Firm doesn't know."

She knelt and whispered to him. "There's an SBS team due here at 4:30 a.m. I guess the safest option would be for us to stay here and await the cavalry."

"Let me guess. You don't like that, and you have a plan?"

Chance and Patrick had been incarcerated in the cell for a while. Little wonder Chance was irritable.

"No, I don't like it, and no I don't have a plan; but I'm working on it."

"Did you give Moss everything he wanted?" asked Chance.

She felt for the plastic bag containing the USB sticks. Gone.

"He took it."

"Did it contain all he asked for?" asked Chance.

A strange thing to ask, George hesitated.

"Yes, he has it all."

Chance sighed, but said nothing. She ignored him, went over to Patrick, and knelt. He was no threat; unshackled, he sat against the wall, one leg out in front of him, the other at an awkward angle. He stank of urine. Patrick rocked backwards and forwards when he saw her, but his face broke into a frown, and he looked down at his crotch embarrassed.

"Hey, Patrick, am I pleased to see you. Don't worry about anything. I'll get you out of here. Okay?"

He made a sound resembling 'okay'.

She turned to Chance. "How long have we been here? How often do they check?"

"We've been here two days. You've been here about an hour, and I guess they'll be back soon. What do you have in mind?"

"It's between one and two in the morning. We have to move," said George.

"Why?" asked Chance. "If this is about revenge, forget it. The SBS can take care of them."

George knelt and pushed her face against Chance's. She spoke to him through gritted teeth. "Look, Chance. I've risked my arse to get in here and save yours and your son's. Less judgement and more constructive ideas. My guess is, they'll kill us when the SBS make their entry and they raise the alarm. Apart from that, yes, I want to kill Moss and the Russian who killed my Mum. You can charge me when we get out of here. If you don't like it, stay here, keep quiet, but keep out of my way."

He nodded, realising he'd been insensitive and misjudged her. She was the loose cannon he'd warned her about. God knows, she'd also worked with her fair share of dipsticks in her service who thought they were the dog's gonads and could win the war on their own. She'd overreacted, but she would not apologise. Neither the SBS nor Chance would stop her. She guessed he knew his wife was dead, otherwise she'd be with them and she regretted being so harsh on him.

Turning her back on Chance and Patrick, she opened her woollen blouse and removed a wire from the base of her bra. The steel wire passed for a bra stiffener. They'd taken Patrick's wheelchair away. With that, she may have stood a chance of finding a tool to cut Chance's ties. But the room was empty, except for the shielded wall light. Walking over to it, she unfastened the two screws holding a wire guard in place. No chance, so she hooked her fingers through it and wrenched it from the wall. The bulb smashed on the floor, leaving them in darkness. The unbent wire fashioned into a handle, which she wrapped around her palm and knuckles. That left six inches free as a stabbing weapon. She unwound it and placed it in her pocket.

She stood between Chance and Patrick and spoke to them both, wondering how much Patrick understood.

They couldn't see her and hoped she sounded confident, at least for Patrick's sake.

"Unless you want to stay here, make noise. I need to get a goon to enter the cell. Okay?"

Patrick understood better than his father, and bellowed like a bear having its claws ripped out. Chance seemed to take his son's lead and roared, "Help!"

No doubt they were busy with Moss inspecting the USBs; she couldn't care less. Several minutes later, someone approached the door. Two voices outside. She stood behind the door, where the guard wouldn't see her. She waited, the garrotte from her bra ready. The goon wouldn't know the light was out, so she guessed she may use it to her advantage. A hammering on the door, someone heard. A bellow from outside in Russian and banging on the metal door. Moss could abandon this place and leave them locked inside the cell, but the SBS would discover them. But that wouldn't advance her mission. Patrick and Chance kept up the cacophony anyway, hoping that their Russian jailers would open the door, eventually. They yelled for half an hour until even Patrick gave up, hoarse with shouting. The noise stopped, but a scraping told her someone was releasing the door fasteners, long metal bars on the outside, on swivels. Simple but effective.

George tensioned the garrotte. As the door opened, Patrick kicked up a ruckus, but Chance remained quiet. The door flew open, and George prevented it from hitting the wall. She waited. The guard flashed an LED light across to where the noise was coming, illuminating Patrick still waving his arms. The guard entered the cell, aiming his automatic weapon using the light. In his peripheral vision, he would see Chance.

The guard cursed in Russian and strode across to Patrick who covered his face as the guard brought back his foot to kick him. Timing was everything. She needed the guard off balance. She pushed the door closed and moved in the darkness. The guard directed the LED light at Patrick and unless his peripheral vision picked her up, this might work, so long as it was quick and silent.

As the guard's foot connected with Patrick's chest, she slid the killing weapon around the guard's neck and wrenched it back, crossing it at the nape of his neck. Patrick continued his wailing, but George realised how smart he was as he grasped the man's foot that had connected with his chest. As the guard dropped the torch and his automatic, Patrick wrapped his arms around the guard's leg and held tight. The guard reached for his throat, but George dragged him back and off balance. She wrenched the weapon tight and hung on. His hands dropped and his heels stopped kicking. Chance hadn't moved.

George pocketed the LED torch and searched the dead guard. Finding a pocket knife, she slit Chance's ties then took the dead man's automatic pistol, shining the torch on the side, and testing the cocking lever and magazine release. Russian markings on the side, she'd never seen one before, but guessed the magazine held at least eight rounds and the action seemed conventional. She'd have no problem with it. Chance went over to his son to calm him.

She stood behind the door and waited for the second guard. She held the dead guard's weapon ready. Nothing.

"Chance, bring Patrick and follow me," she directed.

"Yes, I can carry him."

"The boat is returning in less than 30 minutes. We must reach the landing stage. If possible, without detection. You win, I'll leave the rest for the SBS. I've had enough of this."

"Good, I'm sure Moss won't survive, good for both of us."

They crept along the dank corridor surrounding the Tower. A form appeared, approaching them. They saw each other, but he fumbled with his assault rifle. George had her stolen automatic ready, but she hesitated. If she fired, hell would break loose, they'd never make the boat.

Only four metres from him, she rushed at him before he could raise his weapon. The Russian made automatic in hand. She connected her right shoulder with his stomach, lifting him off the ground and dumped him onto his back, George on top. The man bellowed, which echoed around the corridor as he slammed against the concrete floor, winded. His weapon clattered against the concrete.

George's hand clamped over her adversary's mouth. She embedded her weapon into his stomach and pressed down on it with her own body. She hoped their bodies and clothing would muffle the sound of the weapon going off. Angling the weapon towards his chest, she squeezed the trigger and a muffled 'thwack' ricocheted around them. George lay still for a few seconds until satisfied he was dead. He kicked his heels twice and lay still.

Getting to her feet she whispered, "Come on, Chance, move yourself. Get him in the cell."

She waited, glancing both ways as Patrick sat on the floor, swaying to silent music, Chance dragging the body. As he emerged, he hoisted Patrick onto his back, she handed him the guard's automatic and she took the assault rifle. It looked like an old Soviet AG0-43 5.45 mm automatic. Chance handled the automatic pistol awkwardly, and she guessed he'd be useless in a fight. Anyway, he had Patrick to carry.

George opened a metal door leading to the outside and surveyed the area. Steps descended to the landing stage where the boat would pick them up. A telltale light from a cigarette gave away the guard, the smell of smoke wafting from the landing. He seemed to walk back and forth on the landing point. The guard needed to be neutralised. Chance tapped George on the shoulder and put his mouth to her ear.

"My turn. Look after Patrick, give me the assault rifle."

He lowered Patrick onto the platform and stood at the top of the steps. Chance watched his prey and waited until the guard turned. He unfolded the weapon's stock, locked it into position, and crept down the steps until he was two steps from the bottom. The guard turned and hesitated.

"Chan…," the guard uttered, raising his hands.

What was that? Did the guard know Chance? That's what it looked like.

The rifle came down on the guard's nose, knocking him backwards. The surprised and injured man recovered quickly and faced Chance. Chance fumbled, dropped his weapon, and froze. George pushed Chance out of the way and smashed the guard across the face and fired her weapon into the man's face. The noise would alert others. They had to move.

"Get him over the side," said George.

Chance hoisted the man over the railing and into the sea. A splash from below.

She hoisted Patrick onto her shoulder, fireman's lift style, and carried him down the metal staircase to the landing, hoping they wouldn't have to wait long for the boat. Standing on the deck left them exposed, and eventually someone would check the cell. Chance was a liability and useless in a fight. She's be better off without him.

The wind had increased and was blasting them; and waves were building against the boat. Chance also saw it and lifted Patrick. Speed was important and Moss's men would use a spotlight. Moss would not hesitate to order automatic fire to stop them.

As the boat touched the landing stage, Ted stood, held the metal railing, and steadied the boat as Chance and Patrick boarded. The boat barely moved in the swell and even the wind was dissipating. Both sea and wind waiting for something to happen; to spell the difference between life and death, waiting to see which way it should jump, towards eradication or subjugation? Once she boarded, her mission was over, and no one could criticise her for dereliction of duty. Even the cold summoned her into the boat. She could be warm and safe in her own home by 4 a.m. The boat and sea drew her to them.

It would be easy to board the boat, leave it to the SBS, and live a quiet life. George had always regarded anything beyond her five senses as fluff and bullshit, but she had a notion that if she took the easy option and stepped into that boat, she'd blight and betray the memories of her Mum and sister. She'd also relinquish a future, which she owed to herself and her family. She hesitated for a lifetime, but only a second passed, then stood back. Chance put out his hand to help George, but she shook her head. She could take the lazy option, limp through this night, and the coming years, or do her damned duty, emulate her family. The term 'legacy' touched her mind like evaporating steam, but it was more than that. The events of this night would redefine her future, and she could no sooner take the easy option than betray her conscience.

She sensed Chance scowling, and Ted stood as if to join her. Chance pushed him back into his seat.

"Ted, look after Patrick for me. Okay?"

George held tight to the rusty steel railing, the rough surface digging into her skin. She enjoyed the unyielding indifference of its surface. If she survived this night, she would kill again. Her future lay before her, and she accepted her fate; slotted into this way of life, and feeling more at home than during her time serving in war zones.

Chance ruffled Patrick's hair, took the Soviet assault rifle, and stepped out to join George. He pushed the boat away, and the oarsman made a silent but swift departure towards the coast. Patrick pressed against Ted.

She didn't wait for the boat to be swallowed by the obsidian darkness, and she didn't even look around to see if Chance followed her.

Chapter 54

George and Chance made their way towards the metal stairs to the next level. Her LED torch shone along the curved corridor leading to Moss's office. Running steps behind them alerted George to a guard bearing down on them from behind. They had only a second's advantage over him. The dimly lit corridor cast shadows, and she clicked off the LED. They pressed their backs against a metal doorway, which provided a recess. The guard might have missed them if Chance hadn't knelt, then rolled in front of him, causing the man to run full tilt and stumble over him. The guard landed heavily on his front and grappled for his weapon. George took advantage of his upheaval, and with him lying on his front, used her full weight to drop a knee onto his neck. Removing the wire from the light fitting, she placed a hand over his mouth then stabbed him in the neck, feeling his pulsing blood on her hand. Her victim's hand went to the neck wound, but George lay on him until he lay still. If he wasn't dead, he was out of the fight. She extracted the makeshift weapon and stood.

Raised voices reached them and George realised

whatever or whoever the man had been running towards or from, that was also their destination. A light shone under the wooden doors to Moss's office, and along the corridor where two guards dressed in black, and wearing face coverings, stood guard, and carried MP5s.

They looked a cut above the guards they'd encountered so far. Big but not bulky, lean, and athletic and carrying themselves like professionals. They both spotted George and Chance, but remained unruffled and relaxed. Their weapons remained across their chests, but George knew they could bring them to bear and kill George and Chance before they had time to react. They made eye contact with George but presented no threat. George pointed her weapon down; Chance did the same. They stopped about three metres from the guards.

The regime had changed, but this wasn't SBS either, she'd have heard them. This change had been all but silent. Had Moss drafted in help? How had they arrived unseen? They could have been here for a time, hidden in one of the myriad rooms. Voices filtered from inside Moss's office, and she tried to catch the gist, but her Russian was nearly non-existent, and she didn't even recognise the voice, which seemed calm and deep; like an old bear grinding glass. George braced herself for the worst.

As the guard opened the door, light flooded the corridor.

A voice from inside, "Come in. You're part of this circus. Quickly, we have little time."

An old man in his eighties sat in an easy chair. A shock of white hair and a pallor caused by disease. With his walking stick he beckoned them, then stood on arthritic legs. He looked close to death; sick, terminal. An assistant held a drip. He acted like a nurse, except for the holstered weapon.

"Come now, don't be afraid. No need for those weapons. Chance, nice to see you again, old chap. Been a long time. How are you?"

The old man spoke in near perfect English. In his heyday, a whisper from him would have scared most Russian soldiers. George and Chance walked into the room. Moss sat behind his desk. But rather than a self-confident businessman and apex predator, he resembled a scolded child. No doubt the old man's doing. Tears glazed Moss's eyes. Two guards stood behind him, one of which was Andrei. To George, they weren't there for Moss's safety.

"I'm fine, Anatoly. It's been a long time; I barely recognise you. I thought you'd retired."

The man chuckled and sank into his chair. "I did. And I would have stayed retired if not for my idiot son," he said with bitterness. He pointed towards Moss, and if fingers were weapons, Moss would have died where he sat.

"You, my dear, are Georgina Stone, I'm so pleased to meet you. I shall call you 'George'."

The old man limped towards her and offered his hand. He smiled and his eyes sparkled, as if his mind was with someone else. She remained stony faced.

"I knew your mother well, and we met many times. A fine woman. You should be proud of her. Put your weapon down if you wish. You'll not come to harm here. I must explain. By the way, I'm Anatoly Mosin. You may have heard of me."

A guard relieved them of the assault rifle. She glanced at the guards and knew it would be nigh on impossible to get to Mosin with his goons protecting him.

"So?" asked George.

"I can see you take after your mother for grit," he said with an acerbic grin. "This could take some time. Something we do not have in abundance."

Mosin's eyes focussed on Chance and George with a restrained intensity. "You may sit if you wish, but I suspect, George, you are not the sitting, waiting type. As you wish."

George stood, the automatic hanging from her hand. If she had to use it, she doubted she'd get off one shot before Mosin's men killed both her and Chance. She stood balanced, attentive but not threatening, waiting for whatever rubbish Mosin intended to dispense. Whatever; the outcome wouldn't change. She'd die trying to kill whoever ordered the killings.

"I retired almost two decades ago. Pushed out and given something to run. But the ways of our new Russian businessmen," he spat out the few words as if it offended his palate. "They are nothing more than unconscionable, malfeasant criminals. I handed my substantial interests over to my son Sergei, over ten years ago. But he betrayed me and Mother Russia to feed his own greed."

He pointed a thumb over his shoulder towards his son. His face was full of disdain.

"He was aware of my background, but I made the mistake of trusting him. George, your mother was my bookkeeper in the UK. More than that, she was my provisioner, my fixer, and coordinator, and knew every one of my clandestine shipments between Russia and the UK. She knew every asset and the location of each cache. She knew it all. Julia also knew every illegal in the UK. I'm sure you're familiar with the term. Russian sleepers, pretending to lead a normal life as a Brit. But, as they say, you never retire from the KGB, you wait for the phone call. And I received a phone call directing me to resolve my son's mess."

"Gangland killings by my son were one thing; I knew about them and tolerated them. I told my superiors the boy was learning on the job. But killing former KGB sleepers in the UK was too much. He wanted what Julia Stone had, and what she knew to support his own criminal activities. For refusing to reveal those secrets, he had her killed."

Mosin looked across at Moss who refused to meet his eyes.

"Before I retired, I gave him most of what I had, including my criminal contacts, and I was prepared to accept his nefarious UK activities. The UK is a foreign land, and I convinced myself he'd meet his match and end his days in prison, or dead." He shrugged.

"But he wasn't happy with what I'd given him. He squandered it and wanted more. He had my strictest instructions, never to involve any of my former official KGB contacts in his activities. I made it clear to him, your mother was top of my protected list. He only knew of her existence and that of my network. He didn't know her name or contact details, and none of the others either. That is my guess anyway. Am I right?" he looked over at Moss, who nodded.

"He promised to leave them alone, and I believed him. My death would release him from that promise, to leave my former network to retire in peace."

Mosin sank into his chair, then sat on the edge.

"Well, this corpse isn't dead yet, Sergei."

His raised voice surprised George, and Moss cringed.

"And I won't let you do more damage. George, that man killed the woman I was most fond of next to my dear departed wife. She was an angel, and the most loyal and brave Officer we ever had. I could not tolerate his actions. Sergei created more havoc than he could deal with and risked revealing too much to British Intelligence."

"So, Stephen Moss ordered my mother to be killed? But who did it? Who killed her?" asked George.

"My son ordered the killing, but the killer is standing right there, George. It was Andrei. But, as they say, he was only following orders. Sergei ensnared Andrei, who was previously a loyal soldier and Russian Special Forces, Spetsnaz. I don't blame him, and neither should you. He's now under my protection. I'm sure Sergei wanted to extract the information your mother held and once satisfied he'd have disposed of her, so she would be dead either way. But Julia Stone was a tough woman. No doubt Julia convinced herself you would be safe in the land of war and nightmares. When he couldn't extract the information by asking, he threatened to have you killed in Afghanistan. But to answer a question spinning around in your mind, I didn't give Julia Stone's details to Sergei. Andrei was misguided, that's all. He followed Sergei's orders. But he is also my son."

George let that sink in. Both Sergei and Andrei were Mosin's sons. She exploded. "Your precious Andrei is a murderer. He slaughtered my mother! But, because Andrei is also your son, you're prepared to forgive him, but not Sergei? Do you have no scruples? You're no better than them." She pointed towards Sergei and Andrei.

Anatoly Mosin looked shocked, but spoke softly. "And what you've done over the past few weeks, the deaths. Was every death justified? Ask yourself if you are any better than Andrei. I accept I owe you and your family a great deal and I will repay you. You have my word. George, if the situation had been different your mother and I would have been more than platonic friends. Alas, it wasn't to be. But I once met you and Charlie as babies, and later, when you were small children, I feel as if I know you. There's no reason you should remember. I am as fond of you as I am of my son, Andrei. But Sergei is no longer a son of mine and his termination has been sanctioned."

That still didn't forgive Andrei, who would pay. But she needed her weapon, her only chance. She'd kill Sergei and Andrei with her bare hands.

She pointed a finger at Andrei. "I don't care, you were 'only doing your job'. I don't care 'you're a soldier and that's what soldiers do'. And I don't care for your so-called credentials as a veteran and Special Forces soldier, the next time I see you, I will kill you and I will make you suffer."

"I look forward to it, George. You are a good warrior, but not in my league," said Andrei. No humour in his voice, no gloating, simple facts. She could deal with that.

"I know this is hard for you, George. But these are the facts. So how did Sergei discover your mother's details?

That's the key question you should be asking. Because that traitor effectively killed both your mother and her retired colleagues. Sergei doesn't have the intellect and my precautions were too good. So, let's ask him."

Mosin nodded to Andrei standing over Moss, who took out an automatic and pointed it at Moss's temple.

"No! Don't kill him. He's mine."

"So, Sergei, why don't you tell George who the weak link was? Who was the real traitor?"

Moss looked with a sneer towards his father. "You think you are so clever, Papa. I didn't have to work out who your contacts were. I asked Chance and offered a small pension fund to support his son. He knew almost nothing about the 'Soviet Illegals' network, but he knew Julia Stone. That was enough. You were fools. I paid Chance well for his treacherous work. But it was a two-way street. We did dirty work for him, like killing Marcus Wetherby. He worked for us. And for generous payments, he gave us what he knew, and by the way, he sold you out, Georgina. Chance is dirty." he spat out the words. "Neither loyal to MI5, nor to me. His only interest is himself and his son. Even his wife didn't count. We disposed of her like vermin, with his tacit approval."

"You may kill me, but someone like me will take over. You, old men are yesterday, history, old ways. Look what honour and trust did for Julia Stone. I will not beg for my life, Papa. Neither you nor my brother can kill me. I am your son. And look at you, Georgina, misguided and naïve. We could have been so good together. And we could still have so much together. Give us a chance, please."

Chance the traitor, the Russian in Chance's office told

her the truth. Her mother vouched for Chance. But he'd betrayed them all. Her head reeled. Traitors, all. She didn't trust herself to look at Chance standing behind her, still holding his weapon. Another one on her list.

"I don't have to kill you, Sergei. You will face justice at the hands of the one you wronged. But she'll do us both a favour. You not only betrayed me and disobeyed me by killing my former colleagues, you killed the one woman I was so fond of. You committed a crime of gross immorality and I therefore endorse Georgina's actions," said Anatoly Mosin.

George stared at Sergei. Her eyes widened, and her lips curled in disgust and anger. "I have killed, not because I enjoyed it, nor for personal gain, but because it was the right course of action. It was my duty. But you, I'll enjoy killing you."

Moss's expression didn't change. Even his father seemed to recognise his son's madness, his enjoyment for killing. Even by KGB standards his own son was a monster, his hands red with the blood of his victims; whether he'd killed in person or not.

"So, there you have it, George," said Mosin, looking at his watch. "I have less than one hour to be clear of this fortress."

"What about me?" asked Chance, a whine in his voice.

"Good point. Chance, you were as stupid as my son. Mother Russia does not look kindly on traitors. But I also have my orders. You will come with me. No doubt Mother Russia will herald you as a hero."

With a nod of his head, Anatoly Mosin, Chance,

Andrei, and Moss stood to leave. Chance was first to leave the room with a guard, leaving Andrei and Mosin.

Anatoly Mosin pointed a hooked finger at Moss. "You. Stay."

Moss sat.

Mosin stood in front of George with Andrei behind him. "Georgina, I realise this is not quite the outcome you wanted, but I cannot lose two sons. Andrei is my only remaining son, and I promised his dying mother I'd return him safely. He has learnt his lesson, and we will work to repay the debt we owe you. One day I hope you will understand."

It didn't forgive him, or pay the debt. One day she would hunt Andrei down and kill him. But a sad smile passed over Mosin's face.

"Your mother would be proud of you, George Stone." said Mosin; Andrei nodded in agreement.

"I know the deception orchestrated by your mother, and I admire her ingenuity. Now you and I have something in common. We are the only ones who know your mother's secrets. Use that knowledge wisely. I will be in contact."

Mosin nodded towards Andrei's sidearm, and Andrei withdrew his Russian automatic and handed it to George, butt first. Although tempted to attack Andrei with the weapon, she knew the odds of killing him were slim. And Sergei would also escape. She took the weapon, but couldn't meet Andrei's gaze.

Mosin smiled at her as he would to a rebellious

daughter, shook his head and stumbled out, supported by Andrei, his son.

They left, closing the door behind them. The silence screamed at George to execute the job and leave. The telltale sound of a helicopter landing was barely discernible. Walking towards Moss, she chambered a round, and raised Andrei's weapon. She'd lost the opportunity to kill Andrei and there seemed no chance of her exacting revenge on him or Chance soon, but Moss was hers.

"No final words or a request, Moss? Even this is too good for you."

A look of disbelief on his face. As if he couldn't understand who, besides his father, could resist his charm and charisma. His eyebrows narrowed in a pregnant query.

She fired at the centre of mass, and Moss took a bullet in his chest.

He wheezed as he uttered two words, "Please, why?"

His tone showed sincerity, the first and only time he'd shown that trait. He didn't understand why she was killing him. He keeled over the chair backwards. George moved around the chair to see the result, not to enjoy her action, but to ensure his extirpation.

Two more rounds hit him in the forehead and middle of his face. She emptied the rest of the magazine into Moss's face and chest. Even then, George stood over him, bent, and felt his neck for a pulse. Confirming his death, she turned and left.

George ran along the corridor and down to the landing

stage. Mosin's aircraft turned away from the mainland and headed out to sea. She threw the Russian automatic into the high tide, knowing it would sink into the marshy sand. With only a short hour to leave the Fortress, she peered out to sea. The water was only a couple of degrees above zero. She had two options; wait for the SBS and suffer the humiliation of rescue, or swim to the shore and risk death by drowning and hypothermia. A ladder attached to the Fortress wall led to the sea. Wait for rescue or swim? Prison or death? The wind was forceful, and waves crashed against the concrete leg of the structure. Battling the waves would be treacherous, and the wind chill would kill in minutes. Even the elements were transpiring towards her demise. She estimated her chances of survival as slim to zero and made a shallow dive into the water.

The intense cold shocked her to the core, and the water permeated every fibre. She allowed herself to shiver and struck out for the shore. The waves buffeted her and prevented progress, a quick calculation as she swam. Twenty minutes to swim to the shore; she'd be dead inside ten minutes in this temperature, in this weather, but it wouldn't stop her from trying.

The helicopter taking Mosin away with the traitor Chance barely made a sound. She reckoned it was flying at a height of a few hundred feet. The noise changed and something dropped and splashed into the sea between herself and the shore. The helicopter descended to about a hundred feet above the sea and shone its searchlight for a few seconds to illuminate the object, then banked hard and left, its engine roaring.

George swam towards the object, the dark making it near impossible to track. Had they dropped a dinghy or something else to help save her?

Emotions chased crazy thoughts. Why had Mosin deprived her of the right to kill Chance? But did it matter who killed him? It seemed academic now because the chances of her surviving the next few minutes were slim.

Her swimming was now little more than a weak doggy paddle, her strength flagged, the sea leaching heat from her body, drawing it out and dragging her towards death, but she felt at ease. This was as good as it got. Her family partially avenged, dying struggling to survive, the last in the line of the Stone's. Would anyone remember any of them? She doubted it. Her strokes became feeble until exhaustion and cold ground her to a halt, and she flipped onto her back and waited. How far was she from the shore, a couple of hundred metres? She may as well have howled at the moon.

She fought to remain conscious and paddled with her feet, but her weakness accelerated. Seawater washed over her face, filling her mouth. She spluttered and coughed, but it took too much energy. Darkness overcame her. She mumbled a few words to Charlie and her mother and succumbed to the sea. So near to the shore, yet a million miles from safety. A smile crossed her face. What an exit.

***

The light hurt her eyes, and she struggled to focus. Someone sitting in the corner, watching her.

"Mum? Charlie?" asked George.

"Hardly," replied Ted in his Glaswegian brogue.

She tried to raise her head and flopped back onto the pillow.

"Where am I?" she mumbled.

"At home, in bed. One hell of a stunt you pulled. I don't know anyone except you who'd try to pull such a feat, but we guessed you would."

"We, who is 'we'?" she asked, slurring. Saliva running down the side of her face and onto the pillow.

"I called Colonel Syman before we set off. I knew you'd object, so I didn't tell you. He drove straight across. Him and me took the boat out and waited for a sign of you in the water. The helicopter dropped something, and either it was you they threw out, in which case we had to collect your body, or something else. Then the search light came on and we saw you head towards the object. We hauled you out, emptied you of seawater, and the rest is history. Colonel Syman is downstairs, and he's pretty pissed off, pardon my French. Not because he had to rescue you, but you didn't trust him enough to include him."

"Water, please?" asked George.

Ted put a cup to her lips, and she sipped.

"So, what was the object they dropped?"

"A body we guessed. We'll know when the authorities pick it up. Any ideas?"

"I'd guess it was Chance. Mosin did us a favour and settled a score for my mother."

"Hmm," Ted murmured and smiled.

"Who undressed me?" she asked, both indignation and

humour in her voice.

"I did. I've seen worse. But I was hardly going to molest you or get excited in my condition, was I?"

"You could have been lying, to get my kit off."

They grinned.

"How long?"

"It's midday. You were out for a few hours. The doc gave you a shot of something. Can I ask Colonel Syman to come up?"

"No chance, I'll have a shower and see him downstairs."

Less than fifteen minutes later, as she entered the living room, Colonel Syman stood and grinned sheepishly at her. They sat opposite each other.

"Hello George, how are you feeling?" Syman asked.

"Better than last night. How did the SBS raid go?"

"A bit of a damp squib; they discovered a few dead bodies in a cell. One dead Russian gangster and a few other Russians taken alive. The police will charge them with various offences. You'll be pleased to know that none of the deaths can be attributed to you."

She bit her lip, needing to know if she'd expect a visit from the police, or worse. Syman watched her and guessed.

"You're in the clear. The official line is an internal

Russian gangland problem. Care to tell me what your role in this was?"

She owed him that, but first she had to settle the Melanie Syman issue. George had to avoid Melanie Syman incriminating her. So much had happened, so much damage. Prison courtesy of Syman's wife would not be welcome.

"Colonel, before I tell you, I need to explain what I saw in London a few days ago in a Costa café."

She hesitated, unsure how to tackle this. George, a former SNCO, telling a senior Army Officer his wife was spying for Russian gangsters. Even worse, everything he told her, she passed on.

"You mean her passing on information to the Russians? Yes, I knew a few days ago. Even officers in the Army can make mistakes, especially old ones. I knew she was seeing someone in my unit, and you can guess who. I let it continue, even though it was a weakness. She passed information to a lawyer called Wilson Pinchin and from him to Moss. I stopped the passage of information as soon as Sam paid me a visit and told me. George, anything you tell me now will be between us and will remain so."

She told him everything except details of the information her mother had left her. That would be her inheritance and her mother's legacy to her. George would use it as her mother had used it.

Later, she thought about who else she had to visit, to pay the debt to her mother and sister. It sounded almost gratuitous, but it was her way of thinking. She was an organiser, a planner, a doer. She thought about the details and she dispensed justice. Certainly, the undertaker who'd prepared her mother and killed her sister. Pinchin had to pay, but he was doing his job, as despicable as it was. Gangster or crooked lawyer? The nation would celebrate Chance as a hero. That would be for Sam and his colleagues to spin. The nature of his fate and betrayal would remain a lifelong secret between herself, Ted, and Syman, and of course, Andrei. He'd escape her wrath, but his day would come, she would make sure.

Chapter 55

In the early evening, Templeton Maudlin sat, as usual, in his Library in the Funerarium. His face ticked with evidence of fretting. Moss hadn't contacted him, and he needed a resupply of his therapeutics, and whilst he could last another week, compared to Moss, his secondary purveyor supplied inferior merchandise. Also, he was such a distasteful individual, with whom, under other circumstances, he wouldn't countenance an association.

He read the newspaper avidly, including an account of an unspecified incident on the Grain Fortress. It reported little, or the authorities were keeping things secret. The reporter suggested several bodies had been brought ashore in bags. That showed either a disaster or violence. A separate report also recounted the death of a Director in MI5, a chap called 'James Chance'. The police were investigating suspicious circumstances.

To Templeton Maudlin's distorted opinion, the Grain Fortress was a den of iniquity. Drugs and debauchery were rife and must not be tolerated in a civilised society. An article reporting the death of a woman in an Army barracks caught his eye; ice ran down his back as he recalled the incident first-hand. Reading it twice then mulling over every detail, he concluded there were no clues leading the authorities to him. Reassured, a smile curled the corner of his mouth, and he wondered if he would receive the customer for 'processing'.

"Good evening, Maudlin."

The visitor startled Maudlin away from his concentration on the newspaper, which slid onto the floor. His antediluvian demeanour shot to hell; eyes agape. A splutter escaped him and his jaw hung slack. The visitor looked like Charlie Stone. He shook and tried to minimise his size by pushing himself into the chair and tucking his knees towards his chest.

She smiled, then looked inquisitively at Maudlin. His reaction seemed to fascinate and amuse her. A minute elapsed. To Maudlin it seemed longer than an eternity.

The visitor phased into an image of Moss. "Calm down, Maudlin. Does this help? Lovely to see you again. I thought this poor soul would make you feel safe. Especially since our friend is now employed in a less pleasant but fitting capacity. And as our philosophical friend would say, 'there's nothing more final than eternal emptiness'."

'Moss' reached into his inside jacket pocket and extracted a small package like the one Maudlin had received previously from Moss. "Oh, he asked me to deliver this to you."

'Moss' stretched across to hand the package over, but Maudlin hesitated. "Oh, go on, Maudlin. It won't bite you. Well, it will but… Anyway, Needs must when the Devil drives."

Maudlin took the package and held it to him like a small boy afraid of having his sweets taken away. No matter how often this occurred, it troubled him. For the briefest of moments, thoughts of Moss's demise dispersed like a hoar frost on a warm spring morning. He gripped the package, a precious jewel, and when he looked back at 'Moss', the realisation dawned.

"Moss is dead? When, how?" asked Maudlin.

His mind was still more focussed on his medicinal needs and his business than Moss's welfare.

"Oh, the details don't matter. He's in a better place now," said 'Moss,' grinning.

"Why don't you pour us a drink, Maudlin? You need it and I bear bad news."

"Oh, sorry. Forgive me. Manners," said Maudlin, his hands shaking. He stood and poured two large whiskies from a decanter. With a shaking hand, he handed one to 'Moss' at arm's length.

Maudlin sat, waiting, and watching for the slightest telltale sign of impending perdition. Such was his fear that his first sip of whisky resulted in him having a bout of flatulence, accompanied by both a wind instrument and a vile smell.

"So… sorry. I…" said Maudlin.

"Come now, my dear chap. What's a fart between friends? Relax, I'm not here to take you, or scare you; although seeing you in such a tremulous state does amuse me. There's so little amusement in my line of work."

'Moss' grinned, and Maudlin waited, almost falling off the edge of his seat in apprehension.

"Now to business. There will be an attempt on your life, resulting in your death. Let me explain, something to think about. To plan. I'm not ready for you yet. So, it is best you stay alive, for the moment."

With his medicinals trapped between his buttocks and the chair, Maudlin regained his composure. He wasn't worried about an attempt on his life. This entity had said 'attempt', which meant that he had a plan. It must be within this entity's reach to protect him.

"What do you advise?" asked Maudlin.

'Moss' scoffed. "What would be the fun if I coddled you? No, you will work out the details. For me, it's a sort of '*sanguinaire*', or 'blood sport', as you call it. I will give you clues. You will die here, now," he laughed. "Within one week, but that invaluable information comes with a price. I cannot go back empty-handed; I require a death, a guerdon. After all, even I am accountable. Is that too cryptic for you?"

"Who will make this attempt?"

"Oh, I know, I know nearly everything. Your life and death may go either way." He flip-flopped his hand to show what he meant. "If you don't make suitable arrangements. But, for this enormous favour, I expect you to provide another customer for me. You've heard of a certain Wilson Pinchin have you not? He will visit you. The task will be easy, but the final act is yours. The details will unfold. 'Verbum sap' (enough said)."

'Moss' drained his glass, smiled across at Maudlin with what he fancied was a touch of fondness, which gave Maudlin a sense of reassurance, but a part of his addled brain told him the feeling was fictive. 'Moss' disappeared, but Maudlin sat for several minutes staring at where he'd dematerialised, almost too tormented to move, in case he returned.

As the light faded and the shadows lengthened, he stood, gingerly took 'Moss's' glass between thumb and finger, and dropped it into the wastebasket, glanced at his watch, and started his evening ritual. He called Michael into the Library to give him a task, which couldn't wait.

Chapter 56

It'd been almost a week since she'd left the Grain Fortress. Sam contacted her for an update, but she'd tried to be discreet without appearing to be evasive. Sam told her of Chance's death and that he'd probably been killed by one of Moss's men. He expressed confusion about how Patrick had escaped from the Fortress, but George didn't enlighten him. He was far from stupid, and he'd deduce what happened. The police hadn't called on her, but they didn't have evidence. Sam said he'd be in contact. To George that meant 'don't hold your breath' and don't call us. He asked for her to return her weapon and encrypted phone, which had a finality to it.

George rechecked her kit, as she'd done so often before. She'd wanted to do this without Ted, but he'd insisted. Bradley Maudlin had told her of his father's routines and how he ritualised them.

At 5 p.m., Ted and George parked the car about a mile from Maudlin's Funerarium, and walked the rest of the way. Ted disappeared into the bushes to watch the track leading to the house. George put on her thick black latex gloves, approached the back door of the Funerarium, and retrieved the key from a key lockbox using the code supplied by Bradley. Letting herself into the house, she made her way into the kitchen. From the hanging kitchen knives, she selected a long boning knife. She recalled a saying by Tan Daoji, Chinese General of the Liu Song dynasty, 'Always kill with a borrowed knife'. It made sense. After the mission, the killer could clean and return it without revealing evidence, and with nothing to dispose of. She left the kitchen, walked along the darkened corridor towards the library's open door and watched from the corridor.

Subdued lighting shone from the library. An easy chair faced the window, its back to the door. Maudlin sat in the chair as Bradley had described. Waiting and watching him sip from a whisky tumbler until it was empty. She readied her weapon, feeling the reassuring weight in her right hand. As she was about to act, he arose from the chair, walked to the sideboard, and refilled his glass then depositing it on the table before resettling in his chair.

George gave it another minute and walked behind Maudlin, stabbing through the back of the easy chair into Maudlin's left middle back. She estimated she would pierce his heart, and if he was lucky, he'd die a quick and painless death, which was more than he deserved.

He gasped, but said nothing. He looked over his shoulder to his left. George grasped the handle of the knife and twisted, which elicited a further gasp and a gurgling from Maudlin. Blood seeped from him and soaked into the chair. She wanted to see him die. George walked around and sat in a chair facing him. He looked at peace, barely disturbed by her attack. But Bradley had said that his father indulged in narcotic relaxation. This was doubtless one of those times. She stared into his eyes and he into hers. He rocked his head, as if explaining something, muttering but hardly able to breathe. He muttered something, too quiet to hear; she went across to him and put her ear to his mouth. She expected to hear him ask forgiveness, to beg for his life, to repent. He muttered, "Not."

He looked waxen, and on the point of death, breathing shallow, eyebrows pinched. She sat to watch. Forgiveness was impossible; his crimes were too great, and he deserved to die for the crime committed against his son, Bradley. For his other crimes, he deserved far worse. Whatever his philosophy in life, whatever his reason for his crimes, he seemed to accept his fate. But his eyes questioned why she attacked him; he didn't understand. His look suggested he'd been caught in a piece of theatre, in which a woman had been sawn in half by accident, but in this case, he was the unfortunate woman. George felt no sympathy for this monster who'd killed her sister, helped kill her mother, and terrified his own son. This was a good death for him. Blood spewed from his mouth, and he coughed.

George watched for a few minutes as Maudlin's head flopped to the side, his tongue lolled out of the side of his mouth, and thick bloody gore poured down the front of his waistcoat. She checked his neck pulse. Nothing. She looked at the pathetic character and wished him a tormented death.

There was not only revulsion at what Templeton Maudlin represented, there was also relief. Maudlin's death at her hand had gone some way to assuage her wrath and outrage at this unnecessary death and destruction brought about by folly, greed, ego, and weakness.

George removed the knife from Maudlin's back with a sigh of relief, pulled his head back and sliced the knife across his throat. There was a mere dribble of blood from the wound. George cleaned the knife in the kitchen and returned it as she'd found it.

Bradley had explained to George where to find Maudlin's 'Display Room'. She retrieved the key from Bradley's bedroom and entered the dimly lit room. The fluorescent lights flickered, revealing row upon row of wooden display cabinets. This disgusting pastime may have stretched over seventy years, and Maudlin had carried on the activity from his father. No doubt Bradley Maudlin's revulsion at his father's activity had contributed to Templeton Maudlin's hatred of his son. Each display case held fifty fingers, each with a slip of paper beneath it typed and stuck to green baize. All typed and uniform in Serif font with the date, victim's name and a rating, reflecting his state of mind or the satisfaction he received in taking the fingers. George said a silent prayer. The display, being in chronological order, she went to where she expected to find her mother and sister. Minutes later, she exited the room with a shiver, the fingers tucked in a pouch in her pocket. She left as she'd arrived, and deposited the door key in the key lockbox.

George removed her latex gloves, placed them into a small plastic bag, returned to the liaison point, and she and Ted walked in silence back to the car.

Chapter 57

Charlie Stone's funeral gave a shred of closure for George, the end of a distressing but transformative period. In the last couple of months, she'd seen more than enough pain, suffering, and death to last her a while, and she'd lost her mother and sister. Pain cut deep; but George had peace of mind, she'd avenged her family and exposed Chance for the traitor he was. A strange sense of satisfaction washed over her. It'd been a roller coaster time and a time of loss. Not only relatives and a friend, but her career.

Sam, who had been promoted into Chance's position, seemed impressed with George. He'd invited her to MI5 for an interview, a formality he said. He knew she had PTSD but the Firm's psychologist would assess her regularly for the first year, then annually. She'd received no employment details. But with no job, no income, and time on her hands, she'd accepted the offer.

Ted stood next to her, looking smart in a black suit, and walking with a stick. He was the older brother she'd never had. Syman was also present. She didn't know how the problem with his wife and the Executive Officer would end. But she guessed it would end, as many soldiers' marriages, in divorce. She doubted love played any part in their three-way relationship. If Syman knew of his wife's relationship with Pritchard, why did he let it continue? It showed even an old war horses like Syman could be naïve and stupid. It was unlike him not to put a stop to it. She didn't think Syman was averse to giving Pritchard a good slap, but that would end a senior Officer's career.

The day before the funeral, and after Sam's intervention, Bradley Maudlin was released from prison. Bradley had gained a reputation in prison, especially with his new found confidence. He stood apart from the close family and friends, and George smiled over to him. He had a quirky sense of humour and a healthier view on life than his father. There was no sign when Templeton Maudlin's funeral would be. She neither saw nor heard anything about his death or the funeral, and no one had told Bradley of his father's death. There was no body, so no funeral, and no closure for Bradley. George explained to Bradley she was certain his father had died, but gave away nothing that would incriminate her. He was neither surprised nor upset, but relieved; wanted nothing more to do with either his father's business or his inheritance.

The funeral service carried on around her, and George said a few words, which Ted had helped her write, placed a rose on the coffin and accepted the condolences. She was pleased it was almost over. Whilst it sounded callous, now she could get back to rebuilding her life.

She walked around with Sheila by her side, thanking attendees for coming and shaking hands. George recognised few, which wasn't unusual, some attended as a morbid hobby. One short, stocky man smiled at her and muttered something under his breath. He lingered on the handshake, but she moved on to the next sweaty hand. The grievers had been invited back to Rose Farm Cottage for the wake, where she'd repeat the process.

She walked with Ted and Bradley out of the Crematorium towards the cars. Bradley stopped and pulled George to a halt. She looked around at him questioning. If he had something to say, it could wait until they arrived home. His face was corpse-like, and he stared at George, unable to speak. Ted had also stopped and looked at both.

"What is it Bradley, spit it out?" said Ted.

"You said Templeton Maudlin was dead. He's there, walking towards his car," he said, pointing toward the cars. "I'd recognise that walk anywhere. That is my father."

They were too far to shout and anyway, George knew she'd killed him. So, who was this person? She took a pace to chase after the man, but Ted held onto her arm. "Steady, George; my guess is he'll attend the wake. We can follow him and meet him there."

She turned to Ted. "If Bradley is correct, I killed the wrong person. So, who was he? Who did I kill?"

"It's done, get over it. You can't unkill him, and no good will come of handing yourself in."

They walked towards the car and watched Templeton's car driving along the 400-metre path. Someone approached along the path on foot. Before they knew there'd been an accident, the car increased speed and drove towards the approaching pedestrian. Closer now to the car, George recognised the man at the wheel as the short man with the over lingering sweaty handshake. His eyes bulged, and he shook with the tension, struggling to control the car.

Maudlin's car impacted the pedestrian square on. The tall slim man disappeared underneath the car, which carried on dragging him along the road. There was little noise except for a racing engine, a dull thud, and a gut-wrenching scraping. The car hit a tree head on without slowing.

Ted, George, and Bradley ran over to the car as Templeton Maudlin pushed the driver's door open and fell out onto the grass. As Bradley reached his father, he knelt and looked at his wounds. He hadn't been wearing a seat belt, and from his injuries he'd impacted the steering wheel and the windscreen. Despite his blood-covered face, glass had stripped away his makeup, revealing Templeton Maudlin. He was conscious and gazed at Bradley, bent over him. She hated to admit it, but she would not help save the man's life. Templeton stared at her, his face sheet white. Was it the shock of the accident or something else? He spoke with a clear, strong voice, and talked directly to George, looking expectantly.

She stepped back in shock. Did he think he was talking to her sister, Charlie, and who was Charon?

"I did it. I did what you told me, Charon. I killed Wilson Pinchin for you, in exchange for my life. We did so enjoy our time together, Charlie Stone, and we can enjoy many more times."

She knelt and looked under the car; a head trapped underneath stared at her with dead eyes. The car had dragged the decapitated victim down the road. She recognised the dead face of Wilson Pinchin.

Templeton Maudlin waved to Bradley who put his ear

to Maudlin's mouth. Maudlin talked to his son, but it was a monologue and Bradley's expression never changed.

Thirty minutes later an ambulance arrived and took the delirious and disorientated Maudlin away. Still conscious, he was still talking to someone only he could see. Bradley didn't accompany his father. He seemed unperturbed by his father's condition. Turning to George, he said, "Should we go to the wake?"

Ted shrugged and raised an eyebrow at George.

"What did your father say, Bradley?"

"He told me he'd swapped places with Michael on the night that you visited and that he sat in a dark corner and watched you kill Michael. He told me it was all my fault, and that he loved his only son, Michael, who sacrificed himself for his father. His final words to me were, 'I loved that boy; he was my only son'."

During the wake, no one spoke of the event. A calming fog descended on the gathering. Wilson Pinchin's demise elicited no concern from those watching, despite being trapped headless beneath the car, nor Templeton Maudlin on his way to hospital. After so much tragedy, death, and distress, this event was the finale. Sam attended the wake and engaged Ted in conversation. Sheila took George's elbow and led her into the kitchen.

"George, I have to speak to you. An old friend has contacted me. His name is Anatoly Mosin, he asked me to give you this."

She handed George a card with a name, email, and a Moscow phone number. On the back was a message:

"Until my death, I will look out for you. Make peace with Andrei, you may need him."

George looked at the card and stared open-mouthed at Sheila. "An old friend, you said. So, are you also an illegal Aunt Sheila? Did you work for the Soviets?"

"Yes, your Mum and I worked together, she was my boss, but I'm not an illegal, dear me no. I was one of her 'assets', it was useful for the Soviets to have a Postmistress in their ranks."

"And you contacted Anatoly Mosin to save me and assault the Tower?"

Sheila smiled at George. "Yes, that was me, too. Sam is also an old friend. When your Mum changed sides, so did I. We may work together in the future, George."

George smiled to her Mum's best friend.

Chapter 58

Half an hour before her arrival time at MI5 HQ at Thames House in London, George bought a Styrofoam of tea on the Embankment. MI5's main entrance to Thames House is on Thorney Street, around the back of Thames House. Her walk from Lambeth Bridge, where she'd paid an arm and a leg for car parking, had been bliss, a few daffodils along the Embankment, working ships on the river and the first pleasure boats of the day taking sightseers. The spring sun was over her left shoulder and workers bustled to their 'normal' lives and 'normal jobs'.

Sam had allowed her to complete the paperwork and the exam at home, and her physical fitness report from Colonel Syman at Stanford Hall was accepted by MI5 as proof of fitness and health. Sam had made the process painless.

At the entrance to Thames House, George met her 'sponsor' for 'in processing'. The woman signed her in and led her to Human Resources. The woman talked, but George heard almost nothing, simply observing the atmosphere. She signed the Official Secrets Act, received her probationary contract and warrant card, then went into the canteen with her sponsor, an over talkative and inquisitive member of staff. George would ensure there wouldn't be much to reveal.

"We didn't know about you until a couple of weeks ago. We were really, really surprised. Mr Ghosh told us to keep it to ourselves because there was something hush hush about who you were and what you'd done. He gave us your entry exam papers and your results, you did ever so well, and he told us to file them. So, everyone's been talking about you. Who did you work for before?" asked the woman.

"What do you do here?" asked George.

"I'm only a Secretary, I wanted to do fieldwork, but I failed my entrance exam for the second and final time."

"Secretary's an important job. You keep the system going. Without secretaries, the place would fall apart."

"Let's chat," said the girl, pulling on her curls.

"Look, I have to meet Mr Ghosh now. He called for me to go to his office. Do you mind if I leave you here?" asked George.

"Oh, sure. That's a pity. I'll catch you later, okay?"

"Sure."

Sam's Secretary led George into Sam's office, "Miss Stone to see you, Director."

He stood and offered his hand. "Good to see you, George. Everything taken care of?"

She wasn't sure if he meant personal issues, with the police and the Army or with her 'in processing'.

"Yes, all good. What do I call you?" asked George.

"Everyone except Helen, my Secretary, calls me 'Sam'. Old habits die hard, and Helen's been the Director's Secretary for decades."

George nodded.

"Now then, George, we need to start on a clean sheet. I need to know everything, from when your mother died in the attack to Charlie's funeral. You will write it now, in your own hand. I will read it, take any necessary sanitising action to protect MI5, and its mandate, and to protect you. I will file it in my safe. No one except me will see it, not even Helen. That is to protect you, me and MI5. But I warn you, leave nothing out."

George nodded but uncertainty crossed her mind.

"I once asked you whose side you were on. Will you use the information as evidence against me? Whose side are you on, Sam?"

"I don't walk a wiggly path, George, and I talk straight. But that was also Chance, once. I can give my word. I will read it and lock it away. It will never be read by another, and I will never mention it, never use it in evidence against you… so long as you follow my direction. Clear enough?"

"Clear."

The next time George looked up it was mid-afternoon. Sam had been out all day and she'd written it in his office.

Helen brought regular refreshment.

George handed over the sheath of papers to Sam. She sat and waited as he read. His face remained placid.

"Thank you, George. Is this everything?"

"Yes, all I can think of."

"I'm surprised you survived mentally and physically. Quite remarkable."

Sam gathered the pile of paper together, double enveloped it, wrote on the envelope, and locked it in his safe.

"I will be your sponsor from this point on. Right, let's introduce you to a few of your colleagues, and I'll brief you on your first job."

Chapter 59

Bradley had changed his last name to his mother's maiden name of 'Fulham'. With Bradley, George entered the same hospital that had first cared for Charlie. Although they'd moved on since the assumed death of Templeton Maudlin, this visit gave them both finality. After this, they'd both forget about him and his evil.

Bradley explained to the nurse he was Maudlin's son. That was a lie, but they needed to see him.

"You may have heard, he's comatose because of his head injuries."

"He's been in hospital for a week. Has he had visitors?"

"None. You're the first. Good luck."

The room was silent, and Templeton Maudlin looked at peace. This was the third time George had seen him. The first time she'd seen him was at night, dressed as a Padre, scrambling for the woods to escape. The sun streamed through the window, giving the atmosphere a fresh, clean appearance and smell, which contrasted with the man they were visiting. He had a couple of drips connected to his arm. They sat on either side of the bed, silent. George searched his face for a sign of acceptance of this man's guilt. Had the roles been reversed and Templeton Maudlin had visited her, he'd have used the opportunity to kill her.

"I know you're there, George Stone and Bradley Maudlin."

Bradley Fulham started and stared at Maudlin's face. There was no change, except for the slightest fluttering of his eyelashes. He opened his eyes, turned his head, and looked from one to the other.

"Why are you here? To give me a talking to, or to torment me?" he asked, his face expressionless.

"We want answers. First, why did you kill my sister?" asked George. "Second, why did you let me kill your son? You also owe Bradley an explanation for your criminal behaviour towards him and his mother. Why did you let him go to prison instead of waiting for the police to arrive? Much of this distress was avoidable."

"It was Bradley's fault. He forced this whole predicament on me. His mother was a floozy. I accepted him, cared for him, and he isn't even my son. I had one son, Michael, and he gave his life for me. That is true dedication and loyalty. As for your sister, it was a pleasure. Few things have given me such pleasure. I was with her to the end. I fancy, as I held her hand, she opened her eyes and smiled for me, thanked me. Sublime. But there is no evidence linking me to the death of dear Charlie Stone. So, do your worst George Stone, I am untouchable. As for Bradley Maudlin." He looked at Bradley. "You are a weak, useless simpleton. Useful for nothing but to be used, and I and my friends have plans for you."

"Maudlin, as I am not your son and have no blood links with you, I have no compunction to restrain myself from telling you, you are the most evil, despicable person it has been my misfortune to meet. You and I both know that you killed my mother and Charlie Stone. You may think you are untouchable, but soon you will see the people you have wronged, and beg for your soul. Now, I want to get on with my life."

"Miss Stone, before you go, and I return to my peaceful repose, let me explain something. I not only saw you kill my son Michael, I recorded it. Touch me, and you will feel the full force of the law. I have copied the video and mailed it to myself. Another copy is in a safe place. Your move, George Stone."

Bradley stood over Maudlin with his face inches away from Maudlin's and adopted the crazed look perfected in prison, and for a few moments Maudlin opened and closed his mouth like a landed fish. The same expression had George laughing and in stitches.

Bradley almost whispered. "My name is Bradley Fulham, and I am not your son. I understand you have head injuries, but I hope you survive and return to full health. I shall enjoy inflicting a worse punishment on you as you inflicted on others. Whilst you slumber in your comatose state, think about that, and envisage the pain and suffering awaiting you. If that video ever sees the light of day, I shall keep you alive, until you give me the original and the copies. Your move, Templeton Maudlin."

Some weeks ago, George would have strangled this old man for the crimes against her and her family, and for all the crimes she imagined he'd committed. Now she felt nothing except disgust for this wretched being with malevolence in his heart and wickedness in his eyes. George had exacted revenge and there would be enough time when he left hospital to take any additional action. She watched Bradley who gave Maudlin a final crazed reflective smile.

They left the room and spoke to the Sister. "I told you, no response, right?"

"Sister, we had a long conversation with him. Although he may be asleep now."

"That's impossible," she blurted.

The sister opened the door and looked in at Maudlin. "See, he's still comatose."

George shrugged and smiled. "Sister, could you inform us if there is any change in Mr Maudlin's condition or if you discharge him?"

"I can do that. I expect when we discharge him, he will need specialist care," said the Sister.

"Yes, I can provide that," said Bradley.

"You know that Mr Maudlin is an opium addict. That is why he's on a morphine drip. I'm sorry if you didn't know."

"We knew about that, but we didn't know it was so bad," said Bradley.

"Yes, I'm afraid it is. He may never recover."

As they left the hospital, George made a call to Sheila.

She asked her to trace the package addressed to Mr Maudlin at the Funerarium. Sheila laughed as if it would be easy, and told her she'd contact her that evening.

Later, George and Bradley each received phone calls from the hospital. There was no change to Maudlin's condition; he was still in a coma, but agitated. They'd keep George and Bradley informed.

ABOUT JAKE COREY

Jake Corey served in the British Army for 32 years. The first 12 years he served in the Armoured Corps until being commissioned and retiring in 1999.
Jake Corey served a further 12 years with NATO, travelling widely throughout Europe and Central Asia, first as a civilian policy advisor in NATO's Partnerships and later as the Director for NATO's Partnership Programmes, where he commanded a multinational team of training coordinators and regional specialists.

Printed in Great Britain
by Amazon